VEIL OF THE TRUTHSEER

SARAH CARDEN

CONTENTS

Veil of the Truthseer

Copyright 2023, Sarah Carden

Paperback ISBN: 979-8-9891725-0-4

Ebook ISBN: 979-8-9891725-1-1

For anyone who believes the truth matters, even when the loudest voices say it doesn't.

And to every nerd who's ever wondered if gaming can be their superpower.

But also, and perhaps most especially, for you, Mom. This one goes out to you.

CHAPTER 1

No Good Deed Goes Unpunished

December 4, 2037

RAFE WAS RUNNING AS FAST AS HE COULD TO ESCAPE A world collapsing around him as the steel girders beneath his feet were crumbling in space, hundreds of miles above the ground.

Then he tapped the jump button on his game controller. Sonic the Hedgehog slammed into Doctor Robotnik and the Eggman's hover machine began combusting in countless tiny explosions. The title card for the next level came up, reading "The Doomsday Zone", and as Sonic activated the chaos emeralds to become Super Sonic, the last level of *"Sonic 3 and Knuckles"* was on.

The Doomsday Zone lay in the upper atmosphere, full of asteroids, missiles and flying debris suspended over the planet Moebius, and Rafe was in his element. Put him behind the wheel of a sidescroller, and he suddenly became the master of his world. The game environment scrolled across the screen, and he navigated it with a practiced ease only achievable by someone who knew the level like the back of his hand. He was nearing the end and the setup was perfect. He'd picked up more than enough rings, and he was ready to take the fight to Dr. Robotnik for the last time ...

Except the power died.

"Not again!" Rafe dropped the controller on the coffee table, fuming in frustration. After a moment he stood and carefully navigated the darkened room to the window to pull up the blinds and take a look outside. His small house in one of Greensboro's residential neighborhoods on the east side of town looked out on a series of concrete sidewalk slabs leading out to the road. The houses were slightly dilapidated, but his street was definitely not the worst. There was a street a couple of blocks over where some of the homes were completely abandoned.

The dark cloudy sky outside didn't have a lot of light to offer. No surprise when the weather forecast predicted snow. But with a couple of hours before sunset, there was still some pale illumination cast into his living room.

It would snow soon. He was sure of it. Perhaps it was his imagination, but along with the change in air pressure, he'd always thought he could detect a subtle difference in the way ambient sound carried through the air just before snow. Like it had been slightly muted.

It felt that way now.

He walked to the kitchen, thinking of getting some water. He would have loved some hot coffee, but that would have to wait until the latest blackout ended. They had happened more and more often since the fences had gone up. He took a glass from a cabinet and filled it from the sink before downing about half of it and setting it on the kitchen table.

As he walked back toward the door to the living room, he noticed the trash can that stood at the end of the kitchen counter was nearly full. Was tomorrow trash day? He considered for a second, before deciding that with the power out, he had nothing better to do. He reached for his heavy coat and gloves before pulling on a knit cap over his short, dust brown hair.

His own situation could not continue forever, he knew. He still needed to find a new job, since his last one as a technical writer for a local company had run out about two weeks ago. Prospects were not great. They hadn't been since before college, though he'd managed to keep afloat. He counted himself lucky, in fact. There were plenty of people who had failed entirely.

He sighed, his breath fogging in the cold December air; then he shouldered the garbage bag, carrying it to the trashcan, dropping it inside, and then dragging the can to the road. Snow was beginning to fall around him as he placed the can where it could be accessed by the men on the garbage truck. He was about to go back inside when he spotted a familiar thirteen-year-old boy with mussed brown-blond hair, also pulling a trash can to the road from the house next door. Brushing the snowflakes out of his face, he called out. "Hey Neil, you lost power too?"

Neil nodded. "Yeah." He looked away from where they were, scanning the street nervously as he put the trashcan up on the curb.

"Is something the matter?" Rafe asked.

The boy shook his head. "Not sure. It's just been awfully quiet today..."

Rafe looked around. It was true, there were few people on the streets. He would have thought there would at least be a few going to and from the remote vehicle station, but even for winter the sidewalks seemed deserted. He considered that for a moment and then shrugged, deciding to change the subject. "I heard your dad managed to get through the trial all right."

Neil frowned, rubbing his gloved hands together to warm them. "It shouldn't have happened to begin with. He didn't do anything wrong." His expression was one of disgust that didn't belong on the face of a kid his age.

Rafe, for the most part, kept to himself. He had his own problems and no desire to invite trouble. But a few weeks after Neil's family had moved in the previous year, Rafe had been walking back from the remote vehicle station a couple of streets over and spotted Neil being beaten up by some kids from his class at school. Putting a stop to it had only taken walking up to them on the street, fortunately. Bullies were cowards at any age and while they had initially seemed surprised that someone had intervened, they had taken off running once he had stepped into the alley where they had pushed Neil to the ground. Since he and Neil had both been headed in the same direction, they had walked home that afternoon more or less together. The two had chatted for a bit before reaching Neil's house and when Rafe had noticed he was wearing a T-shirt for the last Final Fantasy released in the states before the war, they had discovered that they shared an interest in video games.

Neil's parents had at first looked at him with suspicion, before he had identified himself as their neighbor, and Neil had explained to them what happened. But that first incident had instilled some trust with the family, and over the last few months, Neil and his parents had occasionally stopped to chat while Rafe was doing yardwork outside, and they had even relied on him for technical advice on occasion. Having gotten to know them a little in the interim, it really didn't seem fair to Rafe that they would have the trouble they were having, or that they would have had to sell their previous house to cover the legal fees. But that was just how things were.

"They really are like piranhas, aren't they," Rafe said sympathetically.

Neil nodded. "I just hope it's all over."

"I hope so too." Rafe looked up at the sky, wishing he had better advice to give, but the chill was getting to him. The snow didn't look like it would let up for a while.

Neil seemed to have come to the same conclusion, because he pulled his heavy coat a little tighter and said, "Well, I guess I'll see you around."

"All right. See you later."

Neil nodded and turned around, heading back toward his house. Rafe turned and headed back to his own. If they were lucky, the power might come back on in the next hour.

October 13, 2029

It was a simple scenario. The party had come across a tribe of goblins who were getting ready to eat a hapless peasant who had wandered into their midst.

"So, what will you do?" Will, the group's Game Master, adjusted his glasses and looked at the other players, who were seated around the coffee table containing the not-yet-filled-in battle map, character sheets, dice, miniatures, and a plastic container filled with cookies Hannah had brought to share.

"Let's just throw some fireballs and move on," Allen suggested. Not surprising, since he'd decided his character would be evil-aligned. Tall and lanky, with skin just a bit lighter than charcoal, he sat in a chair just close enough to the coffee table to see everything without his knees bumping against it.

It was a viable strategy for the popular game *Catacombs and Creatures*, also known as C&C; but there were other factors to consider. "Shouldn't we at least *try* to help the guy?" Rafe asked, a wry smile playing at his lips.

Next to him on the couch, Hannah considered her sheet, fidgeting with the long, brown ponytail that fell just past her shoulders. "Well, what village is he from?"

"Give me a roll for Knowledge, Local," Will said.

Hannah reached for the twenty-sided die, or d20, let it roll across the table, and added up the modifiers. "22," she announced.

There were numerous other polyhedral dice scattered across the table among the character sheets and pencils. Aside from the d20s, there were dice with twelve, ten, eight, six, and four sides – or d12s, d10s, etc., as the players called them.

"All right." Will considered the scenario for a moment and then continued. "He appears to be from a town belonging to one of your patron"s rivals."

"Let's leave him," Hannah suggested.

Rafe gave her a look of mock disbelief. "But what if he knows something useful? Besides, getting eaten by anything kind of sucks."

In C&C, players determined their characters moral stances on two axes; Good versus evil, and chaotic versus lawful. He and Hannah had chosen to play their characters as neutral on the question of good versus evil, but Hannah's Rogue was chaotic. That was to say her actions were more spontaneous and opportunistic with less care for established rules. Rafe's Cleric was lawful, therefore possessing a greater respect for laws and social conventions.

Eric, who played the party's Fighter and had chosen chaotic good for his alignment, nodded in agreement and reached for his d20 with a large hand. While Allen towered over him in height, he was physically more heavy-set than everyone else, in spite of, or maybe because of, regularly working out. "All right, let's go bust some heads." He looked up at Will. "I charge the nearest goblin and attack him with my battle-axe."

Will reached into a box for a dry-erase marker and began sketching the scenery onto the battle map. "Roll to attack. Does anyone else do anything?"

———

December 4, 2037

It was just after sunset, and unfortunately the power had not come back on. Rafe sat in his dark and unheated living room as the gray clouds hung low over the snow-covered street. It had not been a heavy snow. This time of year, snow storms almost never topped an inch or two. One needed to be further inland, toward the battle front and the mountains, to get any kind of volume. Since he was unable to get back to his regular evening pursuits, he'd gotten out some crackers and cheese to tide himself over until he could use the stove to make something that actually counted as a meal. He considered take-out, but dismissed it as too expensive, assuming anything was even open.

In the meantime, he had tried to spend the last hour of fading light going through some old papers, though his heart wasn't really in it. Now that the light was nearly gone, it was hard to read, and he was debating whether to find a candle, pull out his cell phone, or just give it up for the time being. His thoughts drifted as he glanced over at a box near his work desk, filled with his gaming rulebooks and character sheets. It was a shame it was too dark to read over any of them, and there weren't enough people to play in any case. Eric was still nearby, but Allen had gone back to Asheville before the war started. Rafe had no idea what had happened to Will, and the last time he'd talked to Hannah, well ... he preferred not to think about that.

His stomach growled, and he was about to get up and go find something a little more substantial to eat when something else caught his eye out the window. A small crowd was gathering in front of Neil's house. Protesters? Sure, the case had been popular, but now? Here? Hopefully, the Special Peace Keeping Force should be showing up any time now.

Unless they didn't.

It had happened to political dissidents before, based on what he'd heard around the time the crackdown on alternate news sources had started, though it wasn't something he really wanted to consider.

He looked away, going to his refrigerator, retrieving a pitcher and pouring some juice. It wasn't any of his business what was going on out there. Someone would come and break it up, and he needed to stay out of it ...

Did he just hear a window breaking? He looked outside again. Where were the SPKF?

He felt a chill down his spine as he saw that a few men had just advanced onto his neighbor's yard. He reached for his cell phone and dialed the emergency number.

"*911. What's your emergency?*"

"Hi, this is Rafe Turner. There's a bunch of guys picketing next door, and I could have sworn someone broke my neighbor's windows."

"*Where are you located?*" The dispatcher asked.

Rafe rattled off the address, and the woman on the other end of the line took down the information. However, after she was finished, she said, *"Hold on a moment."*

There was suddenly silence on the other end of the line, and Rafe's breath caught in his throat. *Hold on a moment?* Those certainly weren't moments Neil and his family could afford. He paced in agitation, waiting on the silence of the phone connection for what was definitely more than a few moments before the woman finally spoke again.

"Excuse me, but that area has been sanctioned for political protest. I would caution you not to interfere. I would suggest you not leave your home until it's over."

"Are you kidding me?! They look like they might be getting ready to storm their house!" Rafe shouted into the phone.

At that moment, service was suddenly cut off. Rafe cursed into the speaker before angrily thrusting his phone back into his pocket. Couldn't somebody do something?

His eyes widened in disbelief as he looked out the window. Several people had gone into the house, returning a few moments later pulling a man and a woman into the midst of the mob. The rioters spread out, angrily shouting at the couple as a man who was obviously the ringleader climbed on top of a box from which he could address the crowd. He signaled for silence before looking down at the Flynns with nothing but cold hatred evident in his posture.

"Howard Flynn!" the ringleader shouted, loud enough that Rafe could hear him clearly inside his house. "You and your wife have been called to justice by your community for inhumane practices and for aiding and abetting the financial ruin of Greensboro's citizens. You treated your workers like dogs, paid them like slaves, illegally prevented them from unionizing, refused to use equal employment guidelines, and to add insult to injury, you couldn't even be bothered to pay for their health insurance! Yet here you are, living off their blood and their efforts."

Howard said something in response, but his voice was much quieter and Rafe couldn't make out his words.

Everyone jeered, and even though Neil's father seemed to be trying to reason with them, he was quickly drowned out by the shouts of an angry mob that just didn't seem to care. The ringleader motioned for silence once more. "It's the right of every man to have an equal share. You should know that. Especially in this economy, the workers need all the help they can get. You wealthy fatcats do nothing but wallow in your cash and your privilege while the rest of us get poorer every day! Well, your day of reckoning is here!"

Rafe was distracted at that moment by the sound of a door slamming, and out his side window, he saw a figure in a coat, sneakers, and jeans leaping out the back door of the Flynns' house. Moving to his own back door to see what was going on, he recognized Neil running toward his house followed by another dark figure.

Rafe hurried outside, pulling on his heavy coat as he went, and grabbing the Japanese wooden sword he kept at his door. It wasn't the most impressive weapon, just something he'd picked up for mock duels with Eric when they were kids. It was better than his bare hands, though, and hard enough to seriously injure someone. They'd found that out the hard way, when Eric had almost broken Rafe's arm. That resulted in a parental decree to never fight each other with sword-shaped sticks ever again. After that, they had restricted their play-fighting to imaginary enemies.

He sank into the snow in his backyard just as he saw Neil come scrambling over the wooden fence, having not waited for Rafe to open the gate because he was so desperate to get away from his attackers. As the boy began to drop into his yard, Rafe realized where he was going to land, and he was too far away to stop it. An old cement planter box stood just inside the fence, covered in snow just below where Neil was falling. He watched, almost in slow motion as Neil crashed into the planter with a sickening thud. Rafe winced at the sound of the impact before hurrying over to where Neil had fallen. "Are you all right?" he asked.

Neil looked up at him as he clutched his right leg, clearly in too much pain and far too terrified to answer. Then they saw the man who had been chasing him trying to climb over the four-foot-high fence. Rafe couldn't make out much of his features in the dark, aside from the fact that he seemed to be of pale complexion and had a rather unkempt beard.

He lifted the sword in what he hoped was a threatening stance. "Don't you dare come any closer!" He was sure his form wasn't very good, but maybe it was close enough to the movies that it at least looked like he knew what he was doing.

"Let us have the kid, and we'll call it even," the man replied.

Neil looked from him to Rafe with wide brown eyes, not sure what was about to happen.

Rafe did not lower the sword. "He hasn't done anything to you." It was all he could do to keep his voice calm as he did his best to fend off the fear in his heart and keep his hand from trembling. He could almost see the hungry gleam in the other man's eye.

"We should string you up with the Flynns!" the other man screamed. "You're just like them!"

"Better to be like them, than some vicious animal who'd go after a kid," Rafe growled, still amazed he was holding himself together. He stepped to where Neil sat, not taking his eyes off the man. "Can you stand?" he asked.

Neil tried to pick himself up but was in too much pain to move on his own. At that point, the man seized the moment to try climbing over the fence as two others tried to break open the gate. Seeing the threat, Rafe ran at him, clubbing him over the head with the wooden blade just before he cleared the fence. His heart was racing as the pale man let out a grunt of pain and dropped back on the other side. The two men at his gate were still attempting to break the lock. Then he heard glass breaking near the front of his house, and the sound of shouting inside.

It was clear to Rafe that their neighborhood was no longer a safe place. Hurrying to Neil, who was still struggling to get to his feet, he grabbed the kid's arm, pulling him upright. Rafe was not an exceptionally strong man, but adrenaline helped and fear of death was a good motivator. Throwing Neil over his shoulder, Rafe ran to the gate on the opposite side of his yard, carrying the younger boy as he fled into the stand of trees behind his home.

Were the rioters going to destroy his house now too?

Rafe didn't stop or slow to watch the men who had tried to break into his yard. But he could hear them as they made their way around the fence. Once he and Neil were in the trees, he kept going until he was having trouble seeing in the dark, before letting the boy down. He helped him hide under what he thought was a stand of bushes, quickly crawling in after him. Soon enough, he could hear the three men searching nearby. "Where do you think they went?" one of them asked.

"They couldn't have gone far," one of the others said. Rafe glanced at Neil, caught his eye and silently cautioned him not to move. With any luck, the shadows under the trees would keep them from being spotted. He did his best to breathe slowly, lest the sound reveal their location, though he was starting to notice the cold night air in his lungs.

Two gunshots rang out over the gloom and Neil's eyes widened, but he didn't make a sound as the three men looked toward the origin of the noise. "Looks like they got to the good part without us," one of them said.

"Let's go." Rafe recognized the voice of the man he had knocked over the head with his sword. The blow to his head must not have been strong enough to keep him out of the search. "Wherever they are, they won't last long without getting spotted or freezing to death."

There was a collective grunt of agreement as their pursuers gave up the chase and walked back toward the street. Rafe carefully sat up to watch them go as he tried to process what had just happened.

There had been gunshots.

Guns were banned except for use by law enforcement.

Either that was being ignored or they were already here somewhere, just not to arrest those having their 'political protest.' His mind suddenly went back to his 911 call and what the dispatcher had said. This riot had been sanctioned.

The light reflecting off his house flickered in an orange glow, and he looked up, trying to find the source. Had someone lit a fire on the street?

———

Rafe and Neil waited in the woods for some time as the orange light filtered past the shadow of Rafe's house. Once Rafe was sure no one was coming back into the trees, he crawled out of the bushes to get a better look at what was happening. Standing erect and looking out from the gloom, he could see signs of movement in and around his home. He could hear people shouting and chanting slogans in the street, but he didn't dare get any closer. Looking back down, he noticed Neil shivering and decided they couldn't stay here much longer. He glanced toward his house. Every instinct told him he should be able to go there, but the memory of those men and the signs of activity inside ruled that out. He forced himself to take a couple of deep breaths to steady his nerves as he tried to work through the situation they were in.

"Let's go," he said at last.

"But what about Mom and Dad?" Neil asked, his eyes wide with worry.

Rafe shook his head. "We can't go back out there right now, and I'm pretty sure they wouldn't want you getting any more hurt. We'll find out what happened when it's safe." He helped Neil crawl out of their hiding place and then pulled the boy's arm over his shoulder so he could help him limp through the woods. They needed to find shelter.

The further they got from Rafe's house, the quieter things became until at last, they reached a street that was almost empty. In the past few years, Greensboro had become a much different place from the one Rafe had known growing up. First, it had gotten more crowded, and then it had become more destitute. By the time the fences had gone up, he had started seeing parallels with certain parts of larger cities he'd visited. One street could be fine, and the next street over could be a hellhole. Then there were the areas that had been abandoned as folks who couldn't afford their nicer houses had reluctantly consigned themselves to the apartments in the inner city.

Such was the case the next street over. There were houses that were still inhabited, but the one Rafe was making for, he knew, had been abandoned for some time. Dragging Neil over to the back porch, he had him sit on the step, just under the roof. "I'll be right back Neil, I'm just going to make sure no one else is here, okay?"

"Not like I'm going anywhere," Neil said bluntly.

Rafe grimaced at that uncomfortable fact. "True," he said. With that, he walked through the door, which hung open. There was no electricity, and he doubted there was running water, but if he could just find a light in here ... He heard something moving. "Who's there?" he asked.

No one answered, but in the cold twilight filtering in through the boarded-up windows he caught a glimpse of a small animal scurrying across the floor.

"Okay..." he said to himself, "it was just a rat."

Just a rat ... He scoffed at his own cavalier attitude. He could already hear his mother lecturing him on the reality that rats carried diseases. He brought his thoughts back to the task at hand. After a moment, he pulled out his cell phone, letting the screen light his path.

Carefully, he stepped across the floor, cringing at every creaking board under his sneakers as he scanned the area for danger. Finding none, he moved the light up the wall to a bookshelf. Something glinted at the edge of the phone's small radius of light. He moved closer but froze as he felt something – it sounded like a pile of books – brush against his hand and tumble to the floor off a side table. After pausing to catch his breath again, he reached the shelf and the prize that was sitting on it.

A lantern?

Yes!

He shook it experimentally, being careful not to spill the contents. It seemed there was oil in it, and it had a wick. Searching around the shelf some more, he located a box of matches. He quickly brought the match to the wick and after a second, it caught. As he blew the match out, a dim light blossomed through the glass, for the first time allowing him to really see the room.

Pocketing his phone to conserve the battery and looking down, he saw a fireplace and evidence that someone had been cooking with the coals some time ago. It seemed he wasn't the first person to break in, which could mean that someone was planning to come back. He was pretty sure they wouldn't be the house's rightful owner. After looking around with the lantern, the evidence seemed to point to this being a temporary shelter for someone. Good enough for now. If this person returned, Rafe fully intended to avoid confrontation as long as the stranger wasn't a threat.

Decision made, he set the lantern on a nearby coffee table and walked back outside to where Neil was waiting. "It seems to be clear," he said. "Let's get you inside." Neil nodded and braced himself to stand so Rafe could help him into the building.

Neil winced as they reached the door, and Rafe considered what to do next. Once they were inside, and he had lowered Neil to the floor against a wall, he again took his cell phone out of his jacket pocket, but then paused. Under normal circumstances, the correct thing to do would have been to call an ambulance and get his friend to a hospital; but what had happened with the dispatcher bothered him. They had cut him off when he asked for help, because of where he was and what he was asking them to do. Now that they were out of there, he could certainly try again, but ... what would happen to Neil after that?

And given everything Rafe had already done tonight, what would happen to *him*?

Before the Internet had been heavily restricted, there had been stories about children being separated from their families by social services based on political affiliation alone. There had also been reports of people who had stood up to rioters, or friends of the

party in power, being placed in 'protective custody,' or worse ...
disappearing ...

Like Mom ...

He turned the phone off. The authorities had made it clear they
were not going to help. He had interfered. Why should he expect
any assistance now? He needed time to think, and he needed to talk
to someone he knew he could trust.

"Neil, I hate to say it, but I think we're on our own for now."

"What should we do?" Neil asked.

"First, I think we ought to take a look at your leg," Rafe said. "I
don't know if it will help, but I do know some first aid. Hang on a
second, let me see what I can find." He stood up and, taking the
lantern with him, walked further into the house. He remained alert
for danger as he picked his way through the darkened building.
Eventually, he found the kitchen and started searching through the
drawers. Most of them were cleaned out, but in one drawer he
found a standard carpenter's hammer that seemed to have been
overlooked by scavengers. Once he pulled it up, he found that a pair
of pruning shears had been concealed beneath it. He used the head
of the hammer to secure it in the belt at his waist, pocketing the
shears as he brought the lantern up to check the cabinets and the
filthy sink, which didn't look like it had been used in years.

Since the hammer and shears were far from ideal medical tools,
he continued into the back room where an old washing machine
and dryer sat. That was where luck finally favored him. On one of
the utility shelves where someone normally would have kept
cleaning supplies, he found a nearly spent roll of gray duct tape.
"Thank you, MacGuyver," he muttered. Reaching up, he grabbed
the small prize and pocketed it before kneeling on the floor to check
another set of cabinets opposite the old, ruined appliances. That
was where he found a flathead screwdriver. Now that could come in
handy.

Sticking the screwdriver into one of his larger pockets, he
noticed a couple of thin molding boards leaning against the wall. It
looked like they had been taken off the top of a door frame and had

once been a little longer. For his purposes he didn't need to be picky and thankfully, they didn't seem to have any nails in them.

Gathering up his supplies, Rafe returned to the living room. He felt guilty that he'd had to move Neil anywhere before assessing his injury. But if they'd stayed near his house any longer ... He didn't want to consider what might have happened. "All right," he said, getting down on his knees next to Neil, "Are you ready for this?"

"I'll try to be," the boy responded.

Giving him a nod, Rafe leaned in and started examining Neil's right leg. He probably could have done that before, but he had wanted to make sure he had what he needed before he began this particular task. He had a strong suspicion that it was broken. It was hard to see a way around it, the way the kid had landed on the side of that planter's box.

Neil suddenly grunted as Rafe pressed on a point halfway up his lower leg, and he could have sworn he felt something grinding. "I guess that answers that," he looked up at his patient. Neil was gritting his teeth and his posture had visibly stiffened.

"Sorry," Rafe said, jerking his hand from the injury. "That better?"

"What do you think?" Neil groaned, relaxing only a little as Rafe pulled his hand away.

"Yeah, dumb question," Rafe noticed he was sweating and wiped the moisture off his brow. He'd been a lifeguard before, but this was not something he'd ever encountered outside of training. Okay ... where to begin ... He carefully placed the two boards on either side of Neil's leg, and then reached for the duct tape in his pocket.

"Make sure my knee can't move," Neil said quickly.

Rafe glanced in his direction as he tore free a piece of tape. "You've done this before?"

"Summer camp," Neil replied. "One of the other guys fell out of a tree."

"Oh," Rafe tried to think of a way to continue the conversation while he ripped three more pieces of duct tape off the roll and stuck them to the coffee table until he was ready for them. "What happened?"

Neil shook his head as he considered the memory. "He was trying to see how high he could climb before the counselors spotted him and wasn't being careful which branch he put his weight on. When it happened, we were too far away from a road for the paramedics to get to where we were, so one of the counselors walked us through what to do so we could safely carry him out."

"Sounds like he was lucky he didn't break his neck," Rafe said, holding the two pieces of wood in place with one hand and reaching for a piece of tape to wrap them around the boy's ankle.

"That was what they told him when the ambulance got there." Neil winced as Rafe lifted his leg slightly to finish wrapping the first piece of tape.

Rafe paused in his work. "Sorry."

"It's okay," Neil said breathlessly. He looked over at the remaining tape on the coffee table. "Three more left."

Rafe nodded. "I'll try not to move it more than I have to." Maybe he should come up with a new topic. Keep Neil thinking about other things. "So, played any new video games?"

"You know I haven't. We just don't have the money for anything new. Not with the trial..." Neil's expression became more worried. "I hope they're okay."

"I hope so too." Rafe replied as he reached for the next piece of tape. "I'll go take a look to see what happened in the morning."

The boy nodded, steeling himself as Rafe prepared to lift his leg again to wrap the next piece of tape around it. Once the strip was secure Rafe looked it over critically. "It's not too uncomfortable, aside from the obvious, is it?"

"I don't think so."

"Good," Rafe reached for the next piece of tape.

Sensing that he was at a loss for how to continue the conversation, Neil spoke again. "What about you?" he asked. "Played any games?"

"Nothing new. Mostly just some old classics. *Castlevania, Sonic 3* ... "

"You've always liked the older stuff, haven't you," Neil commented.

Rafe nodded sadly. "With my luck, those guys stole my console collection, if they didn't destroy it. Some of those were antiques too." He sighed as he wrapped the third piece of tape. Video game consoles had become prohibitively expensive over the past few years. They were more difficult to keep running too since the Internet had been censored and throttled to the point where regular citizens could barely access it.

Neil gripped his coat as Rafe secured the tape to the boards. "I'm sorry Rafe ... If I hadn't run to you..." He looked down at the floor, trying to hide the anxiety and guilt written on his face. "But I didn't know where else to go..."

Rafe was reaching for the last piece of tape but changed his mind, instead putting his hand on Neil's shoulder reassuringly. "Hey, don't start that. None of this is your fault."

Neil looked up at him and nodded, doing his best to calm down. Once he was sure Neil was going to keep it together, Rafe turned his attention back to the task at hand. Holding the boards in place, he began wrapping the last piece of tape. They were silent for a moment or two before he finished. "Well, how did I do?" he asked, finally. "I didn't make it too tight anywhere, did I?"

Neil looked over Rafe's handiwork for a moment before answering. "I think you pass."

Rafe exhaled and wiped his brow again. "All right, now that's over, let's try to get some rest. I'll go back in the morning to check on things and then..." Then what? The truth was, he didn't know. Neil was not in any position to move anywhere on his own, and it was too dangerous to ask for help at this point without knowing who he could trust.

There was one person who lived nearby, whom he was certain he could trust. "If things don't check out by then, my friend Eric lives on the edge of town, and we can go there. Then ... I guess we'll figure it out from there," he finished at last. He stood up. "I'm going to see if I can find anything to keep us warm, okay?"

Neil nodded. "Okay."

Satisfied with this answer, Rafe picked up the lantern and walked into the back hallway, before beginning his search for anything that would help them get through the night.

CHAPTER 2

THE WORLD AS IT IS

December 5, 2037

RAFE CREPT THROUGH THE SNOW BACK TOWARD HIS AND Neil's houses as quickly as he could. He didn't want to leave Neil alone longer than he had to, but he still had to find out just how much damage had been done and whether Howard and Jane were all right. As the snow crunched under his feet, he found himself rather grateful that the underbrush had served to obscure some of their footprints in the dark. Up ahead, he could see the bush under which they had hidden, and he gripped his wooden training sword, trying to calm his nerves and prepare himself for whatever he may see over the fence behind his house.

Debris was strewn about the yard, mostly broken glass, glittering in the early morning light. A few ruined photos and the remains of several smashed game disks also lay in the area, but he tried to ignore them as he moved toward the back door. He felt a moment of anger as he saw that every single one of his video game systems as well as his laptop computer were absent from their usual places in his living room, but that was inconsequential compared to how he felt when he looked out the smashed front window.

Out on the deserted street, he saw ashes and refuse littered

21

across the area where all those people had gathered; and as he looked more carefully, off in the distance, he saw two bodies hanging from a tree, each with a stain down the front of their clothes that was unmistakably red.

A cold breeze swept loose snowflakes along the sidewalk beneath them, tugging at Howard's coat, and playing disrespectfully with Jane's dark blonde hair.

It was the same color as Neil's.

He wondered, had they already been dead when they'd been hung there? Shouldn't someone cut them down? Or was there someone still around to watch for those who approached to see if they had any other sympathizers?

He watched them hanging there, suspended under the naked tree branches for a period of time he was not quite aware of before forcing himself to focus on what he was there to do. Then, he moved into his bedroom. A few things remained there. A couple of sweaters had been thrown carelessly on the floor, along with the remains of the posters that had once hung on his walls, and promotional art for several of his favorite games and films. Looking around, he spotted something slightly hidden on the wall behind a tattered shred of a vintage Legend of Zelda poster. He smiled sadly as he lifted a corner of the ripped image. It had been obscuring an eight-by-eleven-inch sheet of paper taped to the wall, untouched by the casual vandalism.

He doubted anyone outside his own circle of friends would know the meaning behind the drawing, other than the obvious fantasy genre. His Cleric stood in the back, a shield spell forming in one hand while a morning star mace was held in the other. Allen's Wizard stood next to him, a fireball floating above his outstretched palm. Eric's dwarven Fighter stood in the foreground, a battle-axe in his hands, while Hannah's elven Rogue knelt in a crouch with a dagger, ready to strike. Eric had drawn this near the end of their last semester and given copies to each of the other players.

He reached up and peeled the picture off the wall, removing the scotch tape and folding the paper before stashing it in his jacket pocket. He then picked up the two sweaters and shook off the debris before rolling them into a bundle which he stuffed inside his coat.

In the kitchen, he found the refrigerator still without power and most of its contents gone. Then he heard laughter outside and crept to the window in the living room. He was shocked to see a couple of men standing by the bodies, one of them posing as the other snapped a photo with his cellphone. Then the one posing glanced in his direction, and he ducked out of sight.

Deciding he had lingered long enough, Rafe crept toward the back door and quietly let himself out. Nothing remained for him here. He could have sworn he heard the front door open as he raced back into the trees, trying as best he could to imitate a ghost.

Not long after, he exited the other side of the stand of trees and walked back toward the house where Neil was waiting. He didn't want to believe what he had just seen but there was no way he could unsee it.

When he'd first met Howard, and recognized him as someone he'd seen on the news, Neil's father had told him a bit about the investigation against him. At first, Howard had been under the impression that some of the bigger corporations with political connections were starting to see his company as competition. Maybe they were trying to use those connections to force him out of business. There had been cases like this in other cities, but after the activists got involved, it seemed like it might have been something simpler than that. Scarcities had gotten much worse in the past few years, especially since the war had started. For the politicians, the calculus was easy. To distract the public, they had found one more villain to blame for their own policies, and then told the SPKF to "let the people have their 'day of rage'" as the activists and media personalities liked to call it.

In the end, Howard and Jane Flynn had been publicly murdered, and there had been nothing Rafe could do about it. He stared somberly at the snow in front of him as he walked, anger giving him heartburn as he remembered spending an evening at

Howard's kitchen table, helping him fix his work tablet. How Neil had brought him a couple of Jane's cookies before the sugar taxes had gotten too high, and they'd been really good, even if she had been known to give him the evil eye if he wasn't careful enough about his language. But more than anything, he wondered what they would think about this situation their son was now in and wished that they were walking back through the woods with him.

When he returned to the abandoned house, he found Neil sitting against the wall, waiting for his return. Neil looked up worriedly. "Did you find anything?"

Rafe looked away from him, trying to hide that he was fighting back tears. "I'm sorry. They didn't make it."

Neil let his gaze drop to the ground and seemed dazed for a few silent moments. At last, his voice quiet and distant, he spoke again. "Where are they?"

"Hanging from a tree near your house." Rafe got down on his knees next to Neil, putting a hand on his shoulder, even as he mentally kicked himself for how insensitive the description sounded. He angrily forced himself to dry his own eyes. He couldn't be doing this right now.

He saw Neil's hand clench into a fist on the floor. "Why...?" Neil asked, nearly choking on the question.

Rafe looked out the window, considering his answer. "I don't understand it either," he said at last.

He wished they could stay and give Neil time to grieve but now was not the time. "We need to get out of here and get to Eric. He ought to be able to help us." He offered the boy one of the sweaters he'd retrieved. "Put this on. It's pretty cold out there."

Neil took off his coat only long enough to pull on the sweater. Rafe busied himself with his own sweater and tried not to think too hard about what might be going on in the boy's mind. It was too painful to consider right now. Better to focus on getting to Eric. His hand brushed against his cellphone in his pocket and uncertainty crept back into his thoughts. It might not hurt to at least let his friend know he was coming.

He paused as his thumb hovered over the power button before shaking his head. If he turned that phone back on, it would mean being visible. It was not safe to be visible. Maybe he shouldn't even have it, but he couldn't quite bring himself to throw it away. It was an expensive piece of equipment, even if it was an old model. He placed the device back in his pocket.

Once they were both ready, Rafe hoisted Neil up from the floor, and they began working their way toward the door. Neil did his best, hopping along on his uninjured leg. Getting back out and down the stairs was a challenge, but Rafe knew it would be nothing compared to what lay ahead of them. Eric's family's townhouse was off Jefferson Road, just south of the fence on what had been New Garden. He supposed public transportation might be a possibility. They'd have to keep their heads down and make sure they did not attract attention ... Or maybe not. In his current condition, Neil would stand out like a beacon to anyone watching. Better to stay out of sight.

Would Eric help them?

Rafe shook his head angrily. Now he was just being paranoid. Out of the whole C&C party, they'd known each other the longest. They'd been friends well before Rafe had started attending the same High School; where he and his brother had been forced to enroll after homeschooling had become illegal at the end of his sophomore year. Actually, they'd been friends since before they were preschool age. If he couldn't trust Eric, who could he trust?

The walk to his friend's townhouse would be at least two miles. Not too taxing for someone who was in shape, but dragging an injured person would complicate things, especially someone shorter than himself. That would be on top of the challenge of making sure they stayed out of sight.

Taking one last look at the house in which they'd sheltered, Rafe and Neil began trudging slowly through the snow, heading back toward the tree line. It took them almost ten minutes to reach the small grove of trees between their street and Holden Road. Rafe wasn't used to helping someone walk, and Neil couldn't put any weight on his leg. Although the trees were the only major obstacle separating them from their first landmark, the path they had to take was not easy.

Even so, Rafe felt almost relieved. The road in front of them had not been maintained. Aside from the ones used regularly by the military and other government agencies, most of the roads outside of a certain proximity from downtown were littered with potholes. On the bright side, this greatly reduced traffic on outlying streets, but it also made it that much easier to be noticed.

Rafe took some time to rest against a tree while Neil stood on his good leg, leaning against another sapling. He took note of the snow separating them from the road. It appeared to be melting slowly. Once it fell around here, the snow generally lingered for a while before becoming soggy slush under the sun, and then hardening into ice at night. The snow melting was a good thing in the long run, because not having snow would make it a lot less easy for someone to follow them. In the meantime, though, their prints would be easy to spot.

Rafe straightened up to his full height and looked around the area. No one was visible along what had once been one of the city's busier streets. He turned his attention to Neil. "You ready to cross?" he asked.

Neil was leaning against a nearby tree facing away from him, only a few strands of his dark blonde hair peeking out from under the hood of his coat as he watched the road. On hearing Rafe speak he quickly reached up a hand to his face as though wiping something from his cheek. When he turned to face him though, his expression was determined, and he nodded. "Let's go."

Once Rafe had taken a moment to pull Neil's arm over his shoulder in an assisted carry, they worked their way out of the trees and onto the crumbling asphalt. They then turned their attention to the matter of getting back to cover. Neil hopped along as Rafe helped him, and Rafe wished he was a little stronger and had a better means of doing this, but there was little more he could do.

They were about halfway across the road when he heard a

vehicle off in the distance, and the two of them stepped up their pace, just reaching the other side of the four-lane street and vanishing into the trees before a driverless truck rolled past.

Two hours later, as the sun rose higher, they passed the two stark apartment buildings that had been built along this street a short time ago. That was one problem with having everyone all cooped up in the city, Rafe reflected. Space was at a premium. The only reason he hadn't been living in one of these was because he'd managed to find someone willing to rent a house. They kept to the trees and behind houses that had "For Sale" signs or otherwise weren't occupied. They'd seen a couple of people walking around, but they'd kept well clear of them. Maybe his unkempt dusty-brown hair and four-day beard would help them confuse him for a vagrant, but not if he had Neil with him.

Once they reached Bearhollow Road, they stopped to rest again. Over the time they had been traveling, they had both almost slipped on several occasions, and were nursing some minor cuts from branches. It was better to take advantage of the tree cover than to walk on the sidewalk and run the risk of getting attacked again, but that was a small consolation.

Think of it like a quest, Rafe told himself quietly as they got ready to move again. Yeah. That was the right attitude. Maybe with that, he could keep himself from thinking about the very real consequences for failure.

———

March 9, 2030

"So, tell me again, why did we take this heavy rock, that requires a cart to haul it all the way back to town?" Hannah had been fidgeting with the end of her brown ponytail as she asked the question. "I understand wanting the gold, but that guy who stole it seemed kind of powerful."

"It was for the Temple of ... Bonan Dai? Oh, I forget his name

..." Eric frowned as he tried to remember, before giving up. "You know, the nature god the Druids all worship."

"Orendai," Will clarified.

"Yeah, that one," Eric agreed quickly.

"It was the best way we could transport it," Allen said as he stretched his arms. Even sitting, his long arms seemed to reach halfway to the ceiling, "I don't learn powerful enough teleportation spells until the 9th level."

"That's a problem," Rafe fidgeted with an opened candy wrapper in his pocket.

Allen paused and focused on the floor near Hannah's purse. "Hey, did you drop something?"

Hannah looked down, and her blue-eyed gaze landed on a piece of card stock before she picked it up. "Oh, thanks. That was my national voter registration card. You know since they passed that amendment last month?"

"The one to abolish the Electoral College? I know," Allen shook his head in disappointment as he stood up. "I still don't think that was a good idea. I mean, it takes away so much of the power the states had as 'states,' and then on top of that, our congressional districts are national instead of local too?"

"Well, the idea is to make elections fairer," Hannah placed the card back into her purse as she went back to perusing her character sheet.

"The thing is ... what's the point of even having states anymore? You know it means the cities are going to dominate like crazy." Having given his knees the chance to straighten and pop in a manner that seemed to satisfy him, he sat back down, ready to focus. "But we're getting off the subject. We can debate politics later." He gave Will an apologetic look. "Sorry to interrupt."

"It's okay," Will said. He flipped through his notes for a second and then found the paper he was looking for and turned his attention back to the group. "So, do you continue onward?"

"Yes, we do," Rafe said.

"Well, you continue on for another five miles but then. . . Spot and Listen checks."

"Oh, crap," Eric looked over his results and he gave Will a disappointed half smile. "I seem to be extremely focused on the road ahead," he said by way of an answer. "Don't bother with my rolls."

"I think I succeeded," Hannah said. "16 and 18!"

Will nodded as everyone else tallied their results, which had been rather terrible for the most part, and then turned his attention back to Hannah. "Okay, you look behind you, and you see this guy in dark brown robes riding a spider the size of a small pony. He seems to be barreling down the road at top speed." Everyone looked worried, and with good reason. This was the Wizard from which they'd reclaimed the nature relic.

Hannah looked around at the others before asking humorously "Anyone have a giant can of bug spray guys? We're being followed."

Allen looked around the room, a nervous grin over his goatee. "Yeah ... I cast some caltrops in the road, and then Rafe ... er ... Galen, get those cart horses to a gallop. We're running away!"

"We're not gonna fight?" Eric asked, a little disappointed.

Allen shook his head emphatically. His character's social skills had played a rather large part in the plan to retrieve the rock, and he'd been given a tour of what this particular Wizard liked to do to thieves. "Nope."

December 5, 2037

After about half an hour of walking Rafe and Neil stood in front of a small townhouse. Helping Neil to a seat on the porch steps, Rafe walked to the door and knocked, trying to keep his nervousness at bay. Sounds came from inside, and after a few moments the door opened. Instead of Eric or one of his family, though, Rafe found himself face to face with a stranger, an older woman with a heavyset build and a guarded expression.

"May I help you?" she asked.

"Um, we're looking for Eric Davis. Is he here?" Rafe was certain it hadn't been that long since he'd spoken to his friend, maybe a couple of months at most.

The woman suddenly eyed them with much more suspicion, especially the wooden sword Neil held in his lap. "I'm afraid not. There's no one here by that name."

Rafe furrowed his brow in confusion. "That's weird. I was sure this was the right house."

The woman shook her head. "I'm afraid you're mistaken."

He sighed. "Sorry to bother you, but thanks for your time." He was very aware of how she was watching him as he moved to help Neil up and then left her front step before she shut the door. They didn't stop until they were a couple of blocks away and out of sight.

"What now?" Neil asked as he leaned against a tree.

Rafe didn't answer right away as he was trying to get himself to focus. They certainly couldn't stay around here. He wasn't wrong about the house, he was certain. He'd gone there enough times, yet his friend hadn't even bothered to tell him that his family had moved? With Eric's current whereabouts in question, what was left? He sorted around in his mind for an answer, going through and quickly passing over any number of former coworkers and acquaintances, whom, in all honesty, couldn't use the sort of trouble he'd invite. None of his neighbors had done anything when the Flynns had been murdered, and they probably wanted nothing to do with their current problems either. It was understandable. Most people just kept their heads down, not unlike himself before last night.

"Hey, Neil, do you have any other family in town?" Rafe asked. Maybe he'd taken this far enough. After all, what was he doing out here with an injured thirteen-year-old and what more could he do at this point. . .?

"No one in Greensboro," Neil said. "Everyone else is up north."

Rafe's thoughts went back to Howard and Jane, hanging from that tree.

He'd already done more than the proper authorities had been willing to do. They had allowed this to happen, and had shown no care for Howard's family. Never mind the stories he'd heard about the way Social Services operated these days, and undoubtedly that was where Neil would end up. And then there was his own fate to consider. With the way things had already gone, what could he expect? At the very least, it was probably assault charges for beating that guy with his sword, because self-defense meant nothing anymore, assuming they didn't accuse him of kidnapping Neil, or worse.

No. That was not an option.

He started branching further out, considering the logistics of going to another city. Doing so legally would require special permission, so that wouldn't work. Travel was heavily restricted. No one lived in the countryside anymore, either. There was nothing but abandoned houses … and …

And … his old family home in what had once been Oak Ridge, until the politicians had declared small towns environmental hazards. Rafe gave his friend a grim look as he finally brought himself back to answering the boy's question. "Now? I guess we get out."

"Out?" Neil asked. "Where?"

"Through the fence," Rafe almost couldn't believe his own answer as he was saying it. It had taken him the last couple of hours to get them to Eric's house, but getting out of the city entirely might take the rest of the day, and that was assuming they didn't get caught. On the other hand, there didn't seem to be any other options now.

Neil's eyes widened. "We can do that?"

"Do you want to stick around here?" Rafe asked.

Neil shook his head. "No. It's just … won't someone come after us?"

"I don't know," Rafe spent a few seconds stretching as he continued, "But I don't think I see a better choice here." With that, he walked back over to pull Neil once again into an assisted carry, and they started toward New Garden Road, continuing the trend of staying in the trees where possible.

———

Steam curled up from the coffee cup in SPKF Inspector Richard L. Church's hand as he looked over the files on his desk. A few years ago, most people at least had the decency to file permit papers *before* protests, in case things got out of hand. Now, many people didn't even bother filing them, and sometimes, circumstances transpired in such a way that they never reached a desk in the precinct. It was a sad state of affairs, but an active populous that could root out dangerous sentiments was greatly preferable to those who would turn a blind eye to potential rebels and see their own country crumble. A few misfiled permits were a small price to pay for social progress.

He heard a noise outside the open door and nodded to one of the younger officers who had slipped another set of files into the receiving tray in front of his office. The officer returned the nod with a nervous grimace and quickly left. The younger members of the force had never thought of him as friendly. Rumor had it they were put off by the hardness of his deep-set grey eyes. Not that his wife seemed to mind. He had a rough job, and he was entitled to be intimidating.

There was a knock on the door and after telling the person to enter, he saw that it was Sergeant Everett. He was a heavy-set black man, who was starting to show a few years on him, one of the few remaining old-timers from the Guilford County Sherriff's office, before they were absorbed by the SPKF, in 2035.

"You asked me to gather possible leads on our case, Inspector?" Everett said. "I think I've found a couple."

Church nodded and gestured for the sergeant to have a seat before glancing over the papers. Near the top of the stack sat a picture of the bodies of Howard and Jane Flynn where they had been found at the scene, and he picked it up to get a better view.

"So that's how they looked after it went down." Church dropped the photo back on the desk. "They deserved it, from what I've heard. Hiring people only after forcing them to wait months and months for an interview 'due to competition'; adamantly repelling any attempts to let the workers unionize by insisting on secret ballot elections; only paying contractors by the job rather than giving them an established salary. No wonder his business partners took off for rebel territory the moment the prosecutor filed the charges. It's a disgrace this was allowed to go on for so long, and now there's *this* little mess left for us to clean up." He lifted a file with another photo clipped to it, this one from a yearbook he had picked up from the local middle school. A young boy with dark blond hair smiled nervously, clearly not wanting to be there. Though it was harder to tell with the black and white printing on the page, the file with his information said that he had brown eyes and was about four foot eleven. "Neil Flynn is still unaccounted for?"

"Yes sir," Everett confirmed. They had learned of this about two hours ago, after officers had come in to clean up.

Church perused the file before laying it down in front of him. "Then what are these leads?" he asked.

Everett reached for the last sheet of paper in the stack. "We got a call from a Mrs. Adrian Lee a few minutes ago. She says she bought a house at auction after it was repossessed by civil asset forfeiture last month and was asked to report if anyone suspicious showed up."

"And?" Church prompted.

"She says a man came to her door with a young boy and then left. The description she's giving sounds like Neil Flynn and someone else."

"And you got an ID on this other person, I hope?" Church eyed the older sergeant impatiently.

Everett nodded and reached for one of the other files he'd set on the desk. "Fortunately, we do. I got a profile of the Flynn's neighbor. We've found eyewitness testimony that the boy was seen with him, and his appearance is a match."

Everett passed the new file to Church, and he looked it over for several seconds before his eyebrows raised in surprise. Then his expression hardened. At first glance, Rafe Turner's file seemed rather mundane, with the picture from his photo ID showing a young man with an average build and a clean-shaven face, framed by neatly trimmed dust-brown hair. According to the file, he was twenty-seven years old, stood about five foot eleven and had green eyes. Probably even tucked in his shirts when he'd been employed. He seemed ordinary enough, but it wasn't his appearance that got Church's attention. The real meat was much further down in the report.

"Turner," he growled.

Everett looked at him curiously. "Does the name sound familiar to you?" he asked.

Church nodded. "You bet your ass it does. Do you remember around the time they started resettling people from the country and puttin' up the fences, and we had to root out a few terrorists who didn't want to leave?"

Recognition crossed Everett's face. "Just before the war started, back in '33? You were part of that, weren't you sir?"

"Got shot at as part of it," Church confirmed. He was half conscious of his hand around the spent shell casing he kept in his pocket as a reminder. "There was a lady in Oak Ridge who kissed my shoulder with her twelve-gauge and almost had my wife and daughters down one father. Well, guess who this guy's mother is?"

Everett blinked and then realization hit. "No way ... "

Church nodded. "Carol Turner. Now there's a name that is literally a blast from the past." He gestured to the photo with a self-satisfied chuckle. "And look how clean cut her son is. You'd hardly think he'd started any trouble in his life."

Everett took back the file and looked it over with renewed interest, past the man's serious green eyes to his information below. "Two siblings, father and younger brother's whereabouts unknown, older sister's last known address ... Boone, North Carolina, in rebel territory. Also flagged for trying to search banned news sites during the Internet crackdowns ... And that's only the beginning."

Church nodded until Everett stopped reading. "It's a surprise he hasn't popped up before now with who else he's got in his list of acquaintances. But add kidnapping to the list, and you've got one sick piece of gutter trash. So, what say we pay Mrs. Lee a visit and see if we can find him from there?" He stood and pulled on his coat, taking a moment to stroke back any loose strands of thinning dark hair before pulling on a hat. He closed his hand into a fist around the shell casing. "It's as open and shut as you can get, Everett. We find Rafe Turner, we find Neil Flynn."

———

November 9, 2030

"The Veil of the Truthseer? What's that?" Rafe had asked, looking up from where he'd been playing with his dice.

"It's an enchanted veil, and when you look through it, it shows the world around you as it is," Will explained. Everyone was looking at him with confusion, though; it was clearly a narrative description and really didn't tell them anything in the context of the game itself.

"I'm pretty sure there's nothing like that in any of the rule books..." Eric observed.

"You made it up, didn't you," Hannah accused.

"Perhaps..." Will said innocently.

"Sounds like kind of a boring artifact." Allen was looking at Will with a grin despite his feigned disinterest. "You wear it and the world looks like it already does?"

"Not exactly," Will thought about how he was going to elaborate before continuing, "What makes it special lies more in ... 'how' it shows the world as it is. It can detect when someone has good or evil intentions. It also negates illusions, and while wearing it, you can read a person's thoughts. Anyway, Ardes continues telling his story." He once again adopted his best powerful-yet-lazy-wizard voice. "Rumor has it that it lies in an ancient tower about three days to the east of the town of Rubel; but to get inside, you will need to find three keys that are spread across the land. I need you to help me figure out where they are..."

December 5, 2037

It had been about four years since the fences had gone up around most of the cities, and the countryside had been forcibly evacuated under the new environmental statutes. In a visual symbol of how much power the politicians had over such things, the shopping center on the opposite side of the street had been bulldozed as the media cheered the removal of the "non-environmentally friendly eye-sore." Of course, this had just been a publicity stunt. Countless homes lay vacant in the woods, rotting in place, conveniently out of sight. Now, the length of New Garden was lined by a chain link fence with barbed wire strung across it.

The hulking remains of an overpass connected the hill where the shopping center once stood to a spot where other businesses and a gas station had also once been in place. Homeless people sometimes liked to stay under it, so occasionally the SPKF would come out on a 'humanitarian drive' to force them to take residence in government housing. Interstates 40 and 85 were the only roads anyone cared about once you got out of the inner city.

It was getting close to noon when Rafe and Neil got to Hobbs Road where it neared the fence. Not many people lived beyond that point, mostly out of fear of constant searches by military personnel or the SPKF. As a result, the pines and maples in this area had grown unchecked for quite a while, leaving a small forest.

Once Rafe and Neil had reached the edge of the trees, however, it was a different matter entirely. Much of what used to be New Garden had been cleared away, leaving the area unforgivingly open.

They decided that since it was a little after noon, it might be better to seek cover until nightfall.

They found the emptied remains of a large supermarket on the edge of the open space near the fence and sheltered there for about five hours. Neil hid behind the customer service desk near the front, while, after resting a bit, Rafe went further in, hoping to find anything left behind that was still edible, as neither of them had eaten since yesterday. That hope turned out to be unrealistically optimistic, as he soon realized. Everything here was long gone, even the dog food. The sunlight filtering through the skylights (many of them broken) was starting to dim as he worked his way through section after section of what would have been non-perishables. At last, defeated, he noticed their optimal time for departure was drawing near and made his way back toward where Neil was hiding.

Upon reaching him, Rafe saw that the kid seemed to be asleep. Feeling pretty bad about having to wake him up, he walked over and tapped him on the shoulder. "Come on Neil. Time to go."

Neil looked up at him, blinking the sleep out of his eyes. "Okay..."

Not long after, Rafe helped him out of the building and then over to the side of the abandoned street where they could take shelter in the bushes. Once there, they crawled through the un-mowed grass and the underbrush until they were within sight of the Bryant Boulevard overpass, once a main thoroughfare to the now vacated suburban sprawl beyond. Now, the road beyond the fence was a mess of unmaintained brush and tree saplings.

Rafe had heard stories that occasionally people would dig under the fence or cut holes in it, though someone would eventually fill them in or repair them. Perhaps they would get lucky. Of course, there was also the chance they could get shot, and the way their luck was going...

He turned to his companion. "I'm going to look around and see what I can find. Can you wait here?"

Neil nodded and crawled underneath one of the thicker Virginia pines for cover. It and its brothers looked like they'd been planted there for decoration back when the overpass was still in use, but other plant growth in the area had overtaken it, making it a good hiding place.

Rafe crept across the open area toward the overpass, and down under it, between the concrete pylons, scanning the area for any sign of a security camera. He wasn't as stealthy as they had imagined Hannah's Rogue to be, but he had never imagined he would need to emulate her character in real life. He tried to keep in mind everything he had ever heard about staying out of sight, though he didn't think it was particularly helpful. The chances of being seen by a civilian were slim, because the area was only sparsely populated. Although there was always the chance a helicopter or surveillance drone might fly overhead.

At long last, he made it under the overpass and started to search for any sign that someone might have opened a way for them. As the last of the twilight was starting to fade to darkness in the western sky, it became harder to see, but he could still make out the chain-link fence with barbed wire strung across the top. He picked his way through rocks, chunks of ruined asphalt, and concrete. He felt the butterflies rise in his stomach, and every noise he made seemed far too loud not to attract attention.

Finally, when he was sure there was no other way to get through, he reached into his pocket for the pair of pruning shears he'd picked up at the abandoned house and set to work on the chain links. It was slow going. The shears were not designed for this, and about halfway through his hands were aching. It took probably ten minutes to make a hole large enough to squeeze through, but it felt like hours.

A few minutes later, he was back at Neil's hiding place, and once he had helped Neil to the gap he had just opened, they began slowly crawling through the barricade. Once they had reached the other side, Rafe spared a moment to lean the cut chain links back up against where they had previously hung before helping Neil toward the trees. He knew it wouldn't fool a close inspection, but maybe someone giving it a cursory glance might overlook it. When they were a few feet away, he paused again, thinking, before reaching into his coat pocket and pulling out his cell phone. It was still off.

Earlier, he'd been too busy thinking about getting to Eric, but now something stirred in his memory. He had happened across a web article just before the war about remotely turning on cell phones, and he felt a moment of disquiet. Had he already made a critical mistake before they were even out in the woods?

Through the evening gloom, he heard helicopter rotors in the distance, and he felt a stab of fear as his pulse quickened. Was the helicopter coming for them? He couldn't be sure, but at this point it honestly didn't matter.

Since the time he'd gotten his first phone, it had always felt like a lifeline, a means to contact help if he needed it and to reach out to the world around him. But the truth was it could also be a tether, chaining people to the shores of civilization. If he was serious about not letting anyone find them, then it was a tether he would have to sever.

They had crossed the threshold. It was time to leave their ties to the world behind them at the door. He tried not to think about how putting it that way made it sound like they were already dead.

After a moment's hesitation, he dropped the phone on the ground, and he and Neil ducked into the brush.

The helicopter continued overhead, and Rafe breathed a sigh of relief as he realized it was headed toward the airport. But he decided that from then on, they would keep to the trees or shelter wherever possible. It wasn't just because of helicopters. There were also drones.

As if that wasn't enough to worry about, a few minutes after the rotor noise died away, and the fear of being discovered had abated, he was once again painfully aware that he was really hungry. It had been more than twenty-four hours since the riot, and they had been traveling since this morning without supplies. They would need to find water soon. And food. He had no idea where they would find either.

CHAPTER 3

HAUNTED HOUSES

December 5, 2037

THEY FOUND THE REMAINS OF AN EMPTY NEIGHBORHOOD near the fence. It was hard to shake the unsettling absence of people as he opened a door whose lock had long ago been busted. The house stood vacant, probably looted. But it offered shelter from the cold outside.

As they walked into the foyer, Neil spoke up. "You don't believe in ghosts, do you?"

"No." Rafe tried to sound more sure of himself than he felt. "Why? Are you scared?"

The moon outside was nearly full in the absence of the cloud cover from last night, and he saw the younger boy frown stubbornly. "Of course not."

Rafe helped him to the steps leading up to the second floor so he could sit down, then lit the lantern they'd brought from the first house they'd sheltered in. "Okay, because I'm going to check the area for any surprises, and then we're going to sleep."

Neil nodded but said nothing. Rafe considered for a minute before asking "How's the leg?" He'd been grateful Neil hadn't done much more than weakly say "ow" from time to time, but it was

41

probably more a mark of the seriousness of the situation they were in than anything else.

"It hurts a lot. It's probably not a good thing that we're moving around so much."

"I don't disagree," Rafe said soberly, "but being found would be worse."

His stomach growled. It had been almost thirty-six hours since he'd eaten cheese and crackers in his cold, dark living room. He felt terribly thirsty too. Once he was sure Neil was settled, he turned around and walked into the dark, holding the lantern as he went.

———

February 15, 2031

Will had been warming to the job of setting the scene as he began to lay it out for the players. He leaned forward, his grey eyes twinkling with excitement through his glasses. "As you move through the darkened hallway, you can't help but have an extreme sense of disquiet. Every now and then, you hear the creaking of boards under you, the sigh of loose shutters, and maybe it's just your imagination, but is that the sound of someone moaning?"

"Of course," Allen observed, his posture nonchalant as though encountering spooks and specters was a normal occurrence. "I mean, what else would it be but a ghost?"

"Well, what if it's just your imagination?" Hannah asked.

"I think the odds of that are pretty remote," Eric commented with a chuckle. "This is C&C after all."

"It could be something else that moans," Hannah retorted. "Maybe a window got left open, and it's windy."

"I find that to be very unlikely." Rafe was looking over his dice, picking out the ones he thought he would need the most for this encounter.

"It's not windy." Will said, trying to maintain the suspense. "You hear a louder moan in the next room..."

"I shout into the next room for whoever it is to knock it off," Allen said.

Everyone had been leaning forward, more alert in anticipation of combat; but as he spoke, the mood shifted, and they all snickered. In keeping with a long-honored tradition of player subversion, the Game Master's carefully crafted tension melted away, and the serious party of adventurers had reverted to just a group of friends laughing at a shared joke.

Will shook his head as he composed himself before adding in resignation. "It's a banshee. She screams at you. It's time for my favorite save for everyone." All the players groaned. Of course. It would be a saving throw to test the character's 'will' in the face of something terrifying. This roll would determine whether their characters stood and fought or ran like scared little kids.

"Well," Hannah pointed out as she reached for her dice. "It's not *technically* a ghost."

———

December 5, 2037

As Rafe walked into the kitchen, he saw that this house was in a state of decay, though not nearly as much as the first one they had sheltered in. The floor was covered in vast amounts of dust and grime, and he couldn't readily see anything to eat or drink. However, after poking around, he was surprised to discover a single, sealed bag of potato chips. He had found it in the laundry room, tucked behind a pile of filthy rags. Resisting the urge to open them right away, he gripped his prize to his chest, and made his way over to a tiny bathroom, curious if there might have been any medicine or bandages left behind, or perhaps some towels he might be able to use. There, he also had a little good luck; even though he didn't find any bandages or anything for a better splint, he did find something almost as good in the medicine cabinet, ibuprofen.

He searched around in the kitchen a little more and then

returned to where Neil was waiting, dropping the chips and the medicine into his lap. "Here."

Neil looked up at Rafe curiously as he made his way through another door. "Aren't you going to want some too?"

"Of course," Rafe called over his shoulder, "But we also need water. You go ahead, just make sure you leave some for me, okay?"

"Okay..." he heard the boy's voice echo through the house. He now headed down the hall toward where he thought he had seen a back door while in the kitchen. He found it and, pushing it open, was pleasantly surprised to find a fire pit surrounded by stones underneath one of the larger trees. Perhaps someone had come this way before? He walked back into the kitchen and returned to the fire pit with a medium-sized pot he had spotted on the way out. Looking around further, he found a pile of snow that had not quite melted under a nearby tree. He quickly filled the cooking pot with it before returning to the fire pit. After retrieving some loose paper and some wood from a broken table in the utility room, he used the paper to catch a light from the wick of his lantern.

Soon he had a small fire going. He carefully placed the pot within the fire, hoping he wasn't making a terrible mistake. Part of him worried this would attract attention but being dehydrated was worse.

Much to his relief, the water soon boiled, and a few minutes later, after removing the pot from the fire, he found another armful of snow and used it to extinguish the coals, wincing at the briefly thicker puff of smoke billowing up in the moonlight. He brought the pot inside, setting it in front of Neil on the earth-colored tiles that marked the area in the main foyer. "I'm afraid we'll have to wait a few minutes unless we want to burn our hands," he said, "But at least we'll have water."

"I guess that counts for something," Neil leaned back on the stairs to wait.

"It does," Rafe agreed. He sat down next to his friend. "Hope you didn't eat all the chips,"

Neil paused, looking apologetic before handing him the foil

package. "I stopped before I ate the whole thing, but I might have eaten a little bit more than half before I caught myself. . . I was hungry. . ."

As Rafe looked inside, he saw there was a bit more than a quarter of it left. He sighed, and after a moment he said disappointedly, "Well, it can't be helped now, and you did save some. Try to be a little more careful next time." His stomach growled and he reached into the package and started eating. He could have been angry about it, but at this point, he was too tired and Neil had plenty to deal with already without him adding to the pile. Neil nodded and sat in an uncomfortable silence as Rafe ate. A few minutes later when Rafe was finished, he set the empty bag aside. "I think I saw a bedroom near the kitchen. We'll sleep in there tonight."

Neil nodded and then looked over at the pot. "Do you think it's cooled?"

Rafe licked his finger and then checked the stainless-steel rim. It still felt hot but it didn't seem to be searing anymore. He tested it again, this time letting his hand stay a few seconds longer. It didn't seem to burn. "I think so."

Neil reached out and took the pot by its handles before checking the sides. Then, bringing the rim to his lips, he took one careful sip and then another. Once he was finished, he handed the pot to Rafe. The water tasted sweeter than honey. Rafe had never been a fan of drinking it hot, but the warm liquid against his throat felt wonderful. After they both drank their fill and the pot sat empty, he tied one of the handles to a loop on his coat. He didn't dare leave it behind.

———

December 6, 2037

Rafe sat at the entrance to one of the bedrooms, listening carefully as Neil rested nearby. They had taken turns listening for any sounds that might indicate they had been discovered, but they had passed the night uninterrupted. The old neighborhood was a ghost town.

From a window facing eastward, the sun was slowly beginning to warm the wall behind him through the spider web of broken glass, lacing a shadow burst over the silhouette of the nearby trees. He was relieved to see that, compared to yesterday, today would at least be warm enough to melt the remaining snow. He walked to the window, taking in the frail warmth from the sun shining on his coat and jeans without the wind chill that would result from standing outside. Hopefully they would make more progress today. He returned to where his friend rested and nudged his shoulder gently. "Neil?"

The boy blinked slowly before rubbing the sleep out of his eyes. "What is it?"

"We need to go," Rafe answered. "Do you have the ibuprofen?"

Neil nodded, producing the bottle from one of his pockets.

"All right," Rafe said. "I want you to try starting with two today. I don't want to go any higher than necessary if we don't have to. We don't know when we'll find more."

"These are out of date," Neil pointed to the expiration date on the lid.

"Well, it's the best we've got," Rafe said apologetically. He looked closer at the sticker. "It's only a couple of years past. They worked last night, right?"

Neil nodded and then swallowed two of the tablets. Shortly after, Rafe hoisted Neil up again and together they left the house, moving among the scrub pines to return to the remains of Bryant Boulevard.

———

It took them several hours to arrive at the junction of Bryant Boulevard and I-73, the only part of the road that was maintained to keep the route to the airport open. After reaching the junction, Rafe stayed well away from the road, barely keeping it in sight. The snow was mostly melted, leaving the grass moist and cold under his sneakers. He paid special care to avoid any mud, in case they left more permanent tracks. Eventually, they reached the off-ramp that would have taken them toward the airport. Here, Rafe turned north. Following that, the road led to what had once been the small town of Oak Ridge. Although the population had been forcibly removed, the asphalt had never been taken up.

A few minutes later, an abandoned shopping center with an empty grocery store loomed on the righthand side of the road, and they decided it was a good place to rest. As he had done the last time, Rafe dropped Neil off behind the counter at the customer service desk near the front of the grocery store and walked in deeper. This one had been built to be spacious and airy, with a large glass window over the doors, almost church-like in the way the panels had been framed to give off the appearance of an arch. With the afternoon sunlight peering through the broken glass, he searched through the empty shelves. His stomach growled. If there was any edible food left, he would be happy just for that.

He heard something creak nearby and lifted his wooden sword, backing against one of the shelves to avoid being surprised. "Who's there?"

———

March 22, 2031

"I'm telling you. It makes sense."

Rafe had just arrived at Will's apartment and found him quietly watching Hannah and Allen debate. They discussed such things from time to time, more as a friendly rivalry than anything else, but politics could get heated at the best of times.

"As things stand," Hannah continued, "we're polluting our planet, and we're not using our resources the way they should be used. With every factory, we're putting out so much carbon dioxide into the air, and when we build those nice houses out in the countryside, we're constantly destroying the environment. Wouldn't it be better if we instructed people on a more sustainable means of living?"

Rafe quietly took his favorite spot on Will's couch as Allen gave Hannah a look of consternation. "Essentially what you're saying is that you don't trust the average person to live their lives as they see fit."

"They won't learn if we don't educate them. Haven't we seen what happens when those factories go up?" Hannah replied.

"Well, I don't know if you've noticed," Allen said, tossing a d10 in the air and catching it as he spoke, "But the claim that carbon dioxide is harmful to the environment is still debatable. And further, when we industrialize and the overall population gets more affluent, they pay a lot more attention to the environment without it being forced down their throats because they care about their own property and are more aware of how these things affect it. Didn't some cities clean themselves up eventually? Most people will find the most efficient ways to do things on their own, and they will take initiative if they see how it benefits them. The others will be competed out of the market and find new lines of work. That's how it works. Besides, the people in power are just as human as the rest. Doesn't that make them just as ignorant and corruptible? What makes *them* any better judges?"

"It's only debatable if you ignore what the climate scientists are saying," Hannah said. "If we don't stop killing our planet, things are only going to get worse! People should know what they need to do!"

"Who's ignoring anything?" Allen asked calmly. "Any idiot can see that climate changes. The question is whether or not it's catastrophic or if it even requires human intervention. People can be smart, they can adapt, even without the government nanny looking over their shoulder. They have to because what happens when government fails?"

Hannah gave him an annoyed frown and opened her mouth to continue, but at that moment Will straightened from where he'd been sitting in his desk chair, disinterestedly watching the discussion while resting his chin on his hand, his arm propped up on the arm rest. He glanced out the window and spoke up. "I think I see Eric coming ... "

———

" ... And your Hold Person spell wears off. The vampire takes more damage. He's very weak now, and he's not very happy as the sunlight's burning him to a crisp so he takes a turn to transform into mist," Will narrated.

"I have a spell for that," Allen commented.

"Well, as it turns out, you're next in the initiative," Will's grey eyes were fixed on his friend in anticipation.

Allen pretended to be thinking for a moment and then he raised his hand and said, "Dispel Magic."

Will looked impressed. "The vampire goes back to humanoid form, and he still looks very, very hurt."

They'd laughed when Eric had taken Knowledge: Architecture as a skill. What did a Fighter need with it after all? But Eric had insisted because Kade was a dwarf, and dwarves knew building with stone.

Then, based on an idea Rafe had come up with when they'd learned they'd be facing Count Kirith, Eric had rolled a natural 20 on finding the room in the crypt under the thinnest part of the roof.

Rafe's Cleric prepared some holy symbols along with some Hold Person spells, and Allen's Wizard had prepared a few charges of Dispel Magic along with a Wind Wall, in case the vampire got free of their primary plan by turning into mist. Allen then had Malchior summon a Fiendish Badger to burrow a convex hole down from the roof of the crypt, so it only just opened into the room. They had then placed a crystal ball they'd found in a previous dungeon into the hole to fill the room with refracted sunbeams. They used Hannah's Rogue to lure the vampire to this room, and once he was distracted with everyone else, she climbed to the roof to pull a shroud off the crystal.

Eric had dubbed the plan (out of character, of course) "Operation Disco Ball."

"I use my Holy Symbol to press him into the nearest sunbeam," Rafe said emphatically.

Will nodded, deciding it was time to end this. "All right. Cornered and unable to flee, he tries to fight you, but you prevent him from finding an escape, and he trips, falls into the sunlight cast by the crystal, and begins to disintegrate." He rolled a die and sighed. "Yeah, he pretty much exploded on contact. Nice job guys!"

"Well, you know what they say about sunlight being the best disinfectant," Eric crowed, to the smiles of everyone in the room. He'd let his red hair grow out to curl around his ears. He would cut it back to a more controlled length once finals were over, but at the moment, he looked very wild.

The party cheered and celebrated their victory before Will spoke up, trying to get them back to the matter at hand. "Anyway, as the vampire dies, you see there's a small key sitting in the dust where he once was, and it looks like it goes to that door behind his coffin."

"Okay then," Rafe said, beaming with satisfaction, "I pick it up, dust it off, and then let's go."

Will selected another page of notes. "All right ... you get to the door, and as you turn the key in the lock, you hear the noise of movement on the other side. It's pretty likely the first key to the tower's in there, but..."

Rafe quickly went to his character's list of abilities. "I got a Turn Undead ready, and I'm not afraid to use it."

"You must've really hated those zombies earlier," Hannah teased.

Rafe gave her a very patient look. "I like my brains, and I prefer them where they are, thank you."

———

December 6, 2037

For several tense moments, Rafe stood as still as a statue, surveying the empty store for any sign of what had made the noise. At first nothing happened, but then he caught a flicker of movement in the corner of his vision. A raccoon scurried out from under a piece of paper to streak under what had once been the counter at the bakery.

Satisfied he wasn't about to be attacked, Rafe let go of the terrified breath he'd been holding and walked deeper into the building until he found himself at the doors leading into the rear storeroom. They squeaked as he pushed them open. Beyond it was a mess of rotting cardboard and plastic shelves near a long broken-down refrigerator. In the time since the place had been abandoned, algae had started collecting around a couple of drains in the floor. He was surprised to see a couple of mushrooms in one corner.

Fat chance of those being a good idea, he thought.

In C&C, if his Survival skill had been high enough, he might have been able to figure out if they were edible and the best plants to serve them with to seem like five-star cuisine. Here in the real world, it was just as likely they'd result in a quick and unpleasant trip to the 1960s, followed by death. He turned around, trying not to think how they might taste while going back to his search of the empty aisles.

Finally, he came across a couple of shelves that had toppled over. Getting down on his hands and knees to try and see if he could lift one of them, he was surprised to see something glittering under the darkened shelves. Curiously, he reached out and grabbed at it, pulling it toward him.

"Yes!" It was a small package of chocolates, still sealed in a variety bag. He hadn't had chocolate in over a year. The taxes on sugar were just too much. Pulling the bag open, he reached for one that said it contained peanuts and unwrapped it. The candy was a little discolored, but it still looked edible.

Placing the sweet in his mouth, he chewed as he walked back

toward the service desk, savoring the taste. It wasn't much, but it was good enough. They would need to be careful and make it last.

———

It had taken a little time for the dogs to find the way Turner had gone, since they first had to question the neighbors in the community where he had been spotted. Then a patrol was dispatched to his home to locate a scent object for the K9 unit to pick up his trail. Now, in the afternoon light, Inspector Church found himself standing under the remains of the New Garden overpass, observing the dog handlers as they followed their charges. He took a swig of his coffee as he saw Sergeant Everett walking up to him. "What 'cha got?" he asked.

"There's some flattened grass a short distance from here," Everett pointed in the direction of the evidence.

"We know he's been carrying Flynn," Church wished his coffee was warmer. In this weather, the 'several-hours-removed-from-the-hot-plate' temperature of his drink just wasn't doing it for him. "Judging by what the dogs have been doing, he probably put him down until he could find a way out."

Everett nodded. "Probably," he replied.

Just at that moment, he heard a chain link fence squeaking loudly and saw a segment of it come free under the weight of one of the dogs. Had their suspect cut it open? He'd suspected it already, but that confirmed it.

"Our boy's in much deeper shit now," Church walked over to the fence to look at it. "This alone could put him behind bars for several years, on top of the charges for kidnapping Flynn." His expression became a little more disappointed. "Even if he and Flynn aren't already dead, this is gonna be a lot of paperwork."

Both dogs had stepped beyond the fence and were straining against their handler's leashes to continue the chase. One of them lunged for an object lying in the grass, and Church recognized it as a deactivated cell phone.

"He's covering his bases," Everett noted. "He knows he can't turn it on without being tracked, so he's removing the temptation."

"I'm surprised he didn't destroy it or hide it," Church responded. "Make certain the cybersecurity team goes through it. Maybe we'll get lucky and find other rebels in his contacts list."

He reached for his own phone and dialed the number for his boss with an exasperated sigh. Of course, the Environmental Defense Force would have to get involved now.

———

It was getting dark as Rafe and Neil finally reached the old two-story farmhouse that had been his family home in what had been the town of Oak Ridge. Once a beautiful place, with flowering bushes, a small rose garden, and even an area in the back yard that his mother had set aside for growing vegetables, it had stood empty for the last four years. Now, it was starting to show small signs of decay. While the siding on the exterior remained the same pale blue it had been for as long as he could remember, the white paint on the porch columns and the black trim had been worn by the ravages of nature and the dust and dirt that had accumulated in the absence of someone to maintain the building.

Several windows appeared to be broken. He tried to ignore the holes in some of the walls; holes small enough to have been made by bullets. The door to the sunroom hung open. If not for the pile of leaves on the step leading up to it, he could almost have believed it had been left open for him. He knew his mom had been here on the day of the relocation deadline. He had not heard what had occurred afterward.

Trying not to dwell on that thought, he let Neil sit down on the step. "I'll be right back," he said.

Neil nodded tiredly and once Rafe was sure he was okay for the moment, he walked over to the tool shed. If things had gone according to his mother's plan...

During his junior year at college, on the day of the second stock market crash, his mother had called to let him know about their emergency plans. He had rolled his eyes at the time, but he certainly wasn't laughing now. One thing she had insisted he commit to memory had been where to look for messages. If anything happened, his mother had said, they would leave a message in the tool shed. Specifically, in an old trash can they didn't use anymore. The idea was that anyone looking for something to steal wouldn't care about anything that appeared to be garbage.

Sure enough, the trash can was still there, behind a bunch of old yard equipment. He dragged it out of the gloomy shed and into the fading daylight so he could see what he was doing, and he lifted the lid. He blinked when he saw what appeared to be a scrap of paper on the bottom. Tilting the trashcan over, and reaching a hand in, he brushed aside the litter and dead leaves to pull it out. Much to his surprise, it seemed to have something hand-written on it.

"Rafe?" Neil called out.

"Yeah?" he responded.

"I think I hear something..."

Rafe listened as he tucked the note in his pocket and his green eyes widened as he heard helicopter rotor blades. He knew the sound well since he had heard it all the time as a child. As far away as they were from what passed for civilization these days, this house was still close enough to the airport that it might not be unusual. But Rafe didn't believe that for a moment. Whether it was a military helicopter full of soldiers flying in to hunt them down, or a drone on a routine patrol, it still spelled trouble.

Checking to see that there was nothing in visible range, he ran over to the steps and hurriedly pulled Neil into the sunroom before continuing into the basement. Setting Neil down at the bottom of the steps, he returned to the top of the stairs and listened intently from the door as the chopper approached. The beating of the rotor blades pounded through the windows as his heart rate quickened. Although he was in a basement he had been in and out of more times in the span of his life than he could count, he felt naked and exposed.

What would happen to them if the aircraft landed? Were they searching for him? Were they searching for Neil?

A shadow fell over the open field that separated the pin oaks around the house from the scrub pines and maple trees. Then the shadow disappeared. Over the next few seconds, the sound of rotors began to fade away and then died. Rafe stood, peering out through the dirty windows and was relieved to see that nothing seemed to have landed in the immediate area. He looked down the stairs to find Neil watching him. "I think they're gone."

"Good," Neil said.

Rafe walked down the stairs and hoisted the boy up again, moving them back into the sunroom and through the kitchen. He was surprised the dust covered furniture was still here. He would have thought this place would be looted by now. If not during the chaos of the relocation, then by runners escaping the city.

Rafe set Neil down on a couch in the living room, once he had checked that it was free of mice or spiders. He handed him a piece of chocolate and then returned to the basement to see if there was anything salvageable. He had laughed when his mom had started stockpiling canned goods down there. It was such an old, antiquated idea during the halcyon days before mandatory relocations, when people were still 'allowed' to live out in the countryside. Back then, this scenario had seemed the height of fancy, only played at in the nightmares of the more vigilant adults in the community, the ones most likely to be laughed off as paranoid. Now he just hoped something was left.

The results were not encouraging. The old barrel of sugar his mother kept was gone, as was the flour and the MREs from the times she'd come with them on camping trips. Gone too were the dried apples and survivalist supplies, as well as her once very well-kept collection of spices and the cans of food she'd bought in bulk. There was a small can of powdered mustard that no one had bothered to touch, but it looked like there wasn't much else here, except the memories. Even the old freezer, which his mother had used to store vegetables from their garden and various meats stockpiled from sales she had found, was completely empty.

He had turned to walk back when out of the corner of his eye, something glinted behind an old cardboard box. Getting down on his hands and knees, he was surprised to find a clear plastic water bottle. He pulled it out and squeezed it into one of his jacket pockets before climbing the stairs back to the kitchen.

The sun was starting toward the trees to the west, and the pines were beginning to cast long shadows through the sunroom windows as he reached the head of the stairs. Normally, this time of year, the gas fireplace his father had installed on the room's southwest wall would have been crackling merrily at this time, dispelling the chill from outside. But it lay dormant. Rafe doubted there was gas in the tank.

He turned back toward the kitchen, up a step and walked through one of the opened French doors that his father had installed before designing and adding the sunroom and the master bedroom above it over a period of several years. Standing by the familiar gold oak table and chairs, he took in this room that had been the center of the house in so many ways.

"Well, you know Dad, he never could stand to have a door in the same place for more than a year. . ." Rafe chuckled half-heartedly as he remembered Susan's old affectionate joke at their father's expense. He could almost see his sister bickering good naturedly with Mike while she was chopping vegetables at the kitchen island topped with a large butcher block, also built by Sam Turner. Even after he'd had to travel farther away for work, he'd always tried to be home enough on the weekends to be present and continue improving the house. This whole house had been rebuilt by his parents, most importantly as their home, but also as a labor of love. It felt wrong that the oak cabinets should be so dusty, and that there should be debris on the worn linoleum floor.

April 17, 2029

It had been around the start of Rafe's junior year of high school when his father had been laid off from his job as a computer programmer. He had then spent several months searching for work until he found a job in South Carolina. His mother had also returned to work, determined to continue because the job market remained unstable. His sister, Susan, had been living at home at the time, even while dating the man she'd eventually marry. While she had a part-time job during the day, she was also charged with managing the household.

His father lost his job at the same time that the 'School for All Act' had been implemented, abolishing homeschooling and instituting compulsory public education. But that barely mattered to Rafe, because it was nearing the end of his senior year, and next fall he would start college.

He was coming back up from the cool mustiness of the basement with a bottle of ranch dressing Susan had sent him after. He had just climbed the stairs back into the warm sunlight that was filtering into the sunroom, cutting countless shadowed patterns across the floor, as the sun sank beyond the tall trees to the west.

Susan's boyfriend, Keith, had been in from Blowing Rock that evening and he sat in the kitchen talking with Rafe's sister as she stood in front of the butcher block preparing dinner. They seemed to have plans to go hiking next time she went west to visit him. Just as Rafe placed the unopened bottle down on the table, the door to the outside opened and their mom entered the sunroom, her lunch box in hand. "Hey," she called out, sounding completely exhausted.

"How was your day?" Susan asked, peeling a carrot into a small trashcan. Her short brown hair curled around her ears, and she worked at the task with the skill of one who had done it many times.

Their mother walked in, put her burden down by the doorway leading into the kitchen and then sat down on the couch in the sunroom. "Busy. They had us working at 98% today."

"What does that mean?" Keith asked.

His mom grinned in a way that betrayed this had been an issue to cause her no small amount of suffering. "It means they want us spending as much paid time as possible with patients before we handle all the paperwork. And of course, this is all while they keep adding more red tape." She groaned as she kicked her shoes off and stretched out on the couch, "So what's for supper?"

"I'm doing lasagna and a salad." Susan returned the trashcan to its place under one of the kitchen sinks. "The lasagna should be ready in a few minutes."

"Sounds good," his mom said. "Where's Mike?"

"Upstairs," Susan grabbed a tomato and began dicing it with a knife. "He's probably gaming with his friends online."

"Someone should call him down here soon," his mom said. Rafe had wandered into the sunroom to stand by the fireplace and warm his hands when she looked up at him. "How was school today?"

"I survived." He knew many of the subjects taught at school could be interesting. In their personal library his parents had stacks of books on more subjects than he could count. But the way it was taught at school it either felt dumbed down or in the case of the Social Studies teacher, like an excuse for her to wax philosophical about her pet political issues and how some part of society stood in the way of seeing those issues resolved.

There really wasn't a way to get around it, and he didn't have much further to go, so he gritted his teeth and said nothing. He told himself that it would all be over once he graduated, and then after college he'd be free. Eric had probably only survived this long because his sketchpad had allowed him an escape valve when classes got too tedious. Similarly, Rafe was always glad to get back to his console collection. He'd be working on repairing that old PlayStation 2 in his room right now if Susan hadn't asked him to find ingredients.

His mom gave him a sympathetic look. He never told her everything that happened at school, but she seemed to understand his feelings on the matter anyway. "Well, that's something, I guess. But there's more to life than just surviving..."

The outside door opened again, and Rafe's father walked into the room. "I'm here!" He'd driven three hours to get here from South Carolina. He hadn't been able to find a job any closer after his old workplace closed.

Susan grinned. "You're just in time! We're probably about ten minutes from dinner!"

Soon everyone was seated around the kitchen table with full plates, talking about their day, about the weather, or this hilarious thing some coworker did ...

———

December 6, 2037

Rafe swallowed painfully. The more he looked around this place the less it felt like home and more like an empty shell.

After taking a moment to pull himself back from his memories, he quickly checked the cabinets and anywhere else he could think of where might be food. No such luck. More than a few of his mother's lighter kitchen appliances seemed to be missing too.

After determining the kitchen was empty, he walked down the hall toward the front of the house, past the formal dining room, to the living room where Neil was waiting. He leaned in to check on him and seeing the boy still sitting tiredly on the couch, Rafe turned around and walked by the front door. One of his parents' finds during their many trips through antique shops, it had been painted white, though someone had built an intricate stained-glass pattern into the top half of it which almost seemed to glow as the sun filtered through the colored panes. He paused to look at it for a moment before taking a brief glance into the office. After deciding he didn't see anything immediately useful, he climbed the stairs to the second floor to look through the upstairs bedrooms.

The beds were still there, and the pictures, though there were definite signs that some of the nicer bric-a-brac had been picked through. Mostly though, it was just missing items that were easy to carry. He wandered past a set of built-in shelves along the hall that were covered in dust and saw that many of the books he remembered were missing. He wondered if some of them had been intentionally burned in the old fire pit outside rather than risk having them in circulation again.

Memories of times when he and his siblings had run through this hallway echoed strangely with the awareness that even here, he was no longer safe. He listened intently over the old familiar creaks of the floorboards for the sound of any nearby voices or vehicles as he continued toward the back of the house to his parents' bedroom. The bed was still there, though the sheets, blankets, and mattress pad had long ago been taken. It was then that he noticed a set of dark splotches by the windowsill littered with shattered glass.

There had never been any word on whether his father had returned home, or any subsequent word from his mother. Communications had been cut off. For weeks after, there had been no news, only rumors about a standoff in Oak Ridge. Whether the people there had been taken, had fought to the death, or simply fled, he didn't know. Eventually, he'd given up trying to find out.

Just a few days before that, there had been rumors of a revolt in a small rural town outside of Philadelphia. The next day, there had been three more across the country. The day after that, fifty. Soon, the larger Internet companies began systematically restricting searches of alternative news. There had been rumblings about military desertions increasing in frequency. The major incident to initiate the war had happened shortly afterward, when a convoy that was evacuating a town in western Virginia had been attacked by a rebel militia. The military had defeated them, but it was a hard-fought battle and other militia had appeared to take their place. It was hard to determine the facts after that. One of the few things upon which everyone agreed was that the battle front had held along the feet of the Blue Ridge Mountains for nearly four years.

He walked to the closet that stood at the end of the room, next to a stained-glass window that had miraculously survived. It was one of several antique windows his parents had collected when they were younger, including the one built into the front door. He remembered that his father had kept his grandfather's old shotgun hidden behind a wood panel in the closet. Could it still be there?

With the last of the light of day shining in through the colored glass, he opened the closet to look. It was empty, obviously looted. But, as he looked past the bar for hanging clothes, he could see the old wood panel right where he remembered it. Leaning his wooden sword against the wall, he pulled the panel open and sighed with relief. No one had figured out that it moved, and the weapon was right where it was supposed to be.

He reached in and pulled it out before pawing around deeper in the hole until he found an opened box of shells. Checking it, he found that there were fifteen left. His dad had used the gun to shoot raccoons and possums when they were eating the food the family put out for the cats or the dog. But that was the extent of its usage following his father's inheritance of the weapon. He didn't know whether his mother had made use of her more modern twelve-gauge shotgun at the time of her disappearance, but there was no sign of it in the usual place where she had kept it.

He looked at the shotgun and then the wooden sword in his other hand thoughtfully. Both were large items, and rather unwieldy. It had him thinking back to the inventory list on his character sheet and weight limits. It wasn't a happy reminder, but game physics were much simpler than real life. After all, in C&C you only had to worry about weight. How exactly a character managed to carry everything was, for the most part, quietly ignored in the interest of keeping things from getting tedious. On occasion, someone would comment on mysteries such as whether a character was capable of walking through narrow doorways with a battle axe larger than they were, but that was usually just for the sake of comedy.

This was the real world, and he knew he couldn't take both the sword and the shotgun. Not if he had to carry Neil too. Something had to stay.

The gun was easier to carry thanks to its shoulder strap, and it was a better weapon, but the sword didn't require ammunition. It was also quieter; if he had to use the shotgun, especially out here beyond the fences, anyone within a mile would hear it.

And ... frankly, Rafe didn't *want* to abandon the sword. It wasn't just a weapon. It was a memory of a happier time; just like the house, but this one he could take with him. He and Eric had taken this same sword out into the woods as children countless times. There was a creek out behind Eric's house, down below a ridge, with two boulders on either side of a particularly high point in the terrain. It had been the perfect spot to reenact their favorite scenes from the samurai and giant monster movies Eric used to collect.

Rafe's expression hardened, and he placed the sword in the compartment. It was bigger than the gun, and he had to angle it a little to make it fit, but he managed. He had to bow to practicality, but he wasn't going to just leave the sword lying around for some looter to find. Before he replaced the panel, his hand lingered briefly on the smooth finished wood of the sword with its familiar nicks and dings, quietly saying goodbye to an old friend. He promised himself that one day, he'd come back for it. One day, if the world became sane again.

Pulling the gun over his shoulder by the strap it came with and pocketing the box of ammunition, he returned to the kitchen by way of the back staircase his father had built.

He was on his way back to Neil through the dining room when he remembered the message that he'd found. Pulling it out of his pocket he read it, taking a moment as the sun finally vanished over the trees to light the lantern.

To anyone who's left, I guess that would be you Rafe, if you decide to leave Greensboro. Or maybe Mom or Dad. I don't know where you are. I hope you're alive. I've left Charlotte for good. Came this way only because I wanted to look for news first.

*Didn't find any. I'm going to Boone to find Susan.
I have some food and protection. There's one
container of emergency food left. I buried it on the
left side of the gas tank and left a shovel behind the
bushes. Stay safe.*

Mike

The date was during the summer of last year. Rafe considered for a moment before sticking the note back into his pocket, determined he would add more to it when they left. In the meantime, he walked over to Neil and set the lantern down on the coffee table. "We might have a little more food before we leave tomorrow."

Neil was obviously pleased at that prospect. "Are we going to do watches like last night?"

Rafe nodded before leaning against the couch and dousing the lantern. "You let me know if anything makes a noise or wake me up when it gets to be around 10:00. I'll take over then, okay?"

"Right."

"One more thing." Rafe pulled the shotgun from his shoulder and sat next to Neil. "Have you ever worked a break-action shotgun?"

Neil frowned for a moment as he tried to remember. "I'm not sure. . ."

Rafe opened the break and after checking to make sure that the barrel was empty, he carefully loaded the gun and closed it. "If you see anything moving around outside, wake me up, but if for some reason I'm not quick enough, I'm going to set this down on the table here." He placed the gun on the coffee table within the boy's reach, making sure the barrel was pointed well away from where either of them intended to sit or sleep. "As I said, try to wake me first, but if there's really trouble ... aim and shoot. I should be well awake by the time we'd need a second round. But only shoot as a last resort. Got it?"

"We had a shooting range at summer camp, and they taught us how to use a shotgun. I don't remember if it was the same kind, but I'll be careful." Neil replied gravely. Rafe was relieved that he was aware of the seriousness of the situation.

"All right, I'll be up in a few hours." With that, Rafe shut his eyes and let himself relax. After everything that had happened today, even with the hunger pangs he continued to feel, sleep came a lot more quickly than he could have thought possible.

CHAPTER 4

PARTY DYNAMICS

December 7, 2037

THE NIGHT PROCEEDED WITHOUT INCIDENT. ACCORDING to Neil's wristwatch, which they had been trading off to keep track of the time, it was shortly after 7:30 AM. Rafe was on the fourth and final watch when he saw some light peeking through the room on the opposite side of the hallway, that had once been the family office. Curious, he stood, and walked over to look in. The old piano was still there against the wall by the door he had just entered, though it was smashed to pieces, probably by someone searching for things to steal. Papers were scattered every which way and the empty desk his father had built into the far-right corner was covered in dust, stripped of the computer that had once sat there. However, as he glanced over to the closet to his right, beyond the piano and saw the door hanging open, something on the floor caught his eye.

Walking closer, he realized it was a compass. There had been a few of those in the house, some cheaper than others, from hiking and camping trips, and his parents had insisted he know how to navigate with one. Along with knowing how to use a map. Inspiration crept into his thoughts as he stepped farther into the darkened closet. All his mother's educational materials from their homeschooling days had been kept in there, and if he remembered correctly, that included a box of maps. He searched around in the stacks of papers, workbooks, boxes of dried-out markers, and dusty bins for a few minutes before finding it on a shelf in a corner.

He picked up the box of maps and brought it over to the window. At first glance, most of the contents looked useless. Most of the maps were global, out of National Geographic magazines, or tourist maps from places they'd only been to while on vacation. But near the bottom, he found a map of the old North Carolina roads. He studied it for a moment. It was a relic of a pre-digital past, probably out of date even before the fences went up, but it could at least point him in the right direction. He folded that map back up, returned the rest to the box, and pocketed the compass before walking back to the other room.

As he entered, he saw that Neil was awake. "Hey."

"Hi," Neil replied.

"How're you feeling?"

"Better than yesterday," Neil replied. "But it's probably just the ibuprofen."

They both knew nothing more could be done about Neil's situation right now. Rafe nodded in understanding. "I'll be right back. I'm going to go see if that food I mentioned last night is still around."

Neil smiled. "I like the sound of that."

"I'm leaving the shotgun with you again," Rafe leaned over to see that it was ready for use but not pointed anywhere it shouldn't be. "Be careful with it."

"I will," Neil agreed.

With that, Rafe walked toward the back door of the house and let himself out, making his way to the gas tank. As Mike had reported in his note, there was a shovel in the bushes; so, in the shade of the empty branches of the pin oaks, he commenced digging, wishing the morning air was less frigid as he worked. Heap after heap of dirt was cleared away from the spot, but it was easy to dig; the normally hard-packed red clay soil was softer here. Obviously, someone had dug this hole before.

Soon, he felt his shovel contact something, and he quickly found evidence of a small plastic barrel that had been left in the hole. Digging a little more, he pulled the barrel out and opened it. Inside, there lay a small, sealed bag of beef jerky and another of dried apple slices. It was far better than he could have expected. Probably enough food for a couple of days. Taking the bags, he stuffed them into his pockets and refilled the hole, taking the shovel with him. The morning light was getting stronger as he reached the garage, but that was not nearly as troubling as his thoughts on taking the whole stash. It was silly, his rational side argued, chances were he'd likely be the only one to come this way. Anyone else who would seek out the old family home would probably have been here before him.

The one person he was surprised about was Mike. His younger brother had always been so cavalier about living down in Charlotte, hours away from everyone else in the family. He'd resisted the idea of moving closer even when the regulations about where people could and couldn't live kept getting tighter, and it was getting harder to legally travel, what with expenses rising and fees for practically everything. But the words his brother had written stuck with him.

His dad hadn't been able to get home, and his mom? Who knew? What if either of them managed to come this way too? He walked into the garage and found another plastic barrel, sticking half the jerky into it and shutting the lid before securing it under his dad's old workbench, behind some decaying cardboard.

Finally, he walked back inside, searching the office to retrieve a pen. Once he reentered the old living room, he saw Neil looking up at him hopefully. "Good news," he set the jerky on the table along with the package of dried apples. "It won't last us long, but it will at least keep us another day or so. Maybe three if we're careful."

Neil looked down at their supplies. "Can I?" he asked.

"Sure."

Neil needed no more prompting. He leaned forward and took a

couple of pieces of the jerky before pulling open the bag of apple slices and taking out a small handful. As he ate, Rafe pulled out his share of breakfast and laid out the road map between them. "I know this thing is a little old, but we obviously can't sit here. So, we need to make a decision."

Neil nodded in agreement. "We do."

Rafe scanned the roads on the map. "Seems to me, we ought to avoid the cities. Just about anywhere we go within Union Territory that's populated will be inside a fenced-in compound, and there's a good chance we'll get caught if we get too close. Now, I think we ought to go to Boone."

"Boone?" Neil asked. "Why there?"

"Because my sister is there, or at least she was, maybe my brother too if he made it. Or do you have a better suggestion? I'm open if you can think of something less insane." Part of him hoped his friend did have a better idea. Never mind that Boone would take days from here on foot, there was also the fact that it potentially meant crossing an active war zone as the current battlefront had been along the feet of the Appalachian Mountains for some time now.

Neil frowned thoughtfully and then shook his head. "Not really. Most of my family is in Connecticut, and after what happened, I don't think it'd be good to go there."

"That's definitely too far, too dangerous," Rafe agreed, "and no way am I going anywhere near New York, even if we didn't have to skirt around Washington D.C." With the possible exception of California, New York was arguably the only place in the nation that was more insane than the internationalist nutbars running things from the White House right now. He decided to change the subject. "At some point, we'll need to find someone to look at your leg."

Neil looked worried. "I'll be able to walk again, right?"

Rafe nodded, his green eyes meeting Neil's brown ones as he tried to reassure him. "Of course. We just need to find a doctor when we get there." He considered for a moment. "How's your splint holding up?"

"Okay, I think." Neil looked it over. "It doesn't seem to be falling apart, anyway."

Rafe turned his attention back to the map. "Well, if we didn't have to worry about civilization, I'd say the quickest way to get to Boone would be to just follow Interstate 40 to Highway 421." He traced the route on the map. "But there are about four cities in the way that make that a no-go. Too easy to be seen." He first pointed out Kernersville, then Winston-Salem, Yadkinville, and Wilkesboro. "Our best bet is probably to try and swing around to the north. Maybe head toward Belews Lake and then head west along this road here." He indicated where Belews Creek Road parted ways from Route 65 with his finger.

"How long will that take?" Neil asked.

"A bit longer, but as little time as possible," Rafe said. "The farther we are from Greensboro, the happier I'll be."

"No arguments there, but that wasn't what I asked."

Rafe considered for a few moments. He didn't have personal experience with this kind of thing. As much as he had liked to hike back when there were still nature trails for doing so, he'd never done so for more than a few hours. The closest he ever got to walking for long distances was playing his character in C&C. There were standard charts for travel times in the rules, but that was a game. Although ... people had been playing C&C for a long time, and authors of earlier editions had been particularly eager to incorporate such calculations in the game for realism. Many of the more complicated rules had fallen by the wayside as editions changed, but the overland travel tables still had to be relatively accurate, right? At least enough to keep the more obsessed players from arguing over it too much.

So, let's see ... A normal pace would be up to twenty-five miles a day, but we're going slower because we're trying to use Stealth. And I'm carrying Neil. That means I'm Encumbered. My Strength and Stamina scores are probably not that impressive, and we don't have a lot of food. So, we'd be lucky to make fifteen miles per day. We also have to think about rough terrain because, never mind the mountains, these Piedmont hills are already a challenge. But we're also using some of the roads, so that'll help...

"Getting to the lake might take the rest of the day if we make really good time," Rafe finally replied. "Regardless, it'll probably be dark when we get there. We're going a bit slower than we could, but that can't be helped." He took a bite of jerky and chewed thoughtfully.

There was an uncomfortable silence for a moment. "Sorry about that..." Neil mumbled.

"Not your fault," Rafe reached for the pen, uncapped it and tested it on Mike's note. To his relief, the ink was still good. "Now make sure you're set to go, because once I've got this note placed, we're getting out of here, all right?"

With that, he turned his attention to the piece of paper in front of him and started writing.

———

Church stood by the firepit behind the abandoned house taking note of the marks in the grass. He was no tracker by any means; he was far more comfortable in urban environments. Still, one thing they had going for them was that the snow had mostly melted, aside from patches of white still lingering in the shelter of trees and bushes. While it made it harder to follow footprints, the scent trail left by Flynn and Turner would only be strengthened by the moisture in the area, making it a lot easier for their dog to figure out where those boys had gone.

Inside the building, one of the animal handlers was already walking Mask, a powerful German Shepherd they had brought with them, through the abandoned bedroom where they believed Turner had rested for the night. Outside, the Environmental Defense Force officer who had been summoned to preside over their investigation where it took place on federal property waited a short distance away.

Everett stepped out from the doorway and to the side, allowing Mask to lead the handler out of the house toward the edge of the overgrown back yard. The dog stepped farther out on her leash, sniffing the ground to get a better grasp of the trail as Everett walked over to Church and showed him an empty bag of potato chips. "I found this in the hallway."

Church nodded. "It's a start." He glanced over to a spot on the edge of the yard where Mask had suddenly halted, apparently on the end of her lead. "If he's still carrying Flynn, they may not've gotten far. If only the government bureaucrats at the EDF had granted us permission to expand the search, we'd have probably found them by now."

"Probably," Everett muttered. He was watching the handler follow the dog, which was occasionally sniffing the trail.

Church was hopeful. "Turner is probably heading west in hopes of crossing to the other side of the front; probably going to stop by his parents" house if he hasn't gotten there already. But there are still several cities in his way before he gets anywhere close. The main concern is how he chooses to tackle his situation. It's probably pretty dire by now." He reached down into one of his pockets to finger the shell casing nestled inside it. "I don't fancy the idea of going toward the fighting, but the sooner we get this done, the sooner we're taking no more of Lieutenant Hernandez's time."

Everett made a sound of agreement as the dog continued searching for a trail. The EDF officer silently followed behind them.

———

Once he finished his addition to Mike's note and stashed it away in the trash can under a pile of leaves, Rafe took one last look around to make sure there wasn't anything else he might be able to use. That was when he found a piece of old plastic tarp in the garage, along with some utility rope. After a little trial and error, he managed to roll up what belongings he couldn't fit in his pockets into the tarp, and then used the rope to tie it closed and fashion a couple of shoulder straps so he could secure it to his back. With any luck, they might be able to use it as a tent or a lean-to if they couldn't find better shelter. Finished with his preparations, he returned to the house to retrieve Neil.

It took him a minute or two to figure out a way to carry Neil, the shotgun, and the tarp at the same time. However, after a couple of false starts, the least awkward solution seemed to be Neil keeping the tarp on his back, while Rafe had the gun over his shoulder and supported him with an assisted carry.

They set off through the woods to the north. Not only might pursuers think they would keep to the easier path; the map Rafe had found, plus his childhood memories, told him this would be a shortcut. Sure enough, it was only midmorning by the time they reached Highway 150.

The last time Rafe had been along this road was about a year before the relocation had taken place. He'd come this way to get some groceries, only to see a series of dying businesses beside the grocery cartel that had been allowed a waiver so people wouldn't starve before the final nail was driven into the community's coffin. Seeing no need to go that way, Rafe turned west. As the sun was fast approaching its zenith, they found themselves coming to a street the dilapidated signs identified as "Pepper Road."

When they reached the intersection, Rafe guided Neil over to a tree and sat down, trying to relax the knots from his muscles. "Encumbered movement" was a lot more difficult than the C&C player's handbook would have one believe. He exercised regularly, but this was a far different thing from jogging and doing pushups, or even the hikes he and Eric sometimes took before the fences went up. Even Neil was tired; sure, Rafe was walking for two, but Neil needed to hold on, and that kind of constant effort eventually took its toll. On top of that, they needed to find water again; they were going through more of it than Rafe had expected. He looked across what had once been farmland. He hoped they could get to Belews Creek before they became dehydrated. The land, once covered with tobacco or corn, was now empty of anything except scrub and tall grasses. It was a good thing it wasn't the time of year when most snakes would be active, because aside from getting caught, there were few things he could think of that were more terrifying than a bite from a copperhead in this situation. That, or running into a pack of feral dogs, or a bear. Of course, any animal could have rabies. . .

He frowned to himself. Thinking like that wasn't helping.

Now, if it was a healthy rabbit in the vicinity of a stewpot and spice rack on the other hand. . .

"Do you think anyone's following us?" Neil wasn't looking at him as he asked, but instead, out over the brush by the roadside.

"I hope not." Rafe pulled himself up, rubbing his shoulder in anticipation of carrying his friend again. "We need to keep going."

Neil nodded and, after Rafe lifted him again, they continued, slowing down a little as they started negotiating the brush. "You ever play tabletop?" Rafe asked, hoping to kill the monotony, and get his mind off rabbit stew. He'd never even had rabbit stew, but as hungry as he was right now, it sounded like the best dish ever.

"Not too much," Neil said. "Just some C&C."

They continued a little farther before Rafe spoke again. "Anything interesting happen?"

Neil considered. "The first time I played ... the GM was one of the kids at school, and we started a dwarven civil war."

"How did that happen?" Rafe asked.

Neil chuckled, "The Rogue in the party stole this talisman from their king and tried to ransom it back to them."

"Let me guess, was he evil-aligned?" Rafe took a moment to consider how they would take their next few steps before continuing.

"Yeah," Neil said. He seemed as though he might say more, but paused as they navigated a particularly thick patch of scrub. One of his shoelaces got caught in a branch, and it took them a good minute to untangle it without setting Neil down or taking off his shoe. Once they had reached the other side of the undergrowth, he went on, "It turned out there were two opposing groups in the mountains where we found them. One wanted to use the talisman to take over the kingdom and our Rogue tried to play both sides to create the most chaos behind our backs. It drove the rest of us crazy. The party kind of fell apart after that."

Rafe chuckled. "I'll bet. It kind of reminds me of Will's —" He broke off as he registered the sound of rotors.

Neil heard it too, and they both froze for a moment before they started hurrying toward what looked to be the remains of an old tobacco barn. They rushed under the eaves of a half-collapsed lean-to that had been set up in front of the barn door as the sound of the helicopter came closer. After lowering Neil to the ground just inside the barn's open doorway, Rafe readied his shotgun. Carefully loading it, he waited at the entrance, nervously watching the ground outside for the hint of a shadow. For several seconds, the helicopter sounds became louder and louder, and then slowly died away. Once he was certain the helicopter was gone, he removed the ammunition, pulled the shotgun back over his shoulder and helped Neil up to continue their journey.

From that point on, they didn't bother with conversation. Both were too busy listening for any sign of pursuit and making sure they were never far from tree cover.

———

It was getting close to sunset when they finally reached Belews Lake. Rafe lowered Neil to the ground under a tree near the water. He was terribly thirsty, not to mention famished. They had stopped briefly to eat a couple more slices of the jerky, but he was painfully aware of the fact that they needed to make it last.

Rafe flopped down next to his friend and tried to work the kinks out of his shoulders. Neil was leaning against the tree trunk, massaging his left leg painfully. Between the two of them, they had taken great care to avoid damaging his right leg further. Thank goodness, the splint had held. But it had made the going physically taxing, in no small part due to Rafe doing his best to keep them going at a steady pace. He felt a pang of guilt in addition to the parching of thirst. They couldn't do anything about purifying water from the lake until it got dark. Otherwise, someone might see the smoke when they lit a fire. Rafe didn't care to run the risk of getting sick by not waiting.

He glanced around the area where they had stopped to rest. It was a stand of trees a short distance from what had once been a boat launch. Off to the side, there was a large empty shed, clearly intended for the storage of a boat or a trailer, with an open garage door and peeling white paint. "Do you think that will do for tonight?" he asked, indicating the shelter with his thumb.

Neil looked past him at the building. "I guess so."

"All right," Rafe stood up as the last of the sun's light had been reduced to an amber glow on the edge of the horizon. "Let's see about warming up." He helped Neil up again and they relocated to a spot just inside the building, immediately grateful that it had a packed dirt floor. It was perfect for what he was planning to do. Leaving Neil huddled at the door, he lit the lantern and walked over to the boat launch, looking for a set of large stones with which to make a ring. Once these were in place near the front but still under the roof of the shed, he gathered as many fallen branches as he could find and snapped them into pieces small enough to fit within the improvised pit and lit it. Once he was certain the flame would stay small enough that it wouldn't rise to the height of the roof, he filled his pot with lake water and placed it at the edge of the flames with one handle pointed out. Neil pulled himself closer, and they huddled around their heat source, warming their hands.

Rafe could feel the temperature drop around them, now that it was really getting dark, but the warmth of the fire and the promise of clean water, along with food allowed his spirits to rise. With an actual source of heat aside from their own bodies, this was almost better than the abandoned houses. After a while, he pulled the pot out of the firepit, protecting his hand with the edge of his sweater, and, as it cooled, they ate what remained of the dried apple slices and half of the remaining jerky. They had decided to save the bag of chocolates until things got really dire.

Though he wasn't quite satiated, Rafe felt significantly better than he had an hour or so ago. He sat close to the door so he could listen and watch for any sound or light that had not originated from their fire, or reflections of starlight on the lake's surface. There was so much he didn't know about survival out here. Sure, he had some basics. He knew how to make a fire with modern means obviously, but there were only a few matches remaining in the matchbook, and what was going to happen if they couldn't find any more food? Now that he looked at the map, they were probably sufficiently north that they could follow the old roads toward Boone without having to encounter most of the other city compounds, but ... could they survive long enough that way? What if someone was following them? He looked down at the shotgun at his side. Would he have the nerve to use it if ...

"Rafe?" He blinked and looked up from where he sat to see Neil was watching him.

"What is it?" Rafe sat up straighter to look over at his friend.

Neil wore a thoughtful expression as he spoke. "Why can't people live out here anymore?"

Rafe thought about it for a moment. "You probably already know the official reasons, don't you?"

Neil nodded. "The people on the news said it was because if you lived in the country, you were far more likely to pollute it. That we shouldn't let our natural resources be devastated because it would make more global warming if we kept expanding. What did they call it...?"

"Sustainable development?" Rafe supplied. "That was the official reason," he recalled a long time ago how his parents had talked about it a lot while he still lived under their roof. He remembered far too well the concern they had over what might happen. "There were others," he added bitterly. "Far too many others."

Neil looked at Rafe curiously, and he continued to elaborate. "It doesn't take much to turn good intentions into mud. All it takes is someone who also has other agendas, and when it's a bad idea made out to be a good one and then used as an excuse, not only do you have to deal with the logical conclusion of the bad idea, but the extreme results of the people who use it to further their own ends."

Neil's eyes widened. "So ... if better people had won the election, then we wouldn't have had someone in power that would have made that excuse?"

"Maybe," Rafe said, "Or maybe not. The only way I can see that being effective in the long term is if the person in power managed to roll back the bureaucracy to the point where it would leave everyone alone, and I'm not sure any of the nominees would have done enough. Regardless of which candidate was worse, the only way a powerful government could run well would be if God existed, was innately good, staffed the whole place with angels, *and* got rid of free will, and that sort of defeats one of the big selling points of existing doesn't it?"

"You don't believe in God?" Neil asked.

Rafe winced. That was right. He'd forgotten. Neil and his family were Presbyterian. But there was no point lying. They needed to trust each other. "No. But that's beside the point. Even if someone does, they ought to realize that as far as Earth is concerned right now, there are no angels here, especially not in politics. As you get more and more powerful in a government, and you have the option to help those who helped you, the temptation to reward cronies, punish dissent, take control away from political enemies, and abuse those new powers keeps getting stronger. And it becomes even easier to claim rights at the expense of those whom you think have had 'too much liberty' or 'privilege' as opposed to everyone else. From that point it's all too easy to call those who you claim had those privileges worthy of hate, unworthy of having a voice, and less than human. And saying someone is less than human, makes it easier to justify someone treating them as something less than human. Lives are destroyed when that happens, and it's not just the scapegoats that get hurt."

He sighed as he reached for the water bottle, filling it with water from the pot now that it had cooled sufficiently. It was something he'd had plenty of time to stew over, and it was sort of a relief to say it aloud.

"You were hurt too?" Neil asked.

"Not the way you were," Rafe said, "And to be honest about it, in some ways, I let it happen. That's where I'm not like your parents, or even my own. When push came to shove, up until that last moment when you flew over my fence, it seemed like the only thing I could do was hide."

Neil looked at him for a moment, considering. "That's not what I saw." The fire crackled on as they sat there in silence for a short while, and then Rafe stood and went out again to refill the pot with water for tomorrow morning and to gather a little more kindling. He had returned, placing the shotgun between the two of them when Neil spoke up again. "What's that piece of paper there?"

Rafe looked at where his friend was pointing and reached out to pick it up. It was Eric's picture of their characters. It must have fallen out of his jacket pocket when he'd pulled out the water bottle. "It's something from the last campaign we ran," he unfolded it and showed him the picture, with a small amount of pride. "Eric; he was our Fighter; he drew this near the end of the campaign."

Once again, he was reminded of the fact that he didn't know where his friend was. So many people had disappeared without a word. "So, which one is yours?" Neil asked.

"The Cleric." Rafe pointed to the man in the back. "Galen, Cleric of Saint Alvar."

"Wait a sec. . . You're an atheist, but you decided to play a holy warrior?" Neil teased.

"Somebody has to heal the party." Rafe smiled as he continued pointing, enjoying the distraction. "That's Allen's character, Malchior the Wizard, and in front is Hannah's elf Rogue Falinel, and Eric's dwarf Fighter, Kade Ironbrand. Will sent us across the land, searching for this old artifact that constantly allowed the wearer to see through all illusions and read the mind of anyone nearby. It was a fun campaign. It would have been nice if we'd been able to finish it."

"What happened?" Neil asked.

"Real life."

"Oh. Well, did you at least get to find the artifact?" Neil asked.

"Yeah, we found it. But it took us a heck of a long time, and a lot of challenges, plus there were other people who were looking for it besides us."

———

November 8, 2031

"So, you're saying they want us to hand over our information on the veil because the queen wants it to protect her kingdom, and she wants us to work as a double agent against Ardes?" Allen had asked. "Okay."

"Hang on a second," Eric spoke up. "Isn't the veil like some kind of mind-reader? Isn't that kind of dangerous to leave lying around? Especially in the hands of someone with power?"

"He's got a point." Rafe took a drink from the soda he'd bought when everyone had gone to get take-out for dinner. "Sure, she doesn't sound so bad right now, but what happens if her kid's a jerk?"

Allen grinned. He knew exactly why Rafe was making the argument and countered in-character as the evil Malchior. "All the more need to keep the peasants under control."

Hannah looked thoughtful. "How much do they offer for it?" She looked in Will's direction.

"About fifty thousand gold for the party, or that equivalent in other equipment," Will replied, clearly reveling in the tension between the party members.

Hannah considered before shrugging. "Okay. I say let's do it. That's way more than the wizard's paying us."

"I don't think so. If someone was intending to root out political dissent, it could be abused pretty badly." Eric was fidgeting with a d8 as he considered his analysis. "Should anyone really have that kind of power?"

"Fifty-thousand gold!" Hannah retorted in-character with a grin.

"What about you Galen?" Eric turned to Rafe, clearly asking for support.

"I'm with you," Rafe agreed. "This is a bad idea. I think we ought to stick with Ardes like we said we would."

"We could..." Allen mused, "Or we could use the veil to gain leverage with the queen, which could be really useful..."

"I'm actually kind of surprised at you, though," Eric pointed out. "I would have thought you'd want to claim it for yourself so you could use it to put together that evil empire you're always joking about."

Allen stroked his goatee thoughtfully before a grin of his own spread across his face. "Are we having this conversation in-character?"

"Do you want to discuss your plans for world domination in front of that guy who's trying to make a deal?" Will asked.

"Seems like a brilliant idea," Allen joked. Everyone chuckled, and he continued. "Seriously though, I think I'll side with Eric and Rafe's characters, for my own reasons."

"Aww..." Hannah groaned good naturedly. "But it's so much gold!"

"The queen's representative asks if you're sure," Will said.

"Yes," Rafe confirmed.

"The queen's representative says: 'You'd better think about this carefully; after all, it'd be a shame if anything happened to you on the trip home...'"

"Is he threatening us?" Eric puffed himself up in mock indignation. "I get in his face and look as intimidating as possible."

"Roll the check," Will said with a chuckle.

Eric picked up a d20 from the coffee table and rolled it, adding up the modifiers. "18," he reported.

"The representative looks a little nervous and turns to leave. As he does so, he says 'You haven't heard the last of us!'" Will comically shook his fist for emphasis. "And then he runs away. So, the question is, what are you going to do with the information about that shipwreck where the second tower key is supposed to be?"

————

It was a couple of hours later, and Rafe was sitting in the passenger seat of Eric's car as the two of them rode in a companionable silence back toward the University of North Carolina at Greensboro. It was about 2 a.m. and outside he could see the silhouettes of the bare branches on the maple and oak trees that lined the deserted residential streets in the stark yellow light from the streetlamps. While the inside of the car was quite warm, the first frost of the year was not far off, and he could tell the temperatures outside were continuing to drop as time drew deeper into the early morning hours. They had been grateful for their coats when they'd left Will's place.

"Any news about your dad's job?" Rafe asked.

Eric exhaled, and Rafe could hear the fatigue in his friend's voice. "Not since he spoke out about those new environmental regulations. People say they'll consider him for a new job, but it's obvious they're all afraid. After that riot, no one wants to give him a chance, no matter how good an engineer he is."

"Just because he disagreed with the EPA?" Rafe turned to look at Eric in surprise.

Eric sighed, shaking his head. "There's no rhyme or reason to it. I know the guy who recorded that meeting had ties to the Green Peak Club and you know they've been trying to give the EPA more teeth for years, but still ... how in the world did we get here?" Rafe noticed that his friend's hands were gripping the steering wheel tightly.

"I don't know..." Rafe murmured.

CHAPTER 5

EXPEDITIOUS RETREAT

December 8, 2037

"Rafe," Someone touched his shoulder, and he twitched awake, shivering now that the fire had been reduced to smoking coals.

"What is it?" he whispered. He looked around the shed for a moment before finding Neil's silhouette in the early morning gloom.

Neil was clutching the shotgun tightly in his hands. "I think I heard something..."

Rafe jumped to his feet, still shaking off the light cobwebs of an uneasy sleep as he listened intently through the sound of the nearby flowing water in the lake. He could see the starlight reflecting across the surface, indicating not much time had passed since he had traded the watch with Neil. He turned to look out the filthy glass window that stood to his right, and then he saw it. It was faint, but for a split second off in the distance there was a flash of light that wasn't from the stars.

Not wasting another moment, he grabbed up his improvised knapsack in which he'd repacked their possessions, and after taking the gun from Neil, hoisted him over his shoulder.

"What...?" Neil started.

"Shut up, we're moving," Rafe hissed and started running for the bridge over the lake, not even bothering to kick out the last coals of their fire before exiting the shed. There was no time for that. If he could see the flashlight, then someone was way too close. Distance and obstacles to being followed were better than subtlety at this point. He could see the crumbling asphalt ahead as he raced toward the bridge, and once he was up on it, he spared no time crossing before turning into the woods to the northwest. He could hear a dog barking somewhere behind him as he hurried through the pine trees.

As the coming dawn started to bring a dim illumination behind him, he searched the woods for any brush or rocks he could knock over to make things even more difficult for whoever it was. About thirty feet into the woods, he saw a couple of fallen branches and spared a moment to kick them into the path before continuing, ears alert for any further sounds of having been spotted. It didn't seem that way, but he continued onward.

About a minute later, they found themselves on the edge of a field that had once been farmland but was now overrun with tall grass. He cursed under his breath and then plunged them into the open at the quickest pace he could manage. If they were still exposed when whoever it was caught up, they'd be seen for sure. But maybe luck would be with them ...

The dog behind them barked again. It was closer this time. Looking ahead, Rafe could see the road and just beyond it, a much thicker stand of trees. He tried to run faster, but he was certain he was already moving as fast as he could. Rafe's lungs were burning from the exertion in the cold morning air, and it seemed like adrenaline was the only thing keeping his knees from buckling.

After reaching and immediately crossing the road, he dived into the cover of the woods on the other side. He spared a glance behind him as they hurried onward, and that was when he saw a German Shepherd running through the outskirts of the woods. He narrowed his eyes and turned back to get deeper into the trees. He was winded. As the growth became thicker, he had to slow his pace to navigate through the fallen branches and brush. Throughout all of this, Neil had been quiet, doing his best not to get in the way or make it more difficult for Rafe to carry him, but he asked breathlessly, "What are we going to do now?"

"Keep going." Rafe gasped for breath as he managed to get over a particularly large fallen branch. "They won't catch us if I can help it."

The dog barked again as they reached a stand of thinner scrub pines which bordered their path away from pursuit. Rafe tried to speed up again, but the ache in his muscles told him they were ready to give out. His arms especially were starting to quiver from the weight he wasn't used to lifting. He wouldn't be able to carry on like this for much longer. If he'd been a professional soldier or survivalist, he might have been able to do it, but as things stood, this was about all he could manage. With the dog following them, they couldn't stop and hide either. He looked down at the shotgun in his free hand. If he used it, they would have to move immediately, as that would be one sure-fire way to let the men with the dog know he was there. But at least they would be distracted if the dog was injured, and would proceed with greater caution, knowing he was armed.

Scanning ahead, he spotted a point where the field of open grass dipped slightly into the tree line, leaving a small area that was clear of woods. He cut across it, all the while making sure that he left a clear path in the open before taking cover in the trees. Kneeling as he let Neil off his shoulder, he reached into his pocket and pulled the box of shells out. He hurriedly jammed one into the barrel before shutting the break and stood to take aim at the empty clearing. He tried hard not to think about how cruel this act was to an animal that was just doing what it was trained to do. It didn't have any concept of what its handlers were doing, or what would happen to its prey.

It happened far too soon for his liking. The dog sniffed its way out into the opening, then broke into a run in their direction. Rafe hesitated only for a moment before pulling the trigger.

The gun thundered by his ear and kicked back hard into his shoulder as the dog dropped. Just like that, there was the dog, on the ground, and he could already hear someone yelling in the distance. He forced himself to ease his grip on the weapon before once again gathering Neil and moving out. This time, he changed their direction more due west as much as the tree cover allowed. He didn't stop until he reached a particularly thick stand of pines at the crest of a high hill.

Once he'd taken a few minutes to catch his breath, he pulled Neil up into an assisted carry, and they continued westward, not saying a word for fear someone would hear them.

———

It had been several hours since Church had discovered evidence of Turner's presence at what had once been his family's farmhouse in the former township of Oak Ridge. He would have been able to get there quicker, and potentially even have staked the place out if not for the bureaucrats at the EDF, but there were few things they liked less than someone from a different branch coming in and messing around in their jurisdiction. That being said, runners were SPKF business, so they had no choice but to play ball. Regardless, they had been able to track Turner easily after that. When Mask's ears had perked up, and the handler had taken her off the leash, Church had seen her move toward Belews Lake with an urgency that could only indicate she had a lead.

Then he'd heard the gunshot, and now that he stood with Everett and Hernandez by their wounded dog, watching the handler anxiously trying to comfort the animal and keep her still, his fears were confirmed.

"Seems Turner's armed himself with something a lot more dangerous than that wooden sword Mrs. Lee noticed him with," Church observed.

Hernandez had already called in a helicopter to get the dog out. It really would have been so much easier if the EDF would allow them to land an aircraft wherever they wanted, but officially, the concern over damage to the environment from landing a chopper meant that they were limited to flyovers and emergency pickup only.

"Do you think he's been trained?" Everett asked.

Church gripped the shell casing tighter in his pocket, thinking. "He came of age in the last couple of years where shotguns were still legal, and Mrs. Turner was a damn good shot. I learned that the hard way. I doubt she'd have let him leave the house without knowing something about how to shoot. And if he's using buckshot, he wouldn't even have to aim too well." Mask's wounds had a spread pattern rather than a neat hole, so that seemed likely.

Everett reached for the 9-millimeter in his holster, and pulled it out, checking it, as Church did the same. "Then we'll need to be careful," Everett said.

"If we plan on getting home in one piece," Church agreed. "But even without the dog, it doesn't take a genius to know the direction they're taking." He turned to Hernandez. "We need to set up a perimeter along the old roads west of the Stokesburg/Walnut Cove Precinct. He's likely going to keep heading in that direction. I doubt he'll go near the town itself, but we'll pay a visit to the local Guard station after we're done here and make sure they're on the lookout."

Hernandez looked at him curiously. Church already suspected the man did not like him, and he suspected the man's superiors having given him a job that basically amounted to being a glorified babysitter, had not helped relations. When Church had tried to ask him to help with a couple of tasks since he had joined their party, he had acted as though he didn't understand, even when the purpose of the request had seemed obvious. When it looked like Church was going to try to explain again, slower, he nodded and reached for his phone, walking off a short distance to make the necessary calls.

Putting the issue of Hernandez aside for the moment, Church

turned to Everett. "We're going to search the woods around here, see if we can find any more traces."

Everett nodded.

They were about to turn away when the handler, whom Church only just now noticed was a pale younger man with dark hair and angry blue eyes, looked up at them seriously. "Make sure you get that son of a bitch, Sir. For my dog."

Church nodded, noting the name on the man's uniform patch. "Don't worry, Sanders, we'll get him." As the sound of another approaching helicopter slowly became louder, the two men gave Mask one last look before leaving her with Hernandez and Sanders.

Continuing on foot, especially without a dog to help track their fugitive, was far from ideal; but the terrain and environmental regulations made ground transport inefficient. Besides, their quarry was forced to move slowly; and if their breath was frosting in the morning sunlight, the fugitive and his victim were likely even colder. Under these conditions, it would only be a matter of time before they couldn't run anymore. Then they would be caught, and Turner would face justice. It was simple as that.

"Church." Everett spoke up after a few minutes of silence. "While you were checking out the Turner house, I was doing a little digging into what happened the night he and Flynn disappeared."

"Yes?" Church's eyes did not stop scanning the ground for the fugitive's trail.

"I found an ... interesting recording from dispatch. Apparently, Turner called the emergency hotline before Flynn's parents were killed, and he was told what any normal citizen would be." Everett hesitated, then continued. "But why weren't there any officers stationed in that area that night? Why was there a power outage only on that street? And how did the Flynns die by gunshot wounds when no one there was sanctioned to have a firearm?"

Now Church turned to look at the man, raising an eyebrow. "Tree limbs break, Everett, and power outages happen all the time. It's the dead of winter. I thought you grew up here."

"That doesn't explain our guys not being there," Everett said quietly. "Or the gun."

Church frowned. That wasn't his department, and it wasn't Everett's either. Asking those kinds of questions usually cost far more than he'd ever consider worth paying. "The explanation's probably in some file cabinet somewhere," he said, letting a touch of warning enter his voice. "You can look through all the paperwork for it later, on your own time."

Everett looked at his superior for a few moments, then nodded once. "Of course."

———

Rafe and Neil had pushed on after the incident with the dog, turning north to go around another section of Belews Lake. They'd kept to the trees as best they could, only occasionally using Route 65 to get their bearings and avoid the town of Walnut Cove. It hadn't worked.

Panic threatened to overwhelm Rafe as he stared at the fence, another cage with another lock. Obviously, the map he carried didn't show the fences, but he hadn't expected Walnut Cove's city limits to extend this far north. Being this close was a risk he hadn't wanted to take. The possibility of encountering guards was too high.

What were they going to do? Every second of delay was one more they were in danger of being found. It was barely midday, and he was already exhausted. If a patrol didn't find them, those men with the dog couldn't be far behind. They might even have people waiting for them up ahead somewhere...

"Rafe?"

He looked at Neil, whose eyebrows were also knitted in concern. "Yeah?"

"Shouldn't we get away from this?" the teenager asked.

Rafe nodded and turned east, hoping to get some distance before correcting back into a straighter northerly direction. The reminder seemed to have helped calm his nerves a little, instead leaving him very aware of how sore he was from their exertions this morning, and how exhausted he felt. There was no time for panic. They had stopped earlier only to drink a little of their water before hurrying onward. There had been no time for food. Only now, when he felt they'd gotten a good distance from their pursuers and the adrenaline was starting to wear off, did his stomach suddenly growl with such intensity it startled them both.

"I hope that was you," Neil commented with a grin.

Rafe allowed himself a short, breathless chuckle. "Guilty as charged. We should find somewhere to hide so we can rest for a while."

They made their way through the woods a short distance before coming across a small pond in a gully along one of the hills. After making sure they were as hard to spot as possible from the air, Rafe lowered Neil to the ground and reached into their bag for what was left of the jerky. He decided they should only take half a serving apiece to see if they could extend it a little longer. He didn't relish going hungry; but on the other hand, he knew the chocolates wouldn't last more than a couple of days if that was their only food supply.

He chewed on his allotted share of dried meat as he continued to brood over their food problem. At some point, hunting might be an option, but anywhere near civilization was a risk because someone might hear the gun. It would have to be something they'd do only if it were certain no one was around. Plus, he couldn't waste all their ammunition in the process.

He was now very aware of how tired he was after their escape from the men with the dog, and his eyelids drooped. He tried to fight it, but eventually, he placed the shotgun between himself and Neil. "Hey, could you watch for a little while?" he asked.

Neil nodded. "Okay."

With that, Rafe shut his eyes and leaned back against a nearby rock, thinking he would rest, just for a few minutes ...

_____

October 8, 2029

It was lunch time on a warm autumn day during freshman year. Rafe had been walking through the dining area near the UNCG cafeteria, holding the tray with his lunch in front of him and navigating the tables, looking for a place to sit. Eric had said he'd be there, somewhere.

After searching for a bit, Rafe spotted his friend, sitting with a group of three other people by one of the great arching windows facing the library. His friend had always been tall and a little stocky even when they were kids, and his red hair was also hard to miss, as was the sketch pad that sat next to his food tray. A woman about their age, probably another freshman, with honey-brown hair in a ponytail down her back was talking to a tall man across the table with dark skin and short black hair. This man wore a small goatee. It would go through a few style changes over the next few years, and over those years, he'd often joke about how it proved he was a villain. The third person at the table was a man about the same age. He was slightly shorter, pale-skinned with brown hair that just passed his ears and he wore a pair of glasses. He was half listening to the conversation while reading a textbook in his lap. It looked like a survey course on biology, given the size of the book and what seemed to be printed on the cover.

As Rafe approached, he could hear them talking and instantly realized why Eric had been drawn to them.

"So anyway, in this game, the GM was just as new as the rest of us, and we had a half-orc Cleric, a human Wizard, an elf Rogue, and I'd picked this human Ranger," the darker man said. "We were heading out of town on a mission from this guy to find this mysterious chest, and we were going through this cornfield. So, what's the first thing we do?"

"What?" the girl asked, a grin of anticipation on her face.

"Our Cleric decided to try and throw ears of corn at me. Of

course, since we're all new, no one understands how improvised weapons work, so we spend the next twenty minutes or so goofing off and trying to come up with rules for what kind of damage an ear of corn would do."

"Mostly psychological, I'd guess," the man with glasses said, only briefly glancing up from his book.

"Pretty much," the darker man agreed, "So eventually, we got back on the road out of town, but later, when we got to this dwarven fortress, she used another ear of corn to attack the guard just because she could."

"Sounds like someone who really enjoyed sending the game into mayhem," Eric commented.

"Perhaps," the first man said, "But at two in the morning, everything seems a lot funnier."

At that point Eric noticed Rafe and waved him over. "Oh, hey Rafe. This is Allen, Hannah and Will. You remember how we talked about finding a C&C group? Will was talking about setting up a game."

"Awesome," Rafe said, "That is, I'd be interested if you're looking for a player."

Will sat up straighter. "All right then, come sit down, and we'll talk about it."

Allen held out a hand to shake as Rafe put his tray down in front of Will. "Nice to meet you!"

———

December 8, 2037

Rafe was almost asleep when he heard the snap of a branch a short way down the hill. Almost as quickly, he felt Neil's hand shaking him. "Did you hear that?"

"I heard." Rafe grabbed the shotgun and pulled himself to his hands and knees. "Hang on, I'll be back." He crawled to the crest of the gentle ridge that surrounded the gully, scanning the woods for any sign there might be someone outside their hiding place. His misting breath caught the light filtering through the branches of the leafless trees as he listened, straining for any sound that might indicate they'd been found again.

He felt the barrel of a gun press between his shoulder blades, and a low female voice came from the gloomy forest behind him. "Don't move a muscle."

"Okay. I won't." Rafe shut his eyes, hoping he wasn't about to die a quick, horrible death.

Instead, the gun stopped pressing into his back, and he opened his eyes again to look around. The woman moved into his peripheral vision, pointing what looked to be a military-style rifle at him. She kicked his shotgun out from under his hand. He dearly wanted to retrieve it, but given the situation, he instead studied his captor.

She appeared to be about his age, with dark brown hair in a bun under a knitted cap. He thought she was pretty, despite the gun trained on him and the focused expression on her face. Judging by the military fatigues with a Stokesburg/Walnut Cove patch on the front, she looked to be part of compound security.

Definitely bad news.

Maybe he could use the screwdriver in his pocket? In a pinch, it could probably work as a weapon, assuming he could get close enough and the right moment presented itself. Oddly enough, he couldn't find her name underneath her unit patch.

"Stand up," she ordered, interrupting his thoughts.

He did as she directed, putting up his hands to show he wasn't a threat.

"Rafe?" Neil called out in a low whisper. "Do you see anything?"

Rafe winced. Now they were both caught; there was no way around it. The woman gestured that he walk back into the gully. He obeyed, noting that she picked up his shotgun as they went.

As they came down the hillside, he saw Neil's eyes widen at the sight of the woman behind him. The woman spoke again. "It's the same thing every year. A few idiots think they can survive out in the wild, playing 'mountain man,' rather than staying inside where they should when it's the frigging dead of winter."

"Like we had a choice," Rafe growled.

The woman ignored him, turning her attention to the splint on Neil's leg. "What happened to you? Did you fall and break your leg or something? Or did your 'friend' do this to you?"

"I hurt it running away from the nutbars who were trying to kill me." Neil glared up at her as though she also had some responsibility for his situation. "So, are you going to shoot us and get it over with? Like *them*?"

Rafe's heart leaped into his throat at the thought. "Neil, you need to calm down," he said quickly, trying to keep his own voice as calm as he could manage. "Don't give her a reason to shoot us." He wasn't going to lie by saying it was going to be all right. As far as he could see, things probably wouldn't be, but Neil losing his cool was the last thing they needed.

The woman ignored him, instead focusing on the boy. "By rights, I could've killed you long before now. I had you in my sights before your friend even climbed the ridge back there."

"Then why haven't you?" Neil asked coldly. He was still angry, but Rafe was relieved to see that his friend was at least trying to control his temper.

"Because you're both worth way more to me alive, kid." Her expression was stern. "I've got enough killing to do on my own without adding you to my list."

Somewhere out of the back of his tired mind, Rafe suddenly got an idea. Maybe he was grasping at straws, and it was a stupid idea, but it was worth a try. If this were the game, he would be making a diplomacy check right about now. Will had been known to award bonuses for being persuasive, and that usually meant trying to understand what someone else wanted, and how to make that mesh with what the party wanted.

So, if he were going to strategically roleplay this scenario. . . "How about this?" He almost moved his hand without thinking but paused as he realized that would be a terrible mistake. If he did, she might have thought he was going for another gun. That thought alone was enough to make him feel a little shaky.

Instead, he took a deep breath and looked over his shoulder at the woman, trying to meet her eyes. They were brown, like her hair; and now that they were on even ground, he saw that she was also about five inches shorter than he was. Funny, the sort of things someone noticed when they thought they might be about to die.

"I-I'm going to be really clear here, I do not have any other weapons." Had his voice just squeaked? Rafe plunged on, trying not to think about it. "T-there is a bag of chocolate in my jacket pocket. If you'll let us go, you can have it." Apart from his grandfather's shotgun, the chocolates might be the most valuable thing in their possession.

The woman snorted derisively. "A pretty decent bribe, but you need to work on your delivery. That was pathetic. Smooth it out a bit so it sounds more like you're doing me a favor, and less like I'm about to murder you."

It was Rafe's turn to get angry. "Well, you *are* pointing a gun at my back. I think I've got a pretty good reason to be concerned!"

She sighed and shook her head. "I'm surprised you've even survived long enough to get here from Greensboro. How did you do it?" And then, she grinned, though it didn't touch her eyes. "Actually, I know exactly how you did it. You cut the fence, ran like hell, and hoped to God you wouldn't get caught. Of course, it probably never occurred to you that they'd alert every SPKF and National Guard station from here to the front. You boys must be having a damn lucky day, since it was me that found you first."

"How so?" Rafe asked guardedly.

"No more questions." She slung his shotgun across her back, then knelt down to lift his makeshift knapsack as well, keeping her eyes and her rifle trained on him as she worked. "Pick him up and start walking north. I'll tell you where to turn."

Rafe didn't move. "Is that somewhere I want to go?"

She glared at him impatiently. "We don't have time to argue. You do what I say, and don't you dare try anything stupid."

Something about this felt weird to Rafe. While he was certain she was fully prepared to use threats to get her way, he couldn't shake this feeling that she didn't *want* to do anything to them. Of course, that didn't mean she *wouldn't*, and feelings could be wrong. All told, Rafe wasn't reassured, so he kept his hands visible as he walked over to where Neil sat and helped him up.

They left the gully and continued through the woods a short way until they came to a steep hill surrounded by large pines. A chain-linked fence stood a couple of hills away, cleared land cutting a swath around it. The silhouettes of a few buildings cast icy shadows in the winter sun, which was already beginning to sink in the sky. The fence was blocked from view by trees and four or five untrimmed bushes, bare of leaves in the current season, though in warmer weather they would probably be covered in flowers and new growth.

"Stop," the woman spoke. Rafe stopped behind the bush and waited for her to make the next move. Making sure to keep her eye on them, she pulled a pair of leafless shrubs apart from each other. To his surprise, once the overgrowth had been moved, there was a tunnel behind it, dug into the red clay of the hillside.

"Get inside." The woman gestured with her rifle again and Rafe hurriedly obeyed. The first thing he noticed was that the floor of the tunnel seemed neatly cleared out. He could feel gravel under his shoes, but there didn't seem to be many obstacles. The next thing he noticed as he walked farther into the dark was the soft feel of air being pushed through by a fan in the distance. As his eyes adjusted to the inner darkness, he noticed the occasional wooden support along the walls. Then, as they proceeded beyond where the light from outside could reach. he also became aware of tiny lightbulbs hanging from the ceiling of the tunnel. They passed under what seemed like four or five of these until at last he saw another tiny glow of a light a short distance away. After walking further through the tunnel, they found themselves in a dim concrete room illuminated only by a small electric lamp in a corner. Next to it, Rafe could see a bed roll but that was the most his eyes would reveal in the faint light.

The woman entered the room after them and gestured to the bedroll. "Over there."

"Just who are you?" Rafe was thoroughly confused. He stayed where he was, still holding Neil.

"Call me Rabbit."

Rafe heard stairs creaking near where she was, as someone who had been sitting halfway up suddenly stood and climbed down to join her. She kept her eyes on them as a large man walked into the light.

Rafe eyed the tunnel but knew the two of them could not make a break for it without being caught or shot. Rabbit spent a few moments speaking to the new figure in a hushed tone, after which they both turned to face Rafe and Neil.

It was hard to tell the man's physical features in the dark, but he had a huge black beard that stood out even in the dim light. He surveyed their guarded expressions and then spoke. "I hope Rabbit wasn't too hard on you. But she can't blow her cover, and if one of the other patrols had found you, it would have been best if you believed she was one of them."

Rafe watched Rabbit back toward the wall, her rifle at the ready. She then placed his shotgun and their other belongings by the stairs behind her. Perhaps it was the lack of adequate sleep, plus the exhaustion from having been chased through the woods while carrying all their belongings and carrying Neil. But through the fog of mental fatigue, something finally dawned on Rafe that probably should have when he saw the tunnel. "You guys aren't with the government, are you."

Well spotted, Captain Obvious.

If the man with the beard thought anything of Rafe's mental acuity, he made no sign of it, but instead simply shook his head. "No, we definitely aren't." The man turned to Rabbit. "You should get back out there before you're missed."

She nodded and headed back down the tunnel, leaving them alone with the man. He regarded them quietly before walking over to the tunnel entrance. There, he reached for a square segment of drywall that leaned nearby and fitted it into the room's entrance like a puzzle-piece. When he was finished, it merely looked like someone had tried to renovate and not finished the job. He then approached and offered his hand in greeting. "Call me Badger. That should be good enough for now."

Rafe tried not to groan; or maybe not to laugh, he couldn't tell which, as he took 'Badger's' hand. "This is like a bad movie. Don't tell me we found the Resistance." What else could have given the man the inspiration for such a corny code name?

Who are we going to meet next? The creepy British guy with the opera mask, or Professor X and Wolverine? He decided that question was better left unasked.

Badger replied coolly. "From what I've heard, it sounds like someone in the SPKF is really keen on catching you."

"What do you mean?" Rafe asked. He was still on his guard, but he slowly started helping Neil over toward the light.

Seeing what he was doing, the man walked over and unrolled the bedroll so Neil could be lowered onto it. "An SPKF investigator from Greensboro came by the guard office and told them to be on the lookout for a pair matching your description. Something along the lines of a kidnapping and then shooting a service animal?" Rafe eased Neil down to the bedroll as Badger finished setting it up.

"Well, that's their version." Rafe straightened back to his full height, working the kinks out of his muscles as Neil stretched out his leg with a quiet groan of relief. "The only kidnapping that would have taken place would have happened by the ones who lynched his parents, assuming he was spared the lynching in the first place." Looking closer, he could tell that Badger towered over him. Not as tall as Allen had been, but definitely tall. "The part about the dog is true. We're lucky we made it away with just one injury, as is."

"What happened to his leg?" Badger asked, indicating Neil's improvised splint.

Neil looked up, apparently a bit cowed by the large man's appearance. "I ... uh ... "

"I'm pretty sure he broke it." Rafe still wanted to stay on his guard, but he could already feel a dull aching tiredness coming over him that reminded him, once again, of just what he had been through today. The splint was holding together, but it was starting to show some signs of wear.

Seeming to take a bit of courage from Rafe speaking, Neil finally added "I hurt it jumping a fence when these guys were chasing me back in Greensboro. If Rafe hadn't helped, I don't know if I'd be alive."

"We'll have a doctor take a look at it." Badger considered for a moment and then continued. "Rabbit said that you had a bag of chocolates?" Rafe nodded and Badger continued, his tone apologetic. "We can make this a charity situation if we have to, but I'm afraid our resources are not unlimited. If you can part with five pieces, that should go a long way in helping us help you."

Rafe didn't stop to think, instead reaching into his coat pocket and producing the requested amount. "You can have it. I'm just grateful you guys weren't with Security."

Badger accepted the amount and pocketed the pieces gratefully. "All right then. When Rabbit gets back, I'll have her go get him." He indicated a spot by the bedroll. "Try to rest while you can, it will be a little while."

"Thank you." Rafe was surprised to notice that he felt warm for the first time in a long while. He removed his coat to place it beside Neil and, though he still did his best to keep a wary eye on the area around him, he finally sat down. He never remembered falling asleep.

———

A couple of hours later, Rafe snapped awake as he heard a door opening at the top of the stairs. He sat up abruptly, and it took him a moment before he remembered they were in the basement. Rabbit came down into the light, bringing a white-haired man who turned out to be a doctor. He went straight to work, asking a few questions as he examined Neil's injury. He gently removed the splint, and replaced the planks and duct tape with bandages and a couple of dowels. While the duct tape had held together incredibly well over the course of the trip, it probably wouldn't have lasted more than another day or two. They discussed a cast but, unfortunately, the town was critically short on fiberglass, and plaster was impractical for the situation due to its susceptibility to falling apart on contact with water.

The greatest relief on Rafe's part came when the man revealed that he had also brought the disassembled parts for a pair of crutches. For that, he felt no small amount of gratitude. Finally, something was starting to go their way.

As he watched the doctor adjust the crutches so Neil could use them properly and set the screws into the pre-drilled holes, the doctor asked conversationally, "Where were you headed?"

"West," Rafe sat up from where he'd been leaning against a nearby wall, close enough that he could help if Neil needed him, but otherwise out of the way. "If we can make it across the front, I've got family in Boone, or at least I did."

The doctor nodded as he tightened a screw on a crutch, looking for all the world as though they were just sitting in his office. "I have a brother who lives out that way myself," he commented. "I wonder what he'd think if he could see me now," he chuckled. "He always thought I was the soft one, but here I am." He gave Rafe a good-natured salute as he tightened a nut to secure the crutch he was working on. "Helping runners can get a person disappeared pretty quick, you know ... " his expression turned more serious. "But I guess I just can't help myself. This isn't how Man was supposed to live ... " His voice trailed off into silence and he almost seemed to be speaking to himself as he returned to work.

"So how did you end up doing this?" Rafe asked, turning his attention to the other two people in the basement.

"Fell into it, mostly," Badger paused for a moment, trying to order his thoughts. "We looked at the way the world was bein' run, and how it used to be, and thought 'This isn't the world we want.' So we decided to help people leave. We could leave ourselves, but if we did, there would be no one to tell the truth of what happened here before it was over. Because it will be over one day." His eyes blazed in the lamplight, daring either of them to tell him he was wrong. "One day, there will be a reckoning, if I have anything to say about it."

"It's dangerous though, isn't it?" Neil looked over at Rafe, holding out his hand for assistance. Rafe stood, helping the doctor pull his patient up so he could check if the crutches were sized correctly.

"It is," Rabbit said. She was sitting on the stairs, watching the doctor work – or, more likely, watching their guests. "But if we weren't willing to help, you wouldn't be sitting here now. Speaking of your situation, though, we have some business to discuss."

"Okay." Rafe checked to make certain Neil was balancing correctly on his crutches, then left the doctor to show him how to use them and walked over to the stairs.

"We can't keep you here," Rabbit said bluntly, but with a touch of apology in her voice. She stood and walked down to meet him, holding a canvas bag. "The Guard do random searches, and the risk is too great. However, we can give you some supplies. This has two blankets, a bottle of water purification tablets, and enough rations to keep you going for a few days beyond the fences."

"But we can't pay –" Rafe began.

She gave him a look that told him she wouldn't tolerate any more nonsense. "You paid for it. Do you know how valuable chocolate is on the black market, what with the health food taxes? That bag of chocolates you have, even a little aged, is sufficient to barter enough in goods to last you to Tennessee if you find the right people. Whatever you do, don't eat any more of them."

Rafe blinked in surprise. He knew chocolate was rare these days, but ... "Five pieces bought all this?"

"We bribed a government official with a bottle of homemade

soda last week," Rabbit told him with a smirk. "Don't go out of your way to search for it, but if you find any pre-war bottles or cans in an old house or something, it's worth the weight to take them with you. Especially the cans: They might still have fizz in them."

"Are there a lot of abandoned houses that haven't been looted?" Rafe took the bag from Rabbit.

"No clue. It's hard to scavenge systematically. Too easy to get caught. Anyway, the plan is to lead you to a starting point further north tonight, that will hopefully bypass the most dangerous spots. When you head west, stay south of Pilot Mountain—meaning the actual mountain. That will keep you away from the city of Pilot Mountain."

"Is it a large compound?" Rafe asked as the two of them walked over to where his tarp now sat. It had been returned to him once it was clear what everyone's intentions were.

Rabbit shook her head. "They put a lot of detection equipment around there. It's better just to avoid it entirely if you can."

"Why the extra security?" Rafe wondered aloud as he knelt and started transferring things from the tarp into the bag.

"It used to be one of our larger stations for helping runners," Rabbit said grimly.

At that moment the doctor stepped back so Neil could try a couple of steps with the crutches. Neil swung himself forward experimentally a couple of times and seeing that Rafe was watching him, gave him a thumbs up. Rafe returned the gesture with a smile.

Apparently satisfied with his work, the doctor turned his attention to Rafe. "So, what's the verdict?" Rafe asked, once again getting to his feet.

The doctor walked over to Rafe as Neil continued to practice. "I've done the best I can at this point, though it would be good to get that leg looked at again once you're in a safe location. Unfortunately, you'll have to make do with what you have in terms of painkillers. If I tried to get you anything prescription strength, it'd be noticed."

Rafe folded his arms thoughtfully but gave the man a grateful look. "Well, I guess it's the best we can do. I'm definitely going to appreciate those crutches."

The doctor nodded, reaching for the case he'd brought containing his equipment. "I don't doubt it. I have to leave now, but I wish you the best of luck."

"Thanks for your help," Rafe said.

Neil swung himself over to join the conversation. "Yeah. It's great that I'm not gonna slow us down as much. After what happened with the dog earlier today, we need all the lead we can get."

"It's my pleasure." The doctor reached for his coat and after a couple of handshakes, he pulled it on. "Well then, take care of yourselves." With that, he turned and departed up the stairs.

After he left, Badger turned his attention to Rafe and Neil. "Prepare while you can. Supper will be ready soon, and we'll at least feed you before you go. Once night falls, Rabbit will take you back out to send you on your way."

CHAPTER 6

SLAVE SONGS

December 8, 2037

WHILE HE STILL DIDN'T FEEL FULL, RAFE FELT SOMEWHAT satiated for the first time in a long while. The stars above them were just barely visible through the shadows of the trees. They had walked out the tunnel to find themselves in the dark of a cold night. Even so, Rafe couldn't help but have a new spring in his step. Maybe it was because he wasn't carrying Neil along with all their belongings. In fact, thanks to the new bag, Neil was now actually carrying a couple of the lighter things in their tarp. Rafe certainly wouldn't have begrudged his friend if he needed to be carried once exhaustion set in, but he hoped that wouldn't happen often. The shotgun had also been returned as they departed from the basement, and he felt more secure now that it was back in its rightful place, slung over his shoulder. That was a new feeling, but a soberingly reasonable one. He was in an unfamiliar and violent new world. Wanting some means to defend himself and the discomfort of losing it even for a short while made sense.

As they walked through the dark woods, Rabbit would occasionally pull ahead and then wait as he and Neil caught up. There was a moment where he thought he'd lost her, but then he spotted her again, a uniformed National Guardsman waiting quietly in the moonlight, her brown hair tucked under her knit cap and her rifle at the ready. They seemed to be heading north, unless Rafe missed his guess. He could have checked the compass, but he felt they were better off trusting their guide until they were on their own.

They had been walking for a couple of miles when Rabbit drew to a halt. "This is as far as I go," she said, scanning the area for any sign of company.

"That's fine," Rafe answered. "I think we ought to be all right from here." He and Neil had both pulled up the hoods of their coats for warmth. He thought their jeans and sweaters had done well so far. He hoped they'd remain adequate for the rest of the trip.

The moon was up higher now and as she stepped out of a tree shadow, he could just make out her face where the pale light shone across it. "A few things to keep in mind, just in case you didn't know." She was still all business as her breath fogged in the cold air. "Thermal imaging is more prevalent near Pilot Mountain, that's why I said keep away from there. Don't light any fires. If you're sure you haven't been spotted, hide first, ask questions later. Glass can help with infrared if you can find a house or an old barn, but remember if you can see through it, anyone searching for you can too. Pine trees are your friends, they will help disguise your signature. If you think you've been spotted, it's already too late. Just keep moving and do your best to lose them. That's all you can do."

"Sounds like you've been around a bit." Rafe tried not to shiver. He wouldn't have been surprised at this point to find ice-crystals in his dust-brown whiskers.

"A bit," Rabbit agreed, still scanning the area around them for trouble, "But lots of other people with more experience than me have too, and they've been burned. Most importantly of all, don't use the roads unless you must. I saw you have a compass. Do you know how to use it?" On seeing him nod in confirmation, she continued, "Good. Between that, and keeping the Little Dipper on your right, you should be fine."

Rafe nodded again and set about checking one last time that all their supplies were in order. "Anything else we should know?" he asked as he knelt, tallying the contents in their bags.

"If you somehow end up inside a compound, you can find us by what we carry with us. In this area they keep a flashlight at their left hip. Further west, it changes to keep the authorities on their toes. Near the front line, those who offer help keep a snap ring in the same place with a key hanging from it. If you think you've found them, say a few lines from a Rolling Stones song within earshot of them. For you, any song will do. If they acknowledge you, they'll tell you where to meet them and once they're sure you're alone, they'll ask you if you're looking for Paul. Tell them you're looking for Ringo."

He secured his belongings and stood again as she finished, but when he heard the passwords he chuckled, wondering if he'd actually been shot when the dog found them, or if the organizers of this movement were just always this goofy. "It still sounds like this came out of a bad movie, but okay."

"It's a password," Rabbit said impatiently. "It's not supposed to make sense. Once you've made contact, don't do anything other than what you say you're going to do, pay for what you can, and get going as quickly as possible. That's for your safety, and theirs. Now get going. I can't stay out here." As she turned to leave, she looked back over her shoulder. "Good luck."

Rafe nodded. "You too."

With that, Rabbit disappeared into the woods, and Rafe turned to face Neil. "Well, I guess we'd better get a move on. We're burning moonlight."

"Right."

Rafe looked up at the sky, checking the stars before taking some time to orient their compass. Once he was sure of their direction, they headed west. He held the shotgun at the ready for any potential ambush, occasionally pausing to let his friend catch up.

"How long are we going to walk tonight?" Neil asked, as Rafe started walking again.

"Until you get tired, probably." Rafe moved a branch out of the way so his friend could hobble past it. "The faster we move, the harder it'll be for anyone to catch up."

Neil was quiet as they made their way through the woods. Their path through the hills was by no means easy, but now that he was carrying his own weight, it wasn't nearly as difficult to make progress as it had been before. They did their best to make way through the moonlit woods as silent as ghosts. Neil did slip twice, once on loose ground and the other on a patch of wet leaves, but Rafe made sure to stay close and was there to catch him each time. Several times they stopped moving to listen intently for any indication that someone was coming after them, but there was no sign.

Even though Rafe could tell they were making far better time than before, it was still a surprise to see that it was nearing sunrise when they reached the crest of a hill. From the vantage point, he could see a dilapidated house a short distance away, just beyond the trees and almost lost in a jungle of overgrown bushes.

"How're you doing?" he asked as Neil caught up again.

"You want to stop?" Neil asked. He seemed surprised that Rafe had spoken, but Rafe could clearly see that he looked tired from the past day's ordeals.

Rafe shrugged and gestured to the house. "This looks like about as good a place as any, right?"

Neil nodded. "It'll be less cold than sleeping outside."

"Less cold," Rafe agreed tiredly before offering a small grin. "You know, I tried to get us the 'warm and cozy' suite but those were all booked solid."

It seemed to take Neil a moment to realize he was joking, but when he did, he smiled. "I guess that's what we get for not making reservations early."

The two of them hurried across the small open space separating the trees from the building and crept under the eaves to search for a way in. A brief exploration toward the west side revealed that it was within sight of a road. Rafe felt that might be cause for concern, but he decided they should be all right, as long as they only used the side door on the south wall.

It didn't take long for them to use the hammer and screwdriver to smash the lock open. Once inside, they sequestered themselves in what had once been a living room. The furniture had not been stolen, though it certainly appeared that someone had found their way in at some point, since some of the doors on a china cabinet that stood on one side of the room hung open and the contents had apparently been rifled through. Old magazines were scattered on the decaying carpet, and there was no sign of a television or any electronics, despite the presence of fixtures and stands where they had clearly once been kept. After helping Neil down to the floor against an inner wall and making sure the blinds were closed, Rafe dropped down next to him. He tried to stifle a yawn before reaching into his pack and producing the last of the jerky. "You hungry?" he asked.

"Am I ever," Neil responded.

Rafe handed him his share and they ate in silence. A short while later, Rafe finished licking the crumbs from his fingertips and his thoughts drifted over the events of the past day. "I don't know about you, but I think we were beyond lucky back there."

Neil nodded. "When those guys with the dog found us, I thought we were dead for sure."

"And then Rabbit showed up, and I nearly had a heart attack," Rafe shivered as he remembered her rifle barrel against his back. "If she hadn't been resistance, we really could have been dead. Or arrested."

Neil grunted in agreement and looked toward the window, apparently lost in thought as the sunlight filtering through the blinds was beginning to get stronger. The temperature felt like it was still refusing to rise despite the new day.

"There aren't many people who would do something like that anymore, are there?"

Rafe looked over at him and shrugged. "Not as many as there used to be, I guess. But there's still a few." He considered that for a moment. "Still, that advice Rabbit gave us got me thinking. Kind of reminded me of that song slaves used to sing when escaping north during the first civil war. Did you ever hear about that?"

Neil shook his head and Rafe continued. "Follow the drinking gourd. The reason for that was because the constellation called the Little Dipper has Polaris at the end of the part that looks like a handle. So, you'd use that to navigate north. I think there was more to the song that gave more specific directions. But we have a map and a compass, and we can read, so I guess that means we're a bit better off."

"They didn't really talk about that in school very much." Neil rubbed his eyes. "They spent more time talking about what plantation owners did to slaves."

Rafe shrugged. "It's just something I read about once," he admitted. He leaned back against the wall and offered Neil one of the blankets with a yawn. "Why don't you get some sleep. I'll give you a turn on watch in a few hours."

"Sounds like a plan." Neil accepted the blanket and wrapped it around him before curling up on the floor. "Good night."

"Good morning, actually," Rafe corrected.

"Same difference..." Neil grunted tiredly. He brushed his dark blond bangs out of his eyes and burrowed deeper into the blanket. The room quieted after that apart from his gentle breathing, and Rafe took the shotgun back into his lap, focusing his energy on keeping alert for any sounds of danger.

C&C campaigns frequently resulted in the player characters camping in dangerous, wild areas while out adventuring. It was expected to have the party-members take turns on watch while others were resting, and the instinct to have someone awake at all times had carried over to his current situation. Perhaps it had even saved their lives the previous morning. Not that any knowledge a tabletop RPG could teach would hold a candle to the knowledge someone like Rabbit might have.

However, it was one thing to declare to the GM he would set up a watch, and quite another to sit up through several near silent hours actually doing it. In a game, if a player wanted to keep watch, they just stated it happened, and then maybe rolled to see if they spotted anything during the night. They never had to try staying awake, alone, with no one to talk to, and very real dangers seeming to hide in every shadow. Nor did they have to count those long hours, trying not to drive themselves mad while straining their ears for even the hint of a sound. That part of the experience, Rafe had discovered, was a battle all its own.

———

November 23, 2031

They had all been exhausted by the end of the night. Even Will had sounded tired as he spoke, "Eventually, you find the second key in the hold of the sunken ship. Once you find it, you swim to the surface and make your way to shore aboard the Blue Gull. As you make landfall, and the ship heads off back to its port to the North, what do you do?"

Rafe rubbed his eyes sleepily. His cellphone which sat on the coffee table in front of him said it was 1:34 a.m. "We need to set watches, probably."

"Yeah, and then we'll head back West to report to Ardes in the morning." Allen gave Will an accusing look. "Seriously, Will. A giant spider crab? Under. Water. When half the party can't swim?" Malchior was part of that half.

"You survived," Will calmly pulled a few stray dark brown hairs behind his ears. His grey eyes held no sympathy.

"It hurt," Eric pointed out. "A lot." His dwarf, Kade had managed to use his armor as a weight in order to walk across the seabed, once a water-breathing spell had been applied, but the spider crab had abused him quite badly in terms of damage.

"I almost didn't make it," Hannah pointed out. "Two more hit points, and I would have been gone, and if I'd bought it, we'd've had to go find a temple somewhere to find someone who knows *True Resurrection*, because I'm sure Rafe hasn't learned that yet."

Will leaned back in his chair thoughtfully. "Yeah, maybe I should have given a little more heads up that those things might have been important ... but you *did* survive." He turned to his notes and scribbled something no one else could see.

"No more sea battles for a while, please," Allen said. The rest of the party made sounds of agreement.

"All right." While Will had decided to house-rule a couple of things to make it a little easier, it was still well known in tabletop communities that sea combat could be awkward to run. This fight had taken them a couple of hours past where Will thought they would finish, despite his tweaks.

"So ... focusing now," Rafe could tell everyone was tired and Will wanted to finish up too, judging by the way he was rubbing his eyes behind his glasses. "How about we do our usual watches and then we go back to town in the morning?"

"Yeah," Hannah agreed.

Eric ran a hand through his red hair as he looked over his character sheet with a dissatisfied frown. "I sure hope this Veil thing is worth it."

December 9, 2037

It was late in the evening when Rafe pulled himself out from the warmth of his blanket to see Neil sitting next to him, dutifully holding the shotgun at the ready. The moonlight was shining slightly on the window, illuminating their hiding place. They had rested through the day, hoping the extra recovery time would translate to more miles on their next leg. He glanced at Neil's injured leg and guilt sank into his stomach like a stone. Under optimal circumstances they should have been able to stop somewhere and rest longer. Of course, if things were *optimal*, they wouldn't be on the run at all.

Neil looked in his direction. "You awake?"

"Yeah," Rafe sat up all the way and leaned back against the wall, scratching the brown stubble on his face. "Anything happen while I was out?"

Neil shook his head. "Not a sound."

Rafe found himself thinking he'd kill for a cup of coffee. He attempted to appease his desire for a drink with a small sip from the water bottle. It didn't work.

They'd refilled their bottle at a creek during a rest break the night before, using the water purification tablets rather than boiling it. Rafe was glad they no longer had to run the risk of their smoke being spotted, but he had to admit the chemicals made it taste *terrible.* So terrible, in fact, that he was longing for UNCG tap water, and *that* stuff had been an affront to nature. Still, it was better than nothing. He shivered. If they hadn't been worried about being found, having a fire just for the warmth would have been nice.

He reached for the bag of rations and popped it open to discover it was trail mix. He reached in and only took a small handful before offering it to his friend. Yes, they had enough for a few days. But he reminded himself as he slowly ate his share piece by piece, they never knew when they might have a setback. When something might tip the fragile balance they had reached. What happened if he got hurt? Or one of them got sick? Apart from the people who were chasing them, there might be no one to pull them out of that hole once they fell in. Food, however good it was to have, should be made to last. His stomach growled in complaint almost as though aware of his train of thought, but he forced himself to ignore it as he ate the last few pieces.

"So, are we ready to keep going?" Neil asked.

"Yeah," Rafe agreed. "Just as soon as I get everything packed up."

It was shortly after midnight when they finally left the house and continued into the gloom. On the other side of the road, a hill sloped upward, and the going was not easy, but with a little effort they were able to make their way at a slow and steady pace to the top. As they reached the summit and paused under the shelter of the trees, Rafe caught sight of a larger road as the moon sank closer to the horizon. It hadn't been maintained, but it still cut a recognizable swath through the brush and trees as it headed north. If he was reading the map correctly, it was Highway 89. That meant that they would need to tack in a more southerly direction, toward what remained of that small dot on the map that was labeled King, in order to avoid entering the area they'd been warned against.

"Hey Rafe," he looked over at Neil to see him leaning against the trunk of a nearby tree.

"What is it? Are you tired already?" he asked. He would carry him again if he had to, but his body still ached from their flight from those men at Belews Lake.

Neil shook his head. "Not especially, I was just thinking."

"About what?" Rafe looked out over the darkened hillside to give Neil time to say what he needed to.

"Mom and Dad..." Neil said quietly.

"I'm sorry." It was too dark for Rafe to read his friend's face, but he tried to meet his gaze anyway. "I know it's been hard..."

Neil shook his head again sadly as he tried to think through his words. "Was there anything they could have done to avoid getting killed?"

"Apart from toe the line and keep their heads down?" Rafe asked. "It's hard to say. As long as they continued being honest people in a den of angry vipers, I don't know what would have made a difference. When there's only one acceptable narrative, and people with different views and different ways of life are punished rather than allowed to provide their input, bad decisions are made. And even if the narrative is wrong, to those in power, that narrative can be more important than anything, even the truth."

"Even when that narrative is a lie?" Neil asked.

"Even then," Rafe agreed.

"Then it never mattered to those protestors that Dad said he'd never turn anyone away as long as he thought they'd do a good job."

"Probably not," Rafe agreed.

Howard had not hesitated to tell him the accusation was ridiculously stupid on its face since he had gone out of his way to hire based on merit rather than any racial attribute a person might have. He couldn't have cared less what they looked like so long as they were professional when they came to work in the morning, but that wasn't good enough for the activists. Once they were involved, someone had made an anonymous complaint to the Equal Employment Opportunity Commission about their employment practices. Then, the news organizations riled up a frenzy, and before the Flynn's knew it, there were further trumped-up charges and mobs picketing the company, seemingly every day.

Jane had told Rafe just before the trial officially began that she couldn't blame Howard's two business partners for running. Both had very young children they were worried for, and one of them had found their cat strangled to death on their front porch. All because the only thing that seemed to matter was the story that Howard Flynn's company was racist, for implementing a policy that, as far as Rafe could tell, wasn't racist at all.

Rafe started down the hill gesturing that they continue walking as they talked. "Kind of reminds me of something," he continued. "It's not a happy story, but it's one you might relate to. I was a bit younger than you at the time. We were living in that old farmhouse we stopped at, and my mom ... she was always what you might call 'opinionated.'"

"Around that time, Congress rammed through a piece of legislation to let the Federal Government collect property taxes over top of the states. The politicians said that property owners needed to pay their fair share because of how much they were taking from the poor in rent. Mom always used to say it was because they were running out of billionaires. There was a town-hall meeting about it at a local union office. We naturally didn't expect to be popular, but Mom wanted us there, hoping we'd learn that politics had consequences. She wanted to be allowed to speak, in hopes that the people who went would think about what they claimed to want. Looking back, it seems kind of tame compared to what we saw back in Greensboro, but for that time, it was pretty much a disaster. The leaders in favor of the tax allowed our side to give its views, but only so they could shout our side down. It didn't matter that Mom had spent hours researching and finding evidence to back up her opinions. One woman even called her a liar to her face." Rafe's voice had flattened as he pulled himself over a fallen tree and waited for Neil to catch up.

"It was obvious, even then, a lot of the people there didn't want a debate. They wanted a villain in their little story — someone they could smash like a bug. Only difference was, back then, they still had their heads enough not to use torches and pistols."

Once Neil had pulled himself over the tree, they continued onward in an uncomfortable silence. Then the younger boy spoke. "They didn't even think what those laws they were supporting might lead to?"

Rafe laughed bitterly. "Now that's the irony, isn't it? They were so quick to demonize, that they didn't take the time to listen and consider the opposing view seriously. So instead of taking what could go wrong into account, well ... look where we are now." He gestured at the valley in front of them. "Old houses are rotting on their foundations in empty wilderness, while we're all stuffed into little boxes and pitted against each other like animals. No privacy. No safety. No freedom. Just fear."

"Why didn't you leave a long time ago?" Neil asked.

"For the longest time, I thought my parents were worried about something that would never happen. In my own life, things were okay, so it didn't seem like those people made a difference." Rafe's expression was sheepish, though he wasn't sure Neil could see it in the dark. "I had a job, at least some of the time. My friends were there, and my parents ... I didn't want to believe they were right, even when they tried to show me the evidence. I just wanted to live my own life outside their shadow, and they seemed to be doing fine, until they weren't." He paused for a moment, before he continued speaking, guilt turning his stomach as he spoke. "I never thought ... I didn't want to think it would ever get this bad. I never liked what was going on, but ... I guess it felt safer to carry on pretending I could hide from it and keep acting like the world hadn't collapsed."

They had reached the bottom of the hill and were headed through the woods toward the road now.

"I guess my parents felt the same," Neil admitted. "They didn't want to leave what they'd built either, but it ended up being taken from them anyway."

———

February 21, 2032

"I can't believe you aren't on my side in this, Allen!" Hannah had exclaimed.

"Because I'm black?" Allen returned with a teasing grin.

It was lunchtime one cold Saturday during their junior year. Everyone was sitting in Will's living room, eating takeout and discussing the latest developments in the game. That is, until someone had started talking about a protest that had taken place on campus the previous day. Apparently, some ethnic studies major had decided that 'The Spartans', the name for the sports varsity teams on campus was both racist and sexist, the former because it referenced Western civilization and therefore white culture, and the latter, because historically Sparta was a male dominated society. Some had suggested changing the team's name to the Amazons (proponents claimed the Amazons were non-white as well as a matriarchy) while others didn't think it went far enough. (They complained the new name was racist to South Americans). Regardless, Rafe thought they were always protesting something, and this was just the newest stupid thing to be angry about, so he'd ignored it. To hear Hannah's version of things, he could never understand anyway. He was white. And a man.

Hannah drew herself up as though the answer was obvious. "Exactly, because you're black. Don't you have to deal with it all the time? People making jokes and assumptions about you and not taking you seriously? And people make judgments about you. They don't even know they're doing it half the time because they're privileged. And because they're part of a culture that adheres to that privilege."

"Now who's making blind assumptions? You ought to know better than that," Allen retorted. "Sure, I'm black. But to blindly assume someone's prejudiced just because they're white, or male, or rich, isn't fair. People are individuals, they aren't just their race." He popped a morsel of sweet and sour chicken into his mouth with his chopsticks and waited for the rebuttal.

"Even when those privileges are part of reality? It's the culture itself that holds these stereotypes and prevents people from succeeding in life. It's because of this that men think they can dominate women, and people who are white generally do better than people who aren't." Hannah twisted up a forkful of lo mein with slightly more vigor than she'd intended, and she took a moment to use a napkin to clean the mess off Will's coffee table.

"Kind of funny that. What about those poor white people who are living in Appalachia? Is that white privilege?" Allen asked. "I hear in some areas they use soda as currency because they buy them with food stamps and then use them to trade for other things. Or how about the black rappers and football players and actors and those who run their own businesses? My family makes money, and we're pretty well off. And look at you and me, a white woman and a black man, sitting here in the same living room, arguing about privilege while we're eating Chinese takeout and attending the same school to study pre-law and engineering. Seems pretty equal to me. By comparison, I'd say we're doing pretty well."

"Most people don't even know they're doing it. It's in little micro aggressions where it really comes through..." Hannah began.

"Once again we're back to this trust issue, aren't we?" Allen put his food down for a moment to sip from a bottle of sweet tea he'd picked up next to the Chinese restaurant where they'd gotten lunch. "What you're saying is, not only can't people be trusted to think for themselves, they actually *don't*. Every decision was already made for them by this monolithic over-mind, and free will doesn't exist."

"That's not what I'm saying!" Hannah took a second to realize she'd been waving her chopsticks for emphasis and put them down next to her lo mein carton. "I just think people should check their privileges and be aware of how they affect minorities. Freedom to express yourself doesn't mean you're free to be a racist."

"So basically, people are free to disagree, unless they disagree with you. My grandparents used to tell stories about living in a setup like that. Something about 'separate, but equal?' Of course, in general conversation, they just called it Jim Crow."

Hannah glared at him as she tried to think of a reply but he continued. "That kind of thing leaves the disadvantaged feeling helpless, angry and jealous, and it makes everyone else feel guilty, or resentful." The expression on Allen's face was thoughtful and sad. Picking up his chopsticks again, he pulled up the tin of sweet and sour chicken and crossed his legs, considering Hannah's assertions. He was so tall the image reminded Rafe of a praying mantis. "I've seen it with my cousins. Because when people feel helpless, they don't think they have a chance in life except to cling to politicians, welfare, or whatever it is they think is safest like scared children. They covet what they don't have, because they feel like they should have had it if it weren't for prejudices they assume other people have, while they ignore the decisions they, their parents, and the people in power already made, and the decisions, triumphs, and suffering of millions of individuals. Then they call out to the government for restitution and protection in exchange for freedom, when it was their own calls to the government and relinquishing their own responsibilities that caused their problems to begin with."

"Well, now you're just blaming the victim," Hannah said curtly.

Allen shook his head as he continued playing with his chopsticks. "Societies break down when people become afraid of the responsibility of being free. They don't seek out healthy, honest relationships, and families fail. That society you seem to resent so much – that's what keeps families together, and encourages them to help each other, as opposed to a government paycheck in exchange for your father and your dignity, and a family so fragmented you'd be lucky if you knew what city you were born in, much less who you can go to when you need things the government can't provide."

"That sounds nice and all. Except you already know my family *is* that fragmented, and society couldn't care less for what I went through. It wasn't the government that got my mom addicted to drugs, or told my aunt to kick me out of her house the moment I turned eighteen, because 'she'd done her part.' Not that I didn't find a way to land on my feet, but you remember how I had to find a place to stay at the end of freshman year. You aren't saying people like us are somehow less because our home life wasn't perfect, are you?" Hannah asked.

Allen shook his head, "Of course not. But there's no denying whole and healthy families do better than unhealthy ones, and they are the backbone of society. It's in that society, where people work and trade and create wealth, which lets them come together to make their communities strong. And I will point out, wasn't it a friend of yours who offered to room with you over the holidays to help reduce the cost for you to get an apartment? That counts as part of your community too. For each person that may be racist or sexist, there are plenty of others who are not, and it is those people who form the security net for each other in times of strife. And it is those very citizens who are the technicians that keep the government from breaking. What you ask for is to make the government into a self-perpetuating machine. And that people should depend on it unquestioningly, even when the gears rust, the experts become arrogant, and the politicians become power hungry, abusive, and corrupt. What happens when the machine breaks, Hannah?"

As Rafe listened, he couldn't ignore the feeling that this sounded like an argument Allen had put together over a long period of time, stitching it together as he had formed his thoughts on the matter. He half-wondered what Thanksgivings were like at the Jackson household if that was the germ for his thoughts on this topic.

"And what do you mean by that?" Hannah scoffed derisively.

"A government is a tool, but it's not supposed to be the only tool," Allen supplied. "If it collapses are the people going to be able to function without having to go with their hand out to some politician or bureaucrat who has to tell them when it's okay to breathe? If that's how you live, you aren't a citizen at that point, you're a slave."

"But isn't it the government's job to take care of their citizens?" Hannah argued. "No one should be allowed to suffer just because they're disadvantaged, and there's always going to be people who lord their privilege over others whether you say it exists or not. Most of those people who say that baloney about society don't care enough, especially not about the people who aren't accepted in the community. The privileged are too selfish for any amount of private charity to ever be enough!"

Rafe frowned. That didn't sound right to him at all. How many times in his youth had he watched his parents take part in food drives, and participate in crop walks and charity events through their community? How many times had he seen members of his extended family and friends volunteer, start scholarships, and donate clothes and food? He couldn't deny the tragedy she had experienced in her life, but surely what Hannah said was wrong. He thought about whether or not he wanted to say anything, but Allen had already spoken before he could open his mouth.

"So what *is* enough then?" He asked quietly. When she didn't answer right away he added, "And what is privilege? Each individual has attributes that they are born with, but no one of us has exactly the same. The circumstances of our birth aren't the only factor to consider. We have agency in our own lives, or at least that was what the people who created this country believed."

"For white males..." Hannah murmured.

Allen sighed as he ate one last bite of his chicken and replaced the lid. "For everyone, even if it took us a while to get it right. America is, after all, an experiment; and when you're experimenting, you can't expect to get every single thing perfect on the first try. They set the groundwork, and they made sure we wouldn't strike things out or change things unless we really meant it for a reason.

Besides, does that make the ideals they held to any less worthy, just because they couldn't perfectly live up to them?"

Eric spoke up. "I think I'm ready to get back to the game now." Versions of this debate had already been heard in Will's living room before, over many a box of Chinese takeout. Especially in the last few months, since the presidential elections were this year.

"I agree," Will took a sip from the soda can on the table next to his chair before adjusting his glasses and turning his attention back to his notes for the campaign. "So, the last thing that happened was you encountered Ilaria the Druidess..."

"The one who showed up as a rabbit?" Allen asked.

Will nodded patiently, "Yes, Ilaria, the fair Druidess of the Sacred Whitewood Grove. She came to you as a rabbit and then shifted back into her human form, and offered to help lead you through a safer path back to the Grove so the head Druid could give you more information about the cave system in the forest where the third key's hidden..."

"So, we're following the white rabbit?" Rafe grinned. "That never goes poorly!"

"She could be one of those killer rabbits," Hannah suggested.

Eric was checking his character sheet, but as Hannah spoke he offered a grin of his own. "In that case, she'd be chasing us, and we'd want to make like King Arthur, and run away!"

Allen leaned back in his seat with a chuckle. "It's the old party standby for a reason."

———

December 9, 2037

Rafe and Neil were almost to the road, when a familiar sound suddenly caught Rafe's attention — the violent sound of rotors whipping through the air, keeping a search helicopter airborne. The worst part about it was that it sounded like it was coming from in front of them.

"Are they waiting for us?" Neil wondered aloud.

"Possibly," Rafe agreed. "Though I don't think they could've seen us yet." He checked their compass, safely secured to his wrist, to make sure they were headed in the right direction. Highway 89 now waited about twenty yards away through the trees. He could see the asphalt as a ribbon darker than the silhouettes of the trees around them in the early dawn. What were their options?

They could go south, but that might bring them back to the northern end of the Walnut Cove compound. Or they could go north. He looked to his right, observing the bare trees interspersed with pines, and made his decision.

"North it is then. We'll follow along the road until we're further away and then turn west."

Neil nodded and then maneuvered his crutches to turn around, and they started working their way north along the side of the hill. He couldn't help but think he was becoming something of an expert on the real-world applications of King Arthur's top strategy.

CHAPTER 7

TRUE COMPANIONS

December 9, 2037

"Don't worry, hon, we should find those boys soon; and when we do, I'll be back to Greensboro before you know it."

Church listened as his wife let out a heavy sigh on the other end of the line. *"I know. Just be careful. The girls keep asking why you aren't home for dinner."*

He smiled at the reminder. "I will." After saying their goodbyes, he hung up his cell phone and placed it back into his pocket just as Everett approached his perch on the side of their car, pocketing a cellphone of his own. "What is it?" Church asked.

"A guardsperson from the north end of the compound found footprints indicating two people walked through their patrol area. Based on the appearance of the prints they reported, Flynn seems to be on crutches now," Everett said.

"So that's where they went," Church drawled, "I wondered where they've been holding up since yesterday." He considered the situation for a moment, visualizing the local geography. "There's no way they got past us without help, wouldn't you say? It's unlikely they would have found the crutches in some abandoned house outside the compound, and it's impossible for them to have found food on their own."

"The National Guard have got to be searching the compound for sympathizers right now," Everett agreed.

"Not our problem, of course. But it always looks good in a report to help other agencies find conspirators, so we'll have to remember to add that when we handle our paperwork."

"Yes sir." Everett stifled a yawn. It was still quite early.

"You got coordinates on those prints?" Church asked, pulling on a hat to cover his thinning black hair.

"Right here," Everett handed him a piece of notepaper.

"Good." Church studied it and then headed toward the driver's side of the car. "We'll get as close as we can with our transportation and meet up with the person who found the prints to help track them from there."

———

April 3, 2032

Allen had rushed into the room as Will had let him in. "Sorry I'm late. It's those pro-choicers rallying out in front of the cafeteria. It was so crowded with protestors and counter-protestors, I could barely squeeze through." He took his customary seat in one of Will's chairs and started pulling his dice out on the table. "We're still in the forest tunnels, right?"

"Yeah." Will took his seat by his computer.

"We saw those protestors at lunch earlier, no wonder you were late," Rafe commented, brushing a bit of lint out of his dust-brown hair. He was lounging on the couch next to Eric. "They're still going?"

"Some of them looked a little rowdy." Eric had put on a little more weight this semester. He said it was stress because the programming courses he'd taken were really kicking his ass. "We decided to go around."

"It was a good idea," Allen said, "I think I must have dodged about five different elbows and there was definitely a fight on the stairs down to the cafeteria. Who'da thought murder was such a popular policy position?"

Hannah visibly stiffened in her chair, and Rafe was certain if her ponytail had been a cat's tail it would have been twitching. "I really don't see why you have so little regard for my right to choose," she growled.

"You always have a choice," Allen said. "You can choose not to put that thing in the ... other thing ..." he trailed off awkwardly.

"What about the women who've been raped!" Hannah exclaimed. "They didn't get a choice!" She looked like she might be about to chew him out even harder, but he changed tack at that point.

"Now look, I'm not trying to be insensitive, but you're using the extreme cases to judge every case across the board, and that never makes for good policy." The look on Allen's face said he was already regretting opening his mouth.

"Because forcing a woman to carry a fetus she doesn't want is perfectly okay in every other case," Hannah interrupted sarcastically.

Rafe could tell Allen was starting to get annoyed. "It's not just the abortions either. That executive order forcing every doctor to advocate keeping the number of children in a family at two? One more step, and we'll be no better than China. You say the people advocating for life at the door of abortion clinics are infringing on a woman's right to choose, and yet you're also for requiring people to promote policies that are against their conscience? A life is a life, Hannah. It's bad enough we think we have the right to end it for no reason without forcing everyone else to be an accomplice."

As he spoke, Hannah looked at him more and more angrily. "There's too many people on this planet for the earth to sustain, Allen, we have to do something!"

"So, we have to sterilize or kill everyone, and keep a tight fist around their fertility like we think we own it?"

"No, it's giving women the freedom to live their own lives!" Hannah hissed.

"By encouraging the deaths of children, starting with the ones from neighborhoods of people who look like me," Allen's brown eyes flashed with anger as they locked with Hannah's frigid blue ones. There was a long uncomfortable silence as the two of them stared across the coffee table at each other.

Eric spoke up at that point, "Hey, guys? I know this is a tough subject, and I really don't mean to make this about us or anything, but we didn't come here to fight ... right? We ... we just came here to game and have a good time, didn't we?"

Allen and Hannah were still glaring at each other, but at last, Hannah let out a breath she'd apparently been holding. "Yeah. We did."

There was another awkward silence, and Rafe spent it reorganizing his dice before Eric pressed on doggedly. "So yeah, when we stopped, we were still in those tunnels with Ilaria and the Ranger looking for that giant Venus flytrap; so we could get the last key to the tower where the Veil is, right?"

Will nodded, looking impressed. "That's a pretty good summary actually."

"Okay," Eric began. "Can I start by taking those giant garden shears we found and pruning the roots in this tunnel so we can get through?"

"Sure," Will visibly relaxed as the tense feeling in the room slowly abated.

"I also want to flirt with the Druidess."

"What?" Will pulled up the sheaf of notes he was looking for, but he looked up like a deer in the headlights as everyone else looked his way expectantly. This would, no doubt, be hilarious. "Er ... okay ..."

"So, about this giant fly trap that lives in here," Eric began, pretending to slick back his red hair and adjust an imaginary dwarven beard. "Does it lure flies with anything near as sweet as you?"

The room was filled with chuckles and groans as Will buried his face in his palm, though Rafe could have sworn he heard Hannah mutter "sexist," under her breath even as she was pretending not to laugh. Under Will's hand, his face was already starting to redden as he thought about how he wanted Ilaria to respond.

"Seriously Eric," Rafe said once he'd composed himself, "That's gotta be the worst pickup line I've ever heard."

———

December 10, 2037

The sounds from the helicopter had died away about three hours ago. It was getting close to sunrise when Rafe and Neil passed a man-made lake, and Rafe decided they should cross over the road to make their way into the foothills on a westerly course. Not long after, with the road behind them, they found themselves traveling through a much more deciduous part of the forest. As they reached the crest of a hill, Rafe looked up at the sky behind them through the skeletal branches of the leafless oak and maple trees, squinting against the sunlight. Where they were, he was certain they were as exposed to the searching eye as the trees that surrounded them. There wasn't much he could do about it until they could find better cover, but it still worried him.

They continued onward until they reached the valley and began to scale the next hill which was a bit steeper. He was about halfway up when he noticed that Neil was not immediately behind him. Looking back, he saw his friend had stopped, holding onto a tree for support. Rafe sighed. Just because Neil had crutches didn't mean he could go as fast as an uninjured man. Rafe walked back down the incline, navigating between the trees until he was just above where Neil was waiting.

"Sorry," he said, "I forgot. Are you getting tired?"

"I am, but I wasn't going to ask to stop yet." Neil glanced up at the leafless trees above them.

"You noticed too," Rafe observed.

Neil nodded. "I figured I'd say something when we got to the top. Maybe we could spot some better cover up there. Or you could just go on ahead..."

"Don't sweat it," Rafe assured him. "And you're not slowing me down, all right?"

Neil smiled, but it was clearly forced. Rafe offered his hand, to help pull him up past the tree he was leaning against. The rest of the hill was spent almost climbing through the woods, with each tree almost a rung on a very steep ladder. With each swing, Neil had to be careful that he didn't place the ends of his crutches in any holes or loose dirt, for fear that he'd slip. Rafe soon moved behind him to catch him if he fell. Finally, they reached the summit of the hill, and Rafe looked out through the fading canopy and spotted a familiar sight to the northwest of them in the distance.

"That's the back of the knob at Hanging Rock," he said.

"Really?" Neil asked. "I never got to go before the evacuations."

"My parents used to take us there sometimes," Rafe said. "Eric and I would come up here too, once we were old enough to drive. We'd swim in the lake, and hike to the top of the knob. From there, you can see clear to Winston-Salem on a good day."

Those had been wonderful days, too. The water was always cold, no matter what time of year; but in the summer, the sun would be warm on the sand at the old swimming lake, and in the autumn, when the weather began to cool, the mountainside would turn into endless carpets of reds, yellows, and oranges, interspersed with patches of evergreens and the fields of grass down in the foothills below. Looking out over the woods, he noticed that some snow still dusted the top of the mountain, but within his mind's eye, like it had been yesterday, the autumn colors dotted the rolling hills as if brushed in by a painter.

"It sounds nice," Neil commented, breaking him out of his thoughts.

"Yeah, it was."

Rafe walked ahead a few steps and turned to go directly west, down the hill. He made sure he stayed slightly lower in case Neil fell. About five minutes later they reached the base, and ahead of them he could see a medium-sized lake beyond the trees. On the north shore was an old house, but bearing in mind that they might be followed, they chose to stay well away from it.

Adjusting their course further northwest, they climbed a particularly steep incline and eventually crossed a road that had deteriorated into crumbling asphalt. On the other side, they found a valley that was sloped much more gently and had plenty of evergreen tree cover.

It seemed to take far longer than it should have to reach the point where the depression in the landscape turned further north, leaving them to climb out of it. The sun had passed the apex of its journey across the sky as they reached the top of the hill. They found themselves looking across a cleared area that had once been a lumber farm but was now nothing but scrub and bushes.

"What do you think?" Neil asked before Rafe could bring the topic up himself. "Should we risk it?"

"No, we'll circle around." Rafe decided. Better to play it safe and not run the risk of being spotted from the air. Unfortunately, that meant going still farther north. If he had to guess, he would say they were probably right at the foot of the actual mountain now.

Upon reaching the bottom of this hill, they ended up having to cross over a creek. It wasn't deep, but the fact that the trees were less dense didn't do much to ease their concerns. And even worse, as Rafe finished helping his friend avoid the muddy riverbanks by using several large granite rocks that jutted out over the flowing water, they could both hear another helicopter to the south.

Continuing in their northwesterly track, they found that the slope of the land began to rise dramatically, and soon the going started to get difficult again. Patches of snow began to appear along their path, creating further obstacles to be avoided. At last, as the sun was hovering above the horizon, it became steep enough that Rafe decided they should turn straight west and follow the slope.

Time passed far too fast and yet far too slow as they continued through the woods, doing their best not to tumble. Even with the crutches, there were times Rafe found himself standing between two trees just below his friend on the slope to make sure Neil didn't fall. More than once, they had to stop to catch their breath after a slip that was too close. They continued, not sparing much time to talk for fear that the presence at their backs might finally catch them.

Late in the afternoon, the remains of a clear path with steps constructed out of rocks and railroad ties suddenly entered their field of vision, along with a huge face of rocks to their right.

Neil followed Rafe's line of sight as he glanced upward. The familiarity of the place took a second to register in Rafe's thoughts before he fully remembered where they were. He had quite a few memories of days spent climbing among the rocks above as a young boy, darting among the various crags and crevices as worried parents told him not to get too close to the edge, and friends shared water bottles, crackers and trail mix while taking in the majestic views that surrounded them.

"That's the hanging rock up there, isn't it?" Neil asked.

Rafe nodded. "Yeah. If we follow this trail here, it'll take us back down the slope until we reach the old parking lots and the road to the lake." Taking a few steps along the downward path, Rafe looked behind him at the giant rocks bathed in the dying sunlight. He felt a chill run along his spine as the cold evening wind passed through the trees. "I'm pretty sure there's some cabins once we reach the other side of the lake. It'll probably be okay to stop there."

The path down was much better, once they got to the less rocky areas and could easily negotiate the use of the crutches. It wasn't long before they were able to reach a road. From there, Rafe took them along the west side of the lake until they finally found a path lined with cabins, mostly untouched despite not being maintained for a few years. This didn't surprise him. These buildings were very much designed for rustic appeal rather than amenities.

Rafe walked past the first and second cabin before pausing at the third. "What do you think? Will this do?" he asked.

"Looks good to me," Neil agreed. He followed Rafe as he walked to the back of the building. Once there, they saw that some of the screens were out and crawled through the opening to examine the back door. Rafe reached for his hammer and brought it to bear on the window nearest the entryway. Feeling very much like a burglar, despite the fact the State of North Carolina no longer maintained these places for public use, or any use for that matter, he then reached through the shattered window, unlocked the deadbolt and let himself in. As he entered the living area looking out on the back porch however, he noticed a strange smell in the room and held up a hand to tell Neil to wait outside for a moment. It wasn't a filthy smell or even particularly strong, but it was distinctly enough of an animal smell to get his attention.

Rafe looked around the darkening room for a moment before he heard a growling sound as something moved towards him. That was when he noticed an open window to his right, and then he saw the large shadow covered in thick black fur that was approaching the living area from the bedroom. Not wasting another second, he quickly backed towards the door and firmly closed it after him. He was almost certain he heard a threatening growl through the window as he hurried Neil away from the cabin.

"What was that?" Neil demanded.

"I think it was a bear. . ." Rafe whispered. "And I probably woke it up." He motioned that they make their way deeper into the campground. "Probably saw the window and thought this was a good place for his den."

"Definitely not using that one then," Neil said.

"Nope," Rafe agreed. "I'll try to check the outside a little more carefully next time." They walked a little farther, keeping an eye on the area behind them in case the animal was trying to follow them, but it didn't seem to be.

They passed a few more of the cabins, before reaching an older part of the campground where the screen porches on the cabins were built towards the driveway, rather than the woods. Rafe spotted a mesh panel on one of the screened porches that had been torn loose and after making sure the building had no open or broken windows, he pulled the screen free, helping Neil crawl through. Once his friend was up on the concrete floor of the porch, he checked the door, and once again used the hammer and screwdriver to disable the lock.

Although there was dust everywhere, the simple furniture seemed mostly untouched. A mouse hole had been chewed in the far corner, but there was no food here for the rodents to eat. Instead, there was a simple futon couch, a few chairs, a dining table over a plain linoleum floor, punctuated by a door leading to the bedrooms, and a few windows for getting the best possible view of the outside. There was also a small kitchenette with a refrigerator standing inert next to the stove and sink under several old cabinets. Wood paneling covered the walls to give the place a warm appearance but, in the absence of anyone to properly care for it, it was starting to show signs of decay. The windows had not been washed in a long time, and even though it was getting dark, Rafe could see signs of water damage in places. There was also an especially nasty stain of questionable origin next to the refrigerator.

After taking a moment to survey the area, Rafe turned back to where Neil was waiting at the door. "Nothing's here," he said at last.

Neil let out a sigh of relief and swung himself into the room.

As the last of the light filtered in through the westernmost window, they sat down at the table and Rafe reached into his bag for the trail mix, divvying out their shares. Neither of them wasted words as hunger was too much on their minds for them to consider anything else first. It was getting harder to see Neil's features as the darkness settled in and Rafe leaned against the back of his chair. He didn't feel full, but his stomach had been satisfied enough that he could at least go a few more hours without the constant instinctual nagging to find sustenance. Did his jeans feel more loose than usual?

Taking a swig from the water bottle, he offered it to Neil. As his friend drank, he wiped the water from his own lips, noting their whiskery, unshaven condition under his fingers. Funny how much he'd taken a clean shave for granted before.

"I'm tired," Neil said as he placed the bottle on the table in front of him. He leaned back in his chair, not so much relaxing as just going limp.

"You and me both," Rafe agreed, noting the soreness of his feet. "Once I go refill the water, we should try to get some sleep. Tomorrow we'll need to figure out how we're going to get around Pilot Mountain."

"You sure we'll be okay staying here that long? Seems like those helicopters have been flying around a lot. And what if those men show up again, and what about the bear?" Neil was trying to keep his tone conversational, but it was clear he was looking for confirmation that they were okay here, and Rafe wished he could give it.

"More likely than not, the bear went right back to sleep after we left. It's winter. He's probably hibernating. But for the rest of it, I don't know," Rafe leaned back in his chair glancing warily out the cabin's windows. "I thought we were fine when they found us at Belews Lake, but I know that at some point we also have to rest. We've been going for nearly eighteen hours. We've earned a breather."

"What did we ever do to them anyway?" Neil grumbled.

"Depends who you're talking about." Rafe leaned back in his chair, thinking about the question for a bit before continuing. "Some of the people in charge may think we're at fault simply for having the nerve to act on what we believe, and some of them may think we shouldn't even exist. Some of the people who are after us may feel that way too, but most of them are probably just ordinary people, trying to do their jobs." He stood up and walked to the window, watching the moonlight filtering through the leafless branches outside.

Neil shifted in his seat and rested his elbow on the table, cupping his chin in his hand as he considered their situation. "Should we have left?"

Rafe gave him a surprised look. "Your parents were murdered in the street, and they were coming for you. Do you think the state wouldn't have found every excuse to put you in protective custody?

Mold you into a creepy little Red Guard just like all those other people out there that night?"

"What's a Red Guard?" Neil asked.

"Something my parents said they did in China. They'd take children and teenagers and raise them to worship Mao Zedong and the Communist Party like a god and never to question them. So, when they were told by their leader who they were supposed to hate, they became monsters for him. It never would have occurred to them to think he only wanted foot soldiers. That was what those people back in town were. The American version of the Red Guard."

Neil pulled himself to his feet and picked up his crutches. "They didn't teach us that in school."

"What *did* they teach you?" Rafe asked. Part of him felt a little bad at the question. He was quite willing to say he had a bit of an advantage in that his parents had educated him at home, but it was clear to him that the public school system hadn't done what it claimed to do for a long time.

"I'm not really sure anymore," Neil said with a shrug. He swung himself over to the futon to sit down since it was more comfortable there. "But I know we didn't learn about that."

"And that's how we lose our history." Rafe could have sworn he heard an echo from another time as his mother said the exact same words to him, whenever she tried to point out what the schools had stopped teaching for the sake of inclusivity, or whatever other inane reason. The irony was not lost on him. He returned to the table and picked up the water bottle. "I'll go refill this, and then we'll set up watches for tonight, okay?"

Neil nodded. "Okay." As Rafe neared the door, once again, leaving the shotgun to his friend, Neil spoke up again. "But if they're the Red Guards, then what are we?"

Rafe paused at the door thinking for a moment. "I don't know. I'll be right back." With that, he stepped back outside.

The temperature seemed lower than before, and he shivered. It was probably because of the wind. They would need their blankets tonight. He might even look around in the rest of the cabin when he returned to see if there were any extras.

———

November 20, 2032

" ... But I thought you cared about bodily autonomy. These RFID chips are so clearly in violation of that!" Allen had exclaimed.

Hannah's nostrils flared in anger. "They're only mandatory for the military and for people who can't take care of themselves. It's for their protection. I mean, think about it, Allen, a dogtag or an ID bracelet can get lost, but if you're an elderly person with dementia, something like this could save your life! Don't you care about that?"

Allen glared at her. "It's fine if it's done voluntarily, but Hannah, they are also requiring it of everyone with a disability, or over seventy, even the healthy ones who don't want it!" The law had been passed within the last two days, requiring the aforementioned groups to be implanted with a Radio Frequency Identification chip. These could be scanned in order to identify them. Other people could also opt in voluntarily if they wanted as it could also be used to get through security at transportation hubs and other locations. "We've been losing so many freedoms since President Holdt took power, it's not even funny, and this is just one more," Allen held a d20 in his hand but he wasn't playing with it. He just held it clasped in his fist.

"You just can't stand having a strong woman in power," Hannah bit back. "She's been the best thing for this country since Barack Obama!"

"Can we *please* get back to the game?" Will asked.

"Come on, guys! We've just got a few more rooms in this mountain, I'm sure of it," Eric said.

"And if we're too loud, the dragon might hear us before we can ambush it," Rafe added, trying to bring back a little bit of their group's old levity.

Allen seemed to be having trouble hearing them. "She's a dictator. She's been one since the day she was sworn in. One of the first amendments they got rid of after simplifying the process was the one that said you couldn't serve more than two terms, and you can't tell me the bomb that Antifa guy set up that killed more than half the Supreme Court on Inauguration Day didn't have some amount of planning. Whoever that guy was, he knew what he was doing!"

"So we're talking conspiracies now?" Hannah glared at him.

"You can't deny the results were awfully convenient for her party," Allen intoned.

Will exhaled impatiently and tossed another d20 down on the table with such force that everyone looked at him in surprise. "All right, that does it! This argument is now *over*, and you all hear a roar rumbling through the tunnels. The red dragon whose hoard you're after? You woke him up, he's approaching now, so stop arguing about politics, save it for later. You need to focus on making sure your characters don't get fried."

"Gee, thanks, Rafe!" Eric said mock-sarcastically, but Rafe could tell he was just trying to join in on resurrecting the good mood. "You should know better than to give the GM ideas!"

"Oops," Rafe answered, trying to sound innocent. The two of them waited to see what the other half of the party would do.

Allen and Hannah grudgingly turned their attention to their character sheets, but the tension remained in the room. Maybe it was Rafe's imagination, but throughout the fight, both of them seemed to be taking their frustrations out on the dragon with much greater viciousness than usual.

———

December 10, 2037

As Rafe crept back toward the lake, he was becoming more and more aware of how the higher altitude of the mountain affected night temperatures. Sure, winters had the potential to be cold in this part of the world, but with the higher elevation, it was frigid. He pulled up his hood and did his best to bury his hands into his coat pockets, wishing the bitter night air wouldn't gnaw at his extremities like the hungry beast that had only been partially staved off within his stomach.

Digging his fingers into the palms of his hands tightly, he stepped up his pace to make sure that this errand through the eerie silence of the vacant park would be completed as fast as possible.

Finally, he stepped out into the moonlight on the side of the lake opposite the old swimming area and the large bathhouse and changing rooms. Kneeling on the bank, he filled the water bottle with water from the lake, taking a moment to flip open the pill bottle to retrieve a water tab, slip it into the water bottle, and shake the container to disperse the chemicals. He was slipping the pill bottle back into his pocket, when he froze as he saw a pinprick of light move in the distance.

Slowly straightening, Rafe carefully watched the road to the northeast of the lake, waiting for movement. He hoped it had just been his imagination, but his heart was suddenly thumping, and his instincts were telling him that every second he waited was one less he had to get away. Sure enough, the light appeared again, this time slightly closer.

Someone else was here.

Rafe turned back into the woods to get out of sight, forcing himself to go slow in case sudden movement would be easily spotted in the moonlight. If he didn't do something quickly, there was a good chance that whoever it was could end up tracking them to their hideaway.

Chapter 8

And If I Claim to Be a Wise Man

December 10, 2037

Hernandez had rejoined them as they reached NC 89 ostensibly to provide assistance but just as obviously to provide an unspoken threat. It was more of an annoyance than anything else, but ever since the EPA had become the Environmental Defense Force, they could always be counted on to flex their muscles. It wasn't as if Church was going to stop the search to cut down a few of the EDF's precious trees. After spending the last couple of days with the man it was a bit tempting when Hernandez seemed determined to continue pretending not to understand when it suited him. But even if Church wanted to, it was hardly worth the paperwork.

"Man, that guy sure is a pain," Everett commented in a low voice, almost as though reading his thoughts. "I don't know what he thinks he's trying to pull with that act of his. Any fool can see him doing it."

"I'm glad you said it and not me," Church commented, pulling his coat tighter. His breath formed visible clouds in the light emitted from Everett's flashlight. They trudged through the gloom toward the old park campgrounds. Hernandez was following about a dozen feet behind them, so Church kept his voice low as well. "You might actually have standing, but if I said anything about it, I'd be brought up on hate speech charges." As lily-white as his skin was compared to Hernandez's rough bronze, he'd never stand a chance.

Everett looked thoughtful at that, but continued looking around the area for their target, shivering slightly despite his own heavy coat. Church wished they could have more lights, but even if they weren't trying to alert their quarry, Hernandez had cited some EDF regulation on light-pollution that might interfere with protected species' nocturnal habitats. They couldn't pull out more lights until they were certain of a clear and immediate threat to the environment.

On top of that, he'd been having trouble finding another available K-9 unit to replace the dog Turner had shot. Even under normal circumstances the SPKF were over-worked, but it didn't help that a bunch of them had been sent down to Charlotte to help track down what was believed to be a huge smuggling ring with connections to the rebels. All that meant to Church was that his life was becoming more complicated, and he did not like complications.

Church silently cursed the cold, the woods, the darkness, the smugglers in Charlotte, and the entire EDF agency, but most of all, Rafe Turner for bringing him to this awful place. But of course, Carol Turner's son would be just as ornery and tough as his mother; either that or damn lucky. He fingered the shell casing in his pocket with fingers that were threatening to go numb in the evening cold.

As if in answer to his thoughts, his attention was drawn by a warm light reflecting across the lake. He paused, looking through the trees toward the old bathhouse with curiosity.

"Did Turner light a fire?" Everett seemed to have spotted the light about the same time.

Church turned around and headed back along the north side of the lake, hoping they had just caught Turner in a critical mistake. "He probably did it out of desperation, since it's bitter cold out here," he called behind him, "But that's all we need."

Five minutes later, as they approached the bath house, he

spotted the origin of the warm light. It was a pile of kindling set up over top of what had once been a gravel drive leading up to the old wooden deck and the stairs to the washrooms and changing rooms below. There was no sign of anyone else here. "A decoy," he growled angrily as Hernandez rushed forward to put the fire out, cursing.

"Damn kid coulda set the forest on fire," Church muttered as he looked around for footprints.

Everett folded his arms thoughtfully as he watched the EDF agent pull out a tiny fire-extinguisher and spray it out. "But where is he now?"

Church's thoughts went to the most obvious potential shelters on the map he had found up in the old park records and he exhaled in frustration. The correct location was painfully obvious now that he thought of it. "He was trying to lead us away from the cabins!" With that, he broke into a run back along the road. "We might still be able to catch him!"

———

As soon as the fire looked like it could sustain itself on its own for a while, Rafe tore through the woods around the south side of the lake, hoping against hope that he'd done enough. It had been a lucky thing he'd had the matches in his pocket.

When he saw the cabin they'd broken into, and that no one seemed to be there, he only slowed his gait enough to avoid slamming into the door as he hurried inside. Neil looked up from his place on the futon in surprise. "They're by the bath house!" Rafe gasped, leaning against the table to catch his breath.

Neil groaned but pulled himself up and started toward the door. "No sleep tonight..." he murmured longingly.

"Doesn't seem that way," Rafe agreed. Neil handed him the shotgun, and his sack which he pulled onto his back before following his friend out. "I don't know how much time I bought, but I'm hoping it's at least enough to get us back into difficult terrain."

The two of them hurried to the end of the road leading deeper into the campground as fast as they could and then continued into the woods. After coming up a rise, they passed a small pond and soon found themselves at a set of rocks on a ridge sloping gently downward.

Helping Neil where he needed, Rafe led the way, trying to keep them within the tree cover as he used the ridge as a guide to keep them in a somewhat westerly direction. He felt they were going at an excruciatingly slow pace, but it seemed to work. The moon was sinking below the horizon when they reached another knob-like protrusion in the rocks, and he could see lights off in the distance. They looked like they might belong to a few of the city compounds in the foothills surrounding the mountain on which they were traveling.

The sky behind them was starting to turn gray when they reached an outcropping of rock that looked like it might provide some shelter, and Neil leaned against it in exhaustion. "Have we gone far enough?" he asked, his expression pleading that the answer was affirmative.

Rafe listened for a moment. They had managed to leave whoever it had been with the flashlight without being found, it seemed, because he neither saw nor heard any evidence of them. He looked back at Neil. Going farther was clearly not going to work unless Rafe carried him again, and he was tired too. "We can rest," he decided. "You can take the first two hours, okay?"

Neil nodded and lowered himself fully to the ground, dropping the crutches next to him and shutting his eyes. Rafe reached into their bag and pulled one of the blankets over his friend before sitting down next to him, doing his best not to fall asleep until it was his turn. Eventually he retrieved his own blanket to combat the cold. Still, it was hard to stay awake. He gripped the shotgun hard enough that the joints on his fingers were taut, willing his eyelids not to droop. A few moments later, he saw Neil visibly shivering under the blanket.

"You all right?" he asked.

"J-just c-c-cold," Neil murmured through chattering teeth.

"We can't light a fire." Rafe considered whether there was a way to improve the situation. Then he remembered something he'd read in an Army Rangers survival manual he'd happened across while trying to come up with ways to make Galen's knowledge of wilderness survival seem more realistic. It wasn't a comfortable idea, but still, it was incredibly cold out here. . . He quickly assured himself there was nothing inappropriate about what he was about to suggest, given the circumstances, as long as he took care to be respectful about it. Besides, uncomfortable as it was, it was better than nothing. He turned his back on Neil and scooted closer to him. "I don't know if this will work or not, but ... put your back against mine. I read somewhere that might help."

Rafe felt the younger boy quickly inch closer, leaning against him, and waited a second before asking quietly, "That better?"

"Y-yeah..." Neil answered pulling his blanket tighter around him, "A l-little embarrassing though..."

Rafe sighed. "If only that were our biggest problem. If it makes you feel any better, this is kind of awkward for me too, but it's better than freezing to death."

"It is really c-cold," Neil agreed.

Rafe could still feel him shivering behind him, though it seemed to be less than before, and he tried to adjust his blanket further to trap as much heat as he could between them. "Try to get some sleep, it'll be your turn on watch before too long."

Neil pressed closer against Rafe's back, almost pushing them into the rock in trying to get to the warmest possible spot under their blankets. "I hope that bear eats them. . ." Rafe heard him whisper softly.

"Amen," Rafe agreed.

Neil said nothing more, but that was fine, because despite the new warmth at his back, Rafe was busy focusing on the cold night sky, and the woods around them for any sign of the men who had chased them from their shelter.

December 11, 2037

Rafe blinked, rubbing the sleep out of his eyes as Neil shook him awake. As they had agreed, he had taken his allotted time for sleep, however short. As he looked up, he saw the sunlight behind the outcropping of rock where they were sheltering. He wasn't anywhere near as rested as he wanted, but this was the best that could be done. He shivered. The temperature felt like it had dropped overnight, and while he had no idea how low it had gone, he really did not want to crawl out from under the blanket.

Grow up, you wimp, he thought grudgingly.

Pulling himself up straighter and making sure his hood was secure over his head, he felt Neil shift around behind him. "Hey," Neil murmured softly.

Rafe reached for the sack and shifted around so he was sitting next to Neil instead of behind him. "You hungry?"

"A bit," Neil agreed.

Rafe opened the sack and felt around for their rations. He handed Neil his allotted amount and taking his own, the two of them ate. Putting away their food, he watched the sun slowly push away the shadows between the ridge on which they sat and the smaller ridge that separated them from Pilot Mountain across the gap, thinking about what they should do next. After he'd consumed the last bite of breakfast, he stood and began gathering their belongings to put back in their sack.

"If things work out for us, then I'd like to try going a little farther south," Rafe said at last. "If we can manage to thread the needle between there and King, we'll be getting closer to the front."

"Things are going to get more dangerous, aren't they," Neil observed, using the rock to pull himself upright.

"Probably," Rafe checked their water supply. It was pretty low, and he hoped they would run across a pond or creek soon. Until then, they would just have to be careful not to exhaust what little they had. Once he was done, he waited for Neil to join him in looking out over the gap ahead of them. "You ready?"

Neil paused for a moment before offering a wry grin. "Well, going back to sleep isn't an option."

Rafe chuckled. "Glad to see you still have a sense of humor."

Neil pushed himself forward on his crutches and a cool breeze played at the few strands of blond hair peeking out from under the hood of his coat. "I'll leave you behind if you don't hurry up."

"Now that's something I'd like to see." With that, Rafe cinched up the bag on his back and followed his friend down the mountain.

———

Rafe uttered a short stream of curses under his breath as he kicked the chain links in front of him. The barrier hardly gave a fraction of an inch before rebounding unsatisfyingly back into place. It wasn't doing any good, he knew. Somehow, they would just have to find a way around the fence. But with his current frustrations amplified by lack of sufficient sleep and food over the last couple of days, it didn't make being angry about the situation any less inviting. It had been a couple of hours since noon, and they had slowly been drawing closer to Pilot Mountain when, shortly after passing by a lake, they had somehow ended up facing another fence.

It was Neil who spoke first. "Rafe, are you okay?"

Rafe drew in a breath and let it out in frustration. "Not really," he admitted tiredly, trying to regain his composure as Neil's comment brought him back to reality.

He hurriedly looked around, checking for security cameras. It seemed to quell his own emotions somewhat, leaving him, more than anything else, tired. Now was not the time to lose focus. It was time to back away from the fence and get reoriented.

"I thought you said there weren't any other compounds around the mountain," Neil said as they found a spot safely back under the trees.

"I didn't think there were," Rafe replied. he checked their

compass and map against the mountain toward which they had been heading and found that it was actually on the right-hand end from where they were. "Looks like this fence runs from the southeast to the northwest. . ." It was then that he let out a small groan. "How could I have been so stupid?"

"What?" Neil looked up in alarm.

"Look." Rafe showed him the map, disgusted with himself. He pointed to a spot labeled '*Pinnacle*.' "Based on where I think we are, we should be right on the edge of the town's limits. It's such a small town, I thought for sure it had been evacuated."

"We can go around, right?" Neil studied the map as well, scratching his scalp and dislodging some small debris stuck in it. Rafe hadn't noticed how dirty the younger boy was getting; his blond hair was a lot darker now, and his skin was streaked with dirt. Of course, Rafe was certain the two were a matched pair, but there wasn't much they could do about it.

Rafe was tempted to just take the shears to the fence. He'd carried them this far, why not use them again? But he wasn't certain they could take the time to cut through it, and entering such a small town would no doubt put them in greater danger of being spotted. The local law enforcement probably knew everyone by sight, and they couldn't guarantee they'd meet someone friendly first.

"We'll have to," he agreed finally. He folded up the map and pocketed it, then gestured for Neil to follow him. "We'll backtrack a bit, try to get parallel to the fence, and then keep going." Neil nodded in agreement and then followed him as they resumed walking.

The weather had warmed slightly as they had descended from Hanging Rock, but it had been temporary, and he was sure it was chillier than it had been. As they reached the summit of a hill, they could see the knob of Pilot Mountain rising from the foothills ahead, separated from their current location by two strips of road. The closer of the two was the old Highway 52, abandoned even before the fences, its asphalt crumbling as age and disuse slowly reclaimed it for nature. The other was the *new* 52, cutting its way like a blade through the patchwork of long abandoned fields. They would have to cross it soon, he knew, regardless of the risk of discovery; but they had other concerns before that ... such as the dark cloud bank that hung just beyond the mountain, promising snow.

The bags under his green eyes felt much deeper than they ever did when the worst he had to worry about was staying up late due to homework, or a game; and seeing the weather that was coming in their direction made the fatigue seem all the heavier. He stepped up their pace a little. He didn't want Neil to get too tired or fall behind, but snowfall had dangers of its own for those stupid enough to be out in it.

It wasn't long before a hush fell over the woods. Rafe knew the air pressure had changed, heralding the coming snow. The temperature seemed to have dropped a few more degrees. They were nearing the base of the mountain and the dividing line of Highway 52, when Rafe spotted an old ranch-style house peeking out of the woods. It seemed to have an overgrown gravel drive leading out to an unmaintained road. He had to hope that it would do and that their pursuers would call off the search, at least until the weather improved.

The first flakes of snow were starting to fall as they reached the door of the house. Finding it had already been broken open, they let themselves in. Once inside, he shut the door, waiting for his eyes to adjust as he checked the room for broken windows that would hinder their ability to stay warm. Miraculously, apart from one that had spider-webbed when something had hit it at some point, they all seemed to be functional.

There was nothing in the house. If Rafe had to guess, its previous owners had properly moved out a long time ago. As with the first one they had sheltered in back in Greensboro, whoever had broken down the front door had made camp here at some point. Water damage stained one of the walls, but just below that, there lay a small pile of non-food trash. Someone had not wanted to dump it outside, probably for fear of being discovered. A door to a room with aged carpet on the floor stood to their right. He led them into it.

Neil sat down by one of the walls looking out at the snow through the window across from him. "I guess we're going to rest here for a while?"

"At least until the snow lets up," Rafe replied.

Neil grunted in acknowledgment before shutting his eyes, and Rafe couldn't blame him. If they hadn't had to worry about watching for trouble, he'd have tried to catch some sleep himself. Instead, he pulled out one of their blankets and tossed it to his friend. Neil reached for it without cracking an eyelid and wrapped it around him before his breath slowed. Rafe then walked to the window. Assuming a sentry position, he watched as the snow outside started to become visibly heavier and the fallen flakes started to stick to the ground.

December 12, 2037

The snow did not let up for most of the evening. Fortunately, the room they were in was well insulated, though it was still cold. Throughout the time Rafe was on watch, Neil did not budge an inch, and when his turn came, a short while before midnight, Rafe's descent into slumber felt more like passing out after standing up too quickly than a gentle surrender to restfulness.

When he finally opened his eyes again, sunrise had arrived, and Neil was waiting next to him, facing the window with the shotgun at his side. Outside, Rafe could see that the snow had died down, though the trees and the ground surrounding them were covered in a blanket of white. "Morning," Neil said.

Rafe yawned and sat up a little straighter against the wall. "Morning..." he replied. He stood and walked over to the window, observing the grey clouds overhead. They didn't look heavy with precipitation as they had last night, but the dimmed sky along with the surrounding snowscape made him wish he could curl back under the blanket and shut his eyes again. He certainly didn't relish going out in that.

"Looks pretty heavy, doesn't it?" Neil gestured to the snowfall outside.

"Yeah," Rafe agreed, returning to sit next to their belongings and take in the weather conditions. "Though what worries me about it, apart from leaving tracks, is that we don't have the right shoes for this. We might be running the risk of frostbite out there."

Neil nodded and then asked, "Should we wait a little and see if it melts?"

Rafe was silent for a few moments, struggling with indecision. Speed and caution both had their advantages and disadvantages. On the one hand, there were the risks he had just laid out; and if they did leave, could they guarantee there would be shelter where they stopped? But, on the other hand, the longer they remained close to civilization, the greater the chance someone might happen upon them. Neither choice seemed good. He debated with himself before eventually deciding caution was better. "We'll wait 'till noon and make a decision then."

———

February 12, 2034

Since leaving school, Rafe had jumped from job to job, unable to find one for more than a few months at a time. It was a slow, agonizing struggle to keep his head above water; it was about a year since the fences had gone up, and there were a lot of people looking for work. He considered it an accomplishment that he hadn't had to take welfare, though, and there were a couple of good prospects on the horizon.

One cold winter afternoon, while out job-hunting, Rafe ran into Eric. The two stopped at a nearby coffee shop and were talking over steaming mugs of the bitter drink.

"So, how's life treating you these days?" Rafe asked, once he'd informed his friend of his own fortunes.

Eric fidgeted with his cup. He'd started exercising regularly again since college and, while he was still a little stocky, he looked better. "I've been a useless piece of garbage really..." he said, half-seriously. "Dad keeps asking me when I'm planning to move out, but until I find a job that can actually cover the rent for an apartment, I'm kind of stuck."

"I know how that is," Rafe answered. "You could always move in with me. Half rent's only half as bad, right?"

"I appreciate that." Eric looked out at the street. On the other side stood a gang of young men about high school age, loitering. There had been more of that too, once the age limit for applying for work had been raised to eighteen. "Any news about your parents?"

Rafe shook his head sadly, glancing at his dim reflection in his coffee. "None. I've tried every source I could get my hands on. This whole mess is insane. It's like they dropped off the face of the Earth."

Eric nodded. "I know. To tell the truth, I'm kind of worried about my Dad too."

"Why? What's up?" Rafe looked back up at his friend.

"Well, I don't know if I should say, but..." he paused for a moment, looking around warily for anyone who might be listening. "I don't know, it's just ... I heard him lying to my mom about where he'd been, and we both knew it. He's never done that before. Ever. But when I asked her why, she said he had his reasons. I don't know what it is, but I think something's up."

Rafe was quiet for a while before he nodded. "Well, be careful. I don't want what happened to my Mom to happen to him, or you. But if there's anything I can do..."

Eric nodded. "Like in the game, we gotta look out for each other, right?"

Rafe nodded. "Though this is way different than playing with dice. We don't even have a Game Master to negotiate with anymore."

"I know." Eric turned away from the window as the sky began to darken. "What ever happened to Will, anyway?"

"You haven't heard from him either?"

"Not since graduation. Everyone I asked said the same thing. No one knows where he went."

———

December 12, 2037

The snow had melted somewhat before noon, but not sufficiently to instill Rafe with confidence that they wouldn't be detected, so they had stayed. Unfortunately, they couldn't afford to wait much longer, thanks to an empty plastic bag.

It was late evening, and Rafe crumpled the bag that had once held their trail mix as Neil finished off the last of the crumbs. They had split the last of it equally, but it was nowhere near enough. It had barely been enough before now either, as his gut was quick to remind him, and there were still miles to go before they reached the war zone, or Boone, assuming they could cross it alive without getting caught.

He was distracted from his thoughts when he heard Neil ask a question. "Hey Rafe?"

Rafe looked over at him from where he was standing at the window. "Yeah?"

"Why don't you believe in God?"

At first it caught him by surprise, but then again, he guessed it was only a matter of time before they got to this conversation. It happened with almost every other person of faith he'd spoken at length with, eventually, and it could be a difficult subject to tackle. He decided to open the floor with a question. "Why do you believe in Him?" he asked, doing his best to keep his tone non-confrontational.

"Well..." After a moment of thinking Neil answered, and it was a response that Rafe had heard before. "Because Jesus died for our sins ... and because God is all around us. How could we exist without Him?"

Rafe spent a moment or two debating himself on the correct answer. Neil's hurt and distrust was not what he wanted, but he didn't want to lie either. At last, he said, "I don't believe because I haven't seen sufficient evidence. If the information you have to work with leads you to believe otherwise, that's for you to decide."

"Just because there's no proof, doesn't mean that it's not there," Neil's tone was slightly defensive.

"True," Rafe agreed calmly. He knew very well this could be an emotional subject for some people and had no desire to start a fight. "But at that point, you've taken the question beyond what is rationally knowable to a question of faith. So, the question becomes this: is faith the same as knowledge?" Neil thought about that for a while before Rafe spoke again. "I'm not going to make you answer that if you don't want to."

Neil frowned thoughtfully, "Faith isn't about what you know, really. It's kind of..." He lightly bumped his fist to his chest. "In here, I guess.

Rafe nodded, thoughtfully. "Okay. Well ... here's what I feel ... in here..." He mimicked the motion Neil had made with his hand. "I don't feel like there's any presence watching over me, or that I have any concrete evidence to back up the existence of He or She or It. It's still a pretty incredible world we live in, and before the war, we only just scratched the surface. I think it's unlikely, but I'm only one man with one brain and one set of senses to work with. I don't believe the information I've used to make that call is flawed. But I'm not perfect, and I don't care to silence anyone who has a difference of opinion so long as they're willing to respect mine. Why would I want to when someone else might have a piece of the puzzle that could get me closer to the actual truth?"

Neil pulled the blanket around him a little tighter to keep out the cold. "So, what *do* you believe in?"

Rafe walked over and sat down next to Neil. "That the truth matters. That you shouldn't run from it, even if it's ugly, and if you think you've found it, examine it as thoroughly as you can for cracks or faults." He shrugged, "Of course, there's also the most important and fallible things of all. This," he tapped the side of his head, "and this," he tapped the left side of his chest, "these are the tools we use to sculpt what we know and believe. While they aren't truth itself, they are the lenses through which we are trying to see it and through which we determine what matters to each of us the most while we are enjoying this wonderful gift of being alive. After all, if we weren't alive, none of this would be possible in the first place."

"So as long as you're alive, everything is possible?" Neil gave him a wry look.

"I don't know about 'everything', but there's a heck of a lot more that is than if you aren't," Rafe said. "We're all searching for answers, and we're not always asking the exact same questions, or weighting the same information the same way when it comes in. Is it really so surprising we don't all come to the same conclusions? But the big takeaway is what you do with those answers when the chips are down. That's where you find out who you really are." He laughed self-deprecatingly. "If anyone's been flunking out on facing the truth and its harsh realities the last couple of years, it would be this loser." He jabbed a thumb at himself.

"Well, maybe there weren't enough chips down yet," Neil suggested. "I think I can agree with some of that. Some of it just seems..." He tried to think of a way to describe his thoughts. "I don't know. Lonely. Don't you ever wonder, even a little?" He gave Rafe an apologetic look, as though afraid he'd be offended, and yet there was also something akin to pity there too which made Rafe a little uncomfortable.

In response, he shrugged again, more to shake off that look than anything else, "Every sane person has doubts, and that's okay. It's when people stop asking questions that life gets really scary."

They were quiet for a few moments as Neil considered that thought before he yawned. "Why don't you try to get some sleep?" Rafe suggested "I'll wake you when it's your turn to watch."

Neil nodded. "Okay." With that, he rolled onto his side and

shut his eyes, though, as he did so, Rafe heard him muttering something that sounded very much like a prayer.

As Neil slept, Rafe stood guard and redirected his thoughts away from philosophical matters in favor of more physical needs. Finding food was his first priority. As he saw it, they only had two tools for that. The first was the shotgun, but hunting was out. Any shots fired would attract attention this close to a compound, never mind that he had never hunted before and couldn't guarantee he would hit anything.

That left the second option: the pruning shears.

———

A few hours later, as dawn finally set in, Rafe saw Neil blink the last remnants of sleep from his eyes. "Morning," he mumbled.

"Morning," Rafe replied, walking over from the window.

"Any less snow?" Neil asked, pulling himself to where he was sitting upright and looking around hopefully.

"It freezes at night," Rafe said.

"You say such cheerful things," Neil grumbled as he stretched his arms and his uninjured leg.

Rafe walked over to their bag which he'd set aside before and started looking through it, immediately taking out the lantern and the cooking pot. They were too bulky, and if he ran into trouble where he was going, they would just make running harder. The attention of the authorities was the last thing he needed, and he was only going to take the gun within a short distance of where he planned to cut the fence.

"I guess we're still not leaving then," Neil observed.

"Not yet," Rafe confirmed, his expression turning serious as he explained. "I'm going to try and get us some food." He set aside the water bottle as he spoke, planning to fill it with snow so he could leave it with Neil before he left.

Neil's expression was equally serious. "Anything I can do?"

Rafe shook his head. "For now, just keep your eyes and ears

peeled for any sign that someone besides me is in the area. If you see anyone, hide. I'll try to be gone for as little time as possible. But we need to keep our strength up if we're going to make it."

Neil looked worried but nodded. "You're right."

As morning became afternoon, the snow melted away to a point where Rafe felt confident enough to leave the house. He cinched up his bag alongside the shotgun, placed the chocolates in a pocket of his coat where he could get to them, along with the shears, and set out into the cold. It wasn't exactly warm in the room where they were camped out, but it was still shelter, and he couldn't help but shiver as he was exposed to the elements again. He moved slowly to avoid stepping in the slush that dotted the ground as he made his way into the woods in a southerly direction toward where he knew the fence stood, doing his best to imitate a shadow.

Rafe reflected that, once again, Hannah's elf Rogue probably would have done a much better job. At least she wouldn't have nearly tripped over ice-covered roots, and she'd be much better equipped to avoid the pitfalls of rugged weather. Not to mention, depending on how close of a cousin she was to Tolkien's elves, she could probably walk on snow without leaving a mark. Hell, even his Cleric would probably have done better, if only because of his heavier boots and wool socks. His sneakers really weren't suited to this kind of weather. He could make do when the snowmelt wasn't threatening to soak his cotton socks, but right now, the risk of frostbite made him slowly pick his way around puddles and mud rather than take a more direct route.

After a while, though, the fence loomed ahead through the trees. He paused, scanning the area for any sign of surveillance. Not spotting any, he placed the shotgun in a pile of brush he was sure he could find again and approached the barrier. Fortunately, there wasn't any sign of it being electrified, so he set to work making an opening with the pruning shears. This time, to preserve his hands, he cut only enough to slip under the bottom edge of the chain links, carefully bending the wire back into place when he was through.

Once he was on the other side, he found a portion of old 52 that was maintained, even though the traffic on it was nearly nonexistent. He felt the need to hide twice before he reached the central part of town, which was more of a crossroads by an old church, with one road leading to the middle school and another leading to a store that had recently been built by the grocery cartel.

There was also a driverless taxi station nearby where people could scan their papers, or their RFIDs if they had them, for a ride to the next town. Rafe planned to stay well away from there and the guard that stood nearby.

There were a few older buildings that he noticed built out of red brick, and those that were still in use seemed to play host to an old hardware store and a few small shops. But along with the cartel store, there were also a few newer buildings clearly built with prefabricated materials. As he looked closer, he saw that near one of them was a parking lot containing several vehicles with "SPKF" painted prominently on the side.

Of course, he thought, rolling his eyes at his bad luck, his earlier apprehension about entering the small town returning full force.

This wasn't just a small town with guards who knew all the residents by sight; this was a regional hub for the Special Peace Keeping Force, the very people hunting them. It was probably the whole reason why such a small town was exempted from evacuation. Rafe knew they'd encounter more of these the closer they got to the fighting, but it wasn't as though he'd planned to go for a stroll right into the middle of one. Yet here he was, about to do just that.

I guess that makes me one of those dumb criminals we always used to joke about ...

Rafe almost turned around and left, but practicality – and his empty stomach – kept him there. They needed food. Plus, if there was an SPKF station here, then surely there would be rebels keeping an eye on them, right?

He started scanning the street, hoping for any sign of someone with a flashlight at their hip, and tried to remember a song by the Rolling Stones.

It had been a couple of hours since he entered Pinnacle, and Rafe was waiting behind a small brick building, which had once been a restaurant of some kind. He hoped he hadn't made a mistake.

He'd followed Rabbit's advice and approached a man he'd thought might be who he was looking for, quietly singing a poor rendition of the refrain of "Sympathy for the Devil" as he did so. The man, a rather slim fellow in jeans and a baseball cap, discreetly gestured that they come here to talk, and so he did. Rafe's hands were shoved in his jacket pockets, one resting on the chocolates he brought for barter, and the other on the screwdriver, which was his only weapon. He felt naked without the shotgun, but he was sure there was no way he'd have gone unnoticed if he brought it. He paced nervously for a while, wondering what he would do if this turned out to be a trap and if the other man was thinking the same thing. Perhaps that was what was keeping him.

His breath fogged in front of him, and he forced himself to relax as he took in the last of the melting snow. Hyperventilating wouldn't help. He was already primed to run at the first sign of trouble and, while he was sure the odds were against him, he had used his time to consider his best possible strategy.

At the sound of footsteps coming around the corner, Rafe looked up to see the man from before, rolling a wheelbarrow full of old newspapers and cardboard. He did not meet his eyes but walked over to what appeared to be a burn pile and started loading the paper products onto it. Rafe walked over to stand behind him, watching him work.

"You looking for Paul?" The man asked, still not looking at him.

"Looking for Ringo," Rafe replied.

"A runner, then," The man said, almost to himself as he fed more cardboard onto the blaze. "So, what kind of help are you looking for?"

"Barter for food, if you've got some to spare."

159

———

About half an hour later, Rafe was walking back down the street, his bag now containing a loaf of bread and a large plastic bag of jerky for the price of four pieces of chocolate. After the man had finished loading stuff on the burn pile, he had gone to get another load and come back with the items hidden in his wheelbarrow. It was more than he'd expected by a long shot. Hopefully, this should keep them another few days before they had to start worrying about running out again.

He turned his thoughts toward continuing their journey. With any luck, they could strike out toward Pilot Mountain (the mountain, not the city) first thing tomorrow and be beyond it before the day was out. After that, the foothills would get steeper ... his hands tightened around the strap on his bag at the thought. Things would only get tougher from there.

He was nearing the point where it would be safer to hide in the woods, when he heard a vehicle behind him. Turning to look in the direction of the noise, he spotted an armored truck coming in his direction. He nonchalantly turned down one of the last few side streets before ducking out of sight behind a stand of trees. He didn't bother to check behind him but hurried toward the hole he had cut in the fence, pulling himself through it and yanking the shotgun from its hiding place. He then hurried back toward the house where Neil would be waiting.

As he got closer through the woods, he suddenly heard the noise of an idling vehicle. He paused, fear spiking. Gripping the shotgun even harder, he walked toward the tree line, doing his best not to make any noise.

As he reached the last of the trees, he peered beyond them and at that moment, the worst-case scenario that had been cycling through his thoughts became a reality. Two soldiers stood at the door to the vehicle, and tramping through the melting snow, he could see three figures moving toward their shelter. A heavy black man of about forty in an SPKF uniform approached the building with a woman in the same garb who was partially obscured by the man's larger build, followed by another man in a suit under his heavy coat.

As Rafe watched, they reached the front door, and his heart leapt into his throat when the woman became visible, and he finally recognized her.

Hannah?

CHAPTER 9

CRITICAL FAILURE

December 13, 2037

NEIL CUPPED HIS HANDS AROUND HIS MOUTH AS HE BLEW warm breath into them before nestling them back in the folds of his coat. He was sitting near a window in the room where they had been sheltering. Rafe had been gone for some time now, and he felt colder than he had in a while. Probably because they weren't on the move, he thought. This wasn't the first time Rafe had left him alone, but it was the first time he'd been gone this long. He looked down in frustration at his injured leg. If that hadn't happened, he could be out there now, helping to find food. His stomach growled at the thought, and he tried to redirect his attention to what was outside. There was no sign of anyone, and for a short while the only thing he noticed was his breath fogging the glass.

He was starting to nod off a little when he finally heard something in the distance. He blinked, and realized it was a vehicle – and it was coming closer. Rafe had said to hide, but where? He pulled himself up on his crutches and hobbled out of the room. Near the kitchen, he saw a set of stairs leading into the basement and quickly turned his crutches in that direction, wincing when in his haste he almost slipped on the bare linoleum floor.

Carefully lowering himself down the stairs, one step at a time, he reached the floor at the bottom and paused to let his eyes adjust. It looked like it had once been a playroom for young children, with carpet on the floor and walls painted a faded dark blue. It had no furniture, but it had a storage closet and table set at about a child's height that had been built into the wall on the far side, near a window. Neil hurried toward the storage closet and, pulling the door open, he stepped inside and shut himself in.

He didn't know how long he waited. He couldn't hear the vehicle anymore down here over the sound of his own breathing, but that on its own sounded way too loud for his personal comfort. After what seemed like several minutes, he got tired of standing and so he slowly allowed himself to sink to the floor in the closet, being careful not to strain his splint or make any noise, praying that they wouldn't find him and wondering what they would do if they did.

Then he heard movement upstairs.

Please, let that be Rafe ...

The floorboards creaked above him under the heavy footfalls of two, perhaps three pairs of boots, and then he heard voices. "I think we've found where they were holding up to get out of the snow," said a man with a deep voice.

Not Rafe. Neil did his best to not even breathe, for fear they might hear him.

"Yeah," said another man, "From the prints, someone's been coming in and out, though they were trying to hide it. Looks like they left some of their supplies here."

No, no, no ... Neil thought. He should have planned ahead. He should have hidden their things. *It's all my fault, I'm going to get us caught...*

"Were they planning to come back?" a woman's voice asked.

"Perhaps," the first man's voice responded. "Or maybe ... they haven't left..."

The floorboards upstairs creaked with their movement. They seemed to be exploring the upper floor of the building, and he wished he'd found a better place to hide. Seriously, could he have picked anywhere more obvious than a closet? In the urgency of the situation, where else could he have hidden? Trying to climb into the attic was out of the question, and if he had tried to leave, he'd have been spotted, but there had to be something. Maybe, if he was quick, he could try climbing out the window across the playroom and booking it for the woods...

His thoughts were interrupted by the sound of someone walking down the wooden steps. He did his best to make the sound of his breathing as silent as possible, but it didn't help. The door opened almost immediately, revealing a woman clad in an SPKF uniform, her hair in a short brown ponytail under a winter cap.

"Well, how about that?" The woman said, before yelling up the stairs. "Inspector! I found the kid!"

While the creaking noises from the main floor didn't stop, another figure appeared on the stairs, and in the dying light from a window, he saw what seemed to him a huge black man, also in an SPKF uniform and a heavy coat. He walked down the stairs. "Flynn?" He called out upon seeing him. "Neil Flynn?"

Neil looked directly at him but didn't answer.

"Did you hurt yourself?" the woman asked, getting down on her knees to look over the splint.

"When I was running from an angry mob," Neil said bitterly.

"Where's Turner?" The black man approached to also get a better look.

Neil glared at him. "Who?" He didn't think he was being a convincing liar, but he wasn't going to give them anything.

"Rafe Turner," the woman supplied impatiently. "The man that dragged you all the way out here?"

"I don't know..." Neil considered for a moment and then he added, "I don't think he's coming back."

"Why's that?" the black man asked curiously, now kneeling in front of the door.

"He said I was slowing him down," Neil lied.

The woman frowned thoughtfully and then shook her head. "I'm not sure I buy it."

"That's right. You said you knew him, didn't you?" The black man looked up at the woman for confirmation.

"Why do you think I volunteered when you showed us his details?" the woman answered. "I thought, at the very least, I could talk some sense into him." She turned her attention back to Neil. "Can you stand?"

Everything Neil felt told him he didn't want to, but he had nowhere to run even if he could. Being careful not to bump his leg, he slowly pulled himself back up.

The black man helped him up the stairs, and they walked back toward the front door. Neil had just enough time to see that a white man, wearing a suit underneath his jacket, was searching through the room where they had been sheltering. He was also on his phone talking to someone. "Yeah, we found him just outside the perimeter. It was a good thing they didn't cut the fence again, otherwise it would have been a mountain of paperwork."

Then they were out in the cold. They helped him into the truck and then the woman climbed in after him.

"Don't worry. You're safe now," the woman helped him with a safety harness and put his crutches next to him against another seat.

"Yeah right," Neil murmured.

The woman's eyes narrowed with suspicion "Rafe didn't ... hurt you ... did he?"

"No," Neil looked down at his hands resting on his knees. "He definitely didn't do that."

The woman sighed in relief, but then she asked another question. "Then why don't you feel safe?"

"Would you, if your parents were murdered in the street and nobody tried to stop the people who did it?" Neil snapped, turning to glare at her.

The woman stayed quiet for a little while longer and Neil decided he wasn't going to look at her. *Wherever you are Rafe ...* he begged silently. *Don't come back. Keep running ... Forget about me ...*

Rafe watched the truck pull away as another one approached. There was no further reason to stay here, he decided. Neil was no longer here for him to protect. *What do I do now?* The thought rang through his head as he fought down the urge to panic.

He turned and started running back through the woods, hoping to pick his way back toward the fence, thoughts racing. Maybe, if he was quick enough, maybe he could ... could ...

Rational thought returned when he was about halfway to the fence, and he slowed to a walk, gripping the shotgun in his hands. Maybe he could what? Surrender? Fight to the death in a doomed rescue? That would certainly get him nowhere.

This wasn't a C&C campaign where there was always a way to win. He couldn't go into this half-cocked like some would-be hero. That only worked in the movies and any idiot with half a brain knew that trying to be a hero in real life usually meant digging yourself a six-foot hole. If he was dead, that wouldn't help him, and it certainly wouldn't help Neil. The possibility of something going wrong with a direct approach was too great. Plus, Hannah was there.

"Damn it!" he hissed. At last, he reached the fence and crawled through the hole. His hands shook as he straightened on the other side. He could have walked away, but not until he at least tried to help his friend. This wasn't a problem he'd be able to solve with his grandfather's shotgun, though he carefully tucked the weapon under his coat rather than leave it in the snow again. He needed help.

Once he was through the fence, he began the second walk toward the town of Pinnacle that he had made today. He laughed scornfully. The place was a pinnacle all right; the pinnacle of his own poor judgment.

He quickened his pace as he reached the highway, glaring at the path in front of him and making sure to keep to the trees as best he could while staying within sight of the asphalt. He couldn't be seen with a weapon; that would make an already bad situation worse. The guy from the resistance would be surprised to see him again, but he didn't know who else he could turn to at this point. As much as he wished otherwise, he certainly couldn't ask Hannah. It would be counter to any orders she had, not to mention stupid. Even if she had any inclination to be on his side in this matter, which he was certain she wouldn't, it would have been trouble for her.

For a moment, he remembered the last time they'd talked and cringed, hoping she'd forgot about it. Probably not, but miracles could happen. He shook his head. Now was not the time to think about that. No, the less she was involved, the better.

It seemed like little time had passed when he reached the first house, though he noticed that the sun was beginning its descent toward the west. If he had to guess, Neil would probably still be with the SPKF, but he had no idea where they'd take him. He needed to find that out, and if there was any way of getting to him without anyone sounding the alarm.

To his relief, when he walked back behind the building where he had carried out his transactions earlier, the man was still there, watching the last of his fire burn down. As if sensing his approach, the man turned around in surprise. "You should have been gone by now..." he began urgently.

"Someone I've been traveling with was caught," Rafe interrupted. "I need help."

"If he's been taken by the SPKF, then you may be out of luck," the man said. "Unless they're minors, runners usually get sent north of Durham as soon as they can get a transport."

"That's why I need to get him out of there. He's just a kid." Rafe pleaded. "Please. What can I do? Who can I talk to?"

The man gave him a sympathetic look, but it was guarded. "I'm going to be honest, I have to verify your story. Even if it checks out, I can't make promises. Stay in that stand of trees over there, and don't move. You'd better be telling the truth."

Only then did it occur to Rafe that what he was doing now could be almost as dangerous as walking into SPKF headquarters. The Resistance had no way of knowing this wasn't a trap. If he failed to make his case, he could be a dead man, and really, he had no way to know if this place was still being watched. "Do what you must," he said at last. With that, they parted ways as Rafe went to hide and the man walked around to the front of the building.

———

It didn't seem long at all before the truck pulled to a halt and Neil got a brief look at the SPKF compound and was led inside. The warmth from a heating vent caressed his face as he hobbled along next to the woman. It was the first time he'd felt truly warm since they'd been in that basement with Rabbit and Badger and the doctor had seen to his leg. It felt like weeks ago, though he knew it had been only days. Still, it did nothing to melt the icy fear in the depth of his gut. The seriousness of the situation was enough to keep that sensation chilled to sub-zero temperatures.

It wasn't long before she led him to what looked like a holding area with a small bench. "What happens now?" he asked as she turned to walk out of the room.

"That's what we're about to find out, sit tight," the woman responded, offering him a reassuring smile before shutting the door.

At her departure, he sat down and set his crutches against the wall next to him before taking in the holding area. It was devoid of anything aside from the bench on which he sat and the window in the door through which he could glimpse the outside. Time dragged on, and slowly he began to feel warmth return to his fingers and toes.

He lowered the hood of his jacket so the warm air could filter through his blond hair and wondered if this was how it would all end. Would he spend the rest of his life stuck in a cell somewhere, waiting for the news that Rafe had been caught? Or would they send him to his family in Connecticut? That would be preferable, he guessed, if there wasn't another angry mob there. The thought of seeing his aunts and his grandfather didn't seem like such a bad thing if not for the circumstances. But would these people let him go at all?

He waited, his mind going from possibility to possibility as he counted off the minutes on a clock he could see through the window on the upper half of the door. Finally, after about two hours had passed, the door opened revealing a new woman in a business pantsuit and high-heeled black shoes. As she entered, she brushed a few strands of platinum blonde hair behind her ears. Her hair was cut in a professionally severe bob. As she gave him a sweet smile, he saw that her lipstick was a bright red that demanded the attention of anyone looking in her direction. He couldn't quite place why, but something about her demeanor turned his stomach in knots.

"Neil Flynn?" she asked, coming right up to where he sat and looking down at him as though he was the next box on a list that needed checkmarks.

He looked up at her but didn't provide more of an answer than a questioning grunt.

"I'm Eunice Lord. I'm a youth welfare officer for this district. I'm sure you've had it pretty rough the last few days, but I just want to talk to you." She had a file in one hand which she was looking over as she regarded him.

"About what?" Neil returned her gaze in annoyance.

She shook her head as though he was being coy with her. "Well, about Rafe Turner for one thing. Sergeant Gruben says he didn't hurt you. I'm glad that's the case."

"He wouldn't have," Neil replied. "He saved my life."

"That's what he made you think, anyway," the woman said. "But we need to know where he is." She sat down next to him. Neil immediately felt like his space was being invaded. "Anything you tell us about what happened or where he was headed would be a big help," she prodded.

"He's already gone," Neil turned to see if there was any remaining space to his right on the bench so he could scoot further away. "I don't know where he was going."

"Really?" Mrs. Lord looked a bit disappointed at that, but her expression became more coaxing as she continued. "That's too bad. Because I would think someone who was trying to help you would have done the opposite of most of the things he did. He took you out into the wilderness, and probably exacerbated your injuries, when if he'd just sought protection we would have given it. If he really cared, why did he abandon you?"

"He didn't abandon me!" Neil gritted out, before realizing to his horror that he was contradicting himself.

The woman reached out and put what was probably intended to be a comforting hand on his shoulder, but it felt more like a leopard sinking her teeth deeper into fresh meat. He felt an even stronger urge to scoot away from her, but her grip held him in place. "Then where did he go, Neil? At this point, there isn't a lot that I can do for him, but I can at least help you."

"Like you helped my mom and dad," Neil said darkly, before turning to glare at her.

Her demeanor frosted. She let go of him and stood up, taking a couple of steps toward the door. "We aren't the ones who killed them, Neil. Their greed and bigotry did that."

"Those people would have done the same to me if I'd just sat there," Neil tried not to shout. "And just because my mom and dad had a difference of opinion doesn't mean they deserved to die!"

The mask of sweetness lifted completely as she met him glare for glare. "Get one thing straight. From what I've heard, it wouldn't have been long before they were sitting in prison with the rest of those blind fools in Durham. And if you know what's good for you, you'll cooperate. I don't want to be your enemy, but if that's how it has to be, well, let's just say our next discussion will be far less pleasant."

"What, are you going to torture me?" Neil didn't bother to hide the sarcasm in his question.

"Oh, goodness, no." Her sweet smile was back again, dripping with honey and cyanide. "This is the 21st century, not Medieval Europe. We're going to Winston-Salem in the morning, and then we'll discuss that combative attitude of yours. After all, it's not your fault you were raised that way."

With that she left, though he could hear her voice murmuring beyond the door, apparently discussing something with Church. The noise died down and a little later the door opened again revealing the woman in the SPKF uniform. She was holding a tray balanced on one arm that held a plate of food and a glass of water. "Are you hungry?" she asked as she closed the door behind her.

"A little," he admitted. He hadn't eaten in almost a day. The food on the plate she was carrying was probably from a frozen dinner. But having spent the last few days living on trail mix, he felt ravenous and didn't care. The smell was intoxicating.

The woman sat down next to him on the bench leaving a little space between them for the tray, and he looked down at it. The plate contained what looked like a heavily processed chicken dish with mashed potatoes. With his free hand, he reached for the spoon and put a bite in his mouth. He chewed the soft meat before swallowing and then took another bite while the woman watched.

"I wanted to ask," she began after a moment, "How is he?"

Neil paused and took a good look at her. They hadn't talked any further since getting in the truck. "Why would you care?" he asked through a mouthful of chicken.

"Rafe and I went to school together," she turned to look at him. He could now see the name tag on her uniform. "Sgt. H. Gruben."

"You're Hannah." Having swallowed the chicken he'd been chewing, Neil went for some of the potatoes.

"He mentioned me?" Hannah was looking past him, seemingly at the wall, lost in thought.

"A little," Neil said between bites. "He showed me a picture one of his friends drew."

"He still has Eric's picture." She smiled and shook her head.

"It was one of the last things left in his house after those rioters were done with it," Neil said, letting accusation color his voice. It wasn't hard. The SPKF was *supposed* to stop that kind of thing.

That was the public story, anyway. Whatever Rafe thought Hannah was, she was part of the reason his parents were gone.

At that, she stopped smiling and looked down at her hands uncomfortably. "Oh."

"You can't tell me you didn't know," Neil spat. "You're with the SPKF, after all."

"What happened?"

Neil glared at her. "I think you know very well what happened. My dad's delivery company was all over the news because he had a difference of opinion. So, they got everyone all angry over nothing and used the news and the courts to call up a mob. My parents were murdered, and people just ... let it happen. If Rafe hadn't saved me, I'd be dead too, and it got him into more trouble than *I'm* in. So, if you think my parents deserved what they got like that..." Neil *really* wanted to say something less polite. "That ... *woman*, then you're just as bad as *she* is!" He pulled the tray up onto his lap so he could look away from her as he continued eating.

"He still calls you his friend, you know," he growled through another bite of chicken. "And apart from us having to escape from our homes because no one *else* was willing to do the right thing that night, he's fine. I'm *glad* he left me. He'll get away a lot faster without me to slow him down." He felt something catch in his throat, and it wasn't the baked chicken. Even with the food, being out there was much preferable to where he was.

He finished and lay the tray down next to him without looking at her again. Hannah said nothing more but picked it up before walking out the door. It was then that he noticed the black SPKF sergeant, Everett, if he remembered the man's name correctly, standing in the hall. The man stepped to the side as Hannah passed, almost as though he'd been listening before the door opened. As it swung shut, a silence hung over the room and Neil put his hands together in silent prayer. Rafe couldn't be more different from Eunice Lord, or Hannah even, he decided. *Please God, help me. And let Rafe get away. Let him make it...*

Rafe was uncertain how long he waited alone in that grove of trees, but it felt like an eternity. At one point he thought he caught sight of someone standing at a window in a nearby building. Maybe it was his imagination, because when he looked again, the curtains were drawn. After that, he took a deep breath to steady his nerves before straightening his posture, and slowly started pacing to try and warm up.

It was starting to get dark when someone finally returned from around the side of the building and he saw it was the supplier returning along with someone else. It wasn't until they got closer that he recognized the brown-haired woman in National Guard fatigues.

It was Rabbit.

He stepped out of the tree line, and she gave him a severe look. "So, you lost your friend. What are we supposed to do about it?"

"I don't know..." Rafe said, "But there has to be something I can still do."

"You do know it would be stupid to go storming in there, right?" Rabbit pointed out as though worried that might be what he was contemplating.

"Of course, I know!" Rafe almost yelled, waving a hand toward the general direction of the SPKF installation for emphasis. "That's exactly why I didn't do that..." He paused as he saw that she wasn't arguing and then asked bitterly, "What are you even doing here anyway?"

"Following you," she answered, as though that explained everything.

"What for?" Rafe tried to force himself to slow his breathing and listen.

"Because believe it or not, I thought you could make a useful partner in getting me across the front," she said. "If we go now, then it'll be easy."

Rafe thought about it for a moment, running through in his

mind everything he had done in the last few days. Sure, it would be easy to turn around and leave. Rabbit would probably make it a lot easier. Maybe he had done all he could. . . But even so. . . "Not without Neil," Rafe said quietly.

Rabbit frowned before looking over at him. "I'm not sure you know what you're asking. Do you know what it would take just to get him out? The kind of risks it would require just to save one kid when it would be a lot more effective to secure our footholds in the mountains, regroup and come back later? We could save a ton of kids with an army."

Rafe was quiet for a moment as he tried to think. That was certainly true, but he also had no guarantee Neil would be one of them. While the hypothetical rebel army were off training some-where, his friend could be undergoing any number of abuses, to say nothing of worse things. By the time anyone got to rescuing him any damage would already be done. He tried not to shudder as he thought about what he should say next. Remembering what Rabbit had told him about smoothing it out and making it sound like he was doing her a favor, he took a moment to collect himself.

This would be another diplomacy check, potentially for all the marbles. It was time to roll the d20 and find out.

"What happens if I decide to try anyway?" he asked at last. "I mean sure, you could kill me on the way out of here, but then you lose someone to watch your back on the way to the front. Assuming I leave and try to do it on my own, what are my odds? Not great, and that's assuming they don't kill me outright. . ."

Rabbit interjected quickly, "If you think threatening us is going to work, trust me, you don't want to go there."

Rafe shook his head. "Wouldn't dream of it, just assessing reality here."

"Then get to the point," the supplier growled impatiently.

Rafe nodded. He was still nervous and it was an act of will not to trip over his words as he spoke, but somehow, he managed it. "If you help me, not only are you going to save Neil's life, you're prob-ably going to save mine, and if we work together, maybe all three of us, and to top it all off, you get to stick it to the government you've been fighting so hard on the way out." Trying to appear as determined as possible, he reached into his sack and retrieved what was left of the chocolates. "This is all I have left, and I will let you have it for whatever it will get me. I could really use your help, but regardless, I'm going to help my friend, alone if I have to."

To his surprise, Rabbit grinned in a way that looked positively feral. "Hah! He's learning! You know Turner, I think I've misjudged you. I thought you were just a good boy who ended up in a bad situation. I didn't imagine you had it in you to try something this crazy." She looked thoughtful for a moment, and then chuckled softly. "You might actually have what it takes to pull this off."

"So you *are* Rafe Turner then. The one who disappeared with the Flynn kid after the riot in Greensboro?" The supplier asked.

"That's my name," Rafe said.

"It's a good thing you haven't been near a TV," Rabbit commented. She looked thoughtful for a moment and then picked up the chocolates, before turning to the supplier. "You know, this on its own isn't going to be enough for what we need. But if I add my resources on the pile, I think we can make this work." She looked back at Rafe. "Let's get somewhere warm. I know you've been out here a while."

———

The sky was completely dark when they reached a safe house on the edge of town, and Rafe was now sitting by the fire with a hot mug of soup in his hand. He took a sip from the mug and tapped his finger with impatience. It seemed like this entire day had been taken up by waiting.

An electric light by the drawn curtains died without any signs of a blown bulb or indication that someone had turned it off, leaving only the firelight to illuminate the room. It had been a while since he'd had to think about the occasional blackouts. The military dominated the power grids, and the power companies had not been allowed to expand them. Rafe had heard it was hard to maintain the lines and wind turbines, because of environmental regulations limiting travel and activity beyond the fences. Materials for solar panels had also gotten harder to obtain. It was probably a lot more noticeable out here, closer to the front lines. There were more people in the United States using wood fires and candles for light in the evenings now than there had been since the days of Edison.

The biggest surprise to him though, was that Rabbit was sitting there waiting with him.

"So, what happened?" he asked, taking another sip from his soup mug.

"Isn't it obvious?" Rabbit answered, watching the crackling fire in the fireplace. "I've joined you in becoming a wanted criminal."

"Don't tell me they saw you helping us?" Rafe asked, feeling guilty at the thought.

"Not exactly," Rabbit leaned back in her chair, letting her own soup mug sit on an armrest and using a couple of fingers to keep it balanced. "But after you left, Badger's place got raided. He ... didn't make it. I nearly got caught on the way out."

Rafe sighed in frustration. "Was there anything we could have...?"

Rabbit shook her head grimly, and he noted a few hairs had fallen loose from the bun at the nape of her neck. "Not a thing. I've got nothing left to keep me here, so I figured I'd follow you and join the Minutemen up in the mountains."

"That's pretty noble of you," Rafe observed. From what little he knew about what was going on in the interior, the Minutemen were a large militia supplementing the main rebel army. Supposedly, they were the main obstacle the Union army had to pushing further into the mountains. The news didn't really tell much about what was going on with the rebels if they could help it. But if they'd been defeated it would have been the only thing talked about, so Rafe figured they were still going strong.

The idea that Rabbit had lost everything, but was still focused on joining the fight, made him think of the old samurai movies Eric used to collect, and the Westerns his father watched from time to time. The ones featuring the ronin samurai in Meiji Japan, or the lone gunmen upholding justice in the Old West. It also made him wonder what he would do when he reached the front lines? Should he volunteer, too? He didn't know how to fight like Rabbit did, so would he even be considered worth anything, or just a burden?

"Hardly," Rabbit sounded tired as she spoke. "I'm a heartless butcher, Turner. Do you know I killed three men getting away from Badger's hideout?" She scoffed. "I'm a notorious sociopath who only cares about my personal gain and bringing back the old world of wage slavery, bigotry, and privilege, while the needy starve in the streets." She laughed, but there was no humor in her voice. "If you think I'm doing this just for the greater good, you'd better rethink that idea right now. For their little utopia, they've already taken everything from me that I thought they could take, and then they took more. They'll *never* stop taking, and they'll never start listening. They've already judged me wanting, and they'll cart me off just like everyone else when my bones are all I have left for them to break. You can't reason with people who've closed themselves against you. At that point, you may as well be talking to the raging barbarian they've made you out to be."

"I'm sure there are plenty more people far worse than you, on both sides," Rafe said, neutrally. "It'd be stupid to think otherwise."

"I'm not sayin' there aren't worse people," The flames reflected in Rabbit's eyes as she continued to talk. "I heard through the grapevine there've been some issues across the front with radical churches and End-times cults for instance. But even though they get to say their piece, they and the five or so actual Nazis that exist in the country have no power over there either, no matter what the news over here claims. There's good and bad in any country. It's true. But as far as I'm concerned, those're little annoyances compared to my reality right here in front of me. At least the Central United States aren't run by the people who seem to think we're all their pets." She spat the last word contemptuously. "Coercion in the veil of protection. Intolerance in the guise of equality. Hah! Aren't I a grown woman? If I ever build any kind of life, I've certainly got no plans to build it in this hideous gilded cage." She took a long drink from her soup mug.

Rafe considered for a moment. "I guess you're right. We really aren't supposed to lock ourselves in cages or let other people tell us what we can or can't say. It's not slavery but it's really not so different in a lot of ways. Maybe if I hadn't been so afraid. . ." *If I had been more willing to stand up to this insanity when it wasn't all over the place.*

"It's easy to say what we should have done better, Turner. But regardless of what you did before, I'm pretty sure a coward would have stayed in his house, and let the kid eat lead," Rabbit pointed out.

Rafe looked over at her in surprise. Had she actually said something nice?

The conversation paused as they both heard the door open. They turned to look and saw the supply man enter the room through the door behind them.

"We were able to find news about your friend," he said without preamble.

"Where is he?" Rafe stood up anxiously.

"He's in the SPKF base," the supplier responded. "They're moving him to Winston-Salem tomorrow morning. It looks like he'll be in the custody of Social Services, but with an escort. Given who he's with, they're going to keep him at the Reynolds Building before sending him to a youth education center."

"You got a positive ID on the Social Services rep?" Rabbit was a lot more relaxed as she stood to talk with the supplier.

"A CPS official by the name of Eunice Lord. She handles a lot of the local cases involving juvenile runners. Her husband is some sort of big shot, runs a winery on the edge of the city."

Rafe looked over at Rabbit uncertainly. "What do you think of our chances?"

"Well, like you said, you certainly wouldn't have a prayer on your own." Seeing his expression harden with impatience, Rabbit grinned. "But you're with me now. The first order of business is to get to Winston-Salem," She turned her attention to the supplier. "I'd like you to send a message ahead of us tonight. I'll be writing up a list of supplies we'll need, including means of access, plus an intelligence package on the building and any possible evacuation routes with promise of payment up front when we get there."

The supplier nodded before walking into the kitchen, while Rabbit sat back down in her chair and produced a notepad and pen from her backpack.

"How are we going to get there?" Rafe asked, collecting his mug from where he'd set it on the table between them.

Rabbit responded as she wrote. "One of our vehicles is hidden near here. That'll get us there in time. After that, the Resistance will know we're coming."

"That's comforting, I guess," Rafe drained the last dregs of his dinner and turned to take the mug back to the woman who was in the kitchen cleaning. She hadn't told them her name, and she didn't speak to him, but that didn't matter. He was not supposed to be here, so she had to pretend he didn't exist. He smiled sadly to himself at the thought of how hard that would be for his mother, or even his siblings, all raised to the standards of Southern hospitality.

"We should get some sleep," Rabbit said to him as he came back into the room. She folded up her list, then picked up her own soup mug in her other hand to head for the kitchen. "We've got a long day ahead of us if we're going to rescue your friend. Most of it is probably going to be so stressful you'll miss the days of being hungry in the woods. If we're unlucky, it might be the last chance we get to sleep at all."

"Such an optimist," Rafe said dryly. He nonetheless headed for the door to the basement, where two pallets had already been laid out for them. "Should I be worried?"

"Only if you're smart. If I've guessed wrong, we're already dead in the water."

November 21, 2032

"It drops." Will's voice had held none of its usual fanfare as he made the announcement.

The dragon had been a tough fight, but for once there was no celebrating as their enemy was defeated. Instead, everyone looked at each other uncomfortably.

"We have a problem," Will said firmly, and no one argued. It was long past time to address the elephant in the room. He removed his glasses, cleaning them with a cloth he produced from his pocket, and eyed Allen and Hannah. "Guys, I get that these issues are serious, and I get that you fall on different sides on a lot of things. But from now on, how about we try to keep the politics out of my living room? I hate to put limitations on what we can talk about, but this is really getting out of hand."

Allen and Hannah looked at each other, very grudgingly. "I think that's appropriate," Allen decided at last.

"As long as you do the same," Hannah said, though her tone had not changed.

Allen looked back at the rest of the group, still frustrated, but also apologetic. "We're sorry guys." He looked back at Hannah as though silently asking her, 'aren't we?'

Hannah sighed, "Yeah, me too ... " she said at last.

The rest of the evening wrapped up in relative calm as they calculated XP and divvied out treasure and items, one of which was a rather nice mace Rafe laid claim to for Galen, and then everyone took their leave.

As Rafe and Eric were walking back to Rafe's car, Eric spoke up. "Man, that was rough tonight."

"You're telling me," Rafe agreed, fishing his keys out of his pocket to hit the button to unlock the doors.

"I hope Will can hold them to that promise." Eric pulled open the front passenger door and climbed in.

"I know." Rafe got behind the wheel and pulled his door closed. "To be honest, I'm kind of worried. It's obvious Will wants us to try and crack the tower where the Veil is before graduation next year. I hope they can keep it together. We get enough of this stuff from our parents, and after what happened with your dad, I know you'd rather not deal with it here." He cranked the key in the ignition. It was an older model, one that still used gasoline, though he would probably have to trade it out soon. It was getting harder and harder to justify keeping it when the gas taxes kept getting higher. And with the new travel restrictions they were talking about, what good was a car that could do more than forty miles in a day, anyway?

Eric nodded, warming his hands in his pockets. "Yeah, not right now ... " After what seemed like an appropriate amount of quiet, he changed the subject. "So, what's coming up for Thanksgiving break? Want to spend a day hiking up at Hanging Rock?"

"Sounds great." Well, there was one use for a car, anyway...

CHAPTER 10

CHANGE OF SCENERY

December 14, 2037

RAFE SLEPT UNEASILY AND SOMETIME AROUND 5 A.M. HE
found he just couldn't sleep anymore. Sleeping in dirty jeans and a
sweater that smelled like it deserved the name wasn't the best way to
get a good night's rest, even without the added problem of being a
fugitive. After spending a few more minutes tossing and turning, he
left his pallet, sat down midway up the stairs leading out of the basement and waited until Rabbit sat up. When she started to rouse, he
noticed her look around, note his empty pallet and then finally
spot him.

"Oh. There you are," she stretched her arms, before pulling off
her uniform coat and quickly turning it inside out. Now reversed, it
no longer showed the camo print or the patches with her guard location on it, instead being lined in plain khaki. "You ready to go?" She
had let down her brown hair overnight and it hung just below her
shoulders as she borrowed a brush from a small table that held a few
toiletries the house's owner had left for them.

"About as ready as I'll ever be," Rafe said. With that he stood,
shouldered his bag, and walked over to where he'd set the shotgun
against the wall.

"Okay then," Rabbit gestured that he turn around for a few seconds and as he did so, he heard the sound of rustling cloth. "Because once I lock the back door, there's no turning back. If there's anything you need to take care of before we go, now's the time."

"What is this? The last save point before the final boss?" Rafe asked, keeping his eyes glued to the stairs.

"Nerd," Rabbit murmured, though Rafe was surprised to hear a soft laugh from her general direction. "I'm just saying if you want to use the bathroom or do anything else to prepare before we leave, now's last call. You can turn around now, by the way." He looked behind him and saw that she had traded out her uniform pants for a pair of jeans. Finished with her clothes, Rabbit gathered her own bag and moved past him up the stairs.

"I think I've already played all the side quests I care to do in this game, thanks," Rafe said, retrieving his own belongings. It was meant to be a joke, but it didn't feel like one.

He heard Rabbit sigh as he followed her to the main floor and crossed the living room to the door leading outside.

She picked up a gas can that had been left at the door along with what looked like a car battery. "If side quests are what you want, I could do with some coffee." She handed him the battery and held the door open for him to walk out before turning the lock on the doorknob and pulling the door shut.

"Good luck finding any." Rafe tightened his hood a little bit as he looked up at the stars that hung above them through his fogged breath. He noted the illuminated horizon to the south, glowing from Winston-Salem's city lights off in the distance.

Rabbit chuckled at that. "It might be easier than you think."

From what Rafe understood, Neil would also be headed toward those glowing lights soon and would probably arrive shortly after they did. Wherever he was right now, Rafe hoped the kid was at least warmer than they were.

He followed her through the pines under the graying sky, keeping an ear out for any sign that someone might be following them. It was half an hour later when they reached a large drainpipe hidden behind a decaying building. They crawled through it and found themselves on the other side of the fence. After walking several minutes through the brush, they reached an abandoned lot where Rafe saw several sedans and trucks, some covered in rust while others seemed to have had much better paint jobs and were just covered in debris.

"Now what?" He looked around curiously at the junked cars.

Rabbit spared a moment to look around for any sign of trouble before sauntering over to a dirty grey pickup under a lean-to. She produced a key and a flashlight as she reached the side of the vehicle and used the light to find the keyhole on the driver side door. "First, I need to get this heap running."

"Anything I can do to help?" Rafe followed her to the truck and peered into the window, noting his tired green eyes and unkempt face. He really should have taken the opportunity to shave back at the safehouse.

"Eh ... I don't know, keep watch?" Rabbit pulled the door open and looked inside the truck cab. "Maybe go up to where the main office used to be and see if the place hasn't been looted?"

Rafe glared in mock indignation. "Well, now you're just trying to get rid of me."

Rabbit didn't look up as she responded. "Not at all, I just need time to work. So take a look around, and make sure we haven't been followed." She went around to the front and set the gas can down on the ground next to her before lifting the hood.

Thinking it best to leave the truck to the person who seemed to know what she was doing, he placed the battery down next to the gas can and started a slow walk around the garage. Most of it had been emptied, short of the elevator near the rear that stood inert and unpowered. What could be easily carried away had already been taken, either by the previous owner or looters.

On the bright side, there wasn't much Rafe had to worry about tripping over. After spending a few more minutes wandering through the rows of cars, he returned to find Rabbit closing the hood. "All clear?" She asked as she climbed down off a cinderblock she'd used as a step-stool.

"As far as I can tell," Rafe answered. "Nothing worth carrying with us. It's already been picked clean."

She nodded. "Most of the areas near what passes for civilization are. The only reason the cars are safe to leave lying around is because most people brave enough to come here to loot are looking for things they can carry and trade in town. A truck they can't use isn't worth the trouble of breaking out to steal it." She walked over to the fuel door and pulled it open to pour the gas into the tank. "Could you move that block against the fence there?"

He picked up the cinderblock and dragged it to where she directed. "How do you keep the drones from spotting it while we're on the road?"

"Oh that," Rabbit said, still holding the gas can up to the tank. "All cars have a GPS tracker that transmits their location to a satellite that feeds it to the traffic commission, which in turn feeds that information to computer surveillance."

"Yeah, that's been required since personal cars were made illegal," Rafe said.

Rabbit nodded. "So you know that if you look like a car but don't have a signal, you get flagged and an SPKF officer is sent out to investigate. However, this truck's got a spoofer that randomly generates a legal ID to trick the system into thinking we're an approved vehicle on an approved road and not flagging us." She put the can down under another car and leaned against the hood. "If anyone knew to look, it wouldn't be for hours, and finding the right feed could take years with all the surveillance data they take in. Enough people travel between cities it'd never get noticed unless we left right when the surveillance drones were on top of us, and I got today's schedule from our host last night when I ordered our supplies." She patted one of her coat pockets for emphasis.

Rafe gave her a curious look. "What kind of supplies did you ask for?" he asked.

"The kind for getting in and out, alive." She said gravely. "Whether I got everything I wanted remains to be seen."

Finished with the discussion, she opened the door and pulled herself up into the cab. The engine came to life as she turned the key in the ignition and Rafe walked around the front of the vehicle to the passenger side door.

"Does the heat work?" he asked as he climbed into the front passenger seat.

"It should." Rabbit reached for the dashboard and punched at the temperature controls. Lukewarm air filtered through the truck cab.

"All right, I guess we're set." Rafe pushed his hands against one of the vents. The vehicle hadn't had enough time to completely warm all the air filtering up from the engine, but any warmth at all was a welcome change in this weather.

"Then fasten your seatbelt." Rabbit disengaged the emergency brake and put the truck in drive before easing her foot off the brake pedal. After maneuvering it out of the lot, she turned onto the crumbling road and accelerated.

"You know where we're going?" Rafe asked as she turned the vehicle onto a road that lay just to the side of the old highway.

"I've been there a few times," Rabbit said. "We're skirting around to the west of the Rural Hall compound to Winston's residential zone. We have contacts there, though I haven't met them personally. We'll still need to use passwords."

It was getting close to full daylight. For a few minutes, the truck cab fell into a silence that was almost comfortable, as the two of them lost themselves in their own thoughts and the landscape slid by at a much faster pace than Rafe had experienced since he'd sold his car several years ago.

He allowed his mind to wander for a while, before a thought occurred to him. "Hey."

"Hey," Rabbit parroted, "What's up?"

"How did you know to help us back in Walnut Cove?" Rafe asked. "It definitely got you in trouble, what good did it do you?"

"Apart from helping the cause and that it was our job?" Rabbit asked innocently.

"Well," Rafe said. "We could have been spies. What if I had, as you said, broken Neil's leg on purpose and told him I'd kill him if he said anything?"

Rabbit shrugged. "If I thought that, I would have just followed my orders from the Guard and none would have been the wiser. But I knew you hadn't. Eric used to talk about you all the time, and he showed me some pictures. I recognized you the moment the SPKF sent your photo to the guard station. Took me a moment when I first saw you in the woods, thanks to that scruffy thing you call a beard, but there wasn't a chance of mistaking you."

"Yeah, because personal hygiene has totally been a priority while all this has been going on," Rafe grumbled, self-consciously rubbing the dust-brown whiskers on his chin. "So how did you know Eric?"

Rabbit reached into her jacket pocket and produced a folded piece of paper. Rafe took it and unfolded it to reveal a copy of Eric's drawing of their C&C party. "He drew this for the group ... why do you have it?"

"He gave it to me because I said I liked it," Rabbit admitted. "He did a couple for me, too." She took back the picture before reaching into a pocket on her backpack. She then produced a hand-drawn Valentine's Day card, which she handed to him.

On the front of the card was a forest with a lake and a young couple sitting by it enjoying a picnic lunch. The art style was familiar to Rafe, having watched Eric draw many times. Rafe was about to hand it back when the card accidentally flipped open in his hand.

"*Casey, I just want you to know how much you've meant to me since we met last year. Here's to many more escapades in the future! Love, Eric.*" It was definitely his handwriting, though it was already too late by the time he tried to push it shut again.

"I didn't mean to ... " he started.

Rabbit shook her head. "No, it's all right."

The last thing Rafe wanted to do was pry but seeing she wasn't upset, he let himself relax as he looked down at the card. "So, that's your name, huh? Casey."

"Yeah, I guess it's fair that you know it since I already know yours," Rabbit did not take her eyes off the road as she drove. "Casey Burke. Nice to meet you," she said, as an afterthought. "No real need for an alias at this point. We're involved now, and my position with the Guard's been blown to the moon, so it won't do me any good. Plus, it feels good to be a little more honest about things. I haven't had someone I could do that with in a while."

"Nice to meet you, too," Rafe said in reply to her introduction. "I hope you'll be able to tell the same to Neil once we get him out of this." *If we can get him out of this,* he thought to himself. He glumly surveyed the forest flying by his window for a moment before looking back at her, his face grim as he tucked Eric's card respectfully back into its pocket in Casey's backpack. "What happened to Eric?"

Casey gave him a sympathetic glance before returning her attention to the road. "Most likely, someone sent the SPKF an anonymous tip that he and his dad were helping runners. One week, I came to Greensboro and stopped by to see him. Then the next time I went there, they were both gone, and the SPKF was going over the place with a fine-toothed comb." In her voice now, there was a tone of hopelessness he had not heard before. "Nothing from official Guard sources, nothing from the underground. They just ... disappeared. I looked everywhere I could, but there's only so much you can do without attracting suspicion. The way things are now, no one is safe even trying to find the truth. They're just gone. Like so many others."

"Is that what you meant, about how they took everything from you?" Rafe asked.

"It wasn't everything, but it was a huge part of it."

Rafe clenched his fist. Why hadn't he known? Why had Eric not told him the truth? Was there ever anything he could have done? "I guess that's what'll happen to us if they catch us? We'll disappear?"

Casey's tone became more bitter, and the sharpness returned to her brown eyes. "I won't disappear. I'm going to keep fighting until we're free, and I'm either holding him in my arms, standing in front of his grave, or in the ground."

Rafe did look at her then. "Let's not talk about anyone being in the ground, please. I'd like to hope we're not *that* doomed."

"So, you'd prefer it if we were only slightly doomed. Got it." A wry grin crept out onto her face despite her attempt to remain serious.

"That still doesn't inspire confidence, though I can see why Eric liked you."

———

The sun was visible over the eastern horizon when Casey pulled into a rundown garage, put on the parking brake and opened the driver's-side door. Rafe stretched as he too climbed out of the cab and looked around. They were next to what remained of an old house in a yard that was also full of abandoned cars.

"This is where our ride stops?" he asked.

"You know a better place to hide a leaf than a forest?" Casey asked.

"Good point."

Casey walked toward the trees on the edge of the junk yard. Rafe picked up his pace a little to catch up, following her through the barren undergrowth. The snow was almost completely melted. If only the cold would go too.

Eventually, they reached an old drainage pipe, and Casey knelt to crawl inside. Despite slipping a little on ice that had frozen at the mouth of the pipe, Rafe followed her into the gloom on his hands and knees. "You do know where you're going, right?" His voice echoed along the walls, and he hoped it wasn't as loud outside as it sounded in here.

Casey produced a headlamp from her backpack and slipped it on before continuing forward. "Of course. Only before, I used to come in with my papers like most citizens. Yours have definitely been revoked, and I'm sure mine are too; and even if they weren't, my RFID would give us away the moment I walked through a scanner."

Rafe's eyes widened, not having thought of that before. The government had passed a law some time ago requiring anyone affiliated with the military, or who had health issues that could affect their mental faculties, to be implanted with an RFID chip so that it was impossible to lose their information. It hadn't ever affected Rafe, but as a National Guardsman Casey would have no choice about getting chipped.

Casey continued explaining. "In order to get to the neighborhood we're aiming for, we need to get inside the fence. I don't know if you noticed, but I saw a tag mark near the entrance, so if we can find another one ... here we go." She indicated a small painted mark on the wall that looked like a black smiley faced cat drawn with bright yellow whiskers. It had been painted above the image of a rattlesnake coiled up and ready to strike.

"Tag mark?" Rafe asked.

"Some groups use tag marks in more urban areas because they fit in better with the scenery. You're less likely to be found out if you aren't physically there to give directions. They change their tags periodically, though, because the SPKF gets wise to them. See something enough times and even a kid'll figure out it's important."

"Wouldn't that have been important information when we left you last time?" Rafe asked.

"You were supposed to stay *out* of the urban centers," Casey responded dryly. "I figured you'd go straight west. The tags are mostly for resistance, not runners. There isn't an official list, and teaching every runner would just be too difficult."

She resumed crawling along the pipe and turned left at a fork a short distance from where the image had been placed, and Rafe continued after her. "If there isn't an official list, how do you know for sure it's a resistance tag?"

"The most popular tags are memes from when the Internet was still open to anyone with a connection," Casey said. "The powers-that-be were never good at figuring those out. There are some old standbys, and then there are those that show up and change over time. They attract less attention than, say, uncommon Bible verses, because they're easier to be mistaken for graffiti. That symbol back there was a 'smile-kitty', like the emojis that used to get posted in chatrooms. But as you saw, it was done with two paint colors. 'Smile-kitty' is rarely drawn with more than one. Then there's the obvious clue that it was drawn well inside a drainage pipe and with a rattlesnake underneath. It's a common tag for giving directions. The rattle was drawn to the left. That's your direction. Unless there were some pretty crazy kids before the fences and security went up, I don't see what else it could be."

"Fair enough, I guess," Rafe said. It seemed too open to interpretation to be trusted, but he supposed that ambiguity was what made it safe from the SPKF. From what he had seen, their worldview was pretty rigid.

They crawled along without any more conversation, though Rafe could hear water flowing in the distance. He tried not to think about where this water had been used prior to ending up here. Sure, it was a storm drain, but that didn't mean the water was *clean*. His hands were also starting to go numb, since he couldn't warm them in his pockets without stopping.

A short while later, they reached a manhole cover that had another smile-kitty on it, and the two of them gently pushed it up and to the side. Upon reaching the surface, Rafe blinked as his eyes adjusted to the daylight. They were on the edge of some sort of park, hidden from most of the windows on the nearby buildings by a crumbling brick wall. In the distance, he could see the downtown skyscrapers over several rooftops. But here, they were obviously in a neighborhood full of apartment buildings with the rare older house – the last remnants of owners who had refused to sell.

Judging by the angle of the sunlight, they were north of the downtown area.

"Okay, now what?" he asked, turning his attention to Casey.

"Well, we're inside. The next thing we need is to find them." She traded the headlamp for a scarf from her backpack, moving her loose brown hair aside so she could wrap it around her neck and tuck it under her collar. She scanned the area, then pointed. "Ah, this is it."

Rafe frowned, looking at the wall by a sidewalk leading toward another part of the neighborhood. It didn't look like anything more than random graffiti to him. "You sure?"

"Positive." Casey tucked her rifle under her coat as best she could. It looked awkward, but if they didn't attract too much attention, no one should notice. Hopefully. She walked to the nearby wall, studying it.

Rafe thought it was a collection of letters, but they seemed so heavily stylized he couldn't even read them. They seemed to have been drawn to be one consecutive string covered in an odd diamond pattern that made it very distracting. He thought he saw an 'O' somewhere in there, and an 'E' he thought, but he wasn't quite sure. . .

"There's the smile kitty. So where's the rattlesnake?" Casey frowned as she searched the piece for the icon, and then she slowly backed up almost to the street and suddenly grinned. "Oh wow, hat's off to you friend, whoever you are." She looked over at Rafe. "We need to go that way." She pointed down the sidewalk to the west.

"Where was the rattlesnake this time?" Rafe asked.

"It's the whole piece. The rattle is on the right foot of the letter 'K' at the end," Casey said. "You couldn't read it?"

Rafe shook his head.

"It said 'No step on snek.'"

Casey was already walking down the sidewalk, but Rafe paused where she had been standing, frowning at the wall for a moment. At last he saw it. It was still hard to read, but once he knew what to look for, he even recognized a small eye and a forked tongue coming out of the first post of the letter 'N.' It was an old meme, but he knew exactly where it came from.

"Don't Tread on Me," he whispered with a wry smile. With that, he hurried to catch up with Casey.

———

Church was driving one of the SPKF's specially commissioned driver-controlled SUVs toward the south end of Pinnacle, with Hernandez in the passenger seat. Once he reached a cul-de-sac, he pulled the vehicle to a halt and stepped out into the cold.

Hernandez climbed out after him. As long as his investigation included the wilderness, Church was still saddled with the smug SOB.

The sky was an empty blue, save for the morning sun casting his shadow back behind him over the cracked asphalt. He caught sight of a woman watching him through the window, but as he glanced toward her, she quickly closed the curtains.

That behavior had once bothered him; he was a protector of the people, not something to be feared like the police in decades past. Now, however, he felt it was better for the civilian population not to be curious. Better they weren't exposed to the day-to-day business of keeping rebels and terrorists off the streets and runners where they belonged, and that they respect the power he wielded.

After Mrs. Lord had left with Flynn and Everett, a feed from a security camera that had been placed near one of the fences had been brought to his attention. In it, two figures had passed through, straight toward the fence. Rafe Turner was one of them, though he looked a bit scruffier than the photo that sat in a folder on the edge of the back seat of his vehicle. Another file, containing information on a former National Guardsperson named Casey Burke lay atop the Turner folder. Her presence likely solved the mystery of who had given Turner assistance a few days before.

He leaned over toward Hernandez. "This way," he motioned for the other man to follow him. He played with the bullet in his pocket absently with his free hand as he neared the end of the deserted residential street. Walking between the two easternmost houses, he went into the woods toward the fence. That was when he saw what he was looking for. "Footprints," he said to Hernandez. The man looked where he was pointing and nodded again. They followed the tracks for a bit before the mud ended, also ending their chances of finding where the two pairs crossed the fence.

"He's gone then," Church said.

"Hmm?" Hernandez grunted. He was clearly baiting him again.

"You know what I said," Church muttered to himself, but then he spoke a little louder, "I guess that settles it, Rafe Turner has left Pinnacle."

Hernandez muttered something and started back towards the car.

"Where are you going?" Church demanded.

Hernandez looked at him, clearly surprised he wasn't following before finally answering "They went west." He pointed towards the mountains.

Church considered the answer. "You think they went west huh?" It would be an easy assumption to make, after all, Turner and Burke were runners and possibly (in Burke's case, definitely) rebels. It was the answer that made sense. But one thing Church prided himself on was understanding his suspects. "I don't think you're seeing the big picture here."

Hernandez raised an eyebrow, curiously. "No?"

Church sighed and looked at the man, but he couldn't help but smile in anticipation as he patiently explained his assessment. "Rafe Turner was Carol Turner's son, and she was a true believer. She wasn't the only person to resist on her street, but they all shared the conviction that their property meant something. Rafe Turner undoubtedly believes the same thing, and sick as that is, that would include Neil Flynn."

He regarded the footprints eagerly. "Now, the way I see it, Burke's resistance. She knows the ins and outs of this stuff way better than he does, so I'm willing to bet she's running the show now, and if not for Turner, she'd just go west and we'd never hear from them again. But Turner, he's got too much of his mother in him to leave without a fight, so they're going after the kid. They're going to Winston-Salem."

"Estupido," Hernandez growled. There was no ambiguity as to what he thought of the idea.

"But what if I'm right?" Church said.

"Then you'll be getting your gringo ass out of my forest?" Hernandez asked, this time no longer bothering to play dumb. "They're already talking about closing the case now that they have the kid." He was smirking as he spoke.

Church frowned. He was sure by now that Hernandez would be only too happy to see him take the fall for screwing up, but Church was certain of his hunch, and he intended to prove it. "If you want to keep looking west, go right ahead. I know where I'm going."

———

After dinner, Neil was taken to a more permanent holding cell where he slept uneasily for most of the night. Shortly after 8 a.m., the door clanged open, and Hannah came in to usher him out of the building. Soon they were in a driverless car with Everett and Mrs. Lord, bound southward. Neil pointedly turned his attention out the window, as their transportation sped out through the automatic gate and accelerated down the highway. The trees flew by, casting shadows over him, only to be swiped away with their gathering speed and replaced by others.

"We should be there in about twenty minutes," Mrs. Lord was saying into her cell phone, in between sips of coffee. "Make sure we have the place ready for him and our escorts. Thanks."

Neil wished he had his own smart phone, but he'd left that in his room when he'd gone downstairs to ask his parents what the commotion was about. For the first time in this whole trip, he was more bored than scared or exhausted, and he wished he had something fun to use to distract himself. Why hadn't he taken it? It was probably looted by now, sold on some black market, with all his games and apps, or sitting in some police locker somewhere as evidence.

Then reality came back, and Neil remembered that would have just made things worse. Rafe had dispensed with his when they'd left Greensboro to avoid being tracked. His own cell would not have been any less of a risk. They might even have been found sooner.

A few minutes passed in uneasy silence as the older woman across from him busied herself with her phone. All too soon, another automatic gate opened in front of them and then up ahead, Neil saw a forest of townhouses and apartment buildings on either side. The skyscrapers of the Winston-Salem skyline were also visible, just beyond what remained of the old cigarette factory. A long time ago, before the trial, his dad's company used to run deliveries here. Neil could dimly remember his father telling him what the different buildings were on a trip out this way when he'd been little.

The car rolled off the highway and into the downtown streets before parking at the bottom of a set of steps leading up to a wide plaza between two of the skyscrapers. One was rectangular and the other looked like a smaller version of the Empire State Building. Neil remembered his father talking about that one; according to his story, it was the inspiration for the New York City landmark. It was called. . . Neil struggled to remember. It was so long ago, but he held onto the faint memory as if it alone could protect him from the SPKF. It was the Reynolds Building. That was it! His father had said that once, the Empire State Building staff had even sent the Reynolds Building a Father's Day card.

Neil took some comfort in that. These guys might have left his father to die, but he wasn't really gone if Neil remembered him. God had him, and so did he.

Everett opened the door and climbed out along with Hannah, who held out her hand to help Neil slide over so he could stand and retrieve his crutches. Once he was upright, Mrs. Lord led the way up the stairs and across the plaza toward the Reynolds building. Up close it was a pillar of steel and concrete, painted the color of sand and towering into the sky. Neil noted the stained-glass windows as they walked through revolving clear glass doors framed in polished brass. They crossed an intricately decorated carpet as they walked through the lobby. Mrs. Lord ignored the person at the front desk and instead walked to the elevators, holding the door so that Neil and his escort could follow her inside.

"My husband has arranged a hotel room for you and your escort until we can find you somewhere more permanent." Mrs. Lord balanced primly on her stilettos.

They took the elevator to the sixth floor, where the doors pulled open to reveal a carpeted hallway. Beyond the elevator lobby, several doors stood on either side of the hall. Mrs. Lord led the way to one on the left and knocked. It was opened by an older man in a business suit. His features were dominated by his bulbous eyes, which Neil thought gave him an almost fish-like appearance.

"Sorry to keep you waiting Trent, you haven't been here long, have you?" Mrs. Lord asked, cupping the man's face in her hands in a way that Neil guessed was supposed to be affectionate.

"Not really sweetie. I actually just got here." The man backed away from the door once she withdrew her hands and ushered them inside. It looked like a normal hotel room. Bathroom near the entry door, two queen beds, a single chair, and a television on the dresser, but nothing particularly unique.

"Will this room be sufficient for what you needed?" Trent asked Mrs. Lord as Hannah guided Neil over to the chair by the window.

"I think it should be perfect," Mrs. Lord confirmed, taking the keycards from him. "It's safe, comfortable, and quiet. Just the sort of place for our guest to recover from his recent ordeal." She walked over to Everett, handing him one of the keys before pocketing the other. "I know you'll both do your best to make sure no one disturbs him."

"Of course," Hannah agreed.

Neil looked out the window. No one was going to give him a key to *his* room. The change of scenery meant nothing when he was still as much a prisoner here in this 'safe and comfortable' jail cell as he'd been in Pinnacle.

He tried to ignore what was going on in the room after that, instead preferring to turn his attention outside. The cold sunshine was starting to creep through the clouds and was illuminating patches of the street below.

The talking behind him quieted, and then he heard the door close as Trent and Mrs. Lord left the room.

After an awkward moment, Hannah spoke up. "Um, well ... is anyone hungry? I spotted some bagels in the shop downstairs."

Neil's stomach growled at the thought, and he gave her a half-hearted nod.

"That sounds good to me. If you could find me one with sesame seeds, that would be great." Everett offered her some change, along with the keycard so she could return to the room.

"Sure thing," Hannah pocketed the cash and the card and walked to the door, shutting it behind her with a soft click.

A few moments passed in uncomfortable silence as Everett looked thoughtfully at the door from where he stood, and then he walked over to the bed nearest the window and sat down at the foot of it, so that he was right next to Neil's chair. "Hey kid," he said.

Neil looked in his direction curiously.

The dark-skinned man leaned forward where he sat, clasping his hands in front of him, thinking about what he was going to say before glancing one more time at the door, and then back at Neil. At last, he seemed to come to a decision and he spoke. "I know this can't be easy, but do you think we could talk for a few minutes?"

"About what?" Neil asked.

Everett looked like he was deep in thought for a while longer before speaking again. "I'm an officer of the law. ... It's my job to serve and protect, but that night we clearly weren't doing our job..."

"Ain't that the truth," Neil growled.

If that had offended the man, he didn't show it. Instead, he straightened a little, his expression serious. "To be honest, there's plenty about what happened that night that smells, and I'd like to try and find the truth about why. If you'd be willing to help me out..., do you think you could tell me from your perspective what happened the night your parents died?"

"... *Most of them are probably just ordinary people, trying to do their jobs.*" That was what Rafe had said once, Neil remembered.

What could it hurt? All I have now is time. He started talking.

CHAPTER 11

EMPTY CHURCHES

December 14, 2037

CASEY LED RAFE THROUGH MOSTLY EMPTY STREETS, following vague graffiti signs and keeping away from people who might spot the long guns under their coats. After a few minutes, they reached a shabby-looking street corner on which an old church stood. Judging by its condition, the congregation no longer seemed to be active. Casey surveyed the deserted street, checking the walls and sidewalks for some indication of how to proceed, before she decided to turn down an alley behind the building, finding a fenced-in space with rusted playground equipment. After looking around to make sure the coast was clear, she walked to a door, checked to see if it was locked, and then pushed it open.

Rafe followed her into the gloom of an industrial-looking hallway with peeling white paint over cement block walls. They moved toward a room at the far end that seemed to be better lit, which turned out to be the lobby. The chapel entrance was to their right, through a pair of double doors. From the door Rafe had opened, he could see rows of dusty pews facing a stage framed by intricate stained-glass windows. Even though he felt no religious attachment to the place, he still could appreciate the beauty and skill in the artwork which hung in testament to the beliefs of those who had commissioned it.

But no amount of disbelief in the purpose of this citadel could change the sadness he felt upon noticing that some of the glass in a window on the far-left wall had been smashed, leaving the colored fragments of a rendering of one of the biblical stories strewn on the molding carpet. Rafe also noticed a hole where a flower had once been displayed in another of the windows at the head of the chapel. It now left a sun-bleached pool of light filtering down onto the choir area in front of the gentler hues of the refracted light below it. To see anything made with so much care and detail shattered into ruin by such carelessness, or possibly hatred or cruelty … it was sickening.

Another door opened somewhere, out of sight, and the two of them ducked for cover. The dust fell like snow through the sunbeams around them as they waited for an indication of who was there. Footsteps echoed off concrete as they drew nearer, until at last, he saw a black man enter from behind the choir area and look out over the chapel. From his face, Rafe would have guessed he was around fifty, though it was hard to tell his build under his coat. He did notice the flashlight hanging at the man's left hip.

Casey saw it too, because at that point she stood up and walked out into the open. "Hi. Sorry to barge in like this," she grinned and then, recited the first line from "Paint it Black."

The man didn't seem surprised at what he had heard. "Looking for Paul, are you?"

"George, actually," Casey gestured that Rafe should get up and join her. He straightened and walked over.

The man watched his approach warily and then spoke again. "Well then, let's see if we can find him." He turned back toward the rear of the church and left the chapel, waving for them to follow.

He led them along the corridor, into a meeting hall, and out the door. They continued across an empty lot before following him out onto the sidewalk bound east. As they walked, Rafe saw that the man in front of them was texting on a cell phone. Several minutes later, they turned down another alley, this one a bit further away from the church. There stood another man, this one slightly younger, maybe in his forties, also dressed in a heavy coat with a knitted hat covering his head.

"You must be Rabbit," he said.

"And you must know why we're here," Casey replied, standing confidently as she glanced around.

"Sure, we know." The man was also on the alert, but once he was sure who she was, he went straight to business. "We've looked over what you asked for and determined we will be able to supply it for what you offered. I hope you appreciate what we went through to gather it unnoticed."

"Thank you," Casey responded. "I know it couldn't have been easy."

The man nodded. "Just be careful it doesn't get traced back to us. We've got to keep our own efforts from being compromised."

"Anything helps," Rafe said. He was perfectly happy to let Casey do most of the talking.

The man with the knitted hat turned to lead them still farther into the neighborhood until they reached a townhouse. They entered to find a young black woman in a hoodie and jeans, with tight black curls framing her face. "This is Juno," their guide said. "She'll be your contact. Do you have the payment?"

Casey nodded and reached into her jacket, producing several large bills.

The man looked them over and then nodded. "All right. Juno will take you out to see what we've got, though after you've made your preparations, you're on your own." He placed the payment in his pocket as he spoke.

"That's fine," Casey said, and Rafe noticed her brown eyes alight with anticipation.

The man nodded to Juno, and she motioned them to follow her outside.

As they exited, Rafe asked the question most on his mind. "Casey ... what exactly are you thinking we're going to do?"

"We're going to get Neil out," she whispered, as Juno stayed ahead of them so as not to disturb their discussion. "You didn't think we were going to case the building ourselves, and then fight our way in through the front door with your shotgun, did you?"

Rafe shook his head, though his worry deepened as they continued along the sidewalk. "That sounds more like something some nutjob would do. But I'd rather not shoot anyone at all if it can be helped." He couldn't help feeling creeped out at the sound of that kind of speculation.

Casey's tone remained matter-of-fact as she answered. "Same here. So, we go in quietly, with small firearms we can conceal, and hopefully avoid using."

Rafe nearly tripped over some pavement before he sidestepped a not-quite frozen puddle of water. "So, you do have some idea what we're doing?"

Casey shrugged. "We did simulations of possible scenarios in case something like this came up, and I seriously doubt the security for one kid with a broken leg will be like trying to break into Fort Knox. Compared to a jailhouse, this shouldn't be nearly as complicated."

Rafe stopped at that point to look her in the eye. "Jailhouse or not, isn't this really dangerous...?"

Casey breathed out through her teeth impatiently and grabbed him by the shoulder, leading him along as they walked. "Well, *of course* it's dangerous! But I've gathered everything I can think of based on what we trained for, and what I think would give us the quickest and best possible outcome. You're the one who wanted to save the kid, Turner. It'll be too late to get cold feet just because it's hard once we've got things rolling. So, do you have the will or don't you?"

"How do I even know your plan is going to work?" Rafe glared at her. "You've hardly told me anything!"

Casey gave him a look of exasperation as they continued walking along the pavement after Juno. "That's because I know hardly anything right now *myself*, apart from some educated guesses. This isn't my turf, so we need their help first. We'll have intelligence, basic equipment, and a getaway vehicle. I plan on avoiding any fire-fights where possible, and I'll be right next to you every step of the way. If you go down, I go down, so man up. I have just as much reason to want this to work as you do and more. If we screw up, you just go to prison. If you're lucky, you might even get let out in half a century. I get interrogated, court-martialed, and then probably executed for treason." She let go of him and looked around to make sure they were still in the clear. "Now, once we have the goods, we're going to find a place to hide out. We'll put together the details there, using the information the locals give us. Then we'll go over them until you know them backwards, forwards, and sideways. The last thing we need is you freaking out because you don't know what to do." Casey gave him a look that clearly said *"Like you are right now."*

"That would be ... embarrassing ... at the very least," Rafe agreed. Things were escalating too fast. He felt as though he was sledding down a hill, which had suddenly gone from a gentle slope to a steep drop, and he was dealing with the instinct to flail around for something to help him stop. But it was too late to safely apply the brakes. Doing so meant leaving Neil. As afraid as Rafe was, they'd been through too much together for him to just abandon his friend without a fight now.

They soon reached an appliance repair shop a few streets over. Juno opened the door as they approached, holding it open for them. The way she looked at Rafe clearly indicated she had some concerns about his courage. Not that he could blame her when it felt like he was questioning himself every other minute.

As he thought this, she came in after them and then walked to the register to hit the old-fashioned bell on the counter.

A man with a neatly trimmed mustache appeared from the back. Clearly recognizing Juno, he spoke without preamble or pleas-antries. "Some of our couriers are late. We need a little more time to get everything ready." he said, "You could get some coffee. We'll have it in about half an hour, and then we can direct you to your staging location."

Juno nodded. "Got it. Thanks." She turned to them. "Well, you heard the man, let's go." She paused as though thinking for a moment, "Although, it might be best to leave your weapons here. If we're going to be running around for a while, it's better if we aren't carrying anything that would arouse suspicion."

Casey nodded and walking to a spot that Juno indicated, she removed her coat to hand the man her rifle. Rafe hesitated, reluctant to let go of his grandfather's shotgun; but eventually, he followed Casey away from the windows to also remove his own coat and unsling the weapon. He had tried to make it inconspicuous but there was only so much he could do. The man who had been standing behind the counter carefully took the two weapons and made for the door to the back room. "I'll stick these with your package," he assured them. "We'll keep them hidden until you come back for them."

"All right," Casey confirmed.

After that, the two of them followed Juno back out onto the street, looking around for a place to warm up. Juno soon directed them to a coffee shop. As there was hardly anyone there, it didn't take long for each of them to receive a steaming cup of coffee. They then found a high table set up bar style against a window. It was the perfect place to watch what happened outside.

They drank their coffee in an uneasy silence. To Rafe, it felt like he was looking in on another universe. How was it possible, when there was so much wrong with the world, that the young lady behind the counter could still smile as if she were happy to see them and ask them, in that Piedmont bluegrass twang, what she could get for them today? Of course, she probably wasn't happy at all, at least not to the degree most people would consider true happiness. But the endorphin-producing effect of smiling was probably a lot nicer to her than his own thoughts were to him. At least she wasn't in the planning stages of storming a building in what would no doubt later be called a terrorist attack.

It was all he could do not to let his brow knit with worry at the thought. If he didn't know better, he'd have thought this scenario sounded like something out of one of Will's secret agent campaigns he'd talked of running at some point, using a variant of C&C rules meant for modern-day settings. The party wouldn't have been so slip-shod about it either and tabletop groups were notorious for planning strategy on the fly. . .

Okay, maybe that was a little unfair. Casey did seem to have some idea what she was doing. There really wasn't time for precision right now, Neil could be gone at any moment, and they also had to find time to escape. He still didn't know half of what she thought he was supposed to do during this rescue attempt, and that made him even more aware of that critical distinction between reality and fantasy. As much as he might wish otherwise, he knew far too well that he was not any of his characters. Compared to the idealized and, thankfully, fictitious badassery that emerged in a role-playing game, he felt he'd be lucky if he didn't shoot himself in the foot and bleed to death.

His train of thought was interrupted as a man approached the coffee shop and entered. There was something familiar about him, Rafe thought, but he couldn't place where he'd seen him before. The man was in his forties with an average build and thinning dark hair, and he wore a heavy coat over a rumpled suit. Rafe tried to ignore him as he shuffled over to the counter to order something, checking his phone as he walked. At this point, if they tried to move then they would be noticed, and it was best not to attract attention if he wasn't sure there was anything wrong. Rafe sipped his coffee and continued looking out the window, telling himself he was thinking too much. Not long after, he saw the man sit a short distance from him, also with a cup of coffee and a bagel. He seemed just as intent on his brunch as they were on passing the time.

At that moment, Rafe's attention was diverted to a TV that had been mounted overhead. A woman sat at a news desk speaking about the weather. "*. . . The cold front that held up traffic the last few days has finally moved off the coast, but it will be followed by another wave of colder air and precipitation within the next day and contin-*

uing for the next week or so. It may be a white Winter Holiday this year after all, folks..."

That was right, he realized. It was still December. Christmas was a little less than two weeks away. Before the war, this used to mean returning to his parents' home. Last time they'd all gotten together, his sister Susan had been pregnant, and the anticipation of a new addition to the family had added an extra layer of festivity to a holiday that the whole family enjoyed. That had been almost a year before hostilities broke out, when travel restrictions hadn't been put in place yet, and the evacuations had yet to be enacted.

The memory was almost unreal. Other than Eric inviting him over each year, Christmas had been effectively nonexistent for him since that day. Without family, what was the point?

People who had known them sometimes wondered why his family made such a big deal over Christmas. Where they lived, everyone knew what church everyone attended – or, in their case, didn't attend. But that wasn't what his immediate family valued about the holiday. They valued the part of it that kept them together, seeing each other, enjoying each other's company – the part that was still connected to their heritage and traditions. For a while, he'd half-heartedly explained to anyone who asked that their excuse was just a belated celebration of the Winter Solstice, but eventually, he'd given that up. Christmas was just easier, until everything had been sanitized to the point it was no longer safe to say it. He smiled wryly at the thought. You couldn't say much of *anything* anymore without someone getting offended.

The weather segment had ended, replaced with a news report. It took him a moment to realize why the street shown on the camera was so familiar. It was *his* street, back in Greensboro, or it had been until Neil's parents had been murdered in front of a crowd of people. Why was –

". . .Eyewitnesses report it was a scene of tumultuous chaos as the primarily minority protestors made their grievances known. At first, the protest was not violent. However, according to an eyewitness,

midway through the event, Flynn and his wife came out on their porch with illegal firearms, threatening the peaceful demonstrators."

It cut to a man being interviewed, and Rafe almost did a double take as he noticed a large bandage over the man's left eye. *"I tell you man, it was the scariest thing I've ever seen! They came out of their house and Mr. Flynn just started shout'n "I'll start shoot'n if you don't get lost!"* It was the man Rafe had clubbed over the head with his wooden sword.

"Could you tell us about your injury?" the reporter asked.

"Well..." the man puffed himself up. *"I got it fight'n one o' those white supremacists that tried to get into the crowd to break us up. I mean, we were only here to peacefully let our voices be heard."*

Rafe gripped his coffee mug hard.

The largest lens in the world to reveal the truth, and you decide to lie because your narrative means more to you than what is actually real. Tell the world how that angry mob dragged them out of their house. Tell the world about the boy that lost his parents because of these sickos that you're interviewing right now, who keep trying to find someone else to blame! Tell the world why I saw their bodies *hanging from that tree! Tell the* truth, *God damn it!*

He'd long since concluded that the government-approved media lied, but there was a difference between seeing the evidence and living it. How many people had to have been in on the lie to perpetuate it? How many people had been there and knew the truth? How many cell phone cameras had recorded what really happened?

The TV focused on the reporter. *"According to eyewitnesses, the criminals opened fire on the crowd without giving them time to disperse. Howard and Jane Flynn were dispatched by an SPKF officer who was on security detail for the protest. He is now being hailed as a hero. Some injuries were reported but they were minor.*

"As previously reported, the Flynn's young son went missing during the incident. He has since been recovered, although Special Peacekeeping Force officers are interested in any information about the incident, specifically in connection to this man." Rafe was taken aback for a moment as the photo from his ID card suddenly appeared on

the screen. Perhaps it wasn't such a bad thing that he hadn't shaved at the safe house. At least his scruffy beard gave him something to disguise his face, but he still had to resist the urge to put his hood up as Casey leaned toward him.

"Wow, you're kind of cute when you're all cleaned up," she whispered, tapping his arm warningly. He noticed then how hard he was gripping his cup and forced himself to relax his hold. The thick paper encircled with a cardboard heat guard had been starting to bend under the pressure of his grip. If he had been holding it any tighter, he might have drenched his hand with hot coffee.

The reporter continued, *"Rafe Turner lived on the same street, and was unemployed. SPKF officials report that he is a rebel sympathizer with connections to terrorists. If you have any information about his current whereabouts, please call the hotline number on the left side of the screen, immediately. If you see the suspect, do not approach him. He is believed to be armed and dangerous..."*

Rafe was still watching the news report on the TV when he finally remembered the identity of the man who was sitting a few seats away from them. He didn't know his name, but he recognized him. The man was drinking his coffee and not paying attention to them but Rafe looked away, hoping he hadn't also been recognized. It seemed like he was watching the TV just like they were.

Rafe leaned over to speak to Casey. "We need to go," he whispered.

"Why's that?" she asked, her voice low but much more conversational.

"We just do!"

Casey nodded with a smile as though she wasn't really paying attention, but as she turned back to her coffee, he saw her mouth the word *'Relax.'*

Realizing he was gritting his teeth, Rafe tried to emulate a Zen master, drink his coffee, and not make any sudden moves as Casey looked over at Juno and made a small covert hand motion. They finished their drinks at a leisurely pace, watching as the news moved on to the next story about how President Holdt was signing some trade deal with China, and then stood. He followed them to the trash can to dispense with their cups. Soon they were walking out the door and out onto the street.

"So what's the hurry?" Casey asked once they were back out in the cold.

"That man who sat down next to us was one of the guys who grabbed Neil," Rafe glanced over his shoulder to see if they were being followed, "I don't think he recognized me, but I didn't want to give him a chance..." It didn't look like anyone was coming out of the coffee shop.

"Don't look back," Casey told him, her voice low but firm. "It'll just attract attention."

Juno furrowed her brow in concern before pulling out a notepad and a pen to write with. "I'll go let Apollo know. Come to this address at 1 p.m., I'll have your package for you." She finished with the notepad, pulled off the piece of paper, and pressed it into Casey's hands. "Now, if you go down that alley," she pointed out a small gap between the derelict auto repair shop and a nearly empty strip mall that stood next to it, "There's an abandoned car wash on the next street over. You can hide there."

Casey stuffed the paper in her pocket as Juno ducked down a side street, and the two of them turned in the direction the departing woman had indicated, cutting across an empty back lot behind a shopping center before they reached the car wash. They hunkered down inside what had once been an office, the door now hanging open as someone had broken into it at some point. Rafe was beginning to think that he had been jumping at shadows and that they hadn't been noticed. Maybe they'd been lucky after all.

They waited for some time, but no one even approached the car wash. Once Casey felt it was safe, the two of them exited the building and set a casual pace down the street, alert for any sign they were being followed. Thankfully, there didn't seem to be any indication that they were.

After locating an old map at a bus station, they made their way toward the street they were looking for. More than once, they had to duck into an alley before an SPKF car drove past, or take a different turn before an officer walked by, but it didn't seem like they were looking for them.

The address Juno had given them was in a different neighborhood from where they had started, though no less desolate. The address belonged to an older house that had been built with an attached garage. They walked up to a side door and knocked, and Juno opened the door. "There you are. Did you have any trouble?" She let them inside the garage. Rafe noticed a truck with an extended cab and covered bed waiting inside. On the surface, the truck looked like it had been reworked to public standards, but what Casey had already told him about it suggested otherwise.

"I don't think we were seen," Casey said, pulling off her hat and combing a few tangles out of her hair with her fingers as she walked inside.

Once Juno led them into the house, she stepped ahead of them down the hall. "Good. Don't stay here too long. Nobody lives here, and it's more of a staging location than a safe-house, but the fewer people who see you here, the better."

"Got it," Casey agreed. "We'll just be long enough to grab our equipment, do some prep work, and be on our way."

Juno showed them into what had once been a living room. There, Rafe saw a large crate, almost the size of a small coffee table sitting in the middle of the floor. Casey walked up to it and lifted the lid. Inside, Rafe could see his shotgun and Casey's rifle on top of everything else. Underneath them, he could see that inside the box lay two handguns, and an AR-15 over two backpacks filled with provisions.

Casey lifted one of the pistols, revealing a magazine for the rifle and a couple of smaller mags for the handguns also packed beneath it. "This should be sufficient to get Neil and us out of the city." She turned to face Juno. "Were you able to find a way in?"

Juno handed her a hotel keycard. "Lifted from a night janitor," she said. "It should open all the places you need to go."

"Won't that get traced back to an innocent person?" Rafe asked.

"He's not innocent," Juno told him, her voice cold. "He enjoys turning in people he doesn't like for racist speech or other thought crimes, or just because they don't shout the slogans loud enough. The flack he gets for this will hardly even be a taste of his own medicine."

"We can't thank you all enough." Casey pocketed the keycard.

"Just make sure none of this gets traced to us." Juno gave the two of them a hard look, pulling up the hood on her hoodie over her black curls as she prepared to leave. "And let us know where you plan to leave the truck before you go."

"Will do. And don't worry. Even if we get caught, we won't breathe a word about it. Right, Rafe?" The look Casey directed at him indicated she wanted only a correct answer.

Rafe took a moment to respond. He'd researched a few interrogation techniques before, mostly out of curiosity, and none of them sounded pleasant. Did the Geneva convention apply here? He wasn't technically an enemy soldier, so that meant the answer was no, not that he expected any fair treatment regardless at this point ... He pushed those thoughts aside and nodded. "Right."

Satisfied, Juno left. Rafe took a seat on the living room couch while Casey walked over to the crate to inspect its contents further. After a moment she held up one of the handguns, checking the sights and aiming it at an invisible enemy. "Now then," she said, her tone all business. "If we're going to help your friend, I have one rule for you, so listen carefully."

Rafe nodded. "Okay."

Casey lowered the gun, "While we're in there, you do everything I tell you. No buts, no maybes, and under absolutely no circumstances will I tolerate the word 'no'. I tell you to duck, you duck. I tell you to shoot, you shoot. And if I tell you to run, you get the hell out of there."

"You know a lot more about this kind of thing than I do," Rafe agreed, leaning forward in his seat nervously. "I'll follow your lead."

Even if it means we're going to die? He quickly squashed the thought. "So ... what happens now?"

"First things first," Casey reached into the crate again, producing a cheap computer tablet and started scrolling through several files on it. "We'll check out the intel and determine our injection point, mission details, and escape routes. Then I'll run you through how to handle each of these." She gestured to the weapons in the crate. "We can't do real target practice. Too much noise. But I will school you as thoroughly as possible in the time we have. Are we clear?"

He swallowed hard as he let the reality of what they were about to do sink in, and then he nodded. "Crystal."

Casey nodded in approval. "Good answer. Let's get to work." She sat down next to him and held up the tablet between them so they could go over the contents.

―――――

"There's no way this is going to work," Rafe said. It was getting into late afternoon and after going through an inventory of what they had, Casey had spent the last few minutes outlining their plan for infiltrating the building. That part had been all very well, but she had just started describing the escape route, and what she expected Rafe to do during the retreat. "It's like you just said when we were going over the equipment, that AR-15 was designed for. . . what was it....223 caliber? That's for home defense, not urban warfare. I may as well be chucking rocks out the back of the truck, right?"

Casey was standing by the crate, her arms folded as she listened calmly. "And that's exactly the point," she said, patiently. "I don't expect you to *hit* anyone chasing us. You're an amateur. Yes, I grant that you've had some firearms training, but not for shooting a moving vehicle *from* a moving vehicle. You'd be lucky to even ding the windshield. What I expect you to do is distract them until we get to the checkpoint. Add a couple of flashbangs now and then, and they'll hang back, and expect the countermeasures at the checkpoint to take care of us. After all, *they* don't want to get hurt, and there's always that million to one chance that you'll actually hit something."

"Good thing we're not betting on those odds," Rafe commented.

Casey nodded and returned to the business of describing the plan. "Anyway, as long as you keep up the appearance of a threat, their goal will be to keep us from veering off and disappearing into the city. And they'll keep to that goal until we get to a checkpoint leading out of the compound. I'll handle making sure they don't run us off the road or anything."

"This sounds like a job for an expert driver. Are you sure you're that good?" he asked.

She offered him a reassuring smile. "You just worry about your job. If you can do that, my lead foot will get us through this just fine." She held up the tablet, looking at some notes she had scribbled with a stylus over what Juno had given her.

"Now, moving on to the checkpoint, when we first get there, they will likely try to mess with our vision by shining lasers at us. That won't be a problem for you. You'll be in the back. Of course, then we have to deal with the ADS."

"The what?" Rafe asked.

"The Active Denial System. They first built them way back during the Afghan and Iraq wars. It sends out low frequency microwaves that feel like they're burning without actually harming you."

"That sounds terrible," Rafe stood up from the couch, stretching his arms as he did so.

Casey nodded. "Yeah. I don't think anyone's lasted more than eight seconds under the heat. Though I've heard cold weather can reduce the effect, so with that window, we might be able to handle it for five seconds if we absolutely have to. That'll start at about two-hundred meters from the checkpoint. And then we'll have to deal with the PEVS."

"The PEVS?" Rafe looked at her, confused.

She nodded again. "It's short for a Pre-Emplaced Vehicle Stopper. Silly name, but the equipment is definitely not. It's designed to stop most cars by shorting out the battery. It seems they decided they didn't want to rebuild the entire road so they put in a PEVS system. There will be the way in, the actual speed bump, and the way out, which will have some barriers to navigate."

Rafe looked at her in complete disbelief. "Okay, what's the actual plan? We're not seriously going out that way, are we?"

He spotted the dangerous gleam in her eye once again as she grinned. "That's exactly what we're going to do, and I intend to floor it."

———

March 10, 2033

"Well that's my truth, and I'm sticking to it," Hannah had said. The group had been sitting at their usual table in the cafeteria at lunchtime. It was frigid cold outside, and Rafe wasn't the only one with a steaming mug of coffee on his tray. He sat next to Eric, quietly eating a sandwich while his friend was penciling something in on his sketchpad. It looked like something really detailed, though Rafe wasn't sure what it was yet.

"What does that even mean?" Allen asked coolly. He leaned across the table, toward where Hannah sat next to Eric, resting his goateed chin on his hand with a wry smile on his face. "Your truth?"

"The truth of my personal experience," Hannah replied, just as coolly. "Which you won't acknowledge."

"Well, I suppose there's your emotional experience," Allen conceded, "But I wouldn't call that 'your truth' so much as how you felt about it, and this isn't to mean you aren't allowed to feel. That's not what I'm saying. You can always change your attitude, but in terms of changing reality, that's not worth a teaspoon of salt to the ocean in objective terms."

"Typical." Hannah leaned back in her chair and folded her arms. Thus far, Allen and Hannah had held to Will's truce in his apartment, but this wasn't the first time they'd mixed things up in the cafeteria. Surprisingly though, Hannah didn't seem too interested in fighting today. Instead, she looked out at the sunlight struggling to warm the brick steps on the other side of the cafeteria's front doors. The fountain and the artificial waterfall had been turned off to avoid being frozen, leaving the water feature running along the center of the stairs as a barren multi-layered pond.

Allen shook his head unapologetically. "The question you should be asking, Hannah, is 'What *is* truth?'"

She glanced back at him, raising an annoyed eyebrow.

Allen ignored the gesture and continued conversationally. "If it doesn't exist separately from you, then does that mean your perception is the only thing that exists? That only you matter? Or that only the most powerful person's conception of reality matters? What kind of Orwellian nightmare is that?"

Hannah looked thoughtful for a while, but at last shrugged dismissively. "It's not about what's true, it's about how that truth affects someone's life experience. Those feelings are just as real, and they can hurt, believe it. I think you're thinking too hard on this."

"Actually, I'm pretty sure most people don't think about this enough." Allen settled the tip of his left pointer finger down on the table in front of him. "You see this here? This is me. If only my point of view exists, or the opinion of the person most aggrieved, then how is the rest of the world even real? You've got yourself some freaky matrix situation or something where this is all some illusion being played out in your brain, and how is anyone supposed to move past anything if that's what defines their reality?"

Eric frowned thoughtfully as he looked over the figures he had sketched out on his sketch pad. "There'd be no point in trying to change," he commented. "Because the only thing that would matter is who shouts the loudest."

Rafe figured Eric was thinking about what had happened with his dad. He had managed to find another job eventually, but at reduced pay to the point that they had needed to sell their house in Oak Ridge and move to a smaller townhome in Greensboro. Apart from lifeguarding with Rafe during the summer, Eric was also working as a busboy for one of the local restaurants to help keep things above water, and Rafe knew he'd been taking extra hours when he could.

Allen nodded in agreement as Eric spoke. "Right. But if the truth exists separately from you," he rested his right pointer finger on the table a few inches from his left, "Then it can be discovered," he brought his left finger to meet his right, "and other people can discover it too, and they can grow. And learn. That mutual discovery is the only way that willing consensus and agreement can be truly reached in a sane world." He removed his hands from the table.

"You make it sound so simple. . ." Hannah began.

Allen leaned forward, looking at Hannah. "But it isn't. Our ancestors didn't innately have this understanding. It took centuries for them to develop an effective framework off this idea. But once they worked it out, it proved to be one of the most important cornerstones on which our society was built. So, I hope you can understand why I don't think we should just abandon it because of how people feel about their experiences. I mean, take Will's Veil of the Truthseer for instance. If you think about it, it's so easy to see that it was an item made to facilitate that discovery by pulling back our own perceptions so we could see the world as it is. Why should we want to keep those scales on our eyes?"

As Allen had spoken, Rafe noticed Will looking up in surprise, and then leaning back in his chair and laughing quietly to himself as though he'd just realized what was going on. Hannah, on the other hand, had glanced up at a TV in the corner of the cafeteria. They were playing a commercial for this new organization called the SPKF.

"Hmm ... " Rafe frowned as he considered Allen's words. He'd never quite been able to put it into words, but hearing Allen put it that way ... He wasn't even sure they had intentionally done it ... But he was certain that was exactly the framework his parents tried to use. "That's really interesting," he said softly.

"Yeah," Eric agreed, finally lifting his head of red hair to grace the rest of the table with his face. He had just finished sketching his drawing with a final flourish. Glancing over, Rafe recognized four figures on the page, in pencil lines: a dwarven Fighter, an elven Rogue, a Wizard, and a Cleric, before Eric nonchalantly closed the sketchbook and put it in his backpack.

Allen grinned. "I know, right? Our ancestors put a lot more thought into how we think than we realize." He checked his watch, and Rafe was sure his dark skin had paled a shade or two. "Crap! Speaking of thinking, my engineering class is starting in about ten minutes. I need to get to the science building! Later guys!" He hurriedly gathered his backpack and tray and headed for the exit.

CHAPTER 12

FINAL DUNGEON

March 26, 2033

"You break down the door with a crash loud enough to echo throughout the tower. You see a set of stone steps leading up to another level, and there's evidence that something big lives up there." Will had looked over his stat board at the group with a grin. "What do you do?"

"Check for traps!" Eric called out, gesturing to Hannah.

Hannah and Allen still argued in the cafeteria, sometimes badly enough Rafe tried to find excuses to finish lunch early, but they had done their best to keep their arguments quiet in the living room the last couple of months. Thanks to their partial truce, this semester's gaming sessions had been relatively free of even indirect conflict, and Rafe had been happy to see everyone else even laughing and cracking a smile from time to time. Outside their game, the world was still in turmoil, but in here they could all be friends and relax.

This was their second session in this particular dungeon crawl, and it had already been going for hours, but none of them were ready to call it a night. Most of the semester had been taken up with finding and then navigating this tower, skirmishing with monsters (mostly large spiders), and dealing with puzzles. There had even been an especially long part where the characters had to split up to each deal with an individual challenge. And of course, there was that age-old constant of all C&C dungeons ...

"Of course we check for traps," Hannah agreed. She had been fidgeting with a pencil in her hand, twirling it between her fingers as she listened with rapt attention, but now she grabbed for the dice. "We don't want a repeat of the first floor."

"Roll to search," Will flipped through his notes for one of his other papers.

Hannah let the die roll across the coffee table and then mentally added her own skill modifier to get the total result. "Dang it. 20 total. I really didn't roll that well." She made a face at the die.

Will checked the papers on his desk for a moment before rolling a die, studying it and then looking up dramatically. "You find no traps."

The party looked around at each other nervously. That could either be a fake out, in which case there actually were no traps, or maybe Will had planned something really nasty. The question was... which one was it?

"I guess we'll climb the stairs, then," Allen said at last.

Eric nodded, as he reached out and took one of the cookies Hannah had baked for tonight from a plate on the table. "I take the lead. I'm ready to strike if there's anything coming down."

"So, you go up?" Will asked.

Eric nodded. "I do." He bit into the cookie, chewing as he listened.

Will leaned forward in his chair, very seriously as though he were about to announce something really important, and then he smiled malevolently. "You climb the stairs up to the next floor."

Everyone in the party groaned. It had been a fake out.

"All right Will," Eric said patiently. "What do we see at the top of the stairs?"

Will grinned. "When you get there, you see the room is filled with sticky webbing, covering piles of debris and not a few bodies of previous adventurers. You notice a box in the exact center of the room, nearly buried in it. Oh yeah, and there's this gigantic spider waiting for you. It's twice the size of the last one. Roll Initiative." No one had said anything about how he couldn't have planned both.

"What is it with you and spiders Will?" Hannah demanded with a laugh as she retrieved her d20 from the table.

Will just shrugged and grinned malevolently. "They're creepy."

Rafe rubbed one of his dice with anticipation. This was it. The boss fight...

———

October 8, 2033

"Mom, you need to get out of there," Rafe had been on the phone with his mother. The evacuations were set to begin in a week.

"I absolutely will not," she had said. *"This is our property; they have no lawful right to take it. Don't worry about this, Rafe. We're going to handle this like adults, if possible. If not ... well ... Dad says he'll be home soon and we'll figure something out."*

Rafe tried one last time. "I just don't think this is something you can fight."

There was silence on the other end of the line before she spoke again. *"You may not understand, and that's all right. But ... one day, there may come a time when you'll have to make a stand and be braver than you've ever been. Because fighting for what you've built, for your freedom and for what you love, or what's right, or all those things at once ... you won't protect them by standing down. I love you."*

———

December 14, 2037

The Reynolds Building complex had two main parts. There was the main building, which had inspired the Empire State Building in

New York, built in the 1920s; and then there was the shorter, boxier addition to the north of the plaza which had been added in the 1970s. Rafe's dad had known a man who had worked there who said there was a company joke about how the newer half was the box the older half came in.

While Casey parked the truck near the south entrance, Rafe was walking toward the southwest corner from the plaza between the two skyscrapers.

He was wearing a clean shirt and jeans for the first time in more than a week, as well as a new heavy coat that had also been in their supplies to reduce the risk of someone recognizing him. It also served to better blend in with the local atmosphere. His hood was pulled up, and he had a scarf wrapped to cover his mouth and nose. He was thankful for the cold for once; it gave him a perfectly legitimate explanation for hiding his face.

An armored SPKF patrol car rolled by, and he resisted the urge to back into the shadows as he rounded the corner to the street on the south side of the building. It was dark now, and he shouldn't be noticed, but the best way to attract attention would be to act like he wasn't supposed to be there. And it wasn't that strange to see the SPKF at the Reynolds Building; across the street and a block southeast was the former Sheriff's Department, now the local SPKF precinct. If something were to happen at the Reynolds Building, it would almost be faster for them to run the distance rather than get in their cars.

Not nerve-wracking at all.

Thankfully the Reynolds Building had a fast elevator because in planning they had determined that trying to go down six flights of stairs with Neil in his current condition was not an option. They just needed to make certain no one sounded the alarm too soon.

That was why Rafe was here on his own. His job was to discreetly check the area for unusual activity or witnesses who might alert the authorities. Casey had said it was unlikely at this time of night, but numerous things might affect their departure plans: a security guard or an SPKF officer who got too suspicious, or even a stray civilian who might be familiar with older cars and could spot one being manually driven.

His hand closed around the grip of the illegal handgun concealed in his coat pocket, though his finger stayed off the trigger; his parents had made certain he'd memorized the three rules of gun safety as a kid, but this was the first time it really dawned on him that he might kill someone. He'd been carrying that shotgun for miles, he'd shot that dog, and he thought he'd been prepared to use it on another human, but this was different. This wasn't shooting while running away. This was attacking someone else.

To rescue someone else, he corrected himself. *It's still defending myself and those I care about.* Even so, he tried not to shiver. The three rules were: don't assume a gun is unloaded, don't point it at anything you don't want to shoot, and keep your finger off the trigger unless you're ready to use it. There was also an unofficial fourth rule, though; the one his parents didn't teach him until he was older: *never shoot to wound.* In real life, arms and legs were moving much faster than the torso they were connected to, and so you *always* aimed for center mass. Trying to shoot someone in the knee only worked in bad movies.

Even if he didn't kill someone, the people guarding Neil were no doubt armed, and with much better training. Before, this had just been a chase to keep from disappearing. Now, the odds seemed good that Rafe wouldn't make it out of this building alive.

Well, Rafe, he said to himself, looking up at the Reynolds Building, *now's your chance to find out if you're up to trying this in real life. The question is, did we plan this better than most tabletop parties?*

He let go of the weapon, almost laughing. He hoped at the very least that they had done a lot better than that.

"Rafe?"

He jumped, then looked behind him to see that Casey had joined him. She had also changed into a black winter coat and different street clothes to better blend in with their surroundings, but she was *far* sneakier than he had thought. He took a moment for his heart to stop trying to run to San Francisco and back. ". . . Yeah?"

"I'm ready." She scanned the area, but obviously sensed his mood. "You okay?"

He slowly exhaled, his breath visible as it streamed through his scarf; he tried to expel his nerves along with it, but he wasn't sure how one was *supposed* to prepare for this sort of thing. He supposed Casey might know, but he was just a gamer. "I'll be fine. Let's go."

They were walking towards the South entrance to the building when, to his surprise, a man stepped out of the door to a vacant store front on the ground level, and ducked behind Rafe, pressing the muzzle of a handgun into the small of his back. "I knew you'd be here Turner."

Rafe froze and then his brain worked furiously as he tried to figure out what to do next before pretending to feign ignorance. "Who. . .?"

Casey looked like she might be about to draw her weapon but the man shook his head. "Don't even think about it. Keep your hands where I can see them."

She raised her hands and he quickly reached over to check her jacket pockets, retrieving her pistol and pocketing it, before returning to covering Rafe. "Now, get in there." He gestured that she walk into the empty storefront he'd just left.

She considered for a moment before walking resolutely to the door, staying in his line of sight. Once she was safely inside, he also quickly checked Rafe's jacket pockets, before pushing him to the door as well.

Divested of his weapon, Rafe walked towards the darkened storefront and through the door, trying not to pause and let his eyes adjust as the other man flipped a switch, illuminating the place with a series of sconces. Perhaps there had been a café or a small boutique here at one time. Now the windows seemed to have been covered with white privacy curtains and apart from a few small pieces of furniture, like a folding table near the front, the room seemed to be empty. Someone had left a standing mirror in the back corner, and in it, Rafe recognized the man behind him as the SPKF officer from the coffee shop, grey eyes cold and focused as he held the pistol against Rafe's back with a grizzled hand. A cold breeze blew through the man's thinning dark hair as he shut the door behind them, blocking off their path of escape, and then he pushed Rafe forward so he was in the center of the nearly empty room, next to Casey.

Rafe glanced at her to see what she was going to do. She shook her head, and the message was clear. Unless they wanted to run the risk of getting shot, there wasn't anything they could immediately do.

"Keep your shirt on, cowboy," she whispered. "It's not over yet."

It was an act of will to not hyperventilate. Rafe had not come all this way just to be stopped now, but this was definitely not good.

———

It was around dinner time and Hannah had brought Neil up to a door on one of the highest floors above the hotel. Apart from being allowed to walk around for a brief period under Hannah's supervision, he hadn't been allowed to leave the hotel room until Mrs. Lord had called the room a few minutes ago. Hannah knocked, and after a moment, Mrs. Lord pulled the door open. "Thank you for bringing Neil, Sergeant."

"It was no trouble, Mrs. Lord," she said with a smile.

Well, we're here, Neil thought. *What does she want now?*

The woman returned Hannah's smile with one of her own that was probably intended to look welcoming but to Neil seemed smug more than anything else. "Please, you may call me Eunice, if you like." She beckoned for them to enter the apartment. "Come on in Neil, no sense lingering out in the hall."

Hannah moved out of the way so Neil could enter ahead of her. It was really the last thing he would prefer to do, but running away wasn't an option. With a small sigh, he leaned forward on his crutches and swung himself inside.

What he found was an immaculate living room in white. The white couch against the near wall was upholstered, but visually it was all planes and hard angles over top of a stark rug with some geometric pattern across it. The two chairs on either side seemed similarly angular in their upholstery; the legs on all three pieces were steel, glittering nakedly on top of the rug. The dining area sat a short distance away. The surface of the table and the seats of the chairs were transparent (hopefully clear plastic, as Neil assumed glass would be an accident waiting to happen), with steel legs similar to the living room set. A few paintings hung on the walls between the windows, illuminated by the city lights outside, and punctuated by the view of one of the newer skyscrapers nearby. The pictures hung ramrod straight, despite the chaotic squiggles on the canvas. He wouldn't have been able to tell, had any of them been lying on the floor, which end was supposed to be the top, or if they were supposed to mean anything other than streaks of color.

What kind of place is this? he wondered.

Swinging himself farther into the room, he saw the man he'd met at the hotel room working in the kitchen. Mr. Lord was listening to some tune that had just been released in the last year on the radio while he was slicing vegetables on a cutting board. Apparently it was something about the singer hangin' with her girlfriends. That seemed to be the only idea in the song, as it kept being repeated over and over. Was it really normal for a man this guy's age to listen to music he'd hear some of the girls singing in his class back in Greensboro?

It was kind of annoying after hearing the first two stanzas, but Neil's gaze was more attracted by the lurid neon pink apron the man was wearing. He supposed if Mr. Lord liked it, it didn't do any harm, but he wouldn't be caught dead wearing something like that. He tried not to grimace, but it almost hurt to look at it. As he watched the man with a morbid fascination, Mrs. Lord and Hannah followed him into the room.

Mrs. Lord interrupted his thoughts with a hand on his shoulder. "Please, Sergeant, find him a seat."

Hannah pulled out a chair at the table and gestured that Neil sit. Neil swung himself over and sat down if only so Mrs. Lord would let go of him, allowing Hannah to set his crutches against the wall behind him. Mrs. Lord took a place at the end of the table. "Now, isn't this much better?" the smug smile had returned to her face.

Neil made a noncommittal noise and looked away.

She gave him a flat look and when she spoke, her tone was what one might use with a five-year-old. "Neil, it's impolite to grunt."

"So, what are we doing up here anyway?" Neil frowned at her as Hannah sat next to him. "Didn't you say our next talk wouldn't be so pleasant?"

"Did I?" Mrs. Lord simpered. "Right now, we're going to have dinner. And there are some matters we have to discuss regarding your future."

"What about it?" Neil blinked in surprise.

Mrs. Lord was looking at him as though he were a mouse caught in a trap. "First of all, you can breathe a sigh of relief. It's been confirmed to me that Turner left Pinnacle this morning, and the military has been notified to keep an eye out for him and the other runner he was seen leaving with." She looked satisfied with the news. "We'll have them in custody soon enough, so don't worry, you're safe."

Neil heard Hannah shift in her seat next to him. "Safe," he scoffed.

Mrs. Lord was still smiling, but somehow the temperature in the room seemed to have dropped a few degrees. "*Quite* safe. After all, both Sergeant Gruben here and Sergeant Everett have authorized firearms, and the SPKF precinct is right down the street from us, you know."

Neil stared through the clear table at the rug below his feet. So Rafe really was gone then. He swallowed hard, trying to stay composed. It needed to happen, right? The last thing he wanted was to see his friend die in front of him because he tried to rescue him. But the abandonment didn't make him feel any better. Now here he was, alone.

Mr. Lord walked in and laid a salad bowl in front of his wife. "It's ready," he said. "I'll have the tuna out in just a second."

"Thank you, Trent." Mrs. Lord directed her smile up at her husband before the man walked back to the kitchen. She turned her attention to Neil as she unfolded her napkin and placed it in her lap. "You're in for a treat! My husband is an excellent cook, especially when it comes to wild-caught tuna. And we have a lovely dark chocolate cake for dessert." Neil was surprised. He wasn't an expert on food prices, but he remembered well how his mother used to complain that it was nearly impossible to find a good price on tilapia raised on a farm, much less salmon, or tuna, once the Environmental Defense Force had tightened regulations on fishing. And a cake? With the sugar taxes as they were? That was nearly unthinkable.

Mr. Lord beamed under his wife's praise as he set the fish down in the middle of the table, taking off the apron and hanging it on a hook by the kitchen. "I do my best," he mumbled.

"So, do you like to fish?" Hannah asked, trying to make conversation.

"I've never gotten a license, but I would like to try someday," the man mumbled. It seemed to Neil that mumbling was all he did.

"Perhaps," Mrs. Lord said, her voice a little stiff. "But it's such a brutal sport, and he has so little time. He runs a state winery, you see, and we have to make our quotas."

"It's true, I am pretty busy most of the time," her husband agreed quickly. "Who would like some dinner?"

"It looks good!" Hannah reached for the salad tongs.

"It does indeed," Mrs. Lord selected a serving spatula to pick up one of the pieces of fish. "Well Neil, as I said, we do need to discuss how this is going to go."

"What do you mean?" Neil asked suspiciously.

She gave him a small shake of her head as though pitying him for his denseness. "You can't expect us to keep you here forever. So this can go one of two ways."

She got up to retrieve a piece of paper from a nearby side table and slid it over by his plate as she sat back down. Neil began to read it and he felt a chill run down his spine. It was a pre-typed police statement, about how Howard and Jane Flynn, his mother and father, had pressured and threatened this person to say nothing about their abuses at their company during the trial. That Rafe had helped to cover up evidence for his parents and that Rafe had kidnapped him, dragged him injured through the woods, threatened to do things to this person that Neil could never imagine. The statement concluded by claiming that the writer only wanted to put it all behind him and get back to his life. At the end of the statement, there was a place for a signature, and it took Neil a moment, staring dumbly at it, to realize it was his signature that was supposed to be written there.

"But that's not what happened," he said quietly.

She shook her head at him. "According to whom? Turner? He abandoned you after all, and Howard and Jane Flynn? What does the view of a few racists matter when they had it coming to them? After all this is the general truth in cases like this. Who cares about the particulars? The only thing that should matter for you is whether you are going to cooperate."

Perhaps there was something to the argument. After all, who on this side of the front cared about the truth, and it certainly seemed the easier path, but. . . If Rafe had been here to defend himself, what would he have said? Neil looked over at Hannah. Surely, she'd have something to say about the things they said Rafe had done on this sheet of paper?

The thing that angered him the most, was his parents. They of course would never be able to defend themselves, and they certainly weren't alone, as much as the government and the media lied about it. Because of lies like these, how many others were no longer there to try and set the record straight?

When Neil did not respond, Eunice continued. "I would

encourage you to think hard on it while you are eating our food and enjoying our hospitality. How you are treated from here on out depends on your decision." The tone of her voice made the suggested outcome in that statement a certainty. "I'll have a pen over here, when you're ready to sign, and then we can put all this nasty business behind us. Regardless, we'll stop by the doctor tomorrow to see to your leg of course, but afterward, you will need to continue your education, so you'll be able to live in society. There's a state school on the edge of town that I think might do you some good --"

"You could just send me to my family," Neil cut in.

Her smile disappeared. "Don't be ridiculous. I've looked over your file and not one of them meets the requirements for being a suitable guardian, regardless of what it says in your parents' will."

"Why?" he demanded. "Because they wouldn't insist that I be a good little parrot and repeat whatever you want me to say?"

Mrs. Lord stiffened, narrowing her eyes. "It's because it's for your own good. Two of your aunts are on watch for dissident behavior and it's too risky giving custody to your grandfather when he is far too old to have been properly trained for the job. No, it's better for you to be among your peers and away from dangerous influences. Children only belong to their families *after* they belong to the community. If they fall down on the job, it's our responsibility to step in and repair the damage, and from what I see, there's quite a bit of repairing to do and a long way to go."

Neil saw that both Hannah and Mr. Lord were completely focused on their dinner. He was on his own. Fine, then. "Dangerous influences? Is that why you said my parents deserved to be murdered?"

"It was justice!" Mrs. Lord thundered, gripping her fork tightly in her hand. "They flaunted their white privilege and wealth as though they owned that company, when the real work was done on the backs of their minority employees. But did that make them humble? Oh no, they took a larger cut for themselves and forced their employees to work on an hourly basis and compete for positions based on so-called 'merits'. Of course, that was only a code word to allow them to continue their discriminatory practices. That's what prejudice is. The people had a right to voice their anger."

"Because of my parents' skin?" Neil growled. "I'm pretty sure I know who the racists are."

"Don't be stupid, boy!" she screeched. "Racism requires privilege and power, and your family has both! You should know the oppressed don't have the luxury of prejudice! Now check your privilege and eat your fish!"

It seemed he was getting angrier with her every word, and yet he couldn't find the words he wanted to say. Finally, he said, "I'm not hungry." He'd had nothing since the bagels Hannah had brought him that morning but his mood curdled his stomach so much it didn't matter. There didn't seem any further point to this, and to further illustrate his opinion of the situation, he reached for the paper, and tore it in half.

Eunice watched the paper shred and her eyes shone furiously for a moment before she exhaled and then her expression took on a cold, calculating look. "Very well then. I can see you're in serious need of discipline and must be taught respect, and I will make certain the superintendent knows this when I hand you over. Only a fool could be so unaware of the advantage he's had in life, and I will make sure you learn." She turned her attention to her husband. "Go ahead and take up his plate." As Trent quickly stood to do so, she glared at him again. "You'll have to sit and wait for us until we're finished. Sergeant Gruben still has to escort you back, and I intend to enjoy my meal in spite of your rudeness." She reached for a glass of wine.

"I didn't think it would taste that great anyway," Neil growled.

"Let it go." It was just above a whisper. but it was definitely Hannah.

Mrs. Lord glanced in her direction. "Did you have something to add, Sergeant?" She looked like she heard Hannah clearly but was unsure to whom the plea had been directed.

The younger woman straightened. "No, ma'am." She finally

looked up from her salad, and Neil noticed her bite her lip as she spotted the dangerous gleam in Mrs. Lord's eye. "Please don't take it the wrong way ... I'm not defending him. It's just..."

"Of course you're not defending him," Mr. Lord mumbled as he returned to his seat, giving Hannah an understanding smile. "Such dinnertime conversations are uncomfortable; and when someone has such unconscious biases, it's hard to be civil." He turned his attention to Neil. "Let's have no more arguing under our roof, young man. Once the sergeant has finished her meal and we've prepared a plate for Sergeant Everett, you'll go back to the hotel room. You'll have plenty of time to contemplate your need for education when we deliver you to the school tomorrow."

Mrs. Lord narrowed her eyes at her husband, but at last, she relaxed her grip on her fork. "You're right of course, dear. There will be plenty of time later."

Neil couldn't help but think that Mr. Lord seemed a lot more nervous than he had at the start of the evening.

———

"Put your hands behind your heads, and then turn around," the man commanded. Casey remained calm as she did as ordered, and Rafe did his best not to make any sudden moves as he lifted his own hands, turning slowly to face their captor. The man placed their two pistols on the folding table, well away from them before he looked at Rafe with a self-satisfied smirk. "Well, well. They didn't think you would be this stupid. But we both know better don't we." It wasn't a question, and as he spoke, the smirk became wider. "And we finally meet face to face, Turner. Do you know you've led me through the longest and most frustrating manhunt of my career? If you hadn't resorted to kidnapping, I might be able to respect that."

Rafe tried to keep his expression calm, even as his heart was racing a marathon. "I only kidnapped him in that little story you put out. In the real world, if I hadn't gotten him out of there, he would have been hanging in that tree next to his parents. Of course, if I'd just handed him over after the dust settled, you wouldn't have sent him to his family. He'd have been sent off to a state school and kept there until he was *glad* his parents were murdered. And I'd still be looking at assault and battery charges for attacking the people who tried to grab him."

"That's at the top of a long list of other charges at this point. It's the price you pay for contradicting the vox populi." The man shrugged. "But they had their say, so as someone responsible for carrying out their law, it's my job to clean up the mess." He gestured to a blank stretch of whitewashed concrete behind them. "Keep those hands up, walk over there, and put your hands on the wall. Now."

Rafe walked toward the wall, Casey following slowly behind him. "I guess that mess you're talking about includes the bodies they left behind," Rafe said bitterly to Church, placing his hands on the concrete in front of him. "And loose ends like us."

He felt a hand work its way around the pockets of his jeans, both front and back, patting him down for any other weapons before seeing the man do the same to Casey. "I wouldn't put it that way, boy," the man said. "It's just too bad you decided to be a hero." Rafe heard the click of handcuffs, and then his arms were pulled down one at a time, cold steel fastening around his wrists. "That's what got your mother ... well, that's not important. We've talked enough, I've got a job to do."

Rafe bristled, his green eyes glaring at the man over his shoulder, his fear temporarily replaced by pure loathing. "My mother was a better person than a lemming like you could ever hope to be!" he snarled.

The man shoved Rafe against the wall, then kicked his knees out from under him when he instinctively tried to brace himself. Pain exploded in Rafe's shoulder and head as he hit first the wall and then the floor. He could feel his ear burning from being scraped against the concrete.

"So I *was* right!" the man exclaimed in triumph, "For all that time you stayed quiet like a good citizen, you actually have some fire in you, mama's boy! The most dangerous kind too, the kind that burns hotter because you kept it quiet, stoking it all this time while you did everything you could to keep your head down." He leaned down, gun still pointed at Rafe's head. "I know perfectly well just what kind of woman Carol Turner is, and you're just like her. Hateful. Dangerous. Can't stand anyone who is the least bit different from you, and no respect at all for authority. She clipped me pretty good with her twelve gauge when we closed down Oak Ridge. In the end, though, it made no difference." He straightened, moving on to Casey. "And it won't here either. I knew what way the wind was blowing a long time ago. In the end, you're just two kids on the wrong side of history."

Casey snorted derisively and the man paused.

"Something funny?" he asked.

"Just your arrogance," she said over her shoulder.

The man scoffed. "Well, what do you know anyway?" He turned to give Rafe one more kick.

The gun lifted away, no longer aiming at either of them, as the man lifted his foot, and that was when Casey whirled around under his arm, knocking the weapon away with a sideswipe of her left hand as she brought her right up in a well-aimed strike to his nose.

She hadn't gotten the punch off perfectly enough to break it, but as he tried to recover, Rafe seized the moment, rolling onto his side and delivering some karmic justice with a good hard kick to the man's ankles, knocking his feet out from under him. The man toppled, dropping the gun as he attempted to land without injury. Casey picked up the weapon before he could retrieve it, aiming it at his head.

"Wrong side of history, huh?" Her face was dangerously calm. "What's history but a record of time? Time doesn't take sides, jackass. It just kills everything." She spared a glance at Rafe, though she kept the gun trained on the man. "You all right?"

"I'll live," Rafe groaned as he tried to sit up. His left shoulder still throbbed, as did the side of his skull. "Am I bleeding?"

"It looks like he scratched your ear up a little bit, but you'll be okay." She turned her attention to the man on the ground. "So, who are you...? An SPKF Inspector?" she commented, reading his name badge as she leaned over him, "Well, Inspector ... Church? You're gonna give Rafe the keys to those cuffs now. Otherwise, something drastic is going to happen here, and I don't think either of us wants that."

Church reached into his pocket and tossed Rafe a small key ring. After a few minor gymnastics to pull his cuffed wrists under his backside and then around his legs, he tested the keys until he found the one to his cuffs, finally unclasping them. Rubbing his wrists, he looked up at Casey. "Thanks."

"Any time," She offered a hand to help him up, keeping the gun trained on their would-be captor. "Nice work kicking him over. That made my job a lot easier." She considered for a moment and then turned her full attention back to Church, "Now what to do with you. . . ? Seems to me turnabout's fair play, so let's see how you like it with your hands against the wall." Church slowly pulled himself to his feet and limped to the wall to obey, as Casey issued more orders. "Rafe, I need you to pat him down, take any other weapons or electronics. And Church, don't even think of trying any funny business, got it?"

Church did not respond, and Rafe carefully checked his pockets, producing a cell phone, which she promptly directed him to destroy. Task completed, Rafe walked over to where Casey stood, while Casey looked over at Church.

"What now?" Rafe asked. "Do you think he called in backup?"

Casey frowned. "Here's the thing," she said. "An SPKF officer wouldn't generally pull an ambush like this without his thugs to back him up." She looked over at Church. "You decided to pull this stunt on your own, didn't you."

"And why should I tell you if I did?" Church said.

"If you had backup, they'd already be here, so that can only tell me nobody's coming," Casey said with a smirk of her own. "As long as we can keep you nice and quiet, we can still get back on schedule." She glanced around the room for a moment and then said

"There's a bathroom to the rear. Walk back there. Rafe, you're going to give him the handcuffs, and in case you get any ideas, Church, I can hit a target from across this room. If you move an inch in any direction I don't like, you will become a target. Get the point?"

Rafe retrieved the cuffs and tossed them to Church. Once Casey had directed the officer into the bathroom, she spoke again. "Now, put one cuff around your wrist, and lock the other one around the railing by the toilet paper."

The man narrowed his eyes at them as he secured himself to the metal rail. "You won't get away with this. You have to know that. And you definitely won't get the boy back."

Casey shrugged as she reached for the door. "And how would you know that's what we're up to? Maybe we just decided to plant a bomb or something. That's a sufficiently terroristic thing to do, isn't it? There's a dozen soft targets around here."

Church scoffed. "Not if you've got Carol Turner's son with you."

"How would you know anything about her?" Rafe growled.

"We don't have time for this..." Casey hissed.

Church chuckled derisively. "The way any man knows a woman who shot him in the line of duty. I got sent out to try and convince her to leave. She listened as I told her what to expect. She set me down at her kitchen table, offered me some sweet tea and then told me under no uncertain terms that she wasn't going. The day we came to move everyone out, she didn't bat an eye when she fired off a warning shot, and then the second one hit me. She didn't budge until they dragged her out of that house. My wife nearly lost her husband that day. With a mother like that, I wouldn't be the least bit surprised to find you had the same tendency to stay underfoot and in the way."

Rafe glared at him. "In the way, huh? That day, you took everything from her, just because you put her in your way. I'm sure your wife loves you, but to me, you're just a thug."

"Rafe, I'm sure you find this interesting, but we have to go!" Casey snapped.

"I know," Rafe said.

"Remember," Casey returned her full attention to Church. "Not one twitch."

"Don't worry about that, Burke. It won't be long before the precinct is on to you." Church said with a smirk. "So, you can both forget about Flynn right now."

Casey grinned back at him wickedly as she beckoned for Rafe to start heading back towards the front of the shop. "If we weren't already gambling with our lives, I'd lay down money that you're wrong," With that, she slammed the bathroom door shut.

"Do you think we're still okay?" Rafe asked as he retrieved their weapons from the table.

Casey considered for half a second before tossing Church's pistol into a trash can near the door. They couldn't take it with them. SPKF issued weapons carried transmitters so they could be found if they were separated from the officer carrying them. There was no sign of law enforcement yet, and everything still seemed quiet near the truck as they exited the storefront. "I think we can still do this," she decided at last, turning her attention back to the south entrance of the Reynolds Building. "You good?"

Rafe closed his hand around the pistol now restored inside his jacket pocket. "I think so."

The two of them headed toward the double doors at the south entrance of the skyscraper. Casey pulled out the hotel keycard Juno had given them and put it into the slot by the door. It clicked; the card was still good, then. Rafe waited for Casey to open the door, and then he followed in after her. They went down a hallway and up a short set of stairs, and then they were in the rear of the elevator lobby. A security guard walked by, but as Casey was still holding the keycard quite visibly in her hand, he didn't give them a second look.

Casey hit the call button for an elevator, and one of them dinged open. As they walked in, Rafe hit the button for the sixth floor, and then pulled the scarf down to expose his whiskered face.

He'd be visible on camera, but if they were expecting him the scarf would do nothing, and if they weren't then it would be more suspicious to look like he was hiding his identity while inside. And one way or another, there was no concealing who they were tonight.

Casey had made Rafe memorize some simple gestures, and as the elevator doors opened she signaled *hold ready*; that is, be ready to draw but don't do it yet. Then she strode out ahead of him, her right hand in her coat pocket while she held the keycard prominently in her left, continuing to give the casual observer the cue that they were just here to go to their room. Rafe wrapped his hand around the pistol, but otherwise kept both hands in his pockets, under the pretense that he was just trying to keep his hands warm.

The hallways were decorated with art deco lamps and paneling, with room numbers emblazoned on stainless steel with faux-leather frames. It was all designed to reflect the opulent mid-20th century heyday of the cigarette company that had once owned the building. Even in today's economy, there were people staying in places like this; there just weren't as many places, and the people were usually government officials or union executives. Some of them were in the hall, too: an older man in a suit here, a woman with two children there. They were all headed for their own rooms for what, Rafe hoped, would be a night undisturbed by reports of violence.

Casey found the room they wanted and paused to look around. "I shouldn't be too surprised that they're relying on hotel security," she muttered to him, "but it's almost a little disappointing."

For Rafe's part, he would be perfectly happy not dealing with any more hiccups and he hoped that the incident with Church was the only one they would encounter tonight. He noticed her gripping the firearm she held in her pocket and aiming it at the door through her coat as she knocked with her left hand.

That was when Rafe heard a rhythmic metallic *click-click* coming from the opposite direction from where they had come. He glanced over and saw Neil swinging along on his aluminum crutches, but then pausing as he noticed Rafe.

And Hannah was next to him, carrying a plate of food, recognition slowly dawning on her face.

Oh no. Rafe had known it was possible he might encounter Hannah here, but he had really hoped she had stayed back in Pinnacle. The last thing he wanted was to have her here while he was doing this.

All three of them froze, looking at each other in surprise until the moment the hotel room door opened, and Casey pulled her gun to point it in the face of the black man in a uniform on the other side.

"Rafe?" Hannah broke the silence.

"Drop your weapons and keep your hands where I can see them!" Casey ordered. "Rafe, cover her!"

Rafe heard the *thump* of a sidearm hitting the carpeted floor from inside the hotel room. He only hesitated a little before he pulled the gun out of his pocket and pointed it at Hannah. The plate she was carrying tilted and moved in the direction of her holster. "Not another inch, Hannah," he said, his low voice barely carrying.

Casey exhaled impatiently. "Hannah, was it? When I said 'drop your weapons,' I meant you too. You are going to unstrap that holster and toss it down the hallway behind you. And Rafe, I don't care if you know her; if she doesn't do it, shoot her. Got it?"

"You heard her." Rafe took a step to the left, keeping his angle of fire away from where Neil was standing. He was fighting tooth and nail to keep his hands from shaking.

Hannah's face darkened in anger as she slowly worked her belt buckle. "'Don't be a monster', you said!" she spat. "Was *this* what you meant? The kind of monster that resorts to kidnapping children and holding SPKF officers at gunpoint?!"

Rafe winced. Well, no question she remembered their last conversation ... "Neil, you okay?"

"About as okay as I can be, I guess," Neil answered. He looked at Rafe, then Hannah, clearly not certain what to do.

Rafe turned his attention back to Hannah. "Last time we

talked, I didn't think I'd be rescuing someone from you, no," he said, "but I'm not leaving without my friend!"

"I-I know you don't want to hurt anyone Rafe." Her expression changed, looking sad more than anything else, but she still slid her holstered pistol off her belt. "You need to stop. You both need to put your guns down and surrender."

"No one has to hurt anyone," Neil pleaded, looking up at Hannah. "Just let us go. Or come with us."

"I can't do that." Hannah's blue eyes were still trained on Rafe. He could see she was trying not to cry.

"You're taking too long, Hannah." Casey didn't look at her, keeping her gun aimed at the other officer. "If you want this man to live, you'll drop your weapon and you'll keep quiet. And if you've seen what they got on me, you know I'm not bluffing."

Rafe felt his blood chill to match the outside weather, and silently hoped Hannah would hurry up. *This isn't going to be pretty regardless of what happens,* Casey had said before, when they were still planning this operation. *If it means I have to be the villain to succeed, I'll pay that price. You just concern yourself with the kid.*

Hannah looked from Neil to Rafe, and then to Casey as the holster and the weapon in it finally dropped to the ground and she kicked it across the floor.

"Now your phones," Casey ordered. "Get down on the floor and toss them to me."

The two officers both complied, getting on their stomachs and sliding their phones to Casey, who promptly stomped them to pieces. "You know you won't get away with this," the large black man said.

"Shut up," Casey growled. "I have no use for you if you're going to be difficult. Don't test me."

"Sorry, Hannah." Neil swung himself forward. Once he reached Rafe, he said "I really didn't think you'd follow us. You could have been caught!"

"After all we've been through, why wouldn't I?" Rafe tried to put a little bravado behind the sheepish reply. "I was a little worried you'd gotten tired of being out in the cold."

"Anything's better than that hag upstairs!" Neil retorted.

"Talk later!" Casey ordered. "Get to the elevator. I'm right behind you."

Rafe nodded and lowered his gun, keeping it pointed at the floor as he backed down the hall. Casey followed, as did the two SPKF officers once she told them to stand and follow them. The hotel room door clicked shut behind them as they made their way to the elevator bank. Their pace was set by Neil, but he was going as fast as he could, clearly eager to get away.

"I thought you were smarter than this, Rafe!" Hannah was still glaring at him, real tears streaking her cheeks. "That woman's a terrorist! She'll use you and then abandon you the moment it suits her! Don't go with her!"

"Because it's so much better for me to sit helpless in my home, waiting for the next riot?" Rafe felt anger flare up inside him as he stared her down, his green eyes blazing. "Or in a cell because I finally grew a spine? Bullshit!" He wasn't sure if it was his imagination that she cringed away from him.

They reached the elevators and Rafe slammed his free hand against the call button. It immediately dinged, and the same elevator they had taken before opened for them. Neil swung inside, followed by his two rescuers. The SPKF officers tried to follow, but Casey shook her head and Rafe lifted his pistol again to point it right at Hannah.

"Don't try to follow me, Hannah," he warned as the elevator doors closed. "I'm just as afraid as you are of what I might do!"

The ride down to the ground level was short but felt far too long to Rafe. The SPKF would undoubtedly be on their way soon, the moment Hannah and her partner were able to raise the alarm. That had been the reason for smashing their cell phones and leaving them by the elevator bank, away from their pistols. They would have to choose between finding a civilian with a phone, finding one of the rare remaining landlines that hotels still maintained, or running back for their weapons before coming down after the fugitives. Any of those options would buy them a few minutes.

As soon as the elevator dinged open, the three of them turned back down the hall and hurried toward the south exit. Upon reaching it, Casey looked out the door first. They could hear sirens but they had been faster. Rafe could see their getaway vehicle and no one seemed to have reached this side-street yet. "All right," Casey said, "You get him in the truck. I'll take care of the rest. Ready?"

He nodded, though he could see some movement near the end of the street.

"Hey you!" He caught a glimpse of the security guard at the far end of the hall they'd just come through, but it was too late.

"Go!" Casey ordered. The doors erupted open, and he could hear the distant cries of someone shouting for them to stop, but by then he was at the door to the truck. He heard the *soft* beep of a small device from Casey, and a moment later something exploded near the SPKF precinct. Casey had rigged a firebomb – more smoke and flames than a real danger – in a driverless car and directed it to park in the SPKF lot. The precinct had either just received or was about to receive word of their little escapade, but either way the explosion would distract them for a few precious minutes.

He pulled the door open, and nearly threw Neil into the back. The front passenger seat had been taken out to avoid having to mess with it, leaving only the bench seat in the extended cab. The truck bed was covered in a camper top that was missing its back window. Once Neil was secure in the cab, Rafe hurried to the tailgate and climbed in.

Casey backed toward the truck, her gun trained on the security guard who had followed them out and was already regretting it. "Strap in," she ordered.

Rafe was already putting on the harness they'd rigged to keep him from bouncing around. He knelt on the large foam pad covering the truck bed, secured the tailgate, and pulled out the AR-15. He took over covering the guard as Casey got in, put on a bulky pair of goggles, and cranked the ignition.

"Get ready!" Casey yelled through the open window at the back of the cab. It was as much for Neil as for Rafe; Rafe at least knew the plan. She hit the accelerator, flipping a switch on the dash with one hand to activate a jammer that would disable remote kill signals. "This is where it gets rough!"

He saw the silhouette of two figures at the corner of the street leading toward the SPKF station as she drove the truck along the one-way street. He heard two gunshots, but neither seemed to have hit the vehicle.

Rafe pulled the rifle to his shoulder, ready to use it, even as waves of dread and adrenaline washed over him. This would be the hardest part. Being unnoticed was no longer possible.

The weird thing was, he wasn't freaking out. He was aware of the intense fear tying his stomach in knots, but he was focused. There was no time for joking around, panicking, or debating for twenty minutes about what their strategy would be. There was just him, the moment he was living, and the job he had to do. It was a terrifyingly different world from anything Will had ever conceived, or that Rafe ever thought he'd enter and he'd tumbled down this rabbit hole head first.

Later.

If he lived through this, he would deal with fears, might-have-beens, and mental scars later.

He felt the truck accelerate as Casey increased their speed, scanning the street behind them for the first SPKF cars to come barreling around a corner after them, and tried to ignore his white-knuckled grip on his rifle.

CHAPTER 13

RABBIT RUN

March 26, 2033

"I cast a 'Cure Moderate' on the Fighter." Rafe had rolled a couple of d8's, adding the modifiers in his head and then added "Kade gets 17 hit points back."

"Much obliged," Eric updated his character sheet with a pencil.

"Who's next...?" Will checked the initiative list on his laptop. "Spider-zilla. Okay, so what do I want him to do...?" he consulted the paper on his desk that listed the monster's abilities for a moment before he looked up decisively. "That last fireball from Malchior didn't feel too good so the giant spider's going to bite you. Touch attack of ... 21."

"That hits," Allen responded, looking worried. "So what's the damage?"

"You take..." Will rolled a couple more dice. "Ouch, 14 hit points and 2 Strength."

"Ouch indeed." Allen agreed as he adjusted the totals on his own character sheet. "Any more Strength loss, and I won't be able to carry my own equipment."

"Spider-zilla is going to use his second bite on Kade." Will rolled his d20 again. "Not quite as good. 12."

"Miss." Eric sounded more than a little relieved.

Will glanced at his screen again. "Next on the initiative, Hannah, you're up!"

Hannah looked over the battle map and moved her character miniature behind the model for the spider. "I tumble under him." She picked up her d20 and rolled. "19."

"You make the tumble and take no attacks of opportunity," Will confirmed.

"All right, I now have flanking with Eric, so..." She looked up with a triumphant smile on her face. "Sneak attack!" She rolled again. "For 22."

"It hits," Will said.

Hannah let out a sigh of relief and rolled several d6's along with her d4. "17 damage."

Will corrected the stats on his sheet. "It's really looking hurt." He then gestured to the next player. "Eric."

Eric looked up from his sheet. "I swing my axe, and..." he rolled his d20. "23."

"It hits,"

Eric rolled his damage. "32."

Will looked around at the others dramatically before reaching over to the battle map and knocking the giant spider model onto its side. "It drops."

Everyone else in the room cheered and, after a few moments of celebrating, Rafe turned his attention to the next item of interest. "So what's the status of the chest in the center of the room?"

"It's intact," Will began searching for a document on his computer as he continued. "You can try to open it."

"I check for traps," Hannah said immediately.

"All right, search check," Will found what he was looking for and began typing something while he waited for the results.

Hannah's d20 rolled across the table. "32."

Will finished what he was doing and looked up at them. "You don't find any. The chest is locked, though."

"Well, you know what I'm doing about that," Hannah was already rolling a second check to open the lock. "18."

"It comes unlocked," Will said, "And inside the chest, you find an intricately embroidered veil made of the finest silk with gold threads woven throughout."

"I take it," Hannah looked around as she noticed the dead silence in the room.

Rafe could see everyone regarding Will with the same suspicion and anticipation that was probably written on his own face as their GM smiled mysteriously. "Okay. As you do, you hear a rumbling from the depths of the tower. Also, Eric, roll Knowledge: Architecture."

Eric rolled his d20. "18."

Will's grey eyes twinkled malevolently behind his glasses as he spoke. "This room is now structurally unsound."

Allen groaned and buried his face in the palm of his hand. "Forgot to use Detect Magic to check for enchantments..."

"Sounds like our cue to leave then," Eric picked up his character sheet nervously, as he made sure his d20 was nearby.

"Might be," Allen said dryly, straightening his posture and looking over the map again, "I think it's time to 'port out of here."

"If you recall, this place is not nice to wizards who teleport, what with, you know, that whole 'shunting them into walls' thing?" Will commented, steepling his fingertips as he leaned back in his chair.

"Whoops," Allen grinned sheepishly, "Okay. Plan B. We go with our old standby of running away screaming."

"All righty then," Will cracked his knuckles, and Rafe couldn't help but remember the shirt he'd seen their GM wearing the other week with the caption on the front about how it was indeed the GM's job to try to kill the party. "Get ready for this. You'll be making some Reflex saves on the way down."

———

December 14, 2037

Casey turned the truck down Liberty Street and gunned it towards the exit ramp to Highway 421. Rafe saw two SPKF cars turn onto the street behind him. One of the benefits of their location was its proximity to that highway. It was almost a straight shot to the western checkpoint out of Winston-Salem and they would be there in minutes.

Rafe felt the December wind stinging his exposed face through the opened window at the back of the truck bed. Between it and the rumbling wheels below him he could hear nothing except the sirens outside. He saw the flashing lights behind them and gripped a hand-hold that had been installed under the roof as Casey swerved onto the highway ramp and up onto the bridge.

The ramp was too good an opportunity to waste. Rafe reached into the bag lashed to the truck bed and pulled out a stun grenade. He pulled the pin and lobbed it out the back window, ducking his head to protect his eyes. The flashbang wasn't particularly loud from his perspective, being designed for close quarters, but the light was the main point. There was a loud *bang* audible over the truck's engine, and then Rafe heard the clear screech of metal on concrete as one of the SPKF cars behind them swerved and scraped a barrier. Lifting his head again, he saw that the cars chasing them were still there, but they'd backed off a little. He let out a breath he hadn't realized he'd been holding; maybe this wouldn't be so bad after all.

Then they reached the top of the hill, and he learned why Casey's alias had been 'Rabbit.'

The engine roared once more, and he clutched the handle above him even tighter as the truck rocketed forward. He heard Casey shouting something sounding suspiciously like a war cry as their vehicle screamed down the highway.

Just behind them he saw the two SPKF cars gaining speed as they made another attempt to get close. He lifted the rifle and held it as steady as he could, but each minor bump in the road was magnified at this speed, and he held his fire. They careened down the other side of the hill and under three bridges, one after another; after the third, the pavement smoothed out, and Rafe tried again.

His first shot went wild, and he tried to aim again, but was jolted by another bump. A fourth bridge covered them for a split second. Lining up the sight, he fired once again as the streetlights illuminated the inside of the truck bed once more and a tiny puff of debris blew off the pavement just shy of the lead SPKF car. He continued to fire; after all, as Casey had explained, the point was to threaten, not necessarily damage.

An SUV with flashing lights pulled onto the highway from an entrance ramp they had just passed, far closer than the other cars chasing them. Rafe reached for another flashbang, pulled the pin, counted to two, and threw it. He immediately ducked his head again, barely shielding his eyes before the grenade detonated. He was rewarded with the sound of squealing tires, and looked up to see the SUV go into a spin and clip a road barrier. The two original vehicles swerved around the accident, continuing the pursuit along the bridge they had just climbed.

Rafe was looking around for another target, but at that moment, Casey swerved. She was shouting something, but he couldn't hear her over the noise of the wind screaming around his ears. A moment later, he realized what she must have been trying to tell him. A spotlight illuminated them on the road, and he thought he could hear the rotors of a helicopter above them, but his position inside the truck drowned out even something that loud.

Shortly after that, a new car came hurtling out of the Stratford Road exit and tried to ram them, and Rafe's harness barely kept him from rolling around inside the covered truck bed as Casey evaded their new pursuer. He stole a glance behind him to see Neil, his attention fixed on the road in what seemed like a mixture of fascination and horror. The sign for Silas Creek Parkway flashed in their lights for an instant, and then it was behind them. Rafe could just barely see the speedometer from his position; the needle looked to be at max, and he knew from earlier that it topped out at 120 MPH.

Faster than he'd ever gone in a car before. Faster than he ever wanted to go again.

Casey swerved as they approached a large exit; Rafe realized it must be I-40, and Casey was taking the ramp as planned to stay on 421. He saw a few driverless civilian cars on the side of the road, pulled over by their emergency systems to clear obstacles for law enforcement. Just like they'd been counting on.

Behind them, the two original SPKF cars had been joined by the one that had tried to ram them and missed, and three *more* vehicles came out the I-40 entrance ramp to join them. That actually worked in the fugitives' favor, as they all tried to follow Casey up the 421 ramp and had to slow to avoid hitting each other. Casey had to slow a bit as well to navigate the curve, but once she was on open road again, she floored it.

Rafe took the opportunity to toss another flashbang and take a few potshots at the cars chasing them, as the ramp made them easy targets. He hoped the truck would hold together. It was an older model, and the vibrations were intense.

They blew past a couple of roads; he'd lost track until he spotted a sign for Jonestown Road and realized they were no longer in Winston-Salem proper. The helicopter was still on them, and they were now in the part of the compound that held the small city of Lewisville. Rafe fired a few more shots as another SUV almost clipped them on another ramp. He was about to toss another grenade when the cars giving chase all suddenly fell back in unison.

That meant they were almost there. This was what Rafe had been dreading the most. Flipping the safety on, he put his gun down on the floor next to the stun grenades and undid his harness. Not the best idea at the speeds they were going, but they hadn't had a chance to warn Neil about this part. He hurriedly pulled himself to the cab window and tapped his friend on the shoulder. Neil jumped, surprised, and looked back at Rafe.

"Cover your eyes!" Rafe shouted as loud as he could, pantomiming the action just in case, even as Casey pulled her safety

goggles down over her own eyes. *"And stay low! This is going to sting!"*

Neil looked worried, but nodded and shut his eyes, ducking in his seat. Rafe pulled himself back to the harness, reattaching it and shifting the straps to let him lie on the foam pad. He curled into as tight a ball as he could manage, instinctively covering his head even though that probably wouldn't do anything against what they were about to experience.

For several agonizing seconds, the spotlight from the helicopter continued to shine down on them, sending crazy shadows throughout the truck to accompany the wind that was only biting at him slightly less now that he was no longer upright. And then, just before the spotlight blinked one last time as they went under a bridge, he caught sight of several blue lasers shining through the rear window from the truck cab. Rafe immediately screwed his eyes shut, covering them with his hands for good measure. Apparently, Casey's goggles worked as advertised, because she didn't waver one bit as they hurtled closer. A speed bump rattled the vehicle so hard Rafe was half-afraid the truck would shatter. The harness felt like it barely kept him in place.

Then Casey slowed and started weaving. Rafe was briefly afraid the lasers had affected her, but soon realized she was zooming around the concrete barriers close to the checkpoint. Once, twice, three times he swung violently in his harness as she guided the truck through the last few hurdles that would get them out of the city. The truck scraped against something before it broke free with a screech, and Casey picked up speed again. They were halfway through.

Rafe counted down the meters as he curled up tighter, cushioning his head with his arms to keep from cracking his skull. At two hundred meters the ADS, the Active Denial System, would kick in.

He waited for several more agonizing seconds before another speed bump sent them airborne like hot grease in a skillet. The windows rattled around him, and he tried not to think what would happen if anything came unsecured. Then suddenly, though the vehicle had not slowed further, he felt warm. It was actually rather comfortable at first, and made him realize just how cold it was in the truck bed; but it soon escalated to searing hot. He gritted his teeth as the truck barreled farther into the checkpoint, and he resisted the urge to look out the windows while the number of lasers multiplied overhead.

Two shots fired in the distance as the truck sped along beneath him, and he could have sworn he heard someone cry out in pain before hearing a gate smashing to pieces. He cracked an eye open just long enough to spot, through the windows above him, some of the debris go airborne. He stayed where he was, waiting to hit the last speed bump.

When was it?

Was it there yet?

Damn it, he felt like every inch of his skin was on fire!

The last speed bump hit the tires and as he protected his head one last time and the truck clattered frighteningly around him, the burning was starting to reach nearly unbearable levels. As predicted the truck began to slow and Rafe curled up tighter, clamping his mouth shut to prevent himself from screaming. He had been dimly aware of a small hiss in the background that was far more frightening than anything else about the whole experience, simply because Casey had alerted him beforehand that one hundred and thirty thousand volts had just been sent through their vehicle's undercarriage.

Their vehicle was now dead, killed by an overload. Once they came to a stop, all the SPKF had to do was leisurely drive up and surround them.

For two agonizing seconds, the deceleration continued and the truck swerved a hard left. He could feel that Casey was drifting to avoid the next line of barriers and it seemed like forever that they were floating free over the road ...

Until, at last. At long last, he heard it. Somehow, over the sensory overload of the sirens, the wind, the burning, and his own heavy breathing, he heard a small click just before the right rear wheel of the truck gently nudged another concrete barrier.

The engine roared back to life, revived by the special circuit breaker the Resistance had installed, allowing it to regain power after the PEVS had shorted out the battery.

Half a second later, the spotlight disappeared again as Casey sped up, pulling onto the grass median between the lanes. The poor helicopter pilot probably didn't know what to make of it, as the PEVS had never failed before. The burning finally stopped as she guided the truck out of the range of the ADS and back onto westbound 421. As the chopper's spotlight tried to find them again, she floored the accelerator one last time, and their truck sped off into the darkness.

———

The SPKF cars that had made it through the checkpoint, continued to pursue them for about fifteen minutes before breaking off, presumably because they expected the soldiers at the next compound to take over. That was Yadkinville, but Casey turned the vehicle off the highway and down a smaller road in order to try going around so they could avoid getting too close. She only reduced her speed enough to avoid running off the road. The helicopter broke off entirely not long before that point because beyond here, Casey had told Rafe earlier, enterprising Minutemen had been known to shoot helicopters from the sky with drones if they got too close to contested territory. That didn't mean they wouldn't encounter any more trouble. Wilkesboro lay ahead, and there was an installation there where the army were carrying out operations to attempt further extension of control into the mountains.

When she was certain they were no longer being followed, Casey pulled over to the side of the road. "Is everyone okay?" she called behind her.

"I think so!" Rafe called up from the truck bed. He had sat up once they were past the checkpoint in case he needed to run interference again. But now, he undid the harness and stuck his head into the cab through the window, trying to ignore the slight quiver in his muscles from operating under far too much adrenaline. He never. Ever. Wanted to do that again. "Neil?"

"I'm okay." Neil sounded equally in awe of the speeds they'd just experienced.

"Good..." Casey said. Rafe realized she was breathing heavily, and he felt a chill that had nothing to do with the wind blowing in through the back window. "Because ... I'm going to need a little first aid."

Rafe only hesitated a moment. "Neil, hand me the green backpack. Casey, where?"

"Left side." Her face was a mask of both pain and concentration.

Neil passed Rafe the bag containing their first-aid supplies, and Rafe crawled back out the tailgate to hurry around to the driver side door. He pulled the door open, and Casey let out a small moan. If she weren't belted in, she might have fallen out. But once she had taken a moment to catch her breath, she lifted her right hand to flip on the interior lights. Unfortunately, that just meant her entire left side was cast into even deeper shadow.

Rafe pulled a flashlight out of the backpack and quickly turned it on to survey the damage, hissing through his teeth at the sight before him. Two neat holes poked through Casey's coat right next to each other, surrounded by a ring of blood, still wet on her sleeve. It didn't look like she was injured anywhere else, but it wasn't a small thing either.

She looked up at him. "Good thing I had my tetanus shot, isn't it?" she tried to force her grimace into a grin.

"That's the first thing you think of?" Rafe demanded.

"That ... and that tetanus shots are way better than lead." She looked over her shoulder at the damage, wincing from the pain as she used her good hand to apply pressure to the wound. "I think I must have been really lucky 'cause it seems like it went clean through. I'm pretty sure I'd be bleeding a lot more than this if it had hit a vein or artery."

Marveling at her calm in this situation, he took a deep breath, mentally preparing himself, and then pulled the first aid kit out of his backpack. "Okay, so what do we do?"

"I was able to apply a little pressure by shoving my arm up against the door. So, I think that slowed it down a little..." Casey indicated a smear of blood that he now noticed on the driver's side window. It wasn't what he had asked, but she seemed to still be trying to center herself, so he focused on the task at hand.

He also noticed a hole where another bullet had penetrated through the windshield and several glass fragments on the dashboard. "Did any of the glass get you?"

"I don't think so," Casey said. "Neil, you didn't take any either, did you?"

"I'm fine," Neil said from behind the seat.

She pursed her lips, thinking, before releasing her arm and quickly unzipping her coat with her good hand. "I need you to help me with this."

"Okay." Neil crawled forward in the truck cab and took hold of the right arm of her coat.

Once Casey had pulled her right arm out of her coat sleeve, Rafe helped her pull the coat the rest of the way off, doing his best to be gentle. She still gritted her teeth when they pulled her left arm free. "Now," she said, turning her attention to Rafe, "Give me the scissors, hold up my arm and press a bandage to the wound as tightly as you can," she said, still a little breathlessly, once Rafe had handed her coat to Neil to stow in the back seat.

Rafe nodded. "Neil, could you come out here and hold the flashlight?"

"All right." Getting out of the truck cab was obviously awkward for Neil, but he did it without complaint, and soon he had hobbled around the side of the truck on one crutch to take the flashlight and hold it steady while they worked.

With the light secure, Rafe followed Casey's direction, and she proceeded to cut off the arm of the sweater she was wearing. She drew a breath every time she moved but, otherwise, didn't cry out. Rafe only let go enough so they could pull the fabric from around her exposed arm. She instructed him to tie the sleeve just below her shoulder as a tourniquet, just in case the bleeding got any worse, then walked him through the process of making a pressure bandage.

Once the wound was dressed, she leaned back in the driver's seat and let out a breath, warming herself under a blanket Neil had pulled out of her bag. They had just finished putting together a sling to counter the potential damage walking might do to the injury. Unfortunately, their supply of medicines was not much improved from what Neil had before. They did have a fresh bottle of painkillers of which she had availed herself. At least this one was not out of date. "Glad that's over," she said softly.

At that point, Neil turned off the flashlight and hobbled back to the passenger side so he could carefully climb to the bench seat. "Now what?" He asked.

"Now ... I'm going to join you in the back and Rafe's going to drive this truck to the drop off point." With effort, Casey pulled herself out of the driver's seat while Rafe wiped her blood from the driver's side door and took her place behind the wheel.

"By the way," she said to Neil as Rafe pulled the door shut and turned the key in the ignition, "Hi, I'm Casey."

"Nice to meet you ... again," Neil replied. "Rabbit, right?"

"Yeah." Rafe could hear tiredness in her voice as she spoke. "Anyway ... I'm going to try and get a little rest now. Do you mind if I use your lap as a pillow? I would like to keep my arm elevated."

"Go ahead," Neil said, though before the lights went down, Rafe could have sworn he saw the kid's face go a little red.

"By any chance, have you been through this before?" Rafe asked as he eased the truck back out onto the narrow road.

"Running a checkpoint?" Casey grunted as Rafe hit a bump. "Once before now. Had to evac some heavy equipment without getting ID'd. That was before I joined the Guard, and the check-point wasn't nearly as heavily guarded. Taking a bullet? Not personally, but I had this friend once. Dragged himself into our hideout, bleeding from his thigh. They got him pretty bad while he was looking for a runner who was supposed to be in the area ... He didn't make it ... but while they were trying to stop the bleeding, he said it was no worse than a bee sting ... well, he was a damn liar is what he was..."

"Speak for yourself," Rafe said, and then added with a small chuckle, "Lead foot, my ass. You know your way around a car like I know a Super Nintendo, or my name is Mario."

Casey laughed weakly. "You got me." She was quiet for a moment, and when she spoke again her tone had lost some of its usual edge and defensiveness. "My Dad used to race stock cars. Once I came along, he left the races and opened his own auto shop. He'd let me pretend to drive while sitting in his lap behind the wheel. Taught me everything he knew as soon as I was old enough, even the old tricks he used off-roading with his friends."

"Might have guessed," Rafe carefully guided the car along the road.

"I never drove a race, but every now and then, we'd put his old car through its paces. And we'd talk about it, dreaming of the pit crew we'd put together to make it happen. But it became illegal and the tracks were closed. And then driving your own car got too expensive for regular folks."

"And your father lost his shop," Rafe guessed, hearing the bitterness return to her voice.

"That was the last straw for us," Casey confirmed. "They destroyed my Dad's business, and then they even came and took his stock car, even though he couldn't afford to drive it. They said it was dirty and unsafe. But really, they just couldn't leave a symbol like that lying around where they couldn't tell us what it meant. A car you can control ... that's freedom, you know? A car designed to go fast, that was the embodiment of breaking the rules they were imposing? Of taking control of your own life, and shaping it the way you think it should be shaped?"

"I never thought of it that way," Neil said. "It makes sense, though. There's no pre-set destination. You can get on a different road whenever you want."

"Exactly," Casey agreed. "Life is not meant to be pre-programmed like some computer. It's messy, like a lump of clay, but it's there for you to take in the palm of your hand, as soon as you decide to get in the driver's seat. You might tear it, you might break it, you might crash it, but at least it was done *by* you, and not *to* you. My dad knew that, and he knew exactly what they were doing, and because he wouldn't accept the life they set for him, they took everything from him, and then eventually took him, too. He's been in prison for ... a while."

"Maybe they didn't take everything, though," Neil said thoughtfully.

"Why do you say that?" Casey sounded surprised.

"Because he taught you to drive like him," Neil said. "So, in a way, he got us all out. In a car you could control."

Casey chuckled softly and then winced. "Yeah. He'd love that. If he gets TV wherever he is, I hope we made the news. Just so he can see their faces..." She trailed off after that, but the feeling in the truck cab seemed a little warmer than it had a second ago.

Rafe stayed silent as he drove along the empty road, keeping his focus on what lay ahead and staying alert for any sign that they weren't alone. *Just a little longer. We're not there yet, but we're getting there.*

———

With Neil navigating, Rafe drove west. Mostly west, anyway. The need to keep their headlights off meant Rafe kept missing turns; and the old map didn't tell them where the back roads were washed out or blocked by fallen trees. Once, they had no choice but to cross 421 to go north, and the tension as they exposed themselves was almost unbearable.

Despite years without maintenance, the back roads were still drivable. The streetlamps had long been left behind, but compared to how their night had begun, Rafe found the darkness almost comfortable. He was surprised how easy it was to drive even with the lack of illumination. He wasn't nearly as good a driver as Casey, and it had been years since a civilian driver's license had become useless. Even if he might not remember all the traffic laws, driving a car was apparently like riding a bike. His speed was no doubt unsafe if they happened to meet anyone else taking the roads in the dark, but the odds of that were a lot lower than getting caught by the SPKF if they lingered. It was almost like an old documentary he'd once seen on bootleggers during prohibition, driving fast at night through wooded country to avoid the police.

Soon enough, Neil announced that the road Rafe just turned onto should take them around Wilkesboro. When they hit a T-intersection, Rafe turned the truck to the left, heading west. About twenty minutes later, he stopped in front of a drive leading up to a couple of buildings looming out of the shadows, and after confirming the address by shining a flashlight at the mailbox, pulled in and brought the vehicle to a halt in front of an old garage. Rafe hopped out, walked to the door and lifted it open, before returning to the truck and easing it inside. He shivered. The night air was bitter cold, and he was even more aware of it after spending much of the last day with access to heaters. He blew warm air into his gloved hands and was once again grateful, that among the supplies they had received, there had been a couple of knit caps to wear under their hoods.

Once he'd turned off the truck, he got back out and walked around the vehicle, being careful not to trip on any equipment in the dark before opening the passenger door. "We're here," he murmured.

Casey used her good arm to push herself up and gingerly pulled herself out of the cab, reaching back in to drag her coat and blanket after her as she touched the ground. She leaned against the side of the truck while Rafe helped Neil.

Once Neil was back on the ground, and before Rafe could say anything, Casey dropped her coat and reached back into the cab to pull out her backpack and the rifle strapped to it. Seeing what she had in mind, he walked behind her and picked up her coat. "You might want to put this back on first."

She looked up at him, though he couldn't make out her expression in the dark, and then allowed him to help her get it on, using her uninjured arm to pull her hood up over her hair. "Thanks," she picked up the blanket she had dropped and slipped it back into her pack. "I'm afraid the AR-15 will have to be yours. I don't think I can carry any more than this right now."

"That's okay," Rafe was in the process of organizing his own belongings. "And if you need help, just ask."

"Of course. We're in this together, and we still have several more miles we need to walk." Her attempt to sound enthused about their situation fell flat in the face of the exhausted note in her voice.

"Not tonight," Rafe said firmly. "Once we've shut things down, we're going to find a place to make camp. You really shouldn't be moving as much as you are."

Casey had arranged, via Juno, for a resistance member from Yadkinville to pick up the truck at this garage, which had been set up as a satellite repair shop. They would return it under a hacked GPS, once they had looked it over and cleaned up all the evidence of damage from stray bullets or anything else that might get the SPKF's attention. Trucks and cars like this one were too useful for the Resistance to just abandon. They still had twenty minutes before he would arrive, despite the hour-long delay for emergency first aid. With luck they would be out of here well before then.

Rafe was a little surprised that Casey didn't want to argue; instead, she produced a glove from her coat pocket and, with a little difficulty, pulled it onto her right hand. She didn't bother to slip her injured arm into its sleeve before zipping up her coat. "Fair enough." She hoisted up her backpack and pulled it over the shoulder of her good arm.

"Will you be okay like that?" Rafe asked.

"I'll let you know if I'm not," she assured him.

He nodded and reached for his own pack. Retrieving his grandfather's shotgun and the AR-15, he strapped them to either side of his pack and pulled it on. He noticed Neil standing on the other side of Casey. "I could carry something on my back," Neil offered.

Rafe considered before unstrapping the shotgun again. "This shouldn't be that hard to carry."

"D-don't worry about me. I'm just glad we're not in Winston-Salem anymore," Neil said.

That was when Rafe realized Neil was shivering, and it was obvious why. His coat was probably still sitting in the Reynolds Building somewhere. Rafe reached into the largest compartment of his backpack and retrieved his old coat. He helped Neil pull it on before pulling off his hat and gloves and handing them to his friend. "We can't have you freezing to death after we went through the trouble of rescuing you," he helped him get his head and one arm through the shotgun's shoulder strap.

"I appreciate that," Neil pulled the hat down over his ears.

With that, the three of them limped away from the garage and into the woods. It was then that Rafe really became aware of the toll the night's exertions had taken. His whole body felt like it had been run through a cold tumble dryer. Compared to the others, his injuries from Church were minor annoyances, but he was sure he was stumbling just as bad as the others as they walked.

When they found an empty house along the road, it was the most beautiful sight in the world to him. He didn't even hesitate to break the door open to let them in. Once they were inside, Casey slid her backpack off her shoulder in the living room and dropped down next to it.

"Man, I think I could sleep for years," Neil groaned, leaning against the wall and using gravity to gently lower himself down.

"I'll take the first watch then," Rafe took off his backpack and looked out the window.

Casey reached into her pack with her good arm. "I think I should take it, actually, but before we think about sleep, I've got a little something the two of you might appreciate."

After reaching around in the backpack for a few moments, she produced an object about the size of a small sand bucket, and then a set of matches.

What's that?" Neil asked.

"It's a tent heater," Casey replied. "It doesn't have a huge radius, but it's good enough for this little room. Way better than those cold nights on the way here, wouldn't you say?"

She handed the matches to Rafe. He grinned as he struck one. "What I would say is that you are awesome, and I don't know how we'll ever repay you."

She smiled as she pulled out her blanket and wrapped it around her shoulders before setting her rifle beside her and leaning against her backpack. "I'll accept you making sure no one sneaks up on us once my turn on guard is over."

"Neil and I can cover that, we didn't take a bullet," he said.

She shook her head as she adjusted her blanket. "I'm not dying yet, and I've had the most rest. I'll take the first watch, you take the second, and then Neil can take the last one before morning. You both need sleep too."

Rafe considered arguing, but he had already discovered arguing with Casey was exhausting. He felt pretty tired, and there was a tent heater that needed setting up.

Neil held the flashlight while Rafe lit the heater. Soon, warmth began to permeate the room. It was quickly followed by the sounds of gentle breathing as Neil drifted off next to him. Rafe leaned against his backpack and let his own eyelids close.

He had to agree with Casey about the tent heater. Compared to that night he and Neil sat back-to-back at Hanging Rock, this was living.

CHAPTER 14

THIS HILL BY THE ROADSIDE

December 15, 2037

LIGHT FILTERED THROUGH RAFE'S EYELIDS, AND HE tried to curl tighter into his blanket and keep forgetting what had happened the night before. His shoulder ached where Church had thrown him against the wall, along with his knees where they'd hit the ground, and he was sure he also had several large bruises, all of which he desperately wanted to ignore. However, the smell of something that might be food dragged him back to wakefulness. Rubbing the sleep out of his eyes, he opened them and looked around. Neil was leaning against the wall by the nearest window, watching for any sign of movement. In one hand he held a plastic bag that he was eating out of with a plastic spoon. After watching him for a moment Rafe looked down and noticed a small cardboard box sitting near the heater.

"Good morning," Casey was sitting up, her legs crossed, with another clear plastic bag held open between her combat boots while she was using her good hand to spoon out the contents.

"Shouldn't you be resting?" he asked, sitting up gingerly and trying to comb the bedhead out of his dust brown hair with his fingers as he set the blanket aside.

"I was hungry," she said between bites. "Are you interested in some breakfast? I'm afraid they're not expert chef quality, but MRE eggs are better than nothing."

"I could eat the box they came in, and it'd probably taste good," Rafe said.

Casey chuckled. "The way they usually taste, it's hard to tell the difference." She pointed to her backpack with the spoon in her hand. "They're in the middle pocket."

Rafe reached for the bag and opened the indicated zipper as she continued, "Fortunately, we've only got a day's trip left before we hit the mountains proper so we can be nice to ourselves. Then it's not long before we reach the first town controlled by the Minutemen."

"We're in the war zone now, aren't we," Rafe observed as he found the box she had indicated and tugged it out of the bag.

"Yup, and we've been there since we passed Yadkinville. So, we had better make sure to keep an eye out for soldiers. It'll get more likely the farther we get in, so keep that in mind. And if we find anyone flying the rattlesnake, try to be as nonthreatening as possible. Even if our little road race in Winston got their attention, their regulars might not know who we are."

"If it means not being fired on, I will be as nonthreatening as a newborn kitten." Rafe tugged at a tab on the cardboard box until it opened and then reached for the water bottle he had in his backpack. After pulling open the heater bag and inserting the food packet, he poured in enough water to reach the fill line before he closed it and stuck it back in the box, leaning it against his own backpack.

"You're not cute enough to pull that off, but as long as you don't make any sudden moves or do anything that indicates you're pro-Union, that ought to be good enough for them," Casey said.

He thought about offering some sort of comeback to that, but decided it wasn't worth it. He then noticed something else that had slipped out of the box while he had been focused on its primary contents. Instant coffee.

He prepped it as directed and soon the smell of the beverage filtered through the room. It wasn't anything fancy but when time was up he drained it from the heating bag without complaint, adding a couple of ibuprofen for good measure. Even the powdered eggs, with the texture of mashed potatoes and the taste of something not quite natural, were quickly eaten.

After polishing off his breakfast, he stood and walked over to Neil. "How're you doing?" he asked.

"Better," Neil said. "Now that Mrs. Lord isn't around anymore."

"What happened?" Casey asked.

Neil frowned. "She was a total b..." he mouthed the rest of the word, and Rafe wasn't sure if he felt an evil eye from somewhere that might belong to Jane Flynn. He knew it had to be his imagination. There were no such things as ghosts. But remembering why she wasn't there to give them a reminder of what was appropriate for her son did not help his feelings on the matter either. With some of the profanity he'd dropped the previous night, did he really have the right to say anything?

No, he decided. Now was not the time, and Neil had as much right to curse their situation as any of them.

Sorry Jane...

When Rafe said nothing, Neil tried to explain, "She said what happened in Greensboro was justice, and that I needed to learn about 'my privilege' even though what she tried to make me say happened wasn't true." He glared down at his broken leg, "I know we weren't the worst off in Greensboro before the riot, but ... that doesn't make her right."

"Bolsheviks," Casey murmured darkly.

They looked over at her and she continued, "They demand that you get on your knees and beg for absolution even if you've personally done nothing and harmed no one. It doesn't matter. They already found you guilty and prejudiced because your parents inherited their parent's physical traits and actually listened when they were told to work hard. They cheapen everything by saying the efforts and achievements of you and yours were nothing compared to the color of your skin or what equipment you were born with, while ignoring all evidence to the contrary. Then they have the gall to claim they aren't demanding apologies for who you are when, in truth, that is exactly what they are doing, all in the name of engineering shame and guilt for things that should be inconsequential."

"Falling in line won't save you, even if you do everything they tell you and renounce all that you are. In fact, it's all the better for them, because you've become their co-conspirator in their lie, and they'll hang it around your neck and drag you around with it like a dog on a leash. But the only people who are tying your state of being to that so-called sin is them."

"Never forget that Neil, because as long as you know their game and have the presence of mind not to play along, they will never control you." She pulled off her blanket and began folding it one-handed. "Doing *that* to children..." she growled softly in disgust. She considered the thought and then looked up at them. Her expression had returned to a serious calm. "I think it's time we got going."

"Right," Rafe agreed. The three of them proceeded to gather up their belongings and break camp. Soon, they were leaving the abandoned building and making their way parallel to the road farther west.

April 23, 2033

It had been near the beginning of what would probably be the last game session for a while. Finals were coming up and everyone was likely to be too busy studying for gaming to be practical. Eric had brought copies of the picture he'd drawn for all the players, now beautifully inked and shaded. Since Hannah was running late, they were spending their time talking about it.

"This looks really good," Will said, admiring his copy.

"Thanks," Eric beamed proudly. "I thought since the semester was ending it'd be nice if everyone had a memento. This was a fun game."

"Here's hoping the Internet restrictions the state's pushing don't go through. If that works out, we might still be able to keep playing through cyberspace at least." It was good to see Allen smile a little. He hadn't since he'd gotten the news from his father earlier that day.

"I've got a campaign prospectus all written up for the next part of the adventure, if we do get to keep going," Will said with a grin.

"I can't wait!" Rafe admired the design of the morning star that Eric had drawn for his character, and the little details on the spells, armor, and weapons for everyone else. His friend really was a talented artist.

That was when they heard a knock at the door, and Will stood up to let Hannah enter the room. "Sorry I'm late," she said, "I was finishing up some paperwork with the Special Peace Keeping Force recruiter at the career office."

"You joined the SPKF?" Allen asked with consternation. "When did this happen?"

"I know it's sudden," Hannah agreed. "But with the increasing aggression in the inland part of the state, I felt there was a good chance they might need people." She took a seat next to Rafe on the couch while searching through her pockets for her dice bag so she could place it next to her character sheet.

"Only because the media wants ratings and politicians don't listen," Allen muttered, pointedly looking away from her.

"Yes, they do," Hannah argued, not looking up as she searched for her dice. "Look at how well they've taken care of people since they fixed the health care law..."

"There's been no real change, and you know it," Allen retorted. "We still have a doctor shortage because there's no money in medicine anymore and clamping down harder limits on prices isn't going to help. . ." He exhaled in frustration and looked away from her. "I don't really feel like having this conversation right now..."

"What got into him?" Hannah asked, turning her attention to Rafe.

"There was a riot near his parents' restaurant," Rafe explained as he placed Eric's picture between the pages of one of his notebooks so it would stay flat and placed it in his backpack. Allen's family lived near Asheville and ran a restaurant in an area where there had been protests. It used to be that violence was abhorred by the people in power, at least publicly. But now, it seemed no one among the party in charge was willing to prosecute or arrest anyone from their side anymore. Heaven forbid they should give a damn about the people caught in the crossfire when winning was all that mattered.

"Are they okay?" Hannah asked looking back at Allen again.

"They had a few broken windows, and someone tried to punch my dad in the face. Makes me glad I talked him into getting a gun before the last assault weapons ban came into effect last summer. He was able to keep anyone from actually coming inside." Allen explained dully.

"That's exactly why I joined," Hannah said, "to protect the people."

"You joined the wrong army then," Allen growled.

"What do you mean?" Hannah demanded challengingly.

"Uh ... Guys, let's not fight, please," Eric quietly tried to remind them.

Allen didn't seem to be listening. "They're a special guard detachment authorized by President Holt, Hannah, and they don't protect anyone who doesn't follow her line. If you were smart, you'd go back and tear up that paperwork now, before they pull you too deep to say no when they tell you to ignore something terrible, or worse."

"I don't believe it," Hannah said.

"I know because my parents saw them at Jack Hepburn's rally for his congressional run." Allen's voice was getting louder as he became angrier. "They were sitting around placing bets on whether the protestors were going to beat him up before they kicked him out of the park where he was speaking. Of course, they knew what was going to happen once people started rioting."

Hannah looked livid at that. "And you think you have any room to say anything when those Nazis murdered peaceful protestors on the D.C. Mall last year!"

"Hey! Guys? Stop it! I get you're angry, and I know this needs to be sorted out, but please, take a deep breath and cool off! We did come here to play, right?" Will was firmly holding his campaign notes in one hand as he sat in his computer chair, "I was really hoping we could start soon..."

Allen scoffed as he answered Hannah, completely ignoring Will. "Oh, we're playing *that* game are we? So my parents deserved to get their restaurant wrecked because some assholes who claimed they were on our side, hundreds of miles away, whom every person I know of condemned, did something wrong that my family wanted no part of and had nothing to do with?"

"Well maybe they should have realized what their own side is doing?" Hannah snapped. "They've been eating up the party line so long they wouldn't see the truth if it bit them on the ass..." Her voice trailed off as she finished the insult, but Allen had already stood up. For a moment, Rafe was afraid the other man might actually hit her.

"Is that really how little you think of me Hannah?" He stood there, still as a statue, though his eyes and the tone of his voice betrayed the cold fury beneath. Finally, he picked up his backpack and walked to the door. "I'm not dealing with this crap tonight. Play without me."

Eric stood up to follow him and try to talk to him, while the others waited in Will's living room. For a while, there was an uneasy silence and then Rafe spoke up, "Why did you say that?"

"He's the one who wouldn't see..." Hannah looked away from him angrily.

"You weren't exactly helping," Will's tone was very quiet.

"And I don't need this from you!" With that, Hannah too, stormed out of the room.

Allen didn't return. Neither did anyone else. Eventually, after about thirty minutes of waiting and trying to talk about other things with Will, Rafe took his leave.

The game never resumed.

———

December 15, 2037

The east windows in the conference room Church had borrowed at the Winston Salem precinct sent cool light onto the table where the other two individuals waited. It had been a stroke of luck that one of the building security guards had found him shortly after Turner and Burke had escaped in their truck. As a result, he'd been able to walk to the precinct and tell his version of the story, carefully leaving out the part where the two rebels had left him handcuffed to a rail in a bathroom. Regardless, he had come to them with the fact that he had been right where they had been wrong, and therefore, he should be back in charge of the case. The higher-ups had grudgingly accepted this line of reasoning.

Hernandez had not been pleased, but that was okay, because the search was now leaving his jurisdiction. It was also reaching the edge of Church's domain too, but people were beginning to pay attention now and he wanted results.

"You're absolutely sure, Gruben? That's where he's going?"

"Positive," Sergeant Hannah Gruben responded from her seat. She had been fidgeting with her ponytail until he'd entered the room and then quickly let it fall behind her for the sake of professionalism. "If he were to go anywhere, he would go to Boone."

Church looked down at the map in front of them, straightening his tie. He would probably have to go to a regular uniform before they left. "Normally, I wouldn't even consider going that deep into contested territory, but after they escaped through the checkpoint, the President finally took notice, and now she's got Congress breathing down our necks. If we don't get this kid back, we're going to be a laughingstock. This is our last chance."

"Sir," Everett spoke up. "Is this really how we should be spending our resources? From what Flynn told me, Turner really did save his life..."

He trailed off as Church glared at him. "Are you telling me you think they were right to break every law on the books, Everett? Even when they threatened to kill you?"

The large black man looked back at him, "No sir, but I was a cop for years before the evacuations. Our job was to keep the peace and protect law-abiding citizens. But I can't help but wonder if maybe that mission changed behind our backs somewhere along the way. Maybe because of that change we even failed some people to the point where they had no further recourse but to go outside the law." He did not look away from Church's stare.

Finally, after about five seconds of tense silence, Church spoke, and he was only vaguely aware of how hard he gripped the empty shell casing in his fist. "There are two main routes through the mountains toward Boone," he turned back to the topographical map on the table. "There's an army blockade on 421, but if they go north..." He used a pen to circle a road labeled "Boone Trail". "That would take them along the mountains and into rebel territory with a much lower chance of hitting any of our sentry forces. They must have abandoned their vehicle at some point. Otherwise, Wilkesboro's installation would have detected them on the roads. That, or given how fast they were going down 421, they would have run out of gas before they could take enough of the older back roads to avoid the compound. Let's see if we can get there first."

———

Over the course of the morning, Rafe, Casey, and Neil made a steady pace west. At times they followed roads, and at times they set off through the woods, using only Rafe's compass, the map, and a few landmarks. It was mostly a quiet trek. In the moments when he wasn't watching Neil swing along on his crutches, or Casey with her injured arm nestled inside her jacket, he could almost fool himself into thinking they were just out on a hike, back in the days when that sort of thing was still allowed. The snow was completely melted away, and that catastrophic derailment in Pinnacle that caused all the excitement in Winston-Salem seemed like a distant memory. It wasn't long before they reached the ghostly remains of a small town the map called "Fairplains." Minutes later, by noon, they had completely crossed it.

They soon located a path through the woods that was composed of bushes and tall grass. It had once been the throughway for the towers built for major power lines. No electricity flowed through them. Not after the government had ordered the power cut. But since the overgrown break in the trees seemed to be headed in the direction they wanted to go, they continued following it for three more hours. Once or twice, they had to cross a creek by using rocks to avoid the cold water or tracking their way through mud where erosion had worn away the hillside. A little later, they found a barn at a dilapidated farm where they stopped to rest before continuing. It was getting into the afternoon when, finally, they exited the woods next to an inactive power station to find themselves looking at the main street of another ghost town, which the map called "Miller's Creek." Right in front of them lay a two-lane road going west with the name "Boone Trail."

"Sounds like our road," Rafe said as he read it off the signpost and compared it to the map.

"We've almost made it," Casey agreed, "But we're not out of the woods yet..." she looked around at the intersection in front of them. "Figuratively speaking, of course."

"So, what are we going to do after this?" Neil asked, as they passed the remains of a couple of smaller businesses.

"We'll find 421 again and follow that through to Deep Gap," Casey said, not slowing her step at all. "There, we will have to identify ourselves to the Minutemen, because that's where they hold the line right now. Once that's over, and they've debriefed us, we can get you to where you're going. Hopefully, we'll be able to find some medical attention first, but after that," she turned her attention to Rafe, "you said your sister was in Boone?"

Rafe nodded. "I hope so. Susan and Keith were living there for a while before the fences went up. They were still there last I heard ... " He paused to look over at Casey. "You doing okay?"

She glanced down at the bulge where her arm was still tucked inside her coat, as she considered the question. "I won't be using a rifle for a few weeks, but I'll live."

They had just passed what had been the local high school when Rafe looked up and saw something that caused him to stop. He knew they had been going deeper into the foothills for a while, but it was the first time he saw evidence of the views this area was known for. Rolling under the sky like an endless sea, were the peaks of the Blue Ridge Mountains. At the beginning of this journey, he had known he would see them well before they got where they were going, but it was the first visual sign that they were actually getting there.

He stopped, looking at the sight before him. Just taking it in for a few more moments, as he felt the cold in his toes inside the boots he now wore, courtesy of the Resistance, and the wind on his face where it poked out of the hood of his coat. He heard, rather than saw the other two pause next to him.

"Just past those mountains?" he asked softly. It was only partly a question.

Casey nodded with a smile, "Just past those mountains." That was when they noticed the dark clouds beyond, promising more precipitation. "I guess the weather report was right. It looks like it might snow again soon."

"Let's get going then," Neil swung himself forward on his crutches. He paused after the first step and looked behind him with a conspiratorial grin. "You aren't going to make me race you, right?"

With that, Rafe and Casey resumed walking, soon catching up. They continued along the road for a short way and had just passed a small grove of trees at the top of a rise, when Casey halted and glanced over her shoulder.

"What is it?" Rafe asked.

Casey went for the handgun she had secured to her hip. "We've got company."

Rafe looked behind them down the hill they had just climbed, and his mouth fell open. Several men seemed to be disembarking from a truck at the base of the hill, clad in military gear.

Casey gestured that they hide in the stand of trees and knelt close to the ground next to them behind several large rocks, pulling out a small set of binoculars from her backpack after she dropped it to the ground. "They're not Minutemen." Her expression hardened. "Damn it ... it's Church and our friends from the skyscraper."

"You don't mean..." Neil started.

"Hannah's down there?" Rafe asked.

Casey nodded in confirmation before handing him the binoculars. Rafe brought them to his eyes and scanned the hillside below, taking in the uniforms and body armor. For a split second, he caught sight of Hannah standing next to Church before they disappeared from view behind some bushes. That was all the confirmation he needed. As he returned the binoculars to Casey, he let out a breath and tried to think of what he needed to do. Finally, he turned to Neil, pulling out the map before he began fumbling with the compass on his wrist. "Keep to the trees as much as possible and follow the road until you get to 421. Once you're there, just keep following that highway. You should get to Deep Gap by tonight, but you need to hurry..."

Neil's eyes widened as he realized what was going on. "Are you crazy?"

"Maybe I am," Rafe said seriously, "But I don't want you caught again..."

"Do you see that open field behind us?" Casey pointed past the trees. Rafe could see an open expanse of brush and tall grass. "If we run, they will give chase. If he goes and we stay here, anyone with eyes will see him before he can get to cover," Casey observed. "If we shoot at them to draw their attention, we can't count on all of them focusing on us, and he'll be an obvious target. We've had a full day of travel. We're already tired, he can't run fast, and I'm not exactly in a good situation either. It's a simple equation. If anyone runs, we won't get far."

"Do you think I want the two of you caught either?" Neil gripped his crutches defiantly as he looked between them.

"It's not what I intend to happen," Casey's voice became more musing as she thought aloud, "We might be able to pick them off a few at a time if they decide to rush us, but we're not running from them."

"Pick them off?" Rafe's breath caught in his throat as he realized what that meant.

Casey's brown eyes were stern as she spoke. "Are you committed Turner? I can't hold your hand this time, and I don't think any of us are going to make it unless we defend this hill."

Rafe looked back down the hill, his mind racing. A new thought ramming itself through his brain with every heartbeat.

I could still stop this ...

I have to stop this ...

Dammit, I've got to stop this!

Can I...?

How...?

Deep down he already knew the answer, and it made him sick.

I can't ...

Any choices I could have made to avoid being here passed me by a long time ago.

———

April 30, 2033

It had been a week since the last session of C&C and the last day of classes before Exam Week had been yesterday. Rafe was walking through the quad to get to the gym when he spotted Hannah walking in the opposite direction. He paused. Part of him wanted to wave and say hi. The other part wanted to keep walking and pretend she didn't exist.

That train of thought halted when the decision was taken away from him. "Hi, Rafe," Hannah said, stopping.

"Hi." He also came to a stop, and then, wanting to be polite, he added, "How's it going?"

"It's going all right." She smiled. "I just got done working out. Gotta stay fit, you know. I'm lucky they're letting me stay to graduate before I head off to basic training."

He nodded, "That makes sense."

There was an awkward silence for a moment as her expression became more serious, "How's everyone else?"

"About as well as can be expected," Rafe put his hands in his jacket pockets. There'd been a bit of a cold snap lately.

Hannah sighed. "And what about you?"

"I think you owe Allen an apology at the very least. What you said wasn't very kind, especially given what his family just went through." Rafe did his best to keep a firm tone as he spoke.

She gave him a look that said she was trying not to glare at him. This was probably the first time he'd tried to involve himself in her arguments. "Sometimes the truth isn't kind," she said, her expression stubborn.

"Maybe so," Rafe conceded, "But I don't think you were telling the truth. I think you said what you did because Allen was telling you something that would break your entire world view if you accepted it, and it scared you."

She really did glare at him at that point. "He's been trying to get under my skin since we had our first history class together. Sure, he has his good points, but if he can't see how he's being hurt by the system, someone's gotta show him."

Rafe gave her a hard look, "And you thought the right answer was to tell him he and his family aren't enlightened enough to think for themselves."

"That's not what I said," Hannah replied defensively.

"It was as good as saying it," Rafe said.

"Then how would you have made him see?" Hannah asked, crossing her arms and pursing her lips.

It was his turn to sigh in exasperation. "Well, I wouldn't have felt the need, because I don't think that's actually how things are either."

Hannah shook her head. "With all the evidence to the contrary, how can you not see what's so obvious?"

"Hannah, don't you ever think about the implications of all this?" Rafe asked. He was quickly losing his patience, too. "We've both heard the stuff they've been feeding us here for the last several years. It's pretty easy to come to the conclusion most of these professors are convinced that men, especially white men, and those who don't eat up that social justice crap, are basically the cause of every evil that's ever been committed in the world. Even if I played along out of some misplaced guilt just for being born the way I am, I'd never be an equal to you by their standards. I couldn't even be a friend. Just a so-called 'ally.' And from what I can tell, that's no better than being a toady. You can't really want that from me, can you?"

"No one's asking you to do that," Hannah said dismissively, "You just don't get it. . ."

Rafe cut her off again. "I don't get it, huh? Did it never occur to you that maybe you're the one who's oblivious? We're not here to be your whipping boys, Hannah. I am Rafe Turner, and that was Allen Jackson. We're individuals and have things we think about and value just like any other human being. But if we're just interchangeable names you pulled out of a hat to stick on Allen's monolith, and any disagreement we might have is just our 'fragile toxic masculinity', or our 'internalized misogyny' or whatever ... If you think so little of us that you'd believe something like that ... Well, you should really just think about how messed up that is." He tried not to look around to see if anyone was watching. After the gym he had his own exams to study for and after graduating, he had so much else to do, this social justice stuff just seemed so pointlessly stupid by comparison, and yet if he spoke too loud here it might lock him out of those opportunities for good.

"And how selfish do you have to be to talk about his internalized oppression like it's somehow also about you?!" Hannah bit right back. "You had your white male privilege your entire life to hand you everything you've ever wanted. If you can't see that, then it's clear you're not acknowledging your own unconscious bias either."

Rafe resisted the urge to throw his hands up into the air in frustration. Was this sensation that felt like banging his head against a wall what it was like for Allen whenever he tried arguing with her? He had never wanted anything to do with this crap. Ever. He knew what the school administrators thought. He'd known that since high school junior year when that damned 'School for All Act' had left him to their tender mercies. As long as he got through his education so he could live his life, get a job, and do what he wanted without being bothered, he had long gotten used to tolerating it. Hannah, and Allen too, to be fair, hadn't been able to resist shoving this shit into the one space where it should never have mattered. And now it had been taken to the point where the players' covenant kept in Will's living room lay shattered in ruins. Even as he spoke, Rafe could already see the fragments dissolving infuriatingly into dust before his eyes, and he knew his words were falling on deaf ears.

"I'm being selfish? I'll admit I have had a few things going for me, it's true, and believe me, I am grateful for them. But if you think what *I* bring to the table, how *I* was raised, the choices *I* made, what *I've* achieved, what *I* dream of, what *I* believe in ... If all that means nothing to you, compared to my skin color and whether there's a letter M in the check box on my ID card, I think that's pretty sad. This is not about me, and it's not about Allen either. We're not the ones shoving people into those stupid intersectional boxes to see who has it worst and then assuming that any group who's better off did it by cheating and deserves some kind of payback! It's a false dichotomy and a sick little game I have no interest in playing." He started walking again but paused at her shoulder. He could feel himself trembling as he spoke once more.

He wished he could say the only reason was anger. "Too many people become monsters from drinking that poison, and the last thing I'd want to see is for you to be one of them. If you'd just stop for a moment and open your eyes, you could still try to repair the damage."

Before Hannah could reply, he left her standing there, for once, in a stunned silence. It didn't last long. He could hear her calling after him, probably trying to offer some sort of rebuttal as he exited the quad. But he did not stop, and she was too far away to catch him. He tried to tell himself he was leaving her to think over what he had said. But if he had to be honest with himself, it felt a lot more like running away...

———

December 15, 2037

As if it were someone else lifting his hand, he reached up and undid the strap to which he had secured the AR-15, even as in his mind he was still begging on his knees.

Please Hannah, turn around! Don't make this harder than it has to be ...

Holding the weapon in front of him, he lowered his backpack to the ground and opened one of the pockets to pull out his handgun, handing it to Neil along with a second magazine. "If you're going to stay, I won't let you be defenseless ... but you know how serious this is, don't you? If you take up arms too, they aren't just gonna want to get you back anymore."

I told you not to follow me!

Neil nodded solemnly, taking the gun from his hand. "I know, and I'm not going to let them take us if I can help it." Something about the way he said that sounded vaguely familiar. He wished he could place from where. His conscience gnawed at him even as he pulled out the handgun's second magazine. It was terrifying to hear that kind of conviction in someone that young. It was criminal that he should have to ask Neil to run this risk, when he had already lost so much. In trade for their freedom, was it worth the price?

Run!!!

He wasn't sure if that last thought was for Hannah or Neil. Probably both. He checked the magazine on his own weapon.

"We've got three people, so we need to divide the battlefield into three arcs," Casey said, turning to Rafe. "Center with the rifle, wings with the pistol. Normally I'd take center, but I can't use the rifle with my arm like this, so we need you to take the center arc. Neil, you're taking the left wing. When you run out with Rafe's pistol, go to my rifle. It's only got a few bullets left, but they'll have to do. And Rafe, when you run dry on the AR-15, switch to the shotgun. Of course, if we get to that point, it's probably game over."

She looked around thoughtfully before creeping over to the right side of the rocks. "If they come around, it will likely be this way, the road's there, but it also has some cover they can run to if they get close enough. I need you to try and take anyone you see at a distance so hopefully I can guard this flank. You got it?"

Rafe nodded. "I'll do my best."

"That's all I can ask. For what it's worth, I think we can actually do this. Whether they wait, or decide to come get us, I think there's a decent chance we hold out long enough to attract one of the Minutemen's recon squads. If we're lucky, we can get Church talking long enough to run out the clock." Casey checked the ammunition on her weapon as she spoke.

Is this what we've become?

"I'm sorry," Rafe whispered and lifted the gun as he took a spot behind the rocks between Neil and Casey, kneeling as close to the ground as he could while still being able to see if the soldiers started moving closer. Once again, he wasn't sure if it was for Hannah or Neil.

After taking a moment to move his backpack next to him so he could quickly retrieve the shotgun when he was ready for it, Rafe looked over at Neil, who had just pulled Casey's rifle over next to where he had dropped to a seated crouch behind the rocks to Rafe's left, so he could lift it to cover his side of the empty field. "You okay?" he asked, as Neil took up the handgun and had begun inspecting it.

Neil heard him and nodded.

"All right," Rafe began. "Remember, there are three rules for handling a firearm: Act like your weapon is always loaded, aim only at what you plan to shoot, and only put your finger on the trigger when you're ready to fire. Got it?"

"Got it."

"The safety is here," Rafe demonstrated the features with one hand as he gripped his own weapon with the other. "The magazine goes in through the grip here when you reload. Make sure you hold it firmly, and don't let it kick back on you."

"Got it."

"And please, stay as low to the ground as you can. If you get hit, I won't forgive myself or you."

It was only then that the fear showed through the determination on his friend's face. ". . . Got it."

Rafe gritted his teeth as he looked away. This wasn't right. None of it had been for a long time.

"Rafe Turner! We know you're there! You and Casey Burke are to come out with your hands up and Neil Flynn is going to come out with you." It was Church's voice.

"Actually, I think we're quite comfortable right here, Church!" Casey yelled down the hill. "You should sit back and relax for a bit. Have yourselves a picnic!"

"Too cute by half, Burke!" Church yelled back. "But we're not in the mood. There's snow coming, and we're on a schedule. This is your last chance! If you do not surrender, we will use all force necessary. You have ten seconds."

The three of them shared a glance at each other and then looked out at the hillside as they counted down the seconds. "He sure is impatient," Casey commented, "Probably because we're on the edge of enemy territory."

"Rafe? It's Hannah. I know you'd never willingly hurt

anyone..." He heard her voice crack with emotion as it echoed up the hill. Without the binoculars he could no longer make out which figure was hers. "Please, listen to him!"

Casey looked over at him as though unsure what his response would be, but he met her gaze intently. "Too late to back out now," he said.

"Not even if she cries?" Casey asked.

"I've already made my choices. This hill won't fall because I changed my mind," he answered. He had tried to sound calm, but he wasn't.

5 ... He vainly searched the field for Hannah, and he couldn't find her.

4 ... Where was she?

3 ...

2 ... He couldn't tell which of them she was. They all looked the same from here.

1 ...

"Time's up!" Church intoned. With that, several men began making their way up the hill, running between bushes and patches of grass that gave them cover.

"Here we go," Casey said, lifting her handgun.

Shoving all other thoughts to the back of his mind, Rafe lowered his eye to the sight and searched for a target. He centered it on the nearest approaching form he could find and pulled the trigger. A bullet casing hit the ground in front of him as the gun fired, hammering his ears with the sound. He couldn't tell if it hit, but he saw one of the men on the far left disappear behind a bush. Five more shots rang out. He waited.

After a few seconds he caught sight of someone pulling themselves up and diving behind a rock. He opened fire again. He was sure he hit nothing. Throughout the tall grass behind those bushes, he saw signs of movement. They were too quick for him to risk wasting any more bullets unless he was certain.

The field was eerily quiet for about twenty seconds, and then Casey fired, sending a bullet straight into the face of a man in the brush across the road. He dropped dead as three more shots sounded from a bush to the southeast of them. Rafe shot in that direction, almost immediately feeling something fast whizzing past his ear as someone else returned fire.

Two more shots were fired and he pulled the trigger again.

The smell of gunpowder was strong in his nose as he heard, rather than saw, Neil raise the pistol and fire.

There was movement almost to the far right as a dark-skinned man climbed the hill behind a couple of saplings. He and Casey both fired at the same time. The man dove to the ground, and Rafe wasn't sure if either of their weapons had aimed true, but they didn't see him again.

For several more seconds, there was dead silence. Then just to his left, there was movement and the report of another rifle. Neil shot wildly, but then something moved out of the corner of Rafe's eye, running closer between the taller bushes by the road. Turning, Rafe aimed and fired again. A familiar voice cried out, too late; his eyes widened as his target's helmet flew off mid-fall, and he saw Hannah, blood spattering out behind her in the split second before she dropped to the ground, a bullet to the right side of her abdomen and a look of shock on her face.

He wasn't sure if what he screamed was a curse, a name, or just a guttural cry of sorrow and rage as he turned his attention to another movement to his left and fired again.

After that, and for the next few seconds, he searched the area for any further targets, not really aware of who it was, apart from knowing it wasn't Casey or Neil. *Or Hannah*, a part of him whispered. That meant he needed to shoot. And he did, several times, doing his best to stay low as more bullets whizzed above them. The men were getting progressively closer. He could see some of them at the base of the hill now.

As he fired off one more shot, he saw Church crawling through some bushes. He fired one last time before discovering his own weapon emptied. His shot went wide, and the trigger clicked uselessly as the last bullet casing from his magazine popped to the ground in front of him.

It was time for his grandfather's shotgun.

He snatched it up, opening the break and reaching for a shell from the box. It felt like it had been minutes rather than moments. Frantically, he pulled out a shell and opened the break to shove it into the barrel.

It was all he had left. Snapping the break shut, he lifted the gun to his shoulder, rose slightly to aim, and fired at the first thing that moved.

He didn't know if he hit anything, and to be honest he hoped he never found out, but to his surprise, as he extracted the spent buck-shot casing from the barrel and was jamming another into it, he heard the report of another rifle.

Someone else on the field dropped as the sound of a gunshot rang out again, and Rafe realized it was coming from farther away than any of the SPKF positions.

Two more shots fired, much closer than before. And then out of the woods from across the road to the west, came several more men. They weren't wearing the uniforms of the army or the SPKF, though it was similar. It bore resemblance to that of an army soldier, though those who wore it were carrying lighter equipment. In some ways the uniform also bore a strong resemblance to hunter's fatigues.

Casey smiled as she glanced in their direction. "The Minutemen…"

With the speed of a tactical unit, they spread out over the hill surrounding the area. Rafe heard someone shout, "Drop your weapons and put your hands up! Jackson, take your team and secure the combatants on that hill!"

Casey dropped her weapon in front of her. Rafe and Neil did the same as two men and a woman in uniform joined them under the trees. As they came closer, he could see that each of them bore a grey patch on one sleeve with the Gadsden flag embroidered in a soft green.

Rafe was completely surprised when the second of the three, a tall, dark-skinned man with a goatee below the eye-shield of his helmet, spoke as he got to the crest of the hill. "Looks like we made it. Thank God. Rafe, you okay?"

Rafe's jaw dropped as the man lowered his weapon and lifted the eye-shield on his helmet. "Allen?"

Allen laughed, "Who else? Jeezus man, you look terrible!" Rafe swallowed hard as a host of emotions flowed over him in a wave before his friend threw an arm around him.

After being nearly strangled by the hug, Rafe pulled back to get a good look at him, taking in every detail. "And what about you, running in here like a badass? Am I glad to see you!"

Allen grinned. "Well, I'm not bringing the fireballs these days, but I hope the cavalry works."

"How did you even know we were here?" Rafe asked.

Allen let out a guffaw. "You mean after that hornet's nest you kicked up in Winston last night, you didn't think our intel would pick it up? Dude! Almost all of Deep Gap knows! Once we saw the reports that you actually got out of the city, I went straight to my CO and asked to be put on the team to come find you. Half of the platoon wanted to deploy so they could be out here to shake your hand if you made it!"

Rafe wondered if they were really worth that much attention. He couldn't believe it. "Well, if you want to congratulate the mastermind behind that insanity, you'll want to talk to Casey. I was just along for the ride, really..." That was when he finally remembered where they were ...

And what he had just done ...

"Damn it! Hannah!"

"What?" Allen looked around the stand of trees curiously. "Where?"

"She followed us," Neil said.

Rafe pointed to where she lay. He saw that several of the other Minutemen were clustered around her. Brushing past Allen and running to where she had fallen, he knelt next to her. She had landed on her back and was looking around even as the medic was pressing a thick bandage to her side. The Minutemen had taken no casualties of their own. They had been the clean-up crew. He silently counted his lucky stars he had not killed her. It was a serious wound, and obviously painful. But it had not been fatal. At least, for now.

"Hannah?"

She looked up at him, and he could see the confusion on her face. More painfully, he could also read the accusation in her blue eyes.

"Y-you shot me, Rafe ... You shot me ... Is this how much you hate what we're trying to do? ... Is this how much you hate me?..."

He wanted so much to comfort her, to apologize for hurting her, to beg for forgiveness. But his hand stayed by his side as he looked down at her, doing his best to remain firm. At this point, there could be no turning back.

"No, Hannah. I'd've thought you'd know, for me, hate never even entered the picture. I wish I could say I understood why you want what you want so badly. Or how you reached the conclusion it would ever lead to a good end. But there's too much I love that would be destroyed by the world you're trying to build." He swallowed hard to cover a sob that was threatening to well up in his chest. It was an act of will to keep looking her in the face instead of down at his own coat and jeans.

"What do you mean? Don't you get how selfish you're being?"

He shook his head sadly. "Selfish? Hannah, how is it selfish to want to live in a world where we could both be happy? You could find people who live the way you want to live, and I could live the way I want, and we could coexist in the same place because we wouldn't bother each other. But in your world, there's only your way and no place for someone like me except at the barrel-end of someone else's gun ... and I'm tired of living my life with a gun to my head. I've lived that way more than long enough."

"It doesn't have to be that way..." Hannah tried to begin. He was surprised that she seemed more tired than in agony at this point.

He sensed rather than saw that Allen was standing behind him. "If you make it home before the war is over, Hannah, I hope you go back and take a look around. Just really look," Rafe heard him say, "I doubt you'll ever understand, but maybe you'll at least be able to tell the difference. And maybe you'll have enough time to think about what happened here too." He wasn't yelling, but the coldness of his voice said it all. He was angry, but it had a controlled edge to it that he had not yet mastered back when they were in school together.

She looked up, turning her accusing gaze at him. "Home? Allen? You joined the rebels too?"

Allen did not contradict her, instead his response was direct and to the point. "No more talking. That's a serious injury, and you need to focus on not bleeding."

"We need to take her back to base now," the medic said.

"All right," Allen agreed. Rafe suddenly felt a familiar hand come to rest on his shoulder. "Let her go Rafe. She's already done the same to you."

"Wait!" Hannah was still reaching out to them, "Rafe ... Allen ... don't..."

Rafe stood up and he and Allen watched as two soldiers loaded her onto the stretcher. "Goodbye, Hannah," he said softly. It felt like it could very well be for good this time. As things stood, he couldn't see any way they could ever reconcile, even if a very large part of him still wanted to. Allen was called away to talk to his commanding officer, probably to discuss their next steps.

Not far away, he saw Neil staring at another form on the ground, lying motionless. He walked over to see what he was looking at. It took him a second to realize it was the man who had been guarding the hotel room in the Reynolds Building.

"Neil?" he asked.

"That's Everett..." Neil said quietly. "I don't know if he was telling me the truth or not, but he was the only one who seemed to want to listen in that place."

Rafe put a hand on Neil's shoulder comfortingly, as he added one more crime to the growing list he had committed in the past week or so just to get them to this moment. He had not just ushered Neil into this adult and unforgiving world, he had caused his friend to be faced with the prospect of having to kill to defend himself. Had Neil actually killed someone? The idea of it was too much.

"I'm sorry..." Was his apology more for Everett, or for what he had done when he handed his friend a responsibility he shouldn't have had for years yet?

Neil looked up at him as though begging for some sort of explanation, anything that would resolve what he felt. "If he hadn't come ... He didn't seem like a bad guy."

"I'm sure he wasn't. War kills far too many who don't deserve it," Rafe said.

"Is that what this is?" Neil looked up at the overcast sky, his face creased as he struggled to hold in the emotions that threatened to overwhelm him. Rafe was sure Neil was seeing at least two more faces in his mind's eye than that of the man who lay before them. "It's not fair ... why does it have to be this way? ... Him ... Mom and Dad ... Why did...?"

Rafe tightened his hold around the younger man, supporting him as the dam broke. He didn't say anything. There was nothing he could say that could ever make it all right. Neil was the one sobbing into his coat, but he could not stop the tears falling from his own eyes.

As he glanced around, he noticed Casey sitting on the ground while one of the medics was looking over her wound from the night before. Her brown eyes met his for a few moments. Then, she respectfully looked away. She understood.

In the distance, Rafe saw several of the Minutemen guarding Church and a few others. The rest of the squad was searching the surrounding woods for other survivors. He felt the cold more sharply now than he had ever felt it on their journey. The change in air pressure and muting of sound that heralded snow, along with the oncoming clouds, made the hill on which they stood seem like the graveyard they had made of it with their own hands.

The sky was getting darker, and snowflakes were starting to fall, when Allen and his commanding officer walked over to where they stood. "Rafe Turner?" the man asked.

"Yes?" Rafe reached up to brush the snowflakes out of his dust-brown hair.

The man offered his hand. "Lieutenant Hyundai. I've authorized Sergeant Jackson to provide the three of you an escort to our forward operating base. From there, air transport will get you the rest of the way to our hospital in Boone. I've been informed that your father is waiting for you."

"Dad made it?" Rafe asked.

"Yeah," Allen said.

"Thank you," Rafe responded, taking Hyundai's hand and shaking it firmly.

"I hope you know, that was a hell of a stunt you and Burke pulled off," the man said, before he looked at Neil, who was still leaning against Rafe's side. "Hey kid, you were very brave. I know it couldn't have been easy, but it's over. You're safe now."

Neil seemed too exhausted to do much more than look up at the soldier and nod. He'd pulled his hood back over his blond hair as he'd started getting cold again.

The man gave Rafe's hand a final shake and then turned to Allen, "Get them to base."

Allen saluted, "Roger!" As the officer left, he turned his attention back to the two of them, handing Rafe the shotgun he had abandoned in the trees. "Well, you heard him, let's get a move on!"

As they passed the medics, Casey stood. "It's time?" she asked.

Rafe nodded, pulling the shotgun over his shoulder. "Let's get out of here." As they were joined by Allen's squad, they made their way down the crumbling road. At the base of the hill, Rafe could see a battered armored truck waiting to take them away as the mountains beckoned off in the distance and the snow began to fall heavier around them in the dying evening light.

CHAPTER 15

BEYOND THE VEIL

December 22, 2037

ABOUT FOUR INCHES OF SNOW COVERED THE GROUND outside the modest cabin in Boone. The cold blanket across the yard was almost blue in the dark. It had been exactly a week since their stand on the hill and six days since Neil had been discharged from the hospital. There were still a couple of days before Christmas. Rested, clean, and in Rafe's case finally clean-shaven, they were playing a racing game on the TV in the living area with his younger brother Mike, and Susan's son Ethan. He was several months shy of five years old and not much competition, but they had agreed to let him win every now and then.

Ethan's three-year-old sister Jamie watched from nearby. She was clearly on her brother's side and her golden curls bounced around her head as she cheered with delight whenever he managed to sabotage one of the other racers. Rafe didn't mind. Keeping them entertained while Susan made dinner was the least he could do for occupying half their guest room. Most of the past few days had been taken up with the simple joy of just being there. Neil sat next to him on the couch, a 3D printed plastic cast with a soft sock over it for warmth cradling his injured leg from ankle to knee, his attention on keeping his race car on the track.

Sam Turner, Rafe's father, sat in an old recliner near the back of the room, a pair of reading glasses balanced on his nose and a book in his hand as he tried to ignore the screen. He'd always said video games made him dizzy. It had taken him some time to find the Resistance in South Carolina, especially while being under watch on account of his wife's arrest. But he had managed to find a way to cross the combat zone near Greenville and make his way north.

Rafe guided his car around a hairpin turn, his brother just yards behind him on the track when there was a knock on the door. Mike paused the game as Rafe stood and went to answer it. When he pulled it open, he found Casey standing there, her arm now in a proper sling. Allen stood next to her, and to his surprise, Will.

"Where in the world have you been?" he demanded.

"Nice to see you too!" Will grinned.

As Rafe ushered the three of them inside, Sam stood and walked to the end of the hall to see who was entering. "Oh, we have visitors?"

Rafe nodded. "It's Casey and Allen. . . I don't think you've ever met Will before, though."

Sam shook his head. "He was one of your other friends from school, right?" He walked over to where they stood.

"It's nice to meet you Mr. Turner," Will said.

"Please, call me Sam," his father insisted as he shook his hand. He also exchanged warm greetings with Allen, asking how things were where he was stationed, before moving on to Casey.

"Nice to see you again," Casey said when he got to her.

"How's your wound?" Sam asked.

"I still have a little while before I don't need the sling anymore, but it's definitely better, thanks," she said. Sam had been a huge help in finding her a place to stay once she was released from the hospital.

"Well come on in," Sam said, ushering them down the hall back toward the great room where a wall of picture windows in the living, dining and kitchen area were set up to give a view of the snow-covered woods outside.

After Rafe took a couple of minutes to finish the race, he rejoined them at the dining table. They talked about this and that for a while before Rafe once again broached the subject of what had happened to Will.

"I actually had to get out pretty early," Will explained. "I said something someone didn't like."

"No kidding," Rafe looked over at the TV where Neil, Mike, and Ethan had started a new race, "Story of our lives, huh?"

"It's not all bad though," Will said. "The people running the show here snapped me up for strategic affairs the moment I showed them my credentials."

"I'm not surprised." Rafe offered him a wry grin. "Some of those challenges you used to set for us as our GM? Brutal. I feel sorry for the other side."

"My degree didn't exactly hurt either," Will said with a chuckle before returning to seriousness. "Allen told me about Hannah. You okay?"

"I'd be lying if I said I was happy about it," Rafe said.

He'd thrown up in the bathroom the night after their stand on the hill, and there had been a few nightmares, but he had no desire whatsoever to share that information with anyone.

Hannah had taken a bullet to her gut from his gun and become a prisoner of war. There wasn't anything he could do about any of that right now. And really, it was a difficult thing to examine without wanting to sink into the ground and pull the dirt in after him. At this point, the best he could do was tell himself that somehow he'd find a way to push it to the back of his mind or get used to it. Both options seemed just as horrible. But given the course of action he had recently set for himself, he would have to if he meant to be of any use at all.

Allen gave him a serious look, demanding that Rafe's green eyes meet his brown ones, "Rafe, it's not like you just up and shot her on a whim."

"I know," he tried hard to keep his voice even as he spoke, "I just wish she hadn't followed me. I really could have killed her."

Will sighed, "We all do, but you often can't protect people from the consequences of their own decisions no matter how hard you might try. She was the one who chose to run up that hill after you, in the end."

There was another uncomfortable silence before Rafe spoke again, "Has there been any word about what'll happen to her?"

"None so far that I've heard. Most likely she'll be held with the rest of the prisoners of war. I know she's being cared for though," Allen assured him.

Rafe nodded, "Good ... I was worried ... Well, never mind..."

At that moment, Susan looked over the bar from the kitchen area. "Dinner will be ready soon. Will you all be staying? You're welcome to if you'd like," she said.

"We'd be happy to," Casey answered, followed by Will and Allen also confirming they would stay.

———

May 1, 2033

It had been a few days after the game had fallen apart when Rafe found Will sitting on a bench on campus. He waved as Rafe came over. "How's it going?" He asked as Rafe came close enough to talk.

"Not so great," Rafe admitted, unshouldering his backpack and dropping down next to him. "They still aren't speaking to each other ... I tried to talk to Hannah yesterday, but I'm pretty sure I blew it." He looked at the ground dejectedly.

"It's a shame we couldn't keep it out of the game," Will murmured. "It's so much easier to manage a party when all you have to do is send out a dragon for everyone to fight. Too bad I couldn't even get that to work."

"I know, right?" Rafe nodded in agreement. "So instead of facing down some epic monster and finding out what happened to the veil, we're just going to ... Well, I guess I don't know what we're going to do..." He sighed, resting his hands on his knees and watching as several people walked out of the library a few buildings down from where they sat.

"Drift apart ... keep being mad at each other in Hannah and Allen's case ... most likely," Will said. "They really overdid it this time around."

Rafe returned his gaze morosely to the ground as he contemplated that prospect. "So, what would have happened if we'd been able to play? Since we probably won't."

"Well," Will started. "I was going to have it play out like this..." He leaned forward thoughtfully, resting his chin on his hand as he decided where he was going to start. "You see, I'd thought the party would take the veil to Ardes like they were supposed to. But then it would turn out that he couldn't be trusted with it either. If any of you had decided to wear the veil and look directly at him, you would have discovered he was planning to take over the kingdom by using it to control his enemies and the people in power by becoming their arbiter of truth."

Rafe considered the possibilities that could come from that revelation for a moment before responding. "Yikes."

"I thought so too. I mean, just because you have the Veil of the Truthseer doesn't mean you can't lie about what you see, and if you can make those lies more attractive than the truth, there will be plenty of people who will let themselves be led. Of course, I figured Allen would probably have Malchior join him as his second in command since he was evil aligned. Then we would find some way to set it up so that he would get a replacement character. That way, you'd still have a full party to take the fight to Ardes."

"Sounds pretty crazy," Rafe played with the strap on his backpack as he listened. "What would be left after that?"

"Then you would have to figure out what to do with the Veil," Will said. "The choice would have been yours of course. You could have kept it as an artifact, if you wanted, or found somewhere to hide it. Or you could have given it to the queen, though that would have turned her into a paranoid psycho. Destroying it was possible, but there was also another option I had in mind."

"Oh?"

"You see, the Veil is a divine artifact created by the god of truth," Will said, "Which you probably would have found out at the last session if things hadn't gone so wrong. Sound familiar?"

Rafe grinned as he spoke the name, "St. Alvar." Characters in C&C always picked a deity from a pantheon of gods in the rule-book to worship and for Clerics, Paladins, and Druids, their deity was the source from which they drew their divine spells. St Alvar was Galen's.

Will nodded, "It could have taken you on a quest to return the veil to him. You would either have had to level up enough through your adventure to learn the right spell or else find someone who knew it. I was thinking I'd work Ilaria the Druid and her Ranger bodyguard into the story again somehow, but I hadn't figured that part out yet."

"I take it you were going for the theme that 'no one should have a monopoly on the truth'?" Rafe observed. "Almost anyone we could have given the Veil to would have abused their control of it in some way."

"Something like that," Will agreed.

"That sounds awesome." Rafe smiled sadly as in his mind's eye, the party had any number of adventures across the world Will had built. They told jokes, laughed at absurdities in the rules, dealt with adversity and inter-party disagreements, ordered many a takeout dinner, and trusted their fates to the roll of the dice. They explored musty tombs, great libraries, vast caves, and grand palaces, and the adventure culminated in an epic finale where the Veil was sent back to St. Alvar's plane of existence from whence it came. Eric's Kade, and Hannah's Falinel held the line against an army come to claim it by force, backed by a new, probably good or neutral-aligned, Wizard or Sorcerer who had replaced Allen's Malchior, and a number of non-player-characters they'd picked up along the way. Meanwhile, his own character worked tirelessly to finish the spell before they were overrun. "I wish we could have played that story out to the end."

Will seemed to be looking at the tree across the sidewalk from where they sat. There were new leaves sprouting out from branches that had been bare three weeks ago. The new growth of spring that was coming in as their last semester before graduation drew to a close. His friend leaned back, letting his arms drape over the back slats on the bench, perhaps equally lost in thought over the adventures that might have been. "So do I."

———

December 22, 2037

It was after dinner and Allen, Will, and Casey had just left. Ethan and Jamie were being tucked in by their mother, and Mike was talking with Susan's husband Keith and their father in the den. Rafe had wandered back into the living room, when he saw Neil sitting on the couch, quietly watching the flames in the fireplace. He sat down next to him. For a while, they enjoyed the warmth in a comfortable silence.

"How long do you have before you join the Minutemen for real?" Neil asked after some time had passed.

"I won't start training for a couple more weeks." Rafe had thought hard on the matter since they had been brought into town, reminding himself of what he had seen on the way there, and what he knew lay down this path. The fact remained that he could see no other way around it if anything was ever going to bring this war to an end. About two days ago, he had spoken to a recruiter. They were pulling in anyone they could find. Keith's family was already letting the military rent their ski resort for the war effort, and Susan was volunteering with the city watch when she could in case the army pushed deeper into the mountains.

"You're not afraid you could die?" Neil asked, worry creasing his brow.

Rafe looked over at his friend. "Of course, I'm afraid. Believe me, it's the last thing I want to do. But this has to be done, and I couldn't live with myself if I went back to hiding from it."

Neil didn't look satisfied with that answer, so Rafe explained further.

"I've spent my life doing nothing, just watching, letting others do the fighting, afraid to say anything because of what could happen, waiting for things to blow over that never did," Rafe said. "Maybe I wasn't the only one. Maybe, if more of us had had the nerve to stand up for ourselves and show why what we value matters, we wouldn't be here now. But here we are, and we can't afford to stay out of it anymore. Casey says she's going to join too, as soon as her arm's healed."

Neil frowned. "Then that's what I'll do too."

Rafe shook his head, "Not yet Neil. You're going to stay here with Susan and the others. You're going to get better, and you're going to wait a few years. They don't take anyone under eighteen anyway, so you still have a little time left, I hope."

And if we do our job right, by the time you are old enough, you won't have to.

"But I could help you. I did before, right?" Neil argued.

Rafe let his voice soften, "That's not what I mean. I'm not your parents, and it's not really my right to say this ... And you've had to grow up a lot in the last few weeks. But please, for your mom and dad at least, don't try to rush it."

I won't let you carry anymore burdens that belong on my shoulders. You're having to grow up too fast already...

Neil considered for a moment before relenting. Rafe could see he was at least trying to understand, even if it didn't look like he did. "All right ... But don't come crying to me when I'm not there to save you." He was clearly trying to pass it off as a joke, but he still looked worried.

"That might be pretty tough, but I'll see what I can manage." They were quiet for a while before Rafe spoke again, "Hey, you know this can't go on forever, right? So, how about this? "When all of this is over, let's get a party together and play a game of C&C."

Neil let out a tired sigh, but grinned, "Okay ... I lost all my dice though."

"We'll find new ones," Rafe assured him, "Mine are gone too. And we'll need to find rule books. I wonder if Will still has his..."

"I was a Fighter in the last campaign I tried to play in at school," Neil said, "Maybe I could try a Ranger this time."

"Not a bad choice. Of course, you'll need to decide whether you want to specialize with two-weapon fighting or your bow. But we'll have plenty of time to figure that out." Rafe stood up and walked to the window, taking in the snow that blanketed the ground, pure and serene under the moonlight. He had promised himself before he went to the recruiter that he would never hide from what needed to be done again. He had already let too much of his world slip away because of that mistake.

His thoughts went to his mother and Eric, at best, sitting in prison cells somewhere far away.

No, he would not hide again. And he would give all that he had even if the task before him was to pound those chain link fences and prison walls to dust. A flame of anger and resolve scourged his insides in a hot slow burn. Perhaps it had always been there, but now it burned even more painfully because he knew what it meant and the terrible things it might ... would ... make him do. He had once been afraid when Casey had spoken like this as they were driving toward Winston in a GPS-hacked truck, but the truth was he knew exactly how she felt. He too had found the will to stand, and he was committed. He could no longer afford to stop, and he never would. Not until he was in the ground, or he could say that those he loved were free.

Hang on, he thought, knowing the words only echoed in his mind, though he wished more than anything that they would somehow carry over the many miles that separated Boone from where he might have to go. *We're coming back for you ... I only hope we're not too late.*

VIRGINIA

TENNESSEE

NORTH CAROLINA

N

HIGH COUNTRY

Hwy 221

Deep Gap

Boone

Hwy 421

Blowing Rock

Fairplains

Miller's Creek

Wilkesboro

W. Kerr Scott Reservoir

++ Fences — Roads ∿ Mountains ☙ L.

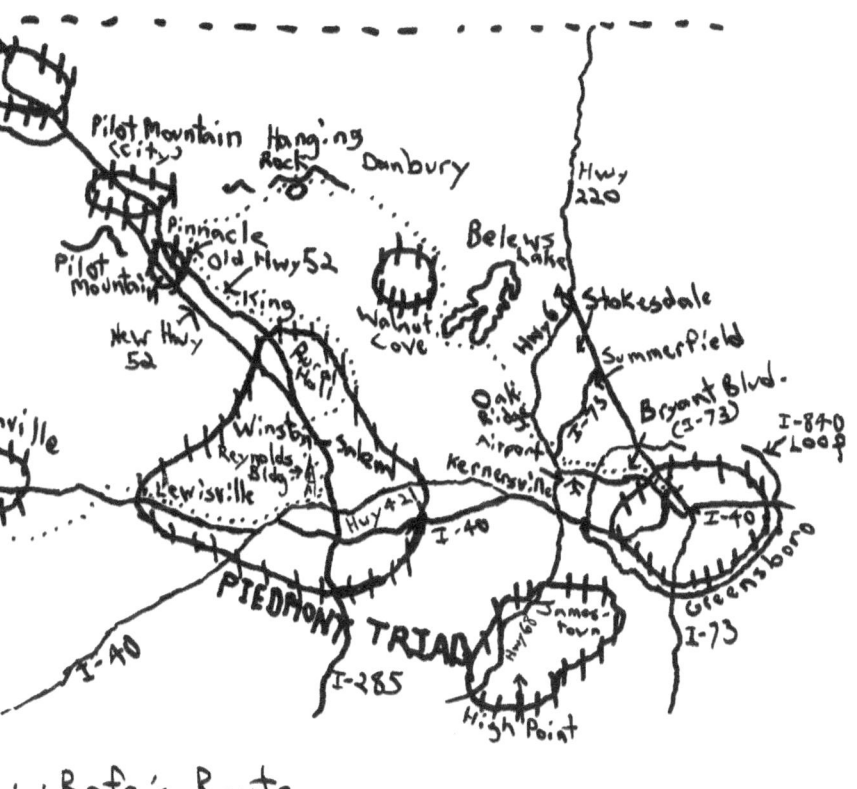

Rafe's Route

GLOSSARY

Ability Scores: In most RPG's these are used to determine the basic attributes a character can have. In C&C, as with multiple real RPG's out there, these scores are: Strength, Dexterity, Constitution, Intelligence, Wisdom and Charisma. Having a high enough score in any of these can give the player character an extra addition to the modifiers they add for certain ability checks or saves. For example: A high Strength is useful for a Fighter's ability to do physical attacks, while a high Intelligence would allow a Wizard to memorize more spells than they would have been able to with a lower score in that attribute.

Alignment (Lawful/Neutral/Chaotic, Good/Neutral/Evil): Determines the moral standpoint of a character in a role-playing-game on the axes of lawful vs. chaotic, and good vs. evil, with neutral being the middle ground for both. Good or evil, as the terms suggest would indicate whether a character acts in a manner demonstrating a respect for morality and the welfare of other people, or not. Lawful would indicate the character has a strong belief in law, obligation, and custom while chaotic would indicate the opposite.

Battle Map: A map, usually divided up into a grid of squares or hexes, often laminated to be used with dry erase markers, on which topography, foliage, and other obstacles can be sketched to simulate a battlefield.

Catacombs and Creatures (C&C): A fictional tabletop role-playing-game in which the players take on roles within a party of adventurers to fight monsters, gain treasure, and collectively play through a story.

Character Class: In Catacombs and Creatures (and many real RPG's too) a character class is used to determine what abilities a character has, and what role they play within an adventuring party.

Character Sheet: A sheet of paper or sometimes more, printed with details of a player's character. This includes their attributes, skills, how much weight they can carry, inventory, spells they can cast, combat capabilities and the benefits of weapons and armor, or any other equipment they may be carrying. They usually have blank spaces for making situational adjustments such as if a character loses hit points during combat.

Check: A roll using a d20 in order to determine success or failure in using a skill or ability, and subsequently adding any modifiers from character abilities or skills in order to get the total number. The higher the number, the more likely the roll succeeds. Rolling a 1 on a d20 is almost always a 'natural' or 'critical' failure. Rolling a 20 is almost always a 'natural' or 'critical' success, and can result in the effort being dramatically more successful. In combat this can translate to doing extra damage.

Cleric: A second-line fighting and spell-casting class that specializes in healing and casting divine spells with about average hit points. They choose a (usually fictional) deity at the beginning of the game to whom they are faithful and gain powerful spells from their faith in that deity. Like Wizards, they do have to plan what spells they have at their disposal during play and usually carry a blunt weapon like a mace instead of a sword. They excel at healing, deterring or controlling undead creatures, and spells that do divine damage, however, at higher levels, reviving the dead, divine miracles, or even asking their deity to personally intercede on their behalf are all possible.

Dice (D20, D10, D8, D6, D4): In C&C, as with various other tabletop RPG's, rolls are made with polyhedral dice. Each die is referred to by how many sides it has. A d20 has 20 sides, a d10 has 10 sides and so on. D20's are used for skill checks, saving throws, and attack rolls. Most other dice are used for damage rolls, determining hit point damage to a target depending on weapon type, or the nature of the spell being cast.

Druid: A second-line character class with average hit points, specializing in divine nature-related spells. They can heal, though not quite to the degree of the Cleric, and are limited by the inability to use metal weapons or armor. But they make up for this with the ability to control natural phenomena like fire, water, wood, or weather, and are able to shape-change into, or communicate with, animals. At lower levels this can be something small, such as a rabbit or a bird. At higher levels, summoning a whale, or turning into a giant eagle, or calling up a typhoon could be options.

Dungeon Crawl: A type of gaming scenario that usually involves a complex of rooms or areas that must be mapped as the party navigates it towards an ultimate goal (often exploring the place for loot, or to achieve a predetermined objective). It usually has treasure hidden in various rooms along with enemies to fight, puzzles to solve, and traps to evade. The party has to decide how to manage their physical condition, spells, items, and equipment while navigating the dungeon in order to complete the crawl.

Environmental Defense Force (EDF): A branch of the military formed in the year 2033 following the Environmental Protection Agency's integration into the Defense Department. They are primarily focused on protecting the environment, claiming it as a matter of national security.

Experience Points (XP): Points awarded by the Game Master that go towards character Levels. These are typically acquired by fighting monsters, gaining treasure, achieving party goals or role-playing major story events.

Fighter: The basic frontline combat character class. They do not cast spells, and are geared primarily towards skills and abilities that help them in combat. What they lack in magical aptitude, they make up for in being specialists with most weapons, and usually having a lot of hit points which allows them to absorb a lot of injuries one might take from being in the thick of combat.

Game Master (GM): The player in a table-top role-playing-game who controls all the monsters, non-player-characters, and anything else not controlled by the other players. They also serve as the referee for disputes and decide what rolls should be made for saves, skill checks, and any other situation where the outcome is uncertain.

Hit Points: Characters in C&C, and most real RPG's, use hit points to determine how healthy they are and how easily they can absorb damage. A character class like a Fighter who generally spends a lot of time on the front lines will generally have a lot which will indicate they can take a lot more damage. Character classes that rely more on magic like a Wizard or being good at dodging like a Rogue, don't generally have as many.

Levels: A metric for determining how powerful a character is. Gaining character levels is done by gaining experience points through succeeding at objectives and fighting monsters. The higher a player character's level, the more abilities and skills they will have at their disposal.

Meme: A joke, image, line from a movie, audio clip, or a short video usually passed around on the internet. Many of them are used as reaction images sort of like emoticons in forums and chat rooms or as a way to generally tell jokes or emphasize emotional reactions in an online conversation. Different memes can be reposted and parodied in an endless stream of variations. They can be as simple as a single image of a cat with a funny face, or as complex as a short clip from a feature film. For instance, 'No Step on Snek' is an image that is a visual riff on the Gadsden flag where the snake is a badly-done pencil drawing with the above phrase intentionally poorly scrawled underneath.

Miniatures: Miniature figurines representing the characters and monsters they encounter. Usually used as a visual aid to indicate where they are on the battle map for the purpose of determining proximity to enemies, range, and how difficult it may be to hit an enemy with a given technique.

Modifiers: Extra values that apply to a given roll, as indicated on a player's character sheet, such as bonuses for having a high strength which can be applied to an attack roll, or ranks in a skill applied to a skill check due to the character being more experienced in that skill and thus more likely to succeed. Negative modifiers can also be given, for example, in a situation such as when a character is shooting a ranged weapon at an enemy hiding behind a tree (because they're trying to hit someone who's using the local terrain as cover).

Party: Collective term for all the players in an RPG as a group, excluding the Game Master.

Ranger: A character class that is combat focused and can function as a fighter, but with some difference in flexibility. They often specialize in fighting with ranged weapons, like a bow, or in fighting with two weapons instead of a main-hand weapon and a shield. At higher levels, they also get access to some healing and nature spells and are typically built with a skillset befitting a person with experience surviving harsh natural environments, and traveling long distances undetected.

Rogue: A character class emphasizing skills related to stealth, thievery, and subterfuge. They do less damage and have fewer hit points, but in trade, they have skills that allow them to pick locks and get to places other characters might not be able to. They have abilities like a dodge bonus, as well as high dexterity to avoid taking hits, and in combat, situational abilities such as sneak attacks allow them to take advantage of other characters distracting a target so they can do more damage.

Role-Playing-Game (RPG): A game usually involving a fictional narrative in which the players play as characters going on an adventure, and played with polyhedral dice. Catacombs and Creatures falls under this category. Many real-world tabletop RPG's can encompass a vast variety of settings, from the more traditional sword and sorcery, to interplanetary adventures in a high science fiction future. Depending on the system used (and the creativity of the GM), multiple settings can even see use in the same game!

Saving Throw (Saves): This is a special type of ability check in C&C as well as certain other real RPG's. Determined with a d20, it is used to show how well a character can resist certain types of effects. A Will save, for example, reflects a character's ability to withstand mental or magical effects. Fortitude saves generally are used to withstand physical effects, while a Reflex save reflects a character's ability to dodge an incoming attack or get out of the way of a physical effect such as falling rocks. Ability scores can provide modifiers to help with these rolls.

'The School for All Act': Passed in the year 2027, this act of congress abolished homeschooling, enacted large numbers of cumbersome regulations on public and private schools and reinforced education as compulsory. Anyone attempting to violate this law was subject to hefty fines and subsequent violations could result in children being removed from the offending household by social services.

Side-scroller: A type of video game in which the gameplay is 2-dimensional, usually viewed from the side, with the player moving the character from left to right, or right to left, across the TV screen.

Special Peace Keeping Force (SPKF): A federal police force created by President Nancy Holdt in the year 2033, ostensibly to bolster local law enforcement, but in practice, to support politically approved criminal activity. They eventually replaced the police and serve as foot soldiers to enforce federal policy.

Skills: As in many real RPG's, in C&C, how many ranks in a certain skill a character has, is related to how much training they've had in a given skill, and can provide a modifier to rolls related to that skill. There is a list of basic skills on a player's character sheet, and some sheets have blank spaces for skills related to specialized knowledge or a trade a character may have learned at some point.

Wizard: A character class almost exclusively focused on the use of magic that is not granted by a deity (usually referred to as arcane spells), they usually have a high intelligence and have to plan what spells they've memorized out of their spell book. They typically have much fewer hit points, have penalties for wearing armor, and are unskilled with physical weapons. But in trade, many of their wide variety of arcane spells have a lot of utility, such as the ability to make light, create magical shelters, send messages, or shoot fireballs at enemies. At higher levels, summoning monsters, creating interdimensional pockets, and traveling to different planes of existence are not beyond the realm of possibility.

ACKNOWLEDGMENTS

This book would not have been possible without the contributions of several individuals, and I could not possibly begin without mentioning my husband, Chris. I've always been able to count on you to tell me when you thought I had something good, and when I needed to go back and try again. A great debt of gratitude to my parents, for their support and patience. Also thanks to Rachel and Don Shive. You've been there to encourage me in my writing since I was a young teenager, and it still means the world to me. Your insights have been so valuable in bringing to life Rafe's journey into maturity in a world gone mad. I would also like to thank Dr. Timothy McGuirk for being willing to advise on medical matters.

My gratitude also to Matthew Bowman for contributions to making the plot more coherent, and reminders not to forget the little details in description. Will's campaign and Rafe's party of adventurers feel a lot more real because of your suggestions. Thanks to Nate Miller, and also to Alex, for helping me to get over that last editing hump.

Also thanks to Patrick Tucker, for his DefenseOne.Com article on military checkpoints. I would also like to convey my thanks to the Winston-Salem Public Records Department for granting me access to all the old newspaper clippings and details on the Reynolds Building.

And last, but certainly not least, a big thank you to all my wonderful friends and family who patiently listened and supported me through my efforts to see this story to it's completion.

ABOUT THE AUTHOR

Sarah Carden is a native of North Carolina, and was raised in the town of Oak Ridge, just northwest of Greensboro. Homeschooled along with her three younger brothers, and an avid reader from a young age, she started writing stories at age thirteen. After spending a year at University of North Carolina at Greensboro, she transferred to Old Dominion University where she acquired her Bachelor's degree, and a love of table-top RPG's. She currently lives in northeastern North Carolina. When not writing, she can often be found reading old books, tending her garden, knitting or crocheting the occasional accessory, or running RPG campaigns with friends.